Charlotte Nash was born in England and grew up in the sunny Redland Shire of Brisbane. Obsessed with horses and riding, she began stealing her mother's Jilly Cooper novels at the age of thirteen, and has been enthusiastic for romance ever since.

Always a little unconventional, Charlotte took a meandering path to writing through careers in engineering and medicine, including stints building rockets and as an industrial accident investigator. Now she writes romantic stories in amazing places, and moonlights as a creative writing PhD student, studying how narratives engage the brain.

Charlotte lives in a cosy Brisbane cottage with her husband and son, and a small flock of lovable chooks.

Also by Charlotte Nash

Ryders Ridge
Iron Junction
Crystal Creek
The Horseman

The Paris Wedding

Charlotte Nash

piatkus

PIATKUS

First published in Australia and New Zealand in 2017 by Hachette Australia
An imprint of Hachette Australia Pty Limited
First published in Great Britain in 2017 by Piatkus
This paperback edition published in 2018 by Piatkus

A CIP catalogue record for this book
is available from the British Library.

ISBN 978-0-349-41716-5

Printed and bound in Great Britain by
Clays Ltd, St Ives plc

Papers used by Piatkus are from well-managed forests
and other responsible sources.

Piatkus
An imprint of
Little, Brown Book Group
Carmelite House
50 Victoria Embankment
London EC4Y 0DZ

An Hachette UK Company
www.hachette.co.uk

www.littlebrown.co.uk

For Mum, who taught me to sew, and who left home in England for new adventures in Australia. The strongest woman I know, who has endured more than one person should be asked to in a lifetime, and who through all of that is still gracious, loving, generous and tenacious. With so much love.

Prologue

Rachael West could not have known that, on the same day her mother died, an invitation was mailed from an upmarket Sydney events firm. She had never met the woman who folded it, whose lacquered nails smoothed the creases, and who slid the creamy envelope into outgoing mail.

The envelope rested in the firm's mailroom for twelve hours, the same length of time it took Rachael to do all the funeral director's paperwork. Over the next two days, as Rachael walked numbly around the farmhouse, and her sister Tess arrived with her husband and children, the invitation made its way through the labyrinth of the Sydney central mail centre. There, its top right corner was creased in a sorting machine and a boot scuffed the front when it was dropped on the floor.

As Rachael sat leaden in the front pew at her mother's funeral, trying not to simply crumble as the community choir sang 'Gone Too Soon', the invitation was finally in a mail truck, headed west.

Afterwards, as Rachael drove her ute in circles around tiny Milton, she could not have known that the invitation was being unloaded into the hands of the local postmistress, Beverley Watkins. All that Beverley knew was that Rachael had mail; Rachael knew nothing.

The town was uncharacteristically silent for a sunny December Tuesday. By now, everyone had made the drive from St George's Church in Parkes back to the Wests' farm. Well, everyone except Rachael. Only Beverley had been required to stop between the funeral and the wake to fulfil her postmistress duties. Rachael was simply avoiding going home.

It was harvest time, and across the paddocks combines worked under grey smudges of dust. Rachael's left hand steered while she chewed the nails of her right down to the skin. The skirt of her black crepe dress stuck to her thighs, and her ragged ponytail was already coming undone. Any moment it might give way completely, like the great dam she'd built around her grief. She had managed to sit through the funeral. She couldn't yet face everyone at the farm.

She waited ten minutes after seeing Beverley leave the post office before she finally turned onto the highway. The radio played country music, fading to static just before the farm's long driveway. The driveway itself was the same as every other time she'd driven it, with the bend in the low spot given to potholes, the verges growing wild wheat, the distant glimpse of the house. The same, except her mother would never again be waiting at the end of it.

The farmhouse came into view: simple block walls with wide verandahs, the tin roof with the knob of an air conditioner perched on top, and tubs of her mother's gardenias in a military row along the front. Cars and utes were parked at all angles down the grassy banks, and Rachael could see black-clad mourners circling the front verandah and milling around inside the house. There must be a hundred people here from all over the district.

She hooked the wheel, pulled the ute up by the side door and went in through the laundry, delaying contact as long as possible. In half an hour, everyone would walk up to the great tree on the rise to cast her mother's ashes among the flowers. Until then, she'd let her sister receive the condolences. Tess was good with that sort of thing.

Rachael knew Sammy would be looking for her; her best friend hadn't been keen on Rachael driving herself from the church. But Sammy was out there somewhere with everyone else, so Rachael sat in her bedroom facing the drawn lace curtains, waiting.

Outside, two women were talking. They couldn't have known that Rachael was there, just behind the curtains, and could hear every word.

'Terrible, isn't it?' said the first. 'She didn't deserve a life like that. First her husband takes off with some blonde, and just when she'd turned it around, she gets sick. Then ten years of being dependent on other people. I'm sure I couldn't stand it. And then to die so young.'

'Marion coped with it very well,' said the other woman. 'She always said it was just one day at a time.'

'It's that daughter of hers who made it possible. Imagine that, giving up ten years of your life to care for someone else. She's made of some stoic stuff. I'm sure none of my lot would do it. No sense of duty.'

'Marion was lucky to have her,' said the second woman. 'However sad her passing is.'

Rachael didn't recognise the women's voices. But their words urged her to march outside and tell them it had been nothing to do with duty or luck. It had been love.

She stood. Her mother was gone, but Rachael would show how much she had been loved. It was time to emerge, to take up the responsibility of hostess, to walk up that hill and finally say goodbye.

'That's not the saddest thing though, is it?' said the first woman. 'It's what happens to Rachael now. Imagine trying to start your life at twenty-eight. Look at her sister – married with three children – and she's a year younger.'

Rachael froze, ears straining for every word.

'I'm sure she'll stay here on the farm. Seems to be doing well enough.'

The first woman tutted. 'She'll never get those years back. She was supposed to be good in school, wasn't she?'

'Arty, I think,' said the other. 'But she did well regardless. I think she was accepted to university.'

'There you go. To think of all the things she must have given up to stay. Well, I suppose we should go and wish her all the best. She'll need it.'

And despite all the things that had happened in the last year, the last week, the last hours, that overheard conversation gave Rachael the distinct sense that however loving her relationship with her mother had been, however much she had chosen to stay, that she had lost something else, just as important and irrecoverable as her mother. Because the women were right. She had given up university. She had given up her future.

And she had given up Matthew.

Chapter 1

The day after the funeral, Rachael, by force of long habit, woke near dawn and made two cups of tea. She dumped the teabags in the sink, then, remembering it would annoy Tess, squeezed them out and tossed them in the bin. It took her longer to register that the second cup wasn't needed.

She poured her mother's tea away and braced her hands on the sink, looking out the window. Their harvest had finished two weeks ago and the wide rolling fields of stubble were grey before the sunrise. A beautiful grey, like a dove's feather, joining the pale soft light at the horizon. As the sun appeared, it gilded the cut stalks, and the single majestic gum on the rise seemed to float on a sea of burnished gold.

Seven, Rachael thought. Seven sunrises without my mother.

She pressed her hand to her mouth. The tears kept boiling up unbidden, the wound still raw and open. Mercifully, Tess, Joel and the children were still asleep. She had time to pull herself together.

'You're up early.'

Rachael jumped and sucked back the tears. Tess had padded into the kitchen in thick, silent socks. Her checked robe was tightly knotted at her waist, her blonde hair stowed in a neat plait. Rachael involuntarily touched the unbrushed, ragged clump behind her head, the result of sleeping on her ponytail. Amidst the frizz were bits of broken elastic sticking up from the overstretched band.

'So, we're getting started on Mum's things?' Tess asked, flicking on the kettle.

'What?'

'Mum's things. I asked you about it last night. You said we'd do it today.'

'When?' Rachael said. She couldn't remember a single thing that had happened yesterday, apart from those two women talking outside her window. The day had been a blur of tears and hymns and the scent of white lilies.

'This morning.'

'No, I mean when did you ask me?'

'After dinner. When Joel was doing the dishes.'

'I don't remember.'

She didn't even remember eating dinner. She took her tea from the windowsill, but didn't drink it. She wouldn't have been able to swallow around the lump in her throat.

'Look, have some breakfast,' she said, dodging around Tess.

'I'll eat later. Where to first – lounge or bedroom?'

'We don't need to start right now,' Rachael said, trying and failing to keep the wobble out of her voice.

'But it'll be a huge job. Her wardrobe is overflowing. What a woman on a farm wanted with all those fancy clothes, I don't know.'

'She made a lot of them for other people – for formals and weddings and things like that.'

'What are they doing in her cupboard then?'

'Because people brought them back and she'd modify them for someone else. She didn't—'

'I bet you don't even know what's in there,' Tess said. 'I bet that ottoman's still stuffed with winter woollies nobody wears. Don't worry, Joel will feed the kids and keep them away.'

Rachael had a vision of her sister striding around her mother's room and stuffing garbage bags with dresses and quilts and other precious things, mixing up what was going where. 'No,' she said.

'I don't understand. We have to get back to the farm in a few days, so I won't be around to help later. You said you wanted to get started.'

Rachael threw her hands up. 'I don't remember what I said! It was her funeral, Tess. Besides, I was here with her the last ten years. I know what she wanted. If you have to go home, that's fine. I can manage.'

'Oh, I see. This is about me choosing to go with Dad when we were kids.' Tess folded her arms, bringing out a well-worn bickering point like a favourite toy. 'Well, someone had to. It doesn't mean I didn't care about her. And I'm just trying to make things easier for you.'

Tess delivered her speech without a shred of sadness. Rachael was utterly unable to understand how her sister was navigating the grief so easily.

'It's not about that,' she said.

Though she couldn't help remembering standing beside her mother on the day Tess and her father drove away. Rachael had pressed herself against her mother, her eight-year-old eyes unbelieving. Marion had squeezed her fiercely, tears in her eyes, though she'd held her voice calm and level. 'She's still your sister,' she'd said. 'This will always be home. She'll be back one day. She'll be back.' Over and over the same words, as if they had the power to make it true.

Now, Tess pursed her lips. 'Well, can I at least make some lists for you? There's all the medical hire equipment that needs to be returned, and someone should throw out all the tablets.'

'Why would I need a list?'

'So you don't forget.'

Rachael stared. Was it possible that Tess still thought of her as a dreamy girl with her sketchbook and pencils, often late and forgetful? Yes, that's what she had been, once. But she'd worked very hard in her last years of school; and then had come ten years of looking after her mother's appointments, medicines and meals, toilets and showers, and the farm. All that had changed Rachael forever. Tess simply hadn't been here to see it.

'I'm not going to forget,' she said.

'You forgot what you said yesterday.'

Rachael gritted her teeth. All she wanted today was to be left alone, to stare down the fields or wander round the house, to be as lost as she needed to be. Choosing retreat, she abandoned her tea and headed for her room.

Tess followed. 'Well, what about cleaning out the fridge? There's tonnes of food from the wake that needs organising.'

'Then take it home for Christmas.'

'Speaking of Christmas, I think you should come up to Dubbo. You shouldn't be here all by yourself. Or, a better idea. I've got someone I want you to meet.'

Rachael spun back. 'Why would I want to be fixed up with anyone?'

'Who said anything about fixing up? It's Joel's cousin, nice man. He's bought a farm near Orange and he doesn't know anyone yet. Family's all in WA, so he's going to be alone too. You can talk shop and keep each other company.'

Rachael rubbed her face. She hadn't slept much this week, her mother's last days in the hospital replaying in her thoughts at night. Worries about the farm and the future were also accumulating like fallen leaves. Couldn't Tess understand how tired she was, how upset? How the smallest things seemed like mountains?

She started back down the hall. 'Will you please just leave it alone? We only just buried Mum.'

'I thought it would take your mind off everything, and besides it's time you found a man. There's been no one since Matthew.'

Rachael froze with that same sick feeling she'd had yesterday, as if his name had dropped a cage around her body, one that was so tight she could barely draw breath. She steadied herself on the wall. Retreat wasn't enough; she needed to escape. The door onto the rear verandah was right there. She suddenly found herself outside, boots on, striding through acres of field, mowing down a row of cut stalks in her haste.

'I'm just trying to help!' Tess yelled at her back.

Rachael didn't turn around. Out under the sky, she pulled out her hair band and sucked in the warming air, trying to shake off the shock. Finding that Matthew's name could still hurt was an unpleasant surprise. She thought she had packed him away so deep in her heart that he couldn't affect her any more.

She strode south, trying to lose herself in her steps, and avoiding the long field where a dip in the ground lay hidden in the wheat stalks. Sadly, avoidance didn't help. If she closed her eyes, she could still imagine lying in that hollow with Matthew, the earth cool against her arms, his body warm beside her. She had lost hours lying against his chest, twisting his curly brown hair in her fingers, staring into his eyes, and listening to his plans for them both. She'd been so excited by the prospects he'd effortlessly sown in her mind: of university, and then coming home to work and build a home together. Dreams that were still tied to the earth and the baked-straw scent of the fields, to everything Rachael was.

He'd broken off and given her his broad smile. 'I'm going on.'

'No,' she'd said. 'I want to hear more.'

So he'd brushed his thumbs across her cheeks, cradled her face, and said, 'I'll love you forever.' Fierce and certain, he'd sealed his promise with a kiss and her heart had lifted with joy.

Rachael wrenched her mind back with an exasperated curse. That same straw scent was in her nose, but everything else had changed. They'd both been seventeen when he'd made that promise, imagining a different life than the one that had happened. And yet she knew she would never love anyone like that again.

She walked until she hit the south fence and still the ache clamped around her like a too-tight belt. The sun was behind a cloud, shooting beams of filtered orange across the sky, and birds wheeled and skimmed low over the stalks. Across the highway in a neighbour's field, a combine turned a lazy circle at the end of a row, the distant grumble of its engines competing with sporadic traffic. Rachael lifted the hair off her sweating neck, but couldn't put it up again; she'd lost the band somewhere in the field. She leaned on a fence post to pick the prickles off her socks, then chewed the remaining nail on her left hand as a truck rumbled down the highway towards Parkes. Another passed a minute later. Rachael lingered, watching.

The next truck had cowboy western murals painted over its cab. Then came two caravans, and two sedans. A sheep truck was next; the driver waved. Then she spotted a green Corolla flying down the highway. Rachael straightened. Just as she made out the mismatched door panel, the car flicked its lights at her and ploughed onto the hard shoulder.

The driver's door flew open and Rachael almost cried again, this time in gratitude. Sammy was here.

'I thought that was you,' Sammy called, negotiating the slope to the fence, the breeze ruffling her choppy fringe. She had a blonde pixie cut, dimpled cheeks and long eyelashes. 'What are you doing out here?'

'Avoiding the house.'

Sammy raised her eyebrows. 'Tess?'

'She wants to get into Mum's stuff.' Rachael's voice caught. 'She's being really awful. I don't understand how she can be so . . .'

'Callous? Invasive?'

'Yeah. She's worse than normal.'

Sammy hugged Rachael awkwardly across the fence. She was wearing her black work pants and blue blouse with *Parkes Country Motor Inn* stitched over the breast pocket.

'Are you on your way to work?' Rachael asked, confused. It was far too early for a shift at the motel; Sammy was more likely to have been at her second job, at the bakery.

'Later. I came to see how you are. I brought food.'

'I'm not hungry.'

'I know. But I bet your nieces and nephew will be. Come on, I'll give you a ride back to the house.'

Rachael glanced over her shoulder, gauging how long it would take to walk, then bent to slide through the fence. 'Probably a good thing. Tess might have decided to clean things out on her own.'

'I'm sure she wouldn't,' Sammy said. 'But leave Tess to me. You've got enough to deal with.'

❧

They found Tess and Joel and their three children – Felix, Emily and little Georgia – in a whirlwind of Weet-Bix, half-empty milk bottles and rejected multigrain toast that had spread from the kitchen to past the dining table. Joel's T-shirt was on inside out and his hair still bed-mussed as he supervised Georgia in the highchair. Tess, who never seemed to eat anything, was sipping tea while simultaneously plunging a knife into the Vegemite jar.

Sammy breezed straight across the chaos, kissed Tess on the cheek, offered some words of condolence, then produced bakery bags. Rachael didn't know what Sammy had said, but as soon as the whole family had finished with breakfast, they dressed and took off down to the sheds, Joel leading the way and the children happily chasing each other.

Sammy stacked the dishes and ran the sink to wash up. Unable to be still any longer, Rachael took up a tea towel. One of her mother's, it was printed with the now-faded words of 'Advance Australia Fair'.

'I did it again this morning,' Rachael said. 'With the tea. Making two cups.'

'Oh, Rach. I'm sorry. I can't believe she's gone either.'

'It's just . . .' Rachael wanted to say *it hurts so much*, but that didn't begin to cover it. Instead, she picked up a bowl and dried it with undue savagery. 'You know, yesterday at the funeral I hadn't seen a lot of those people since school.'

'Yeah, it was really the old crowd, wasn't it?'

Rachael shook her head. 'I realised how long ago that was. How much everyone had—' She broke off, taking a shuddery breath. 'They're all married, Sam. They've got kids, or they've been travelling, or working their businesses. They were all talking about the things they've been doing, and . . . and . . .'

'And you've just been here, looking after your mum?'

Rachael nodded. 'You know I was happy to do it. But then I . . .' Her voice choked.

'What?' Sammy asked gently.

'I overheard someone saying how I used to be good at school and how I'd never make up for losing that time. And then I couldn't stop thinking about that, or about Matthew . . .'

Sammy leaned her head onto Rachael's shoulder, a silent gesture of solidarity and comfort, and hugged her fiercely with one arm. 'Rach, whoever said that is a knob. Let me tell you as a married person, we haven't got something over you. It's not all perfect on this side. You didn't lose time, it was just different. You were utterly selfless in what you did for your mum, and now you've got qualities that other people can only dream about.'

'Like what?' Rachael asked, disengaging herself and hanging a Parkes Elvis Festival mug back on its hook, the same one she'd made her mother's tea in that morning.

'Compassion. Endurance. Patience, for starters. Plus you've been running the property all that time.'

'Mum was the real brains behind it. She might have left it to me, but it was her farm.'

Rachael glanced out the window to the gum tree on the rise where they'd scattered Marion's ashes. She didn't know if she belonged here any more, not without her mother. But where else would she go?

She heaved a huge breath, backing away from a dark pit. 'Talk to me about something else.'

'Well,' Sammy said, putting an encrusted Weet-Bix bowl aside to soak, 'would you like to hear about the suspected rat at the bakery? The disgusting thing I found in one of the motel rooms last week? Or the latest from the Feud Across the Fence?'

'What's happened this time?'

'Well, I saw a police car parked in Bev's drive last week,' Sammy said. 'Taking a statement apparently. I didn't tell you at the time but Bev thought one of her garden ornaments had been stolen, then it turned up later in the bin. Bernie didn't say much about it at work, but I limit him to five minutes boasting about his latest revenge plan, so I don't have all the details.'

Rachael shook her head. For as long as anyone could remember, postmistress Beverley Watkins and Bernie Collins, the town baker, had loathed each other. Their neighbourly dispute was famous in the district, though no one could remember how it had started. Rachael's mother had somehow managed to be good friends with both of them, though never, she was quick to add, when they were in the same room. Rachael knew her mother had been entertained by the ongoing hostilities, viewing them as a harmless farce, but she'd never shared Marion's enthusiasm.

'I always thought it'd burn itself out eventually. They were both so good to Mum, it's hard to believe they hate each other so much.'

'Try living in a shed on one of their properties,' Sammy said. 'Then it feels like it will never end.'

A rumble announced a car coming down the long drive. Sammy put her hand on Rachael's arm and went out to look.

'Speak of the devil,' she said as she came back. 'It's Bev.'

⟶

Rachael opened the door to find Beverley Watkins wearing a pair of Christmas-themed earrings that clashed horribly with her apricot suit. Even so, she managed to project the dignity and authority of a headmistress. Her grey curls had been backcombed into an impressive coif and her half-frames hung on a long chain around her neck. She was clutching a sturdy calico bag and a bucket full of rags and spray bottles.

'I've come to help you clean up,' she said, brandishing the bucket. 'You must have three inches of dirt on the floors after all those people here yesterday.'

'That's very kind,' Rachael said. 'But—'

'Not to mention the state of the toilets. I love a farmer, Rachael, you know I do, but half those men think the toilet brush is some kind of ornament. Let me deal with it and spare you the horror.'

It wasn't the first time Beverley had turned up with rubber gloves and cleaning supplies. She'd taken to coming once a month for the last year or so, and during the worst parts of her mother's decline Rachael's pride had given way to appreciation. The woman was a stain-destroying crusader.

'But what about the post office?' she asked, pushing the door wide to let Beverley through.

'I'm opening late today. Just been in to do the sort. People can still access their mailboxes if they want, and no one much comes in before lunchtime. I brought your post with me. Here.' She dipped into the bag and came up with a thick wad of letters. She squeezed Rachael's hand. 'There'll be some lovely cards in there for your mum. Now, don't you worry about me. Just pretend I'm not here.'

'Bev's cleaning the toilets,' Rachael explained when she went back to the kitchen.

Sammy had finished the dishes and was wiping down the counters. 'I've still got an hour before I need to go,' she said. 'Is there anything else I can—'

She broke off, staring through to the family room window, which gave a glimpse of the drive. Another dust plume was coming, too far away yet to hear, but the vehicle was distinctive enough that Rachael knew instantly who it was.

Two minutes later, she opened the door to see Peter Grant climbing out of a pale-blue van emblazoned with AgriBest logos. Her heart gave a tiny lurch. Peter was Matthew's brother, and there was enough resemblance to remind her of Matthew every time she saw him.

Fortunately, his face was where the resemblance ended. Peter was what Rachael's mother had called 'rough round the edges', a man with a broad country accent, a slow way of speaking and an intense pride in his successful agricultural supply business. Like so many men of the district, Peter was also generous and hard-working, if sometimes overbearing in his enthusiasm. Today he was wearing an AgriBest polo shirt, a snug pair of jeans and a cowboy hat.

'Rach!' He strode over and gripped her in a bear hug. He smelled of soap and cologne, and was all fit muscle under his shirt. 'How're you holding up?'

Rachael was too squeezed to answer, but there was something comforting in his gruff care of her and she patted his solid back. Despite his reputation as a shrewd businessman, Peter had often extended their farm credit long past what was reasonable, saying that the community had to look out for each other. In return, Rachael and her mother had been loyal customers.

'Mum and Dad send their best wishes,' he added. 'They thought it was a lovely service yesterday.'

Rachael nodded and asked him to thank them. Things had been a bit awkward with Greg and Evelyn ever since Rachael had broken up with Matthew, and they maintained a cordial distance. She hadn't been out to their sheep farm in years.

'Just passing by on my way back to Parkes,' Peter said. 'Thought I'd come lend a hand in the shed – you must be still cleaning the harvest gear. Suzi's got the shop under control,' he added when Rachael tried to refuse. 'Oh, hi there, Sam.'

Sammy stood in the kitchen doorway, a tea towel working in her hands. 'Hi.' She turned to Rachael. 'Should I put out another cup?'

'Nah, I'm off down the back,' Peter said. 'Won't come in – dirty boots. Catch you later.'

'Joel and Tess are down there with the kids,' Rachael called after him.

Peter raised a hand in acknowledgement and kept striding. He appeared in the backyard a moment later, growing smaller as he headed for the far shed.

Sammy watched him from the window. 'What's he doing here?'

'Came to help with the harvest gear cleaning.'

Sammy grunted.

A few minutes later, Tess and the children came back from the shed in search of snacks, and Beverley popped in to sip a mug of tea and admire the children before heading back to what she whispered was the 'unspeakable condition' of the second toilet.

This, Rachael reflected, was what her mother had always loved about the country: that people knew and helped each other. But she couldn't help feeling restless. Beverley was cleaning; Peter and Joel were working; Tess had taken over the meals while she was here. Rachael had nothing to do, and into the void came the pressure of lost time, the comments she'd heard at the wake eating like poison into the soft centre of her grief.

She prowled around the kitchen. She picked up the pile of envelopes, then put it down again. Then picked it up again. She couldn't quiet the churning in her chest. Her mother's death had been a terrible shock, but a problem just as large loomed: the *what now?*

She checked the bins for the third time, but they'd already been taken out and replaced with fresh liners smelling of lemon. When she trailed out to the laundry, passing Beverley working on the second shower, she found the hamper empty, the back line nearly full, and a last load already going in the washer. Nothing to do there either.

The children were whining for more of Sammy's pastries while Tess firmly told them no and redirected them to sandwiches. When Joel and Peter came up from the shed for coffee, the noise in the tiled kitchen and family room reached a crescendo.

Overwhelmed, Rachael was hovering in the hall when Sammy came to find her.

Her friend touched her lightly on the shoulder. 'How about we go outside? Sounds like a concert in here.'

Rachael nodded with relief.

'Do you want those with you?'

Rachael looked down. She was still holding the stack of mail. This, at least, was something she could do. She gripped them tighter, and pushed outside into the warm air.

Rachael flipped through the envelopes. Her mother had been a diligent and consistent correspondent. Her Christmas cards went out every year, and she'd kept a diary loaded with birthdates and significant events for just about everyone she'd ever met, which she had checked every week right up to the end, even though Rachael had to turn its pages for her and write her letters. All those years of dedication had been repaid in kind.

Rachael slid open the first card, which offered condolences from the Parkes theatre group, for whom Rachael and her mother made costumes most years. Then another, from the bowls club.

As Rachael was reading it, Sammy came out the door with fresh tea. 'They'll all be gone soon,' she said. 'Bev's nearly finished.'

'Mmm,' Rachael said, taking out another condolence card. The front was pretty, a grove of autumnal trees, but the handwriting was so bad she could hardly read it.

'I've been thinking,' Sammy said. 'Do you want to get away? Even for just a night. I could come and pick you up after work. Tess is here until tomorrow, isn't she?'

'Day after,' Rachael said.

She was about to put the letter pile aside when a particular envelope caught her eye. It was creamy and thick, with her name and address in swirling calligraphy letters on the front. She straightened the tiny fold in the top right corner, and rubbed her thumb over a smudge on the heavy paper.

'Who sent that?' Sammy asked.

Rachael peered at the black letters: *Miss Rachael West.* Each one carefully executed by hand, with little pools of ink at the bends. 'Must be someone arty. Maybe one of Mum's quilting friends.'

She used a finger to break the gold embossed sticker closing the back. Inside was not a card but a heavy tri-folded sheet of paper with a gilded swirl at the top, like expensive letter paper. Two more folded sheets peeped from the envelope.

Rachael read: *Mr Walter Quinn requests the pleasure of your company for the wedding of—* Her eyes skittered down to the names, which struck her in the face like a sledgehammer. 'Oh,' she said. The word came out breathless, as if her lungs had been suddenly punctured.

She read the lines over and over, not believing what they said: *Bonnie Marie Quinn and Matthew Reginald Grant.*

Matthew Reginald Grant.

Matthew.

Rachael's chest twisted in a great knot. She had known Matthew was in Sydney pursuing his medical career while she was caring for her mother. She heard things about him from time to time, mostly from Peter. But she'd never given his life beyond medicine a thought, as if it, like hers, had been on pause. After all, Matthew was the one who'd said he was too busy for a relationship. Now here was immense evidence to the contrary. While she'd been helping her mother to the toilet, and driving to medical appointments, and getting antibiotics for the infections, and organising ring-ins to help plant and harvest, and working at the sewing machine on someone else's wedding dress, or sewing gold braid on costumes for the theatre group, he'd been out meeting people. Falling in love. Getting engaged to a woman called Bonnie Quinn who moved in the kind of circle that sent calligraphied wedding invitations. The movie of Matthew's life had kept playing long after Rachael had been written out of the script.

Abruptly, she realised the gold swirl at the top of the invitation was an elegant monogram of B and M. Bonnie and Matthew. Rachael squeezed her eyes shut as an exquisite pain bloomed between her ribs. This was not what was supposed to happen. It should be her name next to Matthew's.

'What is it?' Sammy asked.

Weakly, Rachael held out the invitation. Sammy extracted her glasses from her pocket and read with her eyes jerking from line to line.

'So he's getting married,' she said finally, then frowned. 'Bonnie Quinn. Wow, really?'

'What? Who is she?' Rachael asked, her voice tiny and faint and frantic.

'Well, you know *the* Walter Quinn, right?'

Rachael thought, slowly extracting where she'd heard that name. On the news, connected with mining and TV stations and a dozen other things. 'The big business guy?'

'Yeah, that's him. I think it's his daughter Bonnie. I've seen her in *New Idea*. She's in some kind of fashion business, but does lots of charity work – raising money for the kids' hospitals and building wells in Africa, that sort of thing. I'm pretty sure she was in *Who*'s sexiest people last year too.'

'How do you even know that?'

Sammy shrugged. 'Working reception at the motel. I can only watch movies if I keep the sound down, so I read the mags instead. It might not be her though.'

'Because Walter Quinn is such a common name.' Rachael sucked in a long, slow breath and forced herself to read the invitation again. Yes, it was all still real. Names. Dates. Location.

'Oh my god,' she whispered. 'It's in Paris.'

'What?'

Rachael pointed, sure she had slipped into some kind of dream. 'Paris.'

She pulled out the other papers in the envelope, which were instructions about contacting a travel agent to confirm flights and the hotel for herself and a partner, compliments of the bride.

Partner. Rachael almost laughed, but it came out as a hiss, like a pressure cooker about to vent.

She stuffed all the papers back into the envelope and squinted at the golden fields under the blue sky, her eyes resting on that dip where she and Matthew had lain together planning their future. She'd seen the whole world in his earnest green eyes. She wanted that moment back; wanted everything as it had been then.

But while the sky was still the same blue, Rachael's hands were rough from work and sun, her face etched with the years of caring for her mother and running the farm. Those days with Matthew were gone and nothing could replace them.

She scrunched the thick envelope and its contents in her fist and lobbed it towards a vintage milk can decorating the verandah. It bounced once off the rim, then tumbled inside with a puff of dust.

Sammy's eyebrows popped above the top of her glasses. 'You okay?'

'You know what you said about getting away for a day?'

'Yeah?'

'How about we do that.'

Chapter 2

Six hours later, when Sammy had finished her shift at the motel, she and Rachael hauled open the door of the second shed, and pulled out two trail bikes. On the tramlines, the dedicated traffic lanes that spared the field soil from compaction, the path was smooth, and they made excellent time to the river. The wind in Rachael's hair was pure liberation after two days spent mostly in the house. The sinking sun cast the low spots of land into pools of grey shadow, and the sky overhead was a pale, unmarred blue.

Two kilometres from the house, they met the river, and there, secreted between the trees, was a rocky bend with a swimming hole. It had been a favourite place when they were in school. They threw up a tent under the trees and, in the last of the sun's heat, peeled down to their underwear to dive in.

The water shocked Rachael like a frozen thunderclap. She surfaced gasping, water streaming down her face, her skin pinched against the cold. Sammy came up nearby with a more controlled gasp.

As Rachael swam, acclimatising, the knots in her body loosened. She floated on her back, exposed to the canopy-shaded sky while Sammy pulled herself onto a rock and ruffled her hair. 'This was a great idea. I thought my shift would never end. My boss is turning into something out of *Psycho*. Did you survive the rest of the day with Tess?'

'Yeah,' Rachael said. 'I finally got down to the shed. Peter stayed for ages helping me and Joel. It was nice of him.'

'But?'

Rachael gave up on floating and pulled herself out to sit in the sun. 'But . . . he reminds me of Matthew.'

'I was wondering about that.' Sammy threw her a towel. 'People usually send a polite letter if they don't want to go to a wedding. But maybe throwing invitations into a milk can will catch on.'

'Funny.'

'You want to talk about it?'

Rachael sighed, squinting into the sun, which had dropped into a gap in the trees. Matthew had stood on that exact rock so many times, in his boardies, dripping wet. 'Rach!' he'd call, looking for her and blowing a kiss before he bombed into the water. Her heart had clenched every time in case he came down too close to the edge, but he always emerged safe, always returned to her, wrapping his arms around her, and telling Peter and their other friends to carry on without him.

'I'm fine,' she'd protested once. 'Don't you want to keep up the competition?'

'No,' he'd said simply. 'I want to sit here with you.'

The others had rolled their eyes at them, the besotted couple in a sea of awkward teenage relationships. Rachael had never minded that, only the bleak emptiness that had followed when he was no longer hers.

'I should be over it, right?' she said to Sammy. 'I haven't seen him in ages. We were only together for a bit over two years.'

Out loud, it seemed a ridiculously short time compared to how long they'd now been apart.

Sammy considered. 'True, but teenage love hits hard. I was still pining over Eric Scott until last year.'

'The red-haired guy who got expelled for drinking behind the loos?'

Sammy shrugged. 'I must like a bad boy.'

Rachael laughed. 'You made that up.'

'I did. Seriously though, I remember what you and Matthew were like. Everyone thought you'd end up together. Hell of an expectation. There's no rules for getting over someone.'

Rachael threw her towel around her shoulders, and dug in the bags for a pair of thongs. 'I'm sure Tess would have some. She's already over Mum.'

'Maybe. Maybe not. People react differently to grief.'

'Mmm. Usually we're pretty civil with each other, even if she is a bit overbearing. I work around her. I just can't find the way this time. Joel is a saint.' Rachael paused. 'How are things with Marty? I've been meaning to ask.'

'Fine,' Sammy said quickly, rummaging in the food bag. 'So, you're not going to Matthew's wedding?'

'I don't know. It just feels ... weird. And I don't like the idea of them paying for me to go.'

Sammy made a dismissive noise. 'Rach, you know I didn't like how he broke up with you, saying he didn't have time for a relationship. I mean, come on. If you do decide to go, I think you've earned the flight.'

'I guess he meant he didn't have time for a long-distance relationship.'

'Whatever. It was the easy route. He didn't even try. He'd only been in Sydney for six months then.'

Rachael said nothing. She could still remember the last time they'd been together when she'd made the trip to Sydney, how she'd counted down the days. Then she was finally there with him, and Matthew had shown her all around campus with enthusiasm, never hinting at any problem before dropping the break-up bombshell. She'd never admitted that part to anyone; it had hurt too much. She preferred to remember coming to the swimming hole with him, and lying out in the fields, and going to dances, and driving the paddock-bashers around his parents' property. She would do all that again in a heartbeat.

'Maybe he just knew,' she said now.

'Don't care. I don't believe in the easy out. You love someone, you try for as long as you can to make it work. Now, we'd better find that gas stove, or all my hunting for marshmallows will be a waste.'

As twilight settled, they dragged in logs to sit on, and scraped fallen leaves aside for their camping stove. Sammy carefully blistered her marshmallows until they were golden and sliding off the stick onto a chocolate wheaten sandwich. Rachael's always caught fire, but she argued she liked the crunch.

'I did also bring soup,' Sammy said. 'If you feel like real food.'

Rachael shook her head. 'Just don't mention any of this to Felix and Emily. They'll be so jealous. They were begging me all afternoon to come. Tess was looking daggers at me like it was my fault.'

When the biscuits ran out, Sammy shut off the gas and the evening drone of insects closed in again. The waterhole was a mirror of branches and sky, and the cooling air promised a quick descent into night.

'Do you want to talk about your mum?' Sammy asked finally.

'Umm . . .' Rachael clammed up. She didn't know where to start.

'I don't know if this is the right time,' Sammy said when Rachael didn't continue. 'But here.' She pulled an envelope from her pocket and from it extracted a tiny folded piece of paper, its edges dark with grime and age.

Rachael's hand flew to her mouth in surprise. 'Where did you find that?'

'Your mum gave it to me at the hospital. It was the same day she passed away, but earlier, when you'd gone to get tea. She said to choose the right moment to give it back to you. What is it?'

Rachael could barely speak through the tears slipping down her cheeks. 'A poem I wrote in school. For Mother's Day. The one right after my father left. She kept it in her purse ever since.'

And from there, all of Rachael's grief came flooding out. How much she missed her mother, the frustration that her life ended too soon, how unfair it was. And yet also the relief she would admit to no one else: that her mother hadn't suffered long in the end. That she'd gone quickly, the way she'd wanted.

After this catharsis, Sammy prompted Rachael for stories about how, after the shock of Rachael's father buggering off, Marion West had calmly taken over the farm.

'She told me once she had no idea what she was doing,' Rachael said, 'but she'd read about no-till farming so she decided to try it. Just like that. Swapped over the machinery and the methods before anyone else around here did. She had guts.'

Sammy laughed. 'That she did. And she didn't suffer fools either. Do you remember when Eric Scott came to that movie-night fundraiser absolutely plastered?'

Rachael giggled. It had happened early in her mother's illness, when she was still walking and able to go out. She'd been sitting next to the refreshment bar where Rachael was serving, and Eric had stumbled in just as the credits for *Star Wars* were rolling and the audience was racing for food and drinks. Marion West had taken one look at Eric and beckoned him over.

'Hello, Eric,' she'd said, with a big smile.

'Oh hi, Mrs West.' Though he was steady on his feet, the slurring 'misshus' gave him away.

Marion had dropped her voice. 'You been drinking, Eric?'

'Nope.'

'That's an interesting smell then.'

'It's Red Bull,' Eric tried, full of hopeful bravado.

'Well, this is a no Red Bull event,' Marion had said. 'You'd better head on out and come back with the truth or a better lie.'

Eric had considered his options then walked. Marion watched him.

When he was almost to the door, she called him back. 'How did you get here?'

When he looked at the floor, Marion had sworn under her breath and held out her hand. 'For all that's holy, Eric. Give me those keys! Rachael and I will drive you home. Then we're going to have a chat about responsibility.'

Over the next year, Marion's fatigue had worsened as the progressive MS took hold. She'd not gone to many more events, keeping mostly to the farm.

'She was always making something,' Sammy said. 'Just like you.'

Rachael smiled. 'I can remember when I was little and she was working on a dress, or curtains, or anything. I'd go to bed and I could hear the sewing machine running seams. And then a bobbin would snag, or the stitches would jam, and I'd hear her saying, 'Shit, shit, shit,' under her breath. It was the only time I heard her swear.'

'Only because she thought you couldn't hear!'

Several hours went by before they ran out of memories, and decided to put on the soup. Afterwards, they leaned back under the twinkling stars with more warm mugs of tea.

Finally, Rachael said, 'I know I had a long time to prepare for this, but I never wanted to think about it. I don't know what to do. Every time I think of running the farm it seems so . . . incomplete without her.'

'What do you want to do then?'

Rachael was silent a long time, staring up through the branches at the stars splashed overhead. She sighed. 'Honestly? I want to go back ten years and do it over. For life to be completely different.'

Dried leaves crackled as Sammy pushed herself up on an elbow to look at Rachael. 'You mean you wouldn't have stayed? You'd rather have gone to Sydney with Matthew?'

'No!' Rachael said, a slimy horror sliding down her back at the thought of leaving her mother to fend for herself. 'I mean I want her never to have been sick. I want to be back at the end of school when everything was still ahead. When Matthew and I were together, and we went to Sydney and did all the things we planned. For Mum to still be here now.'

Sammy let the wish settle in the cooling air. She put a comforting hand on Rachael's shoulder. 'I get it,' she said, her voice husky. 'Lots of us would like to go back. I'd like to have tried harder at school so I could be running a business now and not working at the motel and behind the bakery counter and living in my boss's shed.'

Rachael swallowed her useless desires and wiped her eyes, glad to focus on something else. Sammy's dream job had always been to take over the Parkes video store where she'd worked as a teenager. She frequently lamented that the switch to online streaming had robbed her of her natural calling.

'No new business ideas, then?' Rachael asked.

Sammy gave an exaggerated sigh. 'Not yet. Marty's flat out lost interest in opening his own mechanic shop since he lost his job. He says the industry's down and we don't have enough capital. He's worried about what would happen if it didn't fly. Besides, I have to finish that bookkeeping course so I could hold up my side of things. Not exactly our dream when we got married but . . . well, regrets, you know?'

'Mine's not regret,' Rachael said softly. 'I'm glad I stayed for Mum. I'd do it again. But I'd like my time machine now, thanks very much.'

'Better make that two.'

Rachael peered at Sammy through the dark. 'Are things really okay with Marty? You seem down about something.'

Sammy only paused a fraction of a second before saying, 'Oh, nothing that a glass of wine and a good Japanese horror flick won't fix. He just has to get a new job, that's all. Besides, we were talking about you.'

'Mmm,' said Rachael.

'I was thinking about what you said about overhearing those women at the wake yesterday. You were going to do journalism at uni, weren't you? You did great in English.'

'That was the plan.' The plan she'd made with Matthew at least.

Sammy made a noise. 'Funny. I always thought you'd be an artist or something. You were always sketching or sewing something back then.'

'That's not a real career. Mum was a better dressmaker than me and she still ran the farm.'

'Why don't you look into journalism then? It's not too late.'

'I guess. But there's still the farm.'

'Lots of places do external courses. If you could care for your mum while running the farm, I'm sure you could study.'

Rachael didn't argue, but the ten years of lost time seemed an enormous weight. After seeing all those old friends at the funeral with their families and stories about their jobs and travels, she couldn't just make any decision. It needed to be the right one. She didn't have any time left to make a mistake.

These thoughts stayed with her as they pulled out sleeping bags. The very last thing she did was to take a pen from her bag and write on the back of the biscuit packet, *Are you sure things are okay?* She handed the note to Sammy. This was a long tradition going all the way back to how the two of them had become friends: passing notes in English class. Sometimes the hardest things were easier to write.

Sammy took the pen, wrote, and handed the packet back. *All good*, it said.

⟶

Rachael returned to the farm with renewed hope, but couldn't convert it into any action. A whole day went past, and the night before Tess and Joel planned to leave, she lay awake most of the night thinking.

When the first blush of sunlight showed on the horizon, she slid out of bed and pulled open her dresser drawer. Inside were several sheets of stapled paper detailing her mother's instructions. Rachael knew the list well and had been avoiding it ever since her mother had enlisted Beverley's help in writing it six months ago. It was organised by location: three shorter pages for the linen cupboards where the quilts were stored, and the lounge; and a very long one for her wardrobe and bedroom. Rachael folded that page to the back.

She padded to the lounge, where she'd spent almost all the waking hours with her mother these last two years. Rachael had often been at the sewing table in the evening while her mother dozed in her chair. Standing in the doorway now, she could smell the ashes of the last winter fire in the grate. The large sewing table was still set up in the corner, holding the machine and the overlocker, beneath shelves of offcuts and interfacing and bias tape and tailor's chalk. All of it left to Rachael.

She ran her eye down the list. The nativity play costumes for St George's Church in Parkes were packed in a clear tub under the overlocker. Rachael had carefully cut and stitched each one; Mary's blue satin robe with gold-braid trim was suitably immaculate. She checked everything was there, repacked the tub, and carted it out to the ute. There – she was finally doing something.

Next, she carried out the dying condolence flowers and dug them into the compost heap, then opened the blanket boxes and began matching the long list of her mother's most loved quilts to the list of recipients. By the time the sun was two fingers over the horizon, neatly folded piles covered the lounge floor and the two couches. Only her mother's chair had been left vacant.

'Well, this looks organised.' Tess stood in the doorway in pink satin pyjamas, her hair down but still straight and even.

'Just following Mum's list,' Rachael said. 'She had a long time to plan.'

Tess looked around. 'Want a cuppa?'

'Yes, lovely.' Tess was acting suspiciously like a normal person.

When her sister brought in the tea and set the mugs on the windowsill, Rachael was ready for the inevitable question.

'What can I do?'

'Post bags. There's a stack in the office. Each one of these piles needs wrapping, packing and addressing. Mum wrote notes for everyone,' she added, handing over a stack of cards. She didn't mention that it was Beverley who had written them, taking instructions because Marion could no longer hold a pen for more than a few minutes.

For a while, they worked in silence, then Felix and Emily rushed in to find out what they were doing. Joel, with the baby balanced on one arm, sleepily herded them into the kitchen without being asked, and soon Rachael and Tess were working to a backing track of the toaster popping, the fridge opening and closing, and Joel mediating squabbles. When Rachael smelled cooking butter, she knew he was making pancakes.

The packaging was done by the end of breakfast, and the children carried the bags out to the ute, before Tess told them to go with Joel to begin their own packing.

'What's next?' Tess asked, peering at the list over Rachael's shoulder and pulling the last page to the side. 'The bedroom?'

Rachael tucked the page back and pulled open the last lounge cupboard. 'I want to finish in here first.'

After sorting through a stack of old LPs, Rachael suddenly realised Tess had been silent a long time. She turned to find her sister had pulled open their mother's hinged footstool and was busily emptying its contents. Ringed around her on the floor were all the vintage patterns in their fragile yellowing packets, and the small collection of buttons and trims and braiding affixed to cards that were brown-splotched with age.

'Ugh, what is all this junk?' Tess asked, her nose wrinkling as she dug deeper. 'It smells.'

Rachael lunged. 'No, leave it! You're getting it all out of order. Put it back. That's *not* on the list.'

Tess stared at her with wide eyes, like people did on soap operas when the camera was too close to their face. 'What order? It's all mixed up.'

'It's not. It's ordered by year. Vintage patterns and buttons and trims, plus the fifties' *Vogue*.'

'This old thing?' Tess flicked through the battered magazine. 'Ugh, these clothes are hideous.'

Rachael winced. 'They are not. Put it back!'

They could have been children again, fighting over something of Rachael's that Tess wanted to play with.

When Tess didn't move, Rachael scooped up the spilled contents and retreated to the sewing table, re-sorting the items from memory. When she was finished, she returned them to the footstool, slammed the lid and pushed it underneath the table.

'Fine,' Tess said, as if she'd given up. 'Be like that. I'm going to pack. We can take the mail to the post office when we leave.'

Later, while Joel and the children were in the kitchen fixing snacks for the drive, Rachael walked past her mother's bedroom and saw the door ajar. Prepared to rouse on Tess for rifling through their mother's things after all, she opened the door to find her sister sitting on the central ottoman inside the walk-in robe. The ottoman had a red embroidered silk cover, a shock of colour against the pale carpet. Tess was half-turned towards the three sides of hanging rails, an old jumper of their mother's hugged to her body. She was rocking, silent despite her obvious anguish. Rachael didn't have to see her face to know she was crying.

Surprised, and unsure what to do, she backed out. Maybe Sammy was right and Tess wasn't as iron-hearted as she seemed. In that moment, Rachael forgave her sister all the pushy intrusions. Tess had lost her mother too. They were both hurting. Tess might have left with their father twenty years ago, and a gulf had grown between them because of their separate lives, but they were still sisters. They should talk. Maybe, just maybe, they might find some common ground.

On this last point, however, Rachael's hopes proved unfounded. Tess emerged with dry eyes and jovial spirits, and soon had the kids and bags loaded. She and Joel were just a dust cloud on the horizon before Rachael could even formulate a way to broach a discussion.

⌒

Their departure left Rachael with a long list of farm work – weed control had to be done, and the south paddock prepared for a crop rotation – but first she had two packages to deliver personally.

She drove into town along roads lined with baled straw, the sky daubed with painted clouds. When she pulled up outside Bernie's and Beverley's twin weatherboard cottages, all seemed tranquil. She could almost hear classical music playing. The right-hand house was freshly painted in buttercup yellow with the trims in clean cloud white. Its walls floated in a manicured garden that was divided with low hedges and busily decorated with intricate scenes: garden gnomes, concrete casts of oversized frogs on lilypads and several water features on timed rotation.

In contrast, the left-hand house's only nod to gardening was a large maple tree on the front lawn, though the house itself was neat in dark green and corralled from the street by a low picket fence. The fence that ran between the two cottages, however, was eight feet high, its palings crammed together so barely an atom could squeeze between them. Beneath the maple, Rachael could see Bernie Collins, still in his baker's white shorts and shirt, the latter stretched over his belly. He was busily raking leaves from the lawn and tossing them over the high fence into Beverley's yard.

Rachael grabbed her first package and got out. Only then did she realise that classical music really was playing, at high volume from somewhere inside the houses.

'Bernie,' she called.

Bernie, caught mid-tip, glanced up. He might have reddened, but Rachael couldn't tell through the permanent pomegranate flush across his cheeks.

He pulled out a pair of earbuds. 'Rachael, love! Are you here to see Sammy?'

'No, I have something for you. Thought I'd catch you before you turned in.'

In keeping with his early work hours, it was well known in Milton that Bernie took a long afternoon nap.

He glanced at the large package in Rachael's hands and gestured grandly towards the house. He had flour stuck in the creases of his knuckles, but despite starting work at three in the morning, his winged DA hairstyle was perfect, matching the bakery's logo of Elvis – in full *Jailhouse Rock* dance pose – stitched on his shirt.

Happy barks greeted them at the door.

'Go on, Presley, outside, boy,' Bernie said, shooing the dog into the yard and ushering Rachael past the life-size *Jailhouse Rock* poster in the hall and into a sitting room that paid all homage to the King. The classical music intensified, at odds with the walls crowded with framed Elvis movie and concert posters. Even the cushions on the brown settee were printed with his image. It made Rachael's package all the more fitting.

'This is from Mum,' she said simply, handing it across during a lull in the music.

Bernie raised a questioning eyebrow, but wasted no time in breaking the parcel open. He shook out the quilt: a masterpiece of tiny black-and-white patterned squares that, when viewed from afar, formed an image of Elvis on stage.

'Oh, Rachael. Goodness, look at that. I remember your mum making it for the festival years ago. Got so many admirers, it did. She really want me to have it?'

'She couldn't think of anyone better. There's a note too.'

The envelope looked the size of a business card as Bernie turned it in his thick fingers. 'You want me to read it now?'

'Later. It's for you,' she said. She wasn't ready to hear her mother's words today, even if they were for someone else.

Bernie tucked the envelope in his pocket and returned to admiring the quilt. He shook his head. 'I don't know whether to put it on the bed or frame it!'

A soprano voice pierced the room, a long note on high C. Rachael winced. Bernie seemed unmoved.

'I didn't think you'd like opera,' Rachael said.

'I don't.' He carefully refolded the quilt, then opened a door and beckoned Rachael into the kitchen, where the volume swelled appreciably. 'That's Bev's latest trick – leaving that blasting across the fence from her bathroom window. But if I close this door and keep the earphones in, it doesn't worry me.'

'That's very tolerant of you,' Rachael said carefully, thinking how she wanted to shake them both.

'Can't betray she's had an effect. Besides, she'll have more to worry about when Presley's finished in her garden.' Bernie laughed.

Rachael leaned out the window to see Presley racing about in Beverley's yard, his wagging tail knocking gnomes like skittles.

'Bernie!'

'Don't look at me like that. You don't know what she did last week.'

He launched into an account of Beverley's latest misdeed, but after 'called the police', Rachael didn't hear any more because on Bernie's breakfast bar was a stack of opened mail, and there was no mistaking the envelope crowning the pile with its creamy card and calligraphied address. So Bernie had been invited too.

This fact was still in Rachael's mind as she drove around the block to Milton's main street, where a small run of businesses crowded together. The service station was at the far end, and the community hall alongside it, rather in need of paint. The old surgery was next, and then a truck lay-by. The busiest two buildings were at the end of the row: Bernie's bakery, Blue Suede Choux, whose awning sported a life-size cartoon King singing into a breadstick, and the post office where Beverley was queen. A tour bus had pulled into the lay-by – part of the stream of year-round visitors to the bakery that kept Milton alive. Otherwise, Parkes would have taken over the post years ago and the town would have effectively closed. That the post office was still able to provide a personal and dedicated service to the remaining residents and surrounding farms solely because of Bernie was something Beverley would never openly admit.

Rachael found Beverley writing Christmas cards behind the counter, which was draped in enough tinsel and fairy lights to sink a cargo ship. The stripes in the carpet's pile and faint lemon scent betrayed recent vacuuming. The sparsely stacked shelves were all so neat, the place could have been a museum. Rachael thought of the similarly immaculate gardens around Beverley's house and tried and failed to think of something to say about ending the stupid feud with Bernie.

Beverley accepted the parcel and read the accompanying note with gravity, then briefly clasped it to her chest. 'Bless your mother, Rachael. She was such a good friend.'

Rachael could only nod.

'How are you holding up now Tess has gone home?'

'All right,' Rachael hedged.

Beverley was staring at her intently, as if trying to discern truth from her response by pure confrontation. Seemingly satisfied, she pushed her hands before her on the counter.

'I wasn't sure whether to tell you this today,' she said. 'Because I know you and Matthew Grant were very close once.'

Rachael heard a ringing in her ears, like she was in a movie where a bomb had just gone off. She knew exactly what Beverley was going to say.

'You got an invitation too?'

Beverley plucked the creamy envelope from under the counter. It had been opened with a single surgical incision along the top edge. 'I'd understand if you found this a bit difficult,' she said with a great deal of compassion. 'I remember you had the same envelope in your post.'

Rachael laughed, but even to her it sounded high-pitched and wrong. 'Not at all,' she lied. 'We broke up years ago.'

'Good for you,' Beverley said, brightening. 'It's a windfall then. I must say, it's very exciting. An all-expenses-paid trip to Paris. I always dreamed of going there, but my ex-husband never wanted to travel overseas. I was always very jealous of all the places your mum had been. I'm so looking forward to it – I'm sure we'll have a wonderful time.' Beverley's face had lost ten years, the pinch around her mouth smoothed out, her eyes distant with imagining.

'I'm not sure I'm going,' Rachael said quickly. 'I'd have to leave the farm and it would be right around planting time.'

'Wouldn't Tess and Joel be able to help out again?'

'Maybe, but I'm thinking of going to uni,' Rachael said, casting around for excuses. 'I always wanted to do journalism,' she added, but it did nothing to fill the hollow in her chest.

'Good for you, darling. Your mum would be proud.' Beverley paused. 'But this trip is only for a week. Your timetable should allow that, shouldn't it?'

Rachael shrugged. 'Don't know yet.'

'I'm sure you'd be able to make it work. A holiday is a marvellous thing. Goodness knows, I'm keen to get away for a little while. Is that rotten tour bus still outside?'

Rachael leaned towards the window, her heart pounding. The bus was still there, its disgorged passengers either inside the bakery, posing for photos against the facade, or standing around the picnic tables wolfing their purchases.

'The whole place will look like a shambles when they leave,' Beverley said. 'Paper bags escaping the bins, stones kicked out of the garden. Takes me an hour after I close to set it right. Does Bernard ever thank me that his shop is always neat and tidy? No!'

Rachael didn't mention that Beverley would probably arrive home to find her garden in similar disarray, or that there would be no Parisian respite from Bernie.

'And that's not the worst thing,' Beverley went on. 'Did you know Bernard wants to move the bakery to Parkes? Move the bakery! That would be the death of this town. However untidy the tourists are, we need them, Rachael. Who wants to go all the way to Parkes for their mail?'

As surprising as this news was, Rachael's worries were far more immediate. All she could think was that her private anguish over the invitation was about to become very public. For if Bernie and Beverley had been invited, others would be too, and all of them would wonder why Rachael had decided not to go.

Chapter 3

Rachael tried very hard to ignore Christmas and New Year. In the lead-up, Beverley was particularly persistent in her attentions, promising to leave Rachael a full turkey dinner before going to visit her brother in Bathurst. On Christmas Day, Rachael eventually took the phone off the hook as Beverley's CWA friends called every ten minutes to see how she was. At least Bernie didn't make a big deal of his concern, just stuffing extra bread rolls in her bag along with a wrapped copy of *Elvis Presley's Christmas Duets*.

Rachael left the Christmas tree boxed in the roof, and with it the memories of good-natured arguing over whether lights or tinsel went on first, and putting the star on the top. The star was one Rachael had made in primary school, its points curling now and nearly all the glitter long ago shaken off into the carpet. Tess had one exactly the same. Rachael's mother had loved the idea that they were somehow connected by that star no matter how far apart they were. So after Tess called on Christmas Day, uncharacteristically without any remonstrations, and wished Rachael a happy day and said the children were missing her, Rachael went and got the star out and put it on the windowsill so the gum tree on the rise could see it. Then she went back to work.

Sammy tried to encourage Rachael to go to the Parkes Race Meet on New Year's Eve. Rachael refused, saying she was too busy, and promised she would go to the Elvis Festival in January instead.

It was an almost-truth. She had plenty to do on the farm, and was looking up information about journalism courses. She'd begun the latter task with enthusiasm, but had encountered a problem: she could only read about a course for a minute before she found her fingers had opened a new browser window. A few seconds later, photos of Bonnie Quinn would be splashed across the screen.

Bonnie was tall and leggy, her skin smooth and fine, and she was stylish, whether in a pair of jeans by the beach or on a red carpet. Rachael kept coming back to note the details that made the elements of her outfits work together. Bonnie became burned onto her retinas.

In one particular photo she was wearing a very smart and very fitted white jacket that Rachael spent a long time ogling. It had three-quarter sleeves, rounded corners, a nipped waist and covered buttons – classic fifties' style. It was the sort of jacket that would be paired with a fitted skirt, but Bonnie wore it with three-quarter trousers with an upturned cuff and simple white pumps, crossing the eras. Her blonde hair was twisted elegantly behind her head, with a subtle finger-wave through the front that said she knew exactly what she was doing. Her only accessory was a burnished gold clutch in her left hand, the same colour as the wheat fields in the summer sun.

In many of the photos Bonnie was standing in front of a wall of logos – at a premiere or a high-profile benefit; in others, her arm was linked with an older man who had a sizable paunch but still managed to look powerful and expensive in his tailored suits. This, Rachael discerned, was her father, Walter Quinn, billionaire businessman.

Rachael told herself that all this Google stalking was simply because she was curious. She wanted to understand who this woman was. But as she looked and looked, she realised she was searching for a flaw in Bonnie, something she could point to and say, there, Matthew chose wrongly. But the consolation never came. Bonnie was always smiling directly into the camera, seeming serious and classy and intelligent. She was never bending one knee or putting a hand on her hip like a ditzy model, despite being photographed alongside Hugh Jackman and a bunch of other celebrities.

The crisis point finally came when, after nearly two weeks of this, Rachael stumbled across a rare picture of Bonnie with Matthew. The photo had been taken at some distance, and Bonnie was partially obscuring his face, but it was unmistakably Matthew. He was smiling. The knot that had formed in Rachael's chest when the invitation had first arrived pulled tighter. Her heart thumped as if she'd run all the way from the swimming hole.

She dropped her searching habit after that, hoping the dull ache behind her breastbone would ease. It didn't. It reminded her of the dead-arm craze in primary school when kids had punched each other in the shoulder until the limb went numb. The next day it came up in technicolour bruises that took ten days to fade. Her chest felt like that now, except her heart was the muscle being pummelled. She didn't know how long it would take the bruises to fade, if ever.

And there was a deeper problem. Rachael couldn't concentrate on this potential uni course, couldn't concentrate on anything, while she kept thinking about Matthew. Running the farm with her mother had always given her a bone-tiring satisfaction, but that wasn't enough now. She needed to know what was next. Needed to be able to plan for it.

She pushed out of her chair and through the back door, facing the fields and sky. It was as though the two parts of her life that she'd sacrificed ten years ago – her future career and being with Matthew – were inextricably linked. While one remained unresolved, so would the other.

She paced down the verandah until she stood over the milk can. Several small creatures scuttled away from her hand as she dug inside. She brought out the crumpled invitation and smoothed its pages on the bench. Maybe she had been thinking about this all wrong. Maybe this wedding was the solution.

⌒

The day of the Elvis Festival, as promised, Rachael fought her way into Parkes to meet Sammy and Marty. The footpaths were swimming with people of all ages in costume and Elvis-flavoured sights. The scents of atomised frying oil and hairspray filled the air with carnival excitement.

Rachael had organised to meet Sammy outside the Parkes Country Motor Inn, which was in full view of the main stage across the road in the park. When she arrived, a tribute act was belting out 'Viva Las Vegas', but there was no Sammy. After waiting for fifteen minutes and failing to raise her on her phone, Rachael trekked across to the park and poked her head inside the Blue Suede Choux stall. Bernie, in full Vegas jumpsuit and sunglasses, as though he was due to perform any minute, was serving the tail end of a rush.

'Saw her over by the main stage,' he called when Rachael asked.

So Rachael headed that way, only to spot Beverley ahead in a Lisa Marie wig. With a frisson of guilt, she veered left and ran straight into Sammy, who was jogging through the crowd. She had on a pair of skinny jeans, ballet flats and a tight *Blue*

Hawaii shirt, and looked fresh and appealing except for her red eyes. Rachael instantly forgot Beverley.

'Yes, I know, I'm so sorry I'm late,' Sammy said, looking harried. 'I was just running across to find you. You must have been waiting.'

'What's wrong?'

'Just something silly. I couldn't find Marty.'

Rachael looked around. 'Where is he?'

'Not coming, as it turns out. I finally reached him on the phone and he's gone to see a mate in Orange. So it's just us. Do you want to get some food?'

'Are you sure you're all right?'

Sammy turned away, smoothing her hair. 'Yeah, I'm good. I wish he'd told me, but he says this mate might have a job opening. Now, what's this thing you didn't want to talk about on the phone?'

Rachael took Sammy by the arm and drew her away from the noise of the stage, where the tribute act was demonstrating his best Elvis legs much to the shrieking delight of the ladies in the front row. Across the park and behind a water fountain, she found a space with comparative quiet.

'Do you remember when we went camping what you said about me maybe going back to study?'

'Of course.'

'Well, I've been trying to research it for the last few weeks.'

'That's great—'

'But every time I try, I find myself googling Bonnie Quinn.'

'Oh.'

'I can't split them apart, Sam.'

Sammy frowned. 'I didn't think you were going to try.'

'Not Matthew and Bonnie,' Rachael said, impatient. 'I mean, Matthew and whatever I do next. I don't think I'll be able to move on until he's completely out of my system. I need to decouple him from my life, you know, like, like . . . a tractor and a drill.' She shrugged helplessly.

Sammy laughed at the metaphor, then said slowly, 'That does make some sense. You were saying you wanted to go back in time to when you still had both those things. But how are you going to get over Matthew?'

Rachael pulled the crumpled invitation from her pocket. 'I have to go to the wedding. If I see him get married, I'll know that he's gone and it's over with. Then I can move on properly. What do you think?'

She bit her lip. She had no other ideas. If Sammy thought it was a dud, she was lost.

But Sammy was nodding. 'That might just work.'

Rachael grinned. 'I'm so glad you agree. Because . . . I want you to come.'

'What?'

'My invitation is plus-one. We can see Paris together, and I might need you for moral support. I can't think of anyone else I'd rather go with.'

Sammy's lips parted just slightly to admit a gasp of air, a faint horror brushing her features. It came and went so swiftly that Rachael was unsure she'd even seen it, but she had the deep sense that Sammy was about to refuse.

'You don't want to?' she asked. 'Is this about Marty? Oh, sorry. Of course. You'd want him to come too.'

'It's not that at all,' Sammy said. 'I'd love to.'

'I didn't think . . . I just asked you to go overseas without him.' Rachael shook her head. 'And Paris at that. I—'

Sammy put a hand on her arm. 'You're my best friend, Rach. Of course I want to go. You just surprised me.'

Rachael searched Sammy's face, but could find nothing of the hesitation she'd seen moments before. She smiled. For the first time since her mother's death, she could almost see the glittering possibility of being free of Matthew, of being able to find her own future.

Sammy grinned back. 'Of course, you know what we have to do now, don't you?'

'What?'

'Research! I'll raid the movie shelf at the motel. We have to watch *Midnight in Paris*, *The Da Vinci Code*, *Moulin Rouge* and *The Bourne Identity* to start with. They're all set in Paris.' She seemed completely recovered.

'There is one thing I have to warn you about, and it might make you reconsider,' Rachael said. 'Bernie and Bev both got invitations too.'

Sammy's eyebrows shot up. 'I knew Bernie did, but Bev? Both of them on the same plane? Why do I somehow feel like we might make the news?'

They both laughed.

⟵

Rachael didn't know if it was the festival atmosphere or the rockabilly skirts, but when she returned to the farm in the late afternoon, she pulled out the plastic storage tubs from the shelves above the sewing machine. She hadn't wanted to touch them since her mother had passed away, but now she had purpose.

Rifling through, she found a bolt of salmon-pink Italian slub silk her mother had ordered on sale from Hong Kong years ago and never used. In another tub was a big piece of polka-dot silk chiffon, a remnant of a formal dress from 2008, and a gorgeous blue oriental print that demanded something truly special. Silk again. Rachael had inherited her mother's love of silk – its lightness, its shimmering lustre, the way it draped and sewed. There were other promising finds: a large piece of pale green jersey with an elegant print of blushing red roses. Scraps of lace and tubes of buttons and clasps.

She waited until last to pull the footstool from under the table. Amidst the collections of vintage buttons and closures, patterns and couture books that Tess had rifled through was a packet of corset boning and a huge piece of silk lining, so thin and light it could have been woven from spider's web.

Rachael pulled a few patterns from the box and skimmed her finger over the line of their skirts. If she was going to face Matthew getting married in Paris, she needed to look the part, and a gorgeous project, or three, was just the way to do that. The anticipation of making beautiful things *and* moving on with her life stirred an almost-happiness in her heart. She turned to a blank page in her sketchbook and started with a sweeping line, matching a vintage pattern. She drew and adjusted and redrew as the hours flew away and the sun dragged the blinds down on the day.

Finally, as dusk gathered, Rachael stretched out her aching hand and put the drawings aside. Her plan still lacked one critical element and she couldn't avoid it any longer.

'I have a favour to ask,' she said when Tess answered the phone.

'Can it wait? I've just got the kids to the table.'

'I'll be fast. I wanted to know if you'd be able to come down to the farm for a week in April? I'm thinking of going to a wedding.'

There was a pause, and then the sounds of clattering plates and children became muffled. Tess must have gone to another room.

'Whose wedding?'

Rachael paused. 'Matthew's. It's . . . in Paris.'

She braced herself, but Tess surprised her by saying, 'I heard about that.'

'How?'

'We get gossip up here too. The rumour mill runs all the way to Dubbo.'

Silence followed, until Rachael could no longer bear it. She imagined Tess's face, all the things she might be thinking.

'If you can't come it's not a problem,' she said in a rush. 'I can find someone else. And I don't want to hear anything about it being a bad idea.'

'Keep your pants on. I'm just thinking,' Tess said sharply, 'and looking at the calendar. I do have a few things to work around, you know.'

'Oh.'

'And who said anything about it being a bad idea? Who turns down an all-expenses-paid trip to Paris?'

Rachael said nothing. She could hear Tess muttering under her breath as she looked through the dates.

Finally, she said, 'Should be able to come. But we'd better have a talk about your planting plan to make sure. I'll call you Monday with Joel for a conference.'

'Thanks so much. I owe you,' Rachael said, but didn't hang up.

Another awkward silence. She was simultaneously desperate for advice and wary of Tess's opinions.

'Tess . . .'

'Mmm?'

'I've been trying to decide what to do now that Mum's gone.'

'What do you mean, what to do?'

'With my life. At the end of school I was going to go to university. I was thinking of maybe doing that now.'

'And what, sell the farm after it was just left to you?' Tess demanded.

'No, I would never do that.'

Tess let out a huge breath. 'Listen, Rachael, the grass always looks greener on the other side of the fence. If you want my advice, I'd say stick with what you know. Choose the farm. You can always do side hobbies, but farms are where real work happens. It's a good life.'

Rachael tried to give this the consideration it deserved, but her heart felt absurdly deflated.

'All right, I'll speak to you Monday,' she said.

'Rachael, wait.'

'Mmm?'

'This wedding must be pretty upmarket – you making some new clothes?'

'As a matter of fact, I'm looking at patterns right now,' Rachael said, remembering too late that Tess was openly jealous of the sewing skills Rachael had learned from their mother, which she had missed out on by going with their father.

'What else?' Tess asked.

Rachael's mind went completely blank. 'You mean like shoes?'

'No, I mean sort out your awful nails. What good's a nice dress if you've got chewed stumps on your hands? And make sure you get a haircut too. Do you need me to find a salon?'

Rachael hastily assured her she could manage. But after the call, when she looked at the red ends of her fingers and ragged bitten nails, then peered at her lank ponytail in the hall mirror, she had to admit that maybe Tess was right. Maybe she did need to do something about her chewing habit. And her hair.

She had just over three months to prepare herself to end this silly preoccupation with Matthew. It sounded like more than enough time.

⌐

Two months flew by in a blur of early mornings and late nights. Rachael's sewing station came alive, piles of materials steadily spreading away from the table to occupy the whole lounge. She stopped protesting against Beverley's cleaning visits, and didn't even mind when she came in with bucket and damp gloves to admire what Rachael was doing and ask questions. Rachael was so busy keeping the farm together amidst the sewing that she forgot to chew her nails, and for the first time she could remember there were little white crescents at the ends of her fingers.

Taking it as a sign, the next day she headed into Parkes. Sammy was doing a shift at the motel but the hair salon seemed unintimidating, and this way if the result was a disaster there would be no witnesses. She would never have admitted it to Tess, but the closest she'd come to a hairdresser in the last ten years was trimming the ends of her ponytail with an old pair of craft scissors. What was the point when she wore a hat all the time?

She tugged her cap down as she pushed inside, delighted to find the salon nearly deserted, even if the woman behind the desk had hair an alarming shade of blue and cut in an asymmetrical bob.

'Rachael West,' she said. 'I booked for ten o'clock.'

'Rachael!'

Rachael spun and was mildly horrified to see Beverley coming through the salon door as if she'd been tailing her. There was no hope of hiding now.

Beverley tried very hard to be helpful. When Rachael had no idea what she wanted, she pulled out a magazine and began showing her pictures. When this didn't help, Bev got her talking to Bronwyn about fifties' fashion, causing Bronwyn to suggest a long bob with a fringe cut in.

'The length will be modern, but the fringe is pure Audrey Hepburn. Very chic, and perfect for your face shape,' she added, holding her hands above Rachael's shoulders to illustrate. She tactfully made no comment about the elastic band in Rachael's hair, which was so used it looked like a shrivelled dead spider.

Rachael took a breath. Now or never. 'Do it,' she said.

Beverley clapped her hands in anticipation.

An hour later, the final result was surprisingly sophisticated. Rachael stared at herself in the mirror. Her hair had never been so smooth and glossy, like a perfect sheet of warm brown armour.

Beverley squeezed her arm. 'Your mother,' she began, then broke off, her voice a little choked. 'You look so lovely.'

This moment of warmth somehow led to Rachael going shopping with Beverley and being furnished with a new powder foundation in the right skin tone, an eyeliner pen, and three lipsticks in deep red, bright fuchsia and satin baby pink. Then it was into a nail salon, which Rachael left with the new ends of her nails coaxed into smooth half-moons. The whole time, Beverley kept up a chatter about the history of Paris and all the things she and Rachael must see and do. By the end, Rachael was thoroughly overdone and crowded. She wanted nothing more than to go home and dive into the finishing details of her projects.

She was just summoning the courage to reject Beverley's offer of lunch when they passed the Little Black Dress boutique. Beverley glanced in the window and her mouth twisted into an odd shape.

'Rachael, I have a little problem and I don't have your mother to ask any more.'

'What's that?'

The lines between Bev's brows were deep. 'It might be better if I show you.'

That was how Rachael ended up not back at the farm, but in Beverley's house, standing in front of her open wardrobe. The opera music had been turned off today. Despite the alarming amount of chintz in the room, the clothes Beverley pulled from dry-cleaning bags were surprisingly tasteful.

'These are quite lovely,' Rachael said, admiring a blue dress that was layer on layer of chiffon, and a ball gown in black with a fitted bodice.

'I often showed your mother the pictures before I bought them. Lovely on the hanger, but once I put them on . . .' Beverley shook her head. 'I don't seem able to buy anything that looks any good, except suits, and I can't wear those to a cocktail party in Paris.'

'I wouldn't be so sure about that,' Rachael said, thinking of Bonnie's fifties' white jacket and pants. 'But let's see.'

One by one, Beverley put on the dresses and Rachael could see what she meant. Something that looked wonderful on the hanger looked lumpy or shapeless on Beverley. Finally, Rachael asked if she had a tape measure.

'I think I see the problem,' she said, after taking measurements. 'You're short-waisted.'

'What's that?'

'Your legs are long but your torso is short. It means that the waist is always too low for you in anything you buy off the shelf. All these clothes are made for a standard body shape. That's why they look wrong – they just don't fit right.'

'So everything is going to look horrible?' Beverley looked as though she might cry.

'Not at all.' Rachael was busy pulling out dresses, muttering to herself. 'We can't do anything about this chiffon one because it's all single pieces, though I might be able to dart the underdress. The one with the bodice will be impossible with all the layers. But this and this . . .' She pulled out an attractive satin print dress and a two-piece evening suit made in brocade. 'I can pull these apart and recut the pieces.'

'Do you have time to do that?'

No, thought Rachael, but she could see the look on Beverley's face, the pride of this woman who wanted to keep her house and garden immaculate, and who had lost her best friend in Rachael's mother. Beverley, who came and cleaned and tried to look after Rachael, however much Rachael sometimes wished she would stop. She felt all of this as a great debt, and she was also trying to ignore Presley, who she'd glimpsed through the window earlier, probably stoking the fires of the feud with his activities.

'I can do it,' she said. 'Just let me take some more measurements. I'll do one first and we'll see how it looks. And if you buy anything new, go for an empire cut.'

⟜

That afternoon, Rachael went down to the waterhole, where she floated on her back and mentally reshuffled her time for the next month. As long rays of apricot light turned the fields orange, she climbed out and headed home to change for Sammy's movie night. She hadn't brought a towel so she rode the trail bike wet under her clothes, her squelchy shoes slipping on the clutch. Still, she was fresh and energised in a way she hadn't been in a long time.

She packed a piece of her current dress project to hand sew while movie watching. When she caught sight of herself in the hall mirror on the way out, her sleek bob had dried into pleasing windswept layers around her face and the new fringe framed clear eyes. She looked like someone who was ready to move on.

Sammy said as much when she opened the door to the shed. 'You didn't tell me you were getting a haircut. Let me see. Oooh, glamorous.'

'I wasn't sure how it would turn out.'

'But you like it?'

'I do. It's a bit hard to tie it back, but I'm managing.'

Rachael looked around as Sammy went to check on a pizza in the oven. She and Marty had been living in this converted shed behind Bernie's house for the past five years with the intention of saving money for a house. While the place was small and not strictly legal, Sammy staunchly defended the low rent as a necessary step in their journey to a better place and buying their own business. Boxes were piled in one corner, full of items there was no room to unpack. An exception had been made for Sammy's extensive movie collection, which was stacked two-deep in a bookshelf. All that was normal. But among the magnets pinning various calendars and photos to the fridge, Rachael saw a brochure for marriage counselling services.

'How's Marty?' she asked.

'Same old, still looking for work,' Sammy said as she shoved a garlic bread in the tiny oven. 'He got back from Orange today. He's trying out surrounding towns. Wow, I've just seen your nails.'

'Oh, right.'

Rachael tried to steer the conversation back, but Sammy wanted to know all about what had happened at the salon and when Rachael had stopped chewing her nails, so Rachael ended up relaying the day instead, including about Beverley and her clothes.

'I heard there's a few other locals been invited, mostly friends of Matthew's parents from Parkes,' Sammy said. 'And Pete's the best man.'

'That makes sense,' Rachael said. She hadn't seen Peter in a while, not since she'd gone into AgriBest the week after the funeral to pay some overdue invoices.

Sammy was about to say something else when they both heard a car rumble into the drive. A second later, the shed door opened and Marty appeared, dirty blond hair crammed under a cap, half an inch of stubble on his chin. He was a big guy, not fat, but with the kind of heavy muscle you'd see on a wrestler. He seemed on a mission, as if he hadn't expected Sammy to be home.

'Hey, babe,' she said, dimples showing with a too-bright smile. 'Need something?'

'Hi, Marty,' Rachael added.

'Hi, Rach. How you doing? Just forgot my six.' Marty squeezed past Sammy, went straight to the fridge and extracted a pack of beer. 'Don't wait up, Sam. See you later, Rach.'

He pulled the door closed. Sammy blew out a breath.

Rachael sat frozen. Marty hadn't looked at Sammy, and the tension between them was high and sharp and obvious.

'Is he mad about you going to Paris?' she asked in a hushed tone.

'No, he's totally fine with that.' Sammy poked around in the oven again. 'Look, we've had some problems. Having some problems, I should say. But we'll be fine. It's just a bump in the road.'

'Are you going to counselling?' Rachael pointed to the flyer on the fridge.

Sammy's expression wavered. 'Not yet. But we will. He'll get the hint if I leave that there.'

'Sam,' Rachael whispered. Things were clearly worse than Sammy had been letting on and she felt awful for not having noticed.

'No, don't do that tone,' Sammy said, scooting around the couch to load the movie. 'It's really not that bad. We have good days, and we're working things out. You and I are going to Paris for a week. You're going to get over Matthew and get on with studying, and I'm going to come back refreshed and then get back on track with this house and business thing. It'll all be great, you'll see.'

⟿

The day before they left, Rachael wrote one last to-do list – of things to pack – her stomach twisting with nerves. All those years ago, the break-up with Matthew had felt like being abandoned on the side of the highway, watching the tail-lights of the future disappearing over the horizon. Now, it was as if another ride was just around the bend and she had to be brave enough to stick out her thumb and take it. She was suddenly unsure if she could.

When she'd been with Matthew, everything had seemed possible. He was smart and good-looking and had encouraged her to dream big. He'd been her confidence. No wonder she couldn't move on without getting him out of her system. She wanted to know she was doing the right thing.

Rachael let the door slam as she left the house and tore up the tramline to the majestic gum on the hill. A circle around the trunk was planted with river daisies and into the bark was carved: *Marion West, 1959–2016*. Joel had done the carving, each letter careful and clear.

Rachael had never guessed this was how events would turn out when her mother was newly diagnosed. It had been two days before the HSC and they'd been sitting in a consulting office with white walls and blue carpet.

The doctor said, 'It's the rare type, unfortunately, but there's reason to hope. There are new drug trials all the time, and you're still functioning well.' On he'd gone, about all the services on offer, avenues for treatment.

Marion had finally stopped him. 'All that in its own time. Now, be honest with me. Brutally honest.'

He'd sized her up for a few seconds, and Rachael had wondered if he knew that this wiry direct woman with her sun-kissed face could somehow see through everything.

'It's going to be rough,' he said finally. 'You'll likely lose your balance, your mobility and your continence. We don't have any treatments that work yet. And while other people with this disease have remissions, you probably won't. There'll come a point where you'll depend on someone else for most of your daily living.'

Marion had set her shoulders, tipped her chin up. 'Right. Now that's out of the way, let's talk about the other things.'

Rachael sank down before the daisies and pressed her fingers to the cool earth. She needed her mother's bravery. 'So I'm going to Paris,' she said, offering up her uncertainties, looking for confirmation.

A breeze ruffled the gum. A few leaves drifted down, but no answers came. Rachael's lip trembled. She was on her own now.

When night had settled over the farm and the first stars were pricking the heavens, Rachael's case was packed. She was as ready as she could be. She stood in the doorway of her mother's room. The wardrobe was a shadow, all Marion's things still inside. She had always told Rachael that when things got too much, a way forward would show itself. Maybe this trip was that way forward, its hope winking like Venus in the sky: tiny and distant, but enough to guide her through the darkness.

Bernie insisted on driving Sammy to the airport in his twin-cab Hilux with the bumper stickers that said *Keep Calm Because Elvis Is Still King*, *I've Been to Graceland*, *I Am Australian: What's Your Superpower?* and *Vehicle Frequently Sideways* plastered across the chipped and rusty tray. To complete the look, a longhorn sticker spanned the rear window and a CB radio aerial and spotlight rack adorned the roof. As if to make sure she wasn't outdone, Beverley insisted on driving Rachael. Her Corolla smelled of potpourri. Thanks to her stately observance of the speed limit and Bernie's obvious flouting of it, the two vehicles were never in sight of one another on the highway. By some quirk of Sydney traffic, however, they arrived at airport parking a minute apart.

Rachael wasn't sure how the valet parking attendants – included with compliments of the bride – kept a straight face, especially when Bernie accepted the detailing service and asked them to go easy on the paintwork, then supervised the unloading of their bags as if he was worried about damage. Beverley watched it all with pursed lips.

'Going to do a spot of duty-free,' said Bernie once they'd made it through check-in and security. He rubbed his hands together as if all the vices the airport offered were about to meet their match.

'Good riddance,' muttered Beverley as she turned to Rachael and Sammy. 'Well, girls, what are we going to do with ourselves?'

'Not sure,' Sammy said. 'We might follow Bernie to the duty-free.'

Beverley sniffed. 'Have fun, I suppose. I'm just going to camp at the coffee shop.'

'We'll come and have one with you soon,' Rachael said, but she was buzzing with anticipation and couldn't have sat still. The week had finally arrived; nothing was left to do. Planters were lined up to sow the wheat the week after she got back, assuming the weather held.

All the Parkes area invitees were spread around the flight. Rachael and Sammy were together, with a spare seat on the aisle. Bernie was further back in the cabin, and Rachael caught snatches of his conversation with the crew, who spoke both English and French and ably pretended interest in Blue Suede Choux. Rachael admired the butter-smooth quality of their French. She had been practising phrases from an online French course for two weeks but was having trouble holding even the basics in her head. Beverley was five rows in front on the aisle; Rachael could just see her curls peeking up above the seat back.

She was nervous she might spot Matthew, though it quickly became evident that he wasn't there. Nor were his parents, or Peter.

'They've already gone,' Sammy said when Rachael mentioned it. 'All the family are meeting up first, apparently.'

Able to relax now, Rachael relished even the mundane details of her first ever overseas flight. She watched the safety briefing, then read through the card in the seat pocket three times.

'Nervous?' Sammy asked.

Rachael nodded. 'But excited too. I don't think I'll sleep.'

'Here.' Sammy passed across a bunch of glossy magazines. 'Read about the Duchess losing her baby weight, or Justin Bieber's latest tattoo. That's bound to dull your thoughts. I'm going to see what's on the movie channels.'

Rachael flipped through the magazines, pausing to admire dresses she particularly liked, thinking about how the fabric might have been cut, and then started on a crossword. This lasted her the first ninety minutes. After that, she watched movies, secretly enjoyed the meals in their little partitioned containers, and got up frequently to walk to the bathrooms. When she found herself thinking about Matthew, she chose a different show, or surfed the music selections for non-romantic songs, playing the whole Taylor Swift *1989* album twice.

Sammy seemed able to endure hours in her seat, though she was similarly unable to sleep. She gave Rachael a long explanation of why *The Thing* offered on the movie channel was inferior to John Carpenter's original, after which Rachael demanded to know why she was watching horror movies. Sammy laughed and said they helped her relax.

Finally, the two of them started up a silly paper dot-joining game they'd last played in school, until the plane began its final descent. Rachael found she'd left her nerves behind somewhere over the Middle East. She leaned across Sammy, craning for a glimpse of the city through the clouds.

The wheels bounced twice, and then the co-pilot announced their arrival in both English and French. Rachael gripped her armrest. Out the window was a cloudy sky, the sun just bleeding through like a soft-boiled yolk. The plane taxied. The seatbelt sign blinked off.

And then they were in Paris.

Chapter 4

Rachael stumbled through the airport as if her head was stuffed with feathers and her eyelids replaced with sandpaper. Speakers blared announcements in rhythmic, undecipherable French, and signs directed passengers to unreadable places sprinkled with accents. She loved the exotic, pleasurable disorientation. She was actually *here*. In *Paris*. And at the end of the week, she would be a different person.

In the chauffeured car, at first she could have been in any city. The traffic was dense, with scooters zipping between the cars, and the land either side of the motorway was crowded with warehouses and train tracks. But finally the road swung right and she glimpsed red roofs and trees. She pressed her nose to the window. Beyond the buildings and the winter-bare branches was the dark thread of the Seine, all of Paris anchored to its banks.

They took a low bridge across the water, then hugged the edge for the next ten minutes. Elegant white stone buildings slid by on one side while on the other was nothing but the river. Rachael was enraptured. She had seen the majesty of Sydney harbour, but this was different, far more intimate, so much more than what photos could convey. Under a sky of steel clouds, the city held the river in stone hands, stitching across it with arches and bridges. She remembered snatches of Beverley's guide book: the Seine was Paris, and Paris was the Seine, one creating the other. The river had a pleasing inevitability as it moved ever downstream through the city it nourished. The car followed, before finally turning away from the water.

The architecture became grand: buildings with tall windows, clean stonework and wrought-iron balconies. The chauffeur pointed towards the Musée d'Orsay, the Musée Rodin, and streets of boutiques where famous writers Rachael had never heard of had once created their works. She couldn't keep track. Two days ago she'd woken up in the place she'd spent her whole life, with wide open spaces rolling away to the horizon. Here, every inch was spoken for, hundreds of years of occupation resulting in the city as it existed in this moment. Rachael felt as though she'd stepped into a movie. She hadn't even left the car and yet Paris was a tidal wave of culture and history washing around her.

Then came the Maison Lutetia. Five-star with every convenience, the chauffer told them, one of Paris's oldest hotels; one block from the Church of Saint-Sulpice and booked exclusively for the wedding guests. It was a five-storey stone building with six-panelled windows, the second storey graced with elegant black iron balconies that trailed vines halfway to the street. The driveway was a graceful arc under a portico, where porters wearing blood-red jackets opened the car doors and took command of the luggage.

Inside, Rachael could only gawp. Rich wood panelling covered the tiled lobby, setting off the pale marble of a sweeping staircase crowned with a black iron and gold balustrade. Overhead was a chandelier shaped like a supernova that threw soft yellow light onto the rich cream and burgundy wall panels. Shaded table lamps stood beside chairs upholstered in red and gold. The effect was stately and luxurious, yet soft and sensual, with strategically placed palms offering whispers of natural green.

Rachael gripped Sammy's hand as a porter guided them into an expansive salon where, they were told, the wedding planner would welcome them. Rachael was scared to touch anything. She felt like a shorn sheep that had wandered into a black-tie dinner. How could she face Matthew feeling so intimidated? Had this been a hideous mistake?

Then she spotted Beverley shifting her backside in a deep armchair, Bernie at the end of a couch on the other side of the room, and a few more familiar faces. Angus, the butcher, who had closed his Milton business five years ago and moved to Parkes; Ronald and Jeanette, who ran the service station; and Terry, who'd been the rural fire service coordinator for the last five years. All friends of Matthew's parents and, to varying degrees, of Rachael's mother. Rachael hoped no one was planning to visit Milton this week; they'd find it deserted.

The only person she didn't recognise was a smart-looking woman by the window. She was impossibly slender and wore a tailored mint suit and a harried expression, her phone pressed against the side of her blonde French twist. Her accent was distinctly English. Finally, she snapped the phone shut and came towards them, her expression transforming, her very white teeth bared in a smile.

'Welcome, all, to this wonderful week of celebration. I'm Evonne Grace, the event manager. I know you've had a long journey so I'll keep this brief. Mr Quinn wants you to enjoy yourselves to the utmost so he has chosen the Maison Lutetia as your home away from home in Paris. In your rooms you will find a gift bag courtesy of Bonnie and Matthew. It includes passes to all the museums, and the complete itinerary of all events this week including rendezvous times. Those are important – you need to be in the lobby at the nominated time so we can coordinate the cars. At other times, if you're going out, you simply need to book a car at the front desk. You can also organise a pick-up to come back. Are there any questions?'

Rachael swallowed and raised her hand. 'Can we just . . . go walking?'

'Oh,' Evonne said, with a sparkling shimmer of a laugh. 'Well, yes, of course. You can come and go via either entrance in the day. The rear entrance requires your room key and is closed at night, but the reception is staffed around the clock. You'll notice that security is tight for the events to ensure privacy. For the most part the security team will be invisible, but you can approach any of them at any time if you have a problem. Anything else?' There was silence.

She smiled around at them. 'Excellent. I'm sure you'll want to rest before the welcome tonight. Your keys will be waiting. If I could just have a word with you, please?' This last was directed at Rachael.

Rachael glanced over her shoulder, uncertain. She felt as though she was back in school and being called on for an answer she didn't have. Sammy gave her a questioning look as she followed the rest of the group back to the lobby.

'I'm dreadfully sorry to hold you up,' Evonne said when they were alone. 'Evonne.' She stuck out her hand as though she hadn't just introduced herself to everyone else.

'Rachael West,' Rachael said.

Evonne flashed her teeth. 'Yes, I thought so. And you've all come from Milton in Australia?'

Rachael paused. 'Most of us. Milton or Parkes.'

'Where Matthew grew up, I understand. And just to help me orientate myself – the gentleman with the dark hair is Bernard Collins? And the older woman is Beverley Watkins?'

'Yes,' Rachael said.

Had Matthew mentioned the feud between Bernie and Beverley? Were they expecting trouble? And why did this woman seem to know about her?

'Excellent, thank you. Don't let me hold you up any longer. Lovely to meet you, Rachael. Enjoy the week.'

Rachael retreated to the lobby with her ears burning. Who had spoken to the event planner about her? And what had they said? Was it Matthew's parents, talking about how their friend had died last year and her daughter was invited to the wedding? Or was it Matthew himself?

A dozen times on the way upstairs, Rachael considered relaying all this to Sammy, but it seemed so outlandish she couldn't find the words. Then they reached the first-floor hallway with its thick carpet and buttery light. Rachael swiped a modern card-key in the old, stained wood door of her room and forgot everything else as she swung the door open.

Thick blue drapes like ball gowns framed the full-height windows, and a plush chaise longue reclined on the thick carpet. Light spilled from a bronze lamp atop a heavy wooden desk, and a king-size bed was swathed in a thick down quilt and a mountain of crisp white and Prussian blue pillows. Her case had already been placed on a luggage rack. The air smelled of flowers, leather, furniture polish and vanilla. On an exact corner of the bed was a large box tied with ribbon and sealed with red wax, and another smaller box of fine chocolates.

'We're dreaming, right?' Sammy said from the doorway of her room across the hall. She was just standing there, as if afraid to enter.

She backed up into Rachael's room instead. Rachael pulled at the box's ribbon and peered at the contents: a bound guide to the hotel; a booklet containing the week's itinerary, in classic white with crisp black lettering; museum passes; expensive toiletry samples.

Sammy leafed through the itinerary. 'This welcome thing tonight is a cocktail party at a *secret location*. Cruise tomorrow.

And the hotel's got a gym, a rooftop bar and a smoking room. Is that just what it sounds like?'

'No idea.' Rachael hugged herself. She hadn't heard anything after 'cocktail party'. Matthew would certainly be there.

With the thought, fatigue from the journey finally settled on her like a heavy blanket. She sank onto the edge of the cloud-like pillow-topped bed. The idea of exploring Paris had retreated. She just wanted to sleep.

'I think I'm going to take a nap,' she told Sammy.

'Did you know the east wing of this building belonged to a printer in World War Two? It was a centre of French resistance,' Sammy said, still reading the information pack. She looked up. 'I thought you wanted to be on Paris time?'

Rachael lay back on the bed, the weight of her head holding her down. Beyond the luxurious finishes, tiny nicks were visible in the architraves – marks of character and evidence of a long history.

'Knock, knock!' A jovial male voice came from the doorway.

Rachael sat up, her stomach diving before she realised it was just Peter. He looked uncharacteristically sophisticated in suit pants and an open-neck powder-blue shirt. His hair had been cut, and only the sun-kissed skin visible at his collar showed he was really an agricultural supplies businessman from country Australia.

'Is this place the duck's nuts or what?' he said. 'Are you coming out? Everyone's going for a drink in the bar, warm-up for tonight. Sam?'

Sammy turned to Rachael. 'What about a walk? You wanted to check out the rest of the hotel, and maybe see that church down the street.'

'I hardly slept on the plane. I need a rest. Besides, I need to iron my dress for tonight. You go though.'

Sammy shrugged. 'No, I'll do the same. Sorry, Pete.'

Peter held up his hands. 'Last chance. Come for a quick one, Sam, then you can come back. No rest for the wicked!'

A pause.

'All right, just a quick one. I'll see you later, Rach,' Sammy said.

Rachael heard the door close. After a few minutes, she drew herself up and went to the window. She pulled the white lace undercurtain aside to reveal a broad street faced with elegant buildings where people strolled in red and black coats. She was overcome with longing for her mother as she remembered a cloudy-sky day like this one back in October, when she'd found her mother staring out the window.

'Do you need anything?' she'd asked.

'No.' Marion's eyes were searching, as if trying to see all the features of the farm at once.

Rachael had paused, worried. 'Tea? Biscuits?'

'No.' Her mother had looked around at her then, tiredness in the hollows beneath her eyes, but a serene hint of a smile on her lips. And then she'd said, 'I think this will be my last harvest.'

Rachael had told her not to talk like that, but it was. She had known.

She rummaged in her case, digging out a knitted scarf from the side pocket. Her mother had started it three years ago. The stitches had come ever slower and were increasingly uneven, until towards the end she'd pulled the work into her lap each day but had been unable to add any more. Rachael had finished it with her own neat stitches, but it was the ragged end that she pressed to her face now. It still smelled of her, and was soft as a winter hug.

Rachael curled on the bed with the scarf hugged to her chest, asking for strength. She was here for a purpose. When she woke up, it would be time to begin.

Chapter 5

'Oh, Rach! Where have you been hiding that?'

Sammy stood in the doorway of Rachael's room, her mouth agape. In twenty-five minutes, they were due downstairs. Rachael tugged self-consciously at the hem of her dress, her hair falling forward and sticking to her lipstick.

'I didn't show you because it wasn't finished until two days ago. Mum bought the fabric in a sale and I wasn't quite sure about it.'

'Turn around.'

Rachael did a slow nervous spin. She'd spent many hours on this outfit, modifying one of the fifties' patterns for an oriental dress to match the more modern styling of a runway model she'd found online. The hemline alone had been a nightmare; she'd unpicked it three times and had to take it up to avoid leaving stitch marks. She had thought all the work had been worth it. The finished product was an hourglass of beautiful deep blue satin embroidered with pagodas and willows in greens and golds and reds. The skirt panel flared into a ripple at the mid-thigh and joined the dress at an elevated point at the front, while the halterneck opened in a diamond at the back. A cropped bolero in the same fabric with a tiny gold peg clasp completed the look. Only now Rachael worried about standing out.

'You don't think it's too much, do you?'

'Too much? You could stand on a red carpet in that thing. You make me look like a tramp.'

Sammy's reaction quieted some of the butterflies bashing around in her stomach. 'But you look lovely,' Rachael said.

Sammy's dress was fuchsia with a blue belt at the waist and matching strappy blue heels. It had been a bridesmaid's dress from a few years ago, until Rachael removed most of the ruffles, shortened the hem and added a complementary belt.

Sammy grunted. 'I'm only going to make one suggestion.' She raced back to her room and returned with a pair of pale silver heels. 'Those black shoes are too dark.'

Rachael looked in the mirror and realised she was right. 'You'd better fix my hair too,' she said. 'I've never got the hang of the straightener. It's all uneven in the back.'

'Knock, knock!' Beverley poked her head inside the open door. She was wearing a stylish black dress that Rachael had spent three long nights modifying. 'I've come to see if you need any help. My goodness, that's lovely, Rachael.'

'Thanks,' Rachael said. 'But I'm all right. Sammy's here and we're nearly ready.'

Beverley hovered. 'Right.'

'Did you need something? The dress looks wonderful.'

'It does, doesn't it? I can't thank you enough.' A tense pause. 'No, no, that's all right. I'll just see you downstairs.'

After she'd gone, with obvious reluctance, it took Sammy nearly half an hour to fix Rachael's hair, change her lipstick shade and approve the new shoes. As they descended the stairs late, Rachael saw the other guests had filled the foyer, waiting on the cars that would take them to the venue. The men wore dark suits, and the women cocktail dresses.

A hush rippled through them as Rachael and Sammy appeared. Rachael glanced around. No Matthew, but a number of stares. The conversational hum began again, as though a host of bees had just been taking a break. Sammy and Rachael hovered at the edge of the crowd.

'I was hoping we'd be able to walk,' Rachael said wistfully as the first cars rolled up. 'Did you end up going outside to look around? I only woke up with enough time to iron, and when I asked the front desk for a board, I had to convince them not to send the dress out to a specialist.'

'Not really,' Sammy said. 'A few people were hanging out in the smoking room, which is all cigars and whisky. Not my thing. I went back to my room pretty quickly after Peter showed me the bar on the roof. Besides, I think you'd only go half a block in those shoes before you regretted it. They're not that comfortable.'

The welcome reception venue turned out to be a trendy restaurant and club built into the riverbank underneath Pont Alexandre III, an ornate bridge studded with black iron art nouveau lamps and capped with gold-leaf statues. Security guards had closed off the riverside path on each side of the bridge and were directing pedestrians up to the street. Rachael stared at the river, its surface dark and watching, as the cars negotiated the slip ramp down to the bank.

The entry was through heavy stone archways that, with the yellow lamplight, created the atmosphere of a sumptuous and intimate cave. They were greeted with glasses of rose-tinted champagne that streamed crystal-like bubbles and had heart-shaped candy hanging from the stems.

At first, Rachael couldn't see anyone they knew in the crowd of suits and cocktail dresses, and twisted black shadows fell from the detailed ironwork with every camera flash. The waiters looked more like secret service operatives in their stiffly starched white shirts and black waistcoats, especially with their earpieces. It was all a little threatening. But then Sammy started humming *The Bodyguard* theme song very badly, which had Rachael laughing and distracted her from the imminent spotting of Matthew, which made her stomach clench every time she thought about it. What would he look like? What would he say? Would he even speak to her?

Her mouth was so dry her lips stuck together. She gulped the champagne for some moisture, and the bubbles added a layer of floating giddiness to her anxiety.

A waiter proffered a tray of tiny skewers studded with puffed blue and white globs.

'What are they?' she asked, trying not to sway.

'Black-and-white truffle popcorn finished with a truffle pecorino,' said the waiter smoothly.

'Why is it blue?' Sammy whispered.

Rachael shrugged, and took one to be polite. The corn was light and buttery and delicious, almost good enough to momentarily forget her angst.

'Isn't that Hugh Jackman?' Sammy asked.

Rachael searched the crowd, but saw only a sea of unfamiliar faces. She couldn't even remember what Hugh Jackman looked like in that moment. Matthew was the one she was really searching for, the long anticipation of seeing him now undermining her confidence. She shook herself, needing to find her resolve again. To remember why she was here. She tried to smile and listen to what Sammy was saying.

'Oh, who's that guy taking photos? I'm sure I've seen him somewhere before.'

'Where?'

Sammy pointed, and Rachael caught sight of a dark-haired man wielding a camera. He was dressed in black, and had climbed two steps up a decorative ladder set into the corner, scanning the crowd as if hunting for a rare animal in the rain-forest. In his jeans and long-sleeved shirt rolled to the elbows, he looked like he'd wandered into the elegant cocktail party from a rock concert.

'Does he look familiar to you?' Sammy asked.

Rachael shook her head, still trying to settle her nerves. 'Sorry, I didn't hear anything after Hugh Jackman.'

Sammy laughed. 'Right.'

Rachael decided it was time to be brave. She leaned in to make herself heard over the crowd. 'Should we go and be sociable? Bev or Bernie must be around somewhere, or Peter.'

She paused, because suddenly she did see Peter. He was standing just a few metres away with his wife, Suzi, his suit dark against her white dress. And then, as Rachael took in the man standing half-turned on Suzi's other side, her stomach lurched the way it did from an unexpected fall.

There he was. Matthew. Next to Suzi, his face nearly in profile.

The edges of her vision blurred as she searched his all-too-familiar face. He was the same . . . and yet so different. His hair was the same rich brown, but shorter than it had been in medical school, the soft curls sculpted into something respectable and serious. His face too had lost a softness; his cheeks and jaw were more angular, his face thinner, as if he'd taken up running or boxing. And yet he was still the same man she'd dreamed with in the wheat field at home, lying in those arms, kissing those same lips. The old desire pressed against her breastbone with the force of a hydraulic piston.

'Shit,' she whispered.

The intention of coming here to prove to herself that it was all long ago and ended drained from her body as she stared at him. No matter how brilliant this plan had seemed on the farm in Australia, now that she was standing before him in

Paris, it seemed utterly ridiculous. She still loved him. Still wanted him. Just as fiercely as ever.

'Rach?'

Rachael looked at Sammy, fixing on the iridescent green of her eyeshadow. 'It's him,' she said faintly.

Sammy cocked an eyebrow. 'So it is. And that must be Bonnie.'

Rachael hadn't even noticed the woman standing on Matthew's other side, though she should have from the number of pictures she'd viewed online. Bonnie stood shoulder to shoulder with Matthew, her face and hands animated as she spoke, something gold and sparkly bouncing at her wrist.

'So,' Sammy asked. 'Any fireworks?'

With great effort, Rachael shrugged and lied. 'Completely over him,' she said, hoping to force her heart to see reason.

Her heart ignored the plea. Sammy looked utterly unconvinced too, but anything she was about to say was interrupted as a crystal bell rang out. A hush stole through the crowd, all heads turning towards the corner where the photographer had been moments ago.

A portly man with a red flush across his nose stepped onto a platform so he was head and shoulders above the crowd. It was the same face Rachael had seen next to Bonnie's in so many photos, where he often appeared commanding and brusque. Now, his smile was as warm as the afternoon sun.

'That's Walter Quinn,' Sammy whispered.

'Friends and family,' Walter began, his voice carrying easily over their heads, 'some of you have travelled a long way to be here, and I thank you for shaking off the jetlag so quickly to allow us to bid you welcome.' He raised his glass and a cheer went up. 'A short speech is a good speech, so don't worry, I'll let you get back to your drinks very soon. But first I want my beautiful girl up here. Where are you, Bonnie?'

A flurry moved through the crowd, then Bonnie appeared, her hand over her face as though embarrassed by the attention. She was wearing a short yellow strapless dress that looked like a sack and somehow she was still resplendent.

'And my new son-in-law. Come on, Matty, let's not be shy.'

Matty. The familiarity raked Rachael like a barb.

Matthew moved smoothly through the crowd, his shoulders twisting right and left. His step up was a spring, and then he was standing with Walter, Bonnie's arm linked through his, smiling and dipping his head to hear her whisper in his ear. He drew his own parents onto the platform, along with another woman in shimmering blue who looked an older version of Bonnie. Greg and Evelyn beamed and shook Walter's hand, then Matthew kissed the other woman on both cheeks. The scene faded and muffled until all Rachael could hear was Peter cheering the loudest over the crowd, adding a few piercing whistles. She closed her eyes.

That day with Matthew in the wheat field rushed into her mind, and she felt him stroking her hair.

'Tell me your dreams,' he'd encouraged.

'To lie out here forever.'

He'd laughed. 'If only. I mean in the next few years. When I'm a doctor and you're a journalist.'

Rachael had smiled because his mind was always going ahead, eager to make their plans concrete. She hadn't thought that far into the future.

'I guess that will depend where we can find work.'

He'd nodded. 'Mmm, you're right. It's too early for that. What matters is we'll do it together.'

Rachael remembered his exact expression as he'd said that, so genuine and fervent. It was so vivid that when she opened her eyes she was surprised to find she was still here in Paris.

'Bonnie will always be my beautiful baby girl,' Walter was saying. 'Even though she's achieved so much in her own right. Her foundation is changing lives, her businesses are booming. I promise you all, this week will be a celebration to remember.' He turned to Bonnie, bowing his head as if the next words came hard. 'But if I'm honest, it's as much about me letting you go.'

Bonnie's face crumpled into loving compassion and she kissed Walter on the cheek.

Walter waved away an 'awww' from the crowd. 'Enough of that. This is the natural way of things, and I couldn't be happier with my new son-in-law. Matty, you're a talented doctor. You've got a good head for business, and that makes a good marriage. And you love my girl, which is all a father can ask for.'

'Don't use up your speech early, Walter!' called someone at the front.

Walter grinned and raised his glass again. 'Now, enjoy!'

A camera flash lit all six of them, and Rachael had to turn away. The after-image of Matthew's beautiful smile was etched on her retinas. He'd smiled like that for her once.

Once.

She suddenly realised this could be anyone's wedding, anywhere. Paris, the dresses, the expense – that was all just icing. It didn't change the raw fundamentals. That Matthew was clearly in love. That this was his world now. And that Rachael was still such a long way from accepting it.

Her dress was too tight about her ribs. 'I have to go,' she said faintly, glancing round for escape.

She and Sammy were in the centre of the crowd, hemmed in by couture and canapés. Then a waiter moved through with a tray of toasting glasses held high, parting the guests like an ice-breaker. Rachael rushed into his wake. She heard Sammy call after her, and registered a glimpse of Beverley, but the rest was a blur. Finally, her heels clicked onto the foyer tiles and a bolt of cold air splashed over her cheeks. She'd made it out.

'Madame?' A secret service waiter on his way from the kitchen proffered a tray of shining glasses. More champagne. Rachael took a glass just to have something in her hand. Another waiter offered tiny tartlets of buttery pastry filled with something piped and creamy.

The cheers of a toast came from behind her, after which the edges of the party spilled from the main room and into the foyer. Four young men hustled past her laughing at some joke, their empty champagne glasses askew in their hands as they patted pockets for cigarettes to take outside.

A pair of older men with fat Windsor knots supporting their collars wandered out, drinking what looked like scotch in heavy crystal glasses. One was staring appreciatively at his drink as he talked, but the other man stopped to lean against the wall in a distracted way that caught Rachael's attention. She could see sweat collecting at his temples. The other man carried on, unaware.

Rachael slid her glass onto a wooden counter and stepped closer. 'Are you all right?' she asked.

He looked awful, his arm stiff as he held his glass, his face the shade of putty in the low light. He had trouble meeting her eye. Rachael had seen her mother like this once, and it had turned out to be a clot, part of which had broken off and lodged in her lungs.

Finally, the other man registered he was alone and turned back. 'Nicholas? Come on, man, enough lounging about. This scotch isn't going to—'

'Oh!' Rachael shot out a hand to steady Nicholas as he doubled over, his hand crushed to his chest. The crystal glass smashed on the tiles. His breath came in heaves, and the sweat at his temples became a cascade, turning his royal blue tie to midnight.

'Get a doctor,' Rachael called to the young smokers, who were now staring. They didn't move.

The man's companion had more success, collaring a passing waiter, who spoke urgently into his wrist. The drama caught the edge of the crowd like a wayward curtain blowing into a candle and the call of 'doctor' spread. Rachael steered Nicholas to an ornate chair, reassuring him that help was coming. She hoped it was.

He was still clutching his chest. Rachael kept hold of his other hand, and twisted around, desperate for assistance. She was just in time to see the guests part around a man rushing straight for them.

Matthew.

Their eyes met briefly, enough for Rachael to read in his surprise, recognition, and then a fleet of other emotions that blurred into each other: confusion, gratefulness, regret?

Her own reaction was clear and simple: a searing Cupid's arrow shot clean through her chest. She stumbled back.

Matthew knelt before the chair. 'Uncle Nicholas,' he said calmly as he reached for a wrist pulse. 'What have you been doing?'

Oh, his voice, that hadn't changed either, the same deep timbre she'd always loved. The only difference was the hard edge of assurance as he asked Nicholas questions. That was the product of all the time and experience that he'd had over the last years, and she'd lost.

She crept away, no longer needed.

'Rachael, wait.'

She froze at her name on his lips. 'Yes?'

'Did you see this happen?' His green eyes held her pinned, as if she were some kind of specimen, a moth perhaps, completely at his mercy.

'Um, sort of,' she stammered. 'He was just looking awful, and clutching his chest, like this.' She made a fist.

Matthew's nod was curt. He released Nicholas's wrist.

'Oh, Uncle Nick!' A woman hurtled in, her face twisted with distress.

Matthew gestured her back with one hand and then, to Rachael's utter amazement, he broke into French with one of the security men. Hearing him speak the lilting words was a punch to Rachael's gut. When had Matthew learned French? Their paths seemed to have diverged not years ago but decades. She was even more conscious of how hideously out of place she was, and yet she hovered helplessly because he'd asked her to stay.

An ambulance quickly arrived and Nicholas was taken away. The drama was over, and with the security team's encouragement, the crowd melted away.

Rachael found herself standing on the chequered tiles, alone with Matthew.

Chapter 6

For the longest moment, they simply stared at each other. Rachael was caught in a trance. The yellow lights bled into her vision as if she'd stumbled into a soap opera flashback. She had nothing to shield her from Matthew's full impact. Her desire for him was as fresh as it had ever been. If anything it was stronger, as though all the minute refinements since they'd last met had intensified him, like the flavours in a fine wine. She could see the tiny white scar in front of his left ear where he'd split his skin open at the waterhole when they were sixteen. She'd always loved that scar, as though it marked him as hers forever. But he wasn't, and the despair of it made her quite sick.

She tried to say something, but words wouldn't come.

Matthew gave her a tentative smile. 'Rachael,' he said simply. 'How are you?'

Rachael realised she was holding herself by the elbows. She quickly let go, trying to recover her poise, and then didn't know what to do with her hands. Her fingers scrabbled together in front of her, covering her nails. She'd been biting them earlier while Walter was making his speech.

She found herself returning Matthew's smile, stupidly and maniacally, her cheeks burning hot. 'I'm fine. I—'

'Well, it's good to see you,' he said briskly, as though they were old acquaintances who'd met by chance at a bus stop. 'I wasn't sure you would come.'

He glanced away and Rachael realised he must be searching for an escape. Shame burned up her neck and across her powdered cheeks. She was a fool, stupidly caught in the raw, uncontrollable feelings she still had for him, while he had moved on long ago.

Rachael knew her mother would have had the perfect words to make Rachael feel less stupid. But her mother wasn't here any more. With supreme effort, she built a shell of composure.

'Of course,' she said. 'Thank you for the invitation. I'm very happy for you.'

His expression rippled and an unexpected frown pulled at his brows. He'd opened his mouth to say something when a yellow blur appeared and Rachael found herself face to chin with a woman whose skin was as flawless as the icing on a CWA cake.

A French-manicured hand extended towards her. 'Bonnie Quinn,' the woman said, smiling in such a genuine way that Rachael immediately took her hand. 'Thank you so much for helping Uncle Nicholas.'

'Oh, I didn't do anything,' Rachael said.

'Nonsense. I was told you reacted immediately. You must be one of Matthew's friends from the country?'

Rachael shot a glance at Matthew, her tongue tied with the complexity of what they'd once been to each other. His face was bland and unreadable.

'Yes,' she said quickly. 'From Milton, near Parkes.'

'Ah, one of Matthew's home crowd,' Bonnie said, her eyes lighting up.

Matthew stepped in. 'Bonn, this is Rachael, my girlfriend from high school.'

'Oh, *you're* Rachael? How wonderful. Matthew's told me all about you. Now, you must tell me where you found that amazing dress.'

Rachael didn't know whether to be more floored by the fact that Matthew had so openly admitted who she was, or the fact that Bonnie seemed pleased about it. Rachael had been to two weddings in the past where the presence of ex-partners had caused fistfights once the bar opened. But the present situation seemed far worse. Clearly Rachael was so inconsequential that Matthew was sure Bonnie wouldn't care.

'I, um, made it,' she said, her voice squeezed by the casual disregard of their past.

'Are you serious? My goodness, Matthew, she's a designer. Look at the detail!'

Rachael pulled at her skirt, knowing her smile was about to wobble into tears. Where the hell was Sammy?

'Rachael always did lovely work,' Matthew said.

Rachael. Not Rach, or Rachy, but formal and distant.

'My mother taught me,' Rachael said, as if she was ten years old and speaking to a teacher at school.

She looked around, desperate for escape, then a grey-haired security man appeared, gesturing to Bonnie.

Bonnie took Matthew by the elbow. 'Sorry to rush off, but Dad's probably breaking heads at the hospital. Lovely to meet you, Rachael. Enjoy the rest of the evening.'

And with that, they were gone.

Rachael stood frozen for three long breaths before she realised quite a few people were now watching her, including the photographer, from an elevated position at the end of the foyer. His dark eyes seemed like spotlights, his camera half-raised as if considering whether to take a shot.

As calmly as she could manage, Rachael turned her back and walked away, only stumbling once, following the curve of the wall to what looked like an unpopulated area. She needed air; time alone to stand outside near the river and breathe space back into her lungs.

All she could think was how wrong she'd been to come to this wedding. Seeing Matthew and Bonnie together had done nothing to move her on. If anything, it had made the hopeless yearning to undo the last ten years even worse.

⟜

She finally paused in an unfamiliar hallway that ended with a door. Not wanting to go back, she tentatively pushed it open, and heard the clatter of crockery and smelled caramelised onions. She must be near the kitchens. Before she could retreat, she spotted bathroom doors. She would wash her face, then go back and find the way outside.

As she entered a surprisingly large bathroom, complete with chairs, the first thing she saw was a pile of discarded clothes on the tiled floor. Odd. She stopped, wondering if she'd missed an out-of-service sign. Then she realised that the pile was a beautifully dressed old woman lying on the floor. She had clearly fallen, her thin arms and legs as fragile as a bird's.

Despite her age, she had no short blue curls or knitted shawls or sensible shoes. Her hair was a sleek silver bob, her dress an elegant slip of lavender silk and beads, and a fur stole lay crumpled behind her. Long strands of pearls the size of marbles hung from her neck, and a colossal ruby ring had twisted around her middle finger.

Her eyes were open as Rachael bent and put a hand on her shoulder. 'Are you hurt?'

The woman struggled to get up.

'No, don't move,' Rachael said. 'I'll get someone to help.'

'*Non!*' the woman gasped.

'I'll be as fast as I can—'

Her hand closed on Rachael's arm, her wrinkled eyes wide and imploring, her accent thick. '*Non, chérie*, please. Tell no one. Wait.'

Rachael hesitated, but the woman's grip was firm, the skin of her hand smooth and warm. She relented. 'Do you think you can sit up? Here, use your hand to help.'

She guided the woman's arm down to the floor to help push up off the tiles. She'd done the same thing for her mother several times when she'd fallen at home. When the woman had eased to sitting, Rachael asked her again if she was hurt, if she had any pain, before helping her to her knees, then pulling over a chair.

The woman sat, took a shuddery breath, smoothed down her hair and pulled her elegant tasselled bag into her lap. 'Thank you,' she said after a long minute of recovery. 'It is terrible to grow old.'

'I really think I should find someone, just to make sure you're okay.'

'*Non*. I slipped, a silly thing. I am not hurt.'

'Yes, but—'

'Please, *chérie*.' Her tone was different now, lower and secretive, as if imploring came with difficulty. 'I have already lost so much freedom. Besides, this is Bonnie's party. One ambulance a night, hmmm? You do not have to stay. I will be fine here. Just a few minutes to recover, you see?'

She raised her eyebrows, and from her bag extracted a thin cigarette holder, the kind Rachael had only ever seen in movies. It was a glamorous act from a bygone era, confidently illustrating her improvement. Rachael was fascinated, but not fooled. She might keep the secret of the fall, but there was no way she was leaving the woman here alone.

'I'll stay a while,' she said. 'Just in case.'

'No, no,' the woman said. 'Surely the party is more interesting?'

Rachael shrugged in an elaborate way, but she knew that for a moment her expression had betrayed how much she wanted to stay away.

The woman watched her shrewdly from under her precision-cut fringe. 'Who is it you are avoiding, *chérie*?'

'No one,' Rachael said quickly. 'I just wanted some fresh air.'

The woman loaded her holder with a cigarette. '*Bon*. You may stay. In fact, you may help me outside, as long as you do not talk about business, politics or polo.'

'I don't know anything about polo or politics,' Rachael said as she offered her arm. 'And the only business I know is wheat farming.'

They passed back through the hallway and then into the foyer, the woman moving smoothly but slowly, her silver bob shifting like a sheet of snow. Calmer now, Rachael's earlier wrong turn seemed obvious. They soon exited through one of the stone arches and a security man nodded as they passed. The woman turned towards him and issued a flowing sentence of French, and the man stepped away to speak into his wrist.

Only when the woman was seated on a stone bench under the bridge, her stole pulled around her and her cigarette lit, did she speak again. 'I grew up also on a farm,' she said, a thin curl of blue smoke rising from her cigarette. 'A lifetime ago, my father and mother grew wheat far from Paris. But I always wanted to run away to the bright lights.' She gave a little flick of her wrist as if to capture all of Paris around them.

Despite the cold, which had turned Rachael's arms to goosebumps, she leaned forward. 'And you did?'

The woman tilted her head. 'You do not know who I am, do you, *chérie*?'

'Oh dear, should I?' Rachael said. 'I'm sorry.'

'No matter. It is refreshing to be anonymous. How do you know Bonnie and Matthew?'

Rachael had a moment to think as a waiter appeared with two glasses of red wine. The woman gestured to her to take one, and the slug of wine at least made her chest warm.

'I, um, went to school with Matthew.'

'Ah, a childhood friend.' The woman leaned forward, pearls swinging, the lit end of her cigarette scribing a cedilla in the air. 'You know him well?'

'Um, once maybe,' she hedged.

'So what do you think of them?'

'I'm sorry?'

'Has Matthew found a good match?'

'I, uh, I don't know them like that. I haven't seen Matthew in years,' Rachael said, and took another gulp of wine.

If she was honest, all she could see was how perfectly Bonnie and Matthew matched. She thought of Matthew calling her 'Rachael', and Bonnie being all pleased to meet someone from his long-ago past.

'A pity. I only met him this week. I am still forming my opinion,' the woman said, tipping her finished cigarette from the holder and taking up her wine. 'That is an immaculate dress, *chérie*. Where did you buy it?'

'I made it,' Rachael said, then at the woman's lifted eyebrow, added in a rush, 'I like to sew.'

'May I?' the woman asked, putting down her glass. Soon her fingers were shifting along the hemline, moving the fabric between the pads of her fingers. She pulled a pair of gold-rimmed glasses from her bag to peer at the stitches. 'Exquisite,' she said, retrieving her wine glass and sitting back. 'You did not make this from a standard pattern.'

"Well, no. I did use one, but I made some changes to it to match another dress I saw. I like to draw too,' she added.

The woman regarded her steadily. 'This dress reminds me of Tom Ford.'

'Who is that?'

'A designer.' The woman shook her head. 'Never mind. What pattern did you use?'

'A fifties' *Vogue*. I changed the skirt and added the cut-outs. The original design seemed too . . . heavy for the fabric.'

The woman made a satisfied noise. 'I see. After I ran away from the farm, I worked in fashion all my life. Your work is very good. But you are a farmer?'

Rachael blushed. 'Well, yes. It was my mother's farm.'

'And will you run away to work in fashion too? Perhaps stay in Paris after this week?' The woman was watching her intently.

'Oh, it's just a hobby,' Rachael said quickly. 'The farm's a lot of work, especially now it's just me.' She had to look away as tears rushed into her eyes. 'Sorry. My mum died a few months ago.'

'Ah.' The woman clucked her tongue. 'I am so sorry to hear it.' She reached out to pat Rachael's arm. Her skin was soft as chamois. 'You are a kind person, I think. You need to be with people you know. Are you here with friends?'

'My best friend.'

The woman drew her hand back and used it to push herself up off the seat. 'I will leave you to find her. Do not be out too long in the cold. And be careful of the river. Remember, one ambulance is enough. I must go to be sociable again.' She paused. 'What is your name, *chérie*?'

'Rachael. Rachael West.'

'A good name for a designer. I am Yvette. Come and talk to me at the next party. Ask Bonnie if you cannot find me. I am her grandmother.'

She beckoned a security man, who offered his arm and guided her inside. Rachael was left staring after her, the soft slosh of the Seine and the hum of passing boats keeping her company.

﹏

Cold finally drove her inside. Rachael crept through the stone arch back towards the restaurant, trying to stop her teeth chattering. Her toes were pinched in her shoes, and the uneven stone of the pathway was cold through the thin leather soles.

She finally found Sammy searching for her at the end of the bathroom hallway.

Sammy's face lit like sunshine. 'There you are! I was worried something had happened to you. Did you know someone collapsed?'

Rachael was forced to give a quick account. She stuck to the facts, leaving out her worst reactions and everything about Yvette, hoping that if she didn't acknowledge her feelings for Matthew, it couldn't be true that she still loved him.

Sammy didn't let her off the hook. 'And how do you feel now?'

Rachael put her hands over her face. 'I don't know if coming here was a good idea after all, Sam.'

Three men emerged into the foyer, dapper in their suits, cigars in hand. One, Rachael didn't recognise. The other two were Peter and Matthew. Peter saw them first and waved.

Sammy grabbed Rachael's hand. 'Okay, how about we call it a night?'

Rachael didn't need encouragement. Heedless of the cold, she clipped along the stone path by the river and up a long uneven ramp, hoping this was the way back to the Maison Lutetia.

'Slow down, Rach,' Sammy panted. 'You'll break your ankle.'

At the top of the ramp, a security man barred their way. Despite Rachael's protests, he wouldn't allow them past. Prepared to break through by force if necessary, Rachael was disarmed when he calmly asked them to wait, and spoke into his wrist. A car arrived two minutes later to take them to the hotel.

On the ride back, Rachael thought with dismay about how many events the week still held. She rushed through the lobby, and by the time she'd climbed the staircase, she'd sweated through the blue fabric of her dress, her hair had separated into curly chunks, and the bolero had swung sideways like an oversized bib. She tugged it off, breaking the stitches on the clasp in her haste.

'Okay, something's clearly wrong. What really happened?' Sammy asked as soon as they were in Rachael's room.

Rachael pressed her hands against her cheeks. Her fingers felt like icy water on her burning skin.

'What on earth did he say to you?'

'Nothing,' Rachael said, unable to voice how much the exchange had hurt. 'He didn't say anything. But still . . .' She faltered.

'You felt like the last time you saw him?'

'Yes. And meanwhile, he's completely over it. He has a gorgeous fiancée and a career and this amazing life, and I'm just . . .' She waved her arms, then dropped them, her energy gone. She sank leaden onto the bed. 'I'm still the girl from the farm who hasn't been anywhere or done anything, and still isn't over the man who left her years and years ago. Pathetic.'

'You don't look it in that dress,' Sammy said. 'Everyone was talking about it.'

'They were?'

'Oh yes. You don't realise how amazing you look. Are you sure he just didn't know what to say to you?'

Rachael shook her head. 'He was pretty clear he couldn't care less. He'd even told Bonnie about me.'

Sammy made a dismissive noise. 'So is that where you were the whole time? I was looking for you.'

'Um, not the whole time. I was outside for a while, talking to Bonnie's grandmother.'

'Yvette de Richelieu?' When Rachael expressed her surprise, Sammy added, 'Beverley was gossiping about her. She must have read up on the family. Yvette is a reclusive fashion icon who started out as a model, then became a muse and then a designer herself. She's supposed to be releasing a new collection, but it's long overdue and no one thinks it will ever happen. Apparently, she's famously prickly and never gives interviews. Anyway, then Bernie showed up and Bev stopped talking – you know, to give him the silent treatment as always – and do you want to hear something funny?'

'What?' Rachael asked.

'As I left, the photographer was getting them to pose together and Bev was pulling her best cat's-bum mouth.'

Rachael tried to smile, but her body hurt like it was harvest time and she'd been up from dawn till midnight. Both her heels were blistered, her calves ached, and her dress was rumpled.

'Sam, I know I said coming here would help me move on, but I think it's just going to make it worse.'

'Don't say that. This is just the wobbly beginning.'

Rachael shook her head. She didn't tell Sammy how lost she still felt without her mother, how she missed hearing her voice. She thought of her mother's tree all alone on the top of the rise. It would be late morning now, the sun shining on the river and the fields. She was so far away from it all here, in her tight dress and a room that someone else deserved, just pretending it would help her get on with her life. She was frightened. She wanted to see the familiar fields of home, smell the straw and the gardenias, even the diesel of the machinery. To feel safe.

'Bev reckons all Walter's business buddies are on their third heart attack,' Sammy was saying. 'So there's bound to be more entertainment at the next party. Sorry, that wasn't very funny.'

Rachael lifted her eyes. Sammy was trying, but she didn't have the strength.

'I want to go home,' she said.

Chapter 7

The decision to leave was enough to calm Rachael and allow her a good night's sleep. She only woke twice. The first time, she heard a man's voice in the hall and a door closing. She'd glanced at the clock – the other guests must be coming back from the party. The second time, she thought she heard a possum shriek, but when she dragged herself out of the pillowy down and peered through the door's peephole, all was quiet, only the lamp outside Sammy's door burning in its sconce. Rachael had sighed; she must be terribly homesick to be imagining nocturnal wildlife halfway across the world.

She went back to bed, and woke just after six when the room was still dark. Only then did she consider the questions that would arise back home if she left early. She couldn't claim that she'd felt unwell – that wouldn't explain getting on a plane. Ruefully, she remembered Yvette saying that anonymity was refreshing.

She already knew what Sammy thought, and it was too early to wake her and ask again. What she really wanted was to talk to her mother, and then she found herself remembering Tess crying in their mother's wardrobe, and did the maths on the time difference between Paris and Australia.

'What are you talking about? You've only been there a day,' was her sister's response when Rachael said she was considering coming home.

'It's not like I imagined,' Rachael said, uncharacteristically open with Tess. 'It's hard seeing Matthew again, and I just want to get back to what's normal.'

Tess laughed. 'You think I didn't feel like that when I had my kids? But I couldn't send them back, could I, and it's worth it when you stick out the bad bits. This is an amazing opportunity, paid for by someone else. You don't throw that kind of thing away. Don't you dare come home.'

Rachael burst into tears.

Tess sighed. 'Look, give it another day,' she said, more gently. 'And call me tomorrow. I bet by then you'll think differently. All new things are hard at the start.'

'You're supposed to be my sister,' Rachael said.

'I am. That doesn't mean I'm just going to tell you what you want to hear.'

Rachael put the phone down wondering why on earth she'd thought Tess would be a good person to call.

As she packed her case, she imagined trying to explain the wasted airfare to Matthew's parents, or the Quinns. 'I couldn't bear seeing my old boyfriend with his new fiancée,' she said out loud, and it sounded immature and weak.

She said it again, and hearing the silliness of the words somehow bled the intensity from the feeling. It *was* only a few days. Maybe Tess was right. After all, if she went home now, what would she be doing tomorrow? Still searching for photos of Bonnie on the internet?

Just to be sure, she put in a call to the travel agent who'd booked her flights. It was after-hours for their office in Australia and all she got was a message with numbers to call in an emergency. She almost laughed. A broken heart didn't really qualify as an emergency, no matter how she spun it.

When Sammy knocked just after nine, Rachael was unpacking her case.

'Were you really serious?' Sammy asked.

'I had a weak moment.'

Sammy flopped on the bed beside Rachael's half-empty bag. 'What changed your mind?'

Rachael sighed. 'I thought about what I'd do tomorrow if I left now. And also, I called Tess. She basically said she'd leave me at the airport.'

'Have to hand it to Tess – at least you know where you stand with her.'

Rachael grunted. 'So now I have to try not to make another arse of myself today.'

'Would it help if I told you Matthew's not going to be on the cruise later?'

'He's not?' Somewhere in Rachael's chest, a pressure-relief valve opened.

'Something about a suit fitting. I couldn't quite hear all the details last night. Bernie and Peter were trying to talk at the same time. Did you know Bernie's planning on moving the bakery to Parkes?'

Rachael hung last night's dress in the wardrobe. 'Bev mentioned it a while ago. She thinks it'll close Milton down.'

Sammy was frowning. 'Probably will. Peter's practically got the shop picked out for Bernie. Anyway, you must be starving and I haven't eaten anything either.'

At the prospect of a day without running into Matthew, Rachael's dull, dark worries finally gave way to shimmering possibilities. Paris was waiting. It was time to go and discover it.

In deference to her blistered heels, she pulled on her well-worn soft leather boots, jeans and a polo shirt, and tucked her hair behind her ears. 'Do you think we can find some croissants?'

'Sure. If the fashion police don't find us first.' Sammy laughed as Rachael threw a pillow at her. 'I love that after that amazing dress last night, you're still comfortable in jeans. What are you planning on wearing later?'

'You really want to see? It's a bit crushed.'

Rachael extracted a plastic dry-cleaning bag from the wardrobe. She opened the zip to show Sammy the shining pink silk formed into a smooth bodice and airy bell skirt.

'Curse your talent, Rachael West. That's gorgeous. See if you don't give another old guy a heart attack.'

Rachael laughed, but her heart filled with pride. She smoothed the fabric. 'I hope you're right about Matthew. Because if this cruise turns into a repeat of last night, I'll just have to swim. And I rather like this dress.'

⟶

Rachael and Sammy stepped into the Parisian morning with nothing but a map, a guidebook and country-girl confidence in their sense of direction. For a long while, they simply stood on the corner nearest the hotel, adjusting to the differences.

'Not even Sydney was this big and crowded,' Sammy said. 'I keep feeling claustrophobic.'

'Or this beautiful,' Rachael said as they picked a direction and struck out.

She had never seen anything like Paris. Not a concrete facade in sight, and no high-rises at all. The buildings were all stone and iron, with glimpses of trees and parks between them. It wasn't green – all the trees were winter naked – but the potential was there, as if life was just waiting to break free. The one time that Rachael had explored The Rocks in Sydney, the worn stone steps and tiny laneways had spoken to her of a long history, but it was nothing compared to the weight of Paris.

The ground floors held boutiques and restaurants, many of them not yet open, and people strolled the streets in bright coats and boots. Rachael nearly walked into a lamppost when a woman strode by in a coat with an asymmetrical cut she'd never seen before. Sammy teased her about that for half an hour.

They found a café with footpath tables, a board proclaiming *Le Petit Déjeuner Parisien* and a counter piled with golden pastries. With some hesitation, Rachael ordered, satisfyingly wrangling her tongue around *croissant*, *pain au chocolat* and *jus d'orange pressé*. And despite all she'd heard about the rudeness of the French to foreigners, the waiter treated them with patience, even after her broad Australian 'sill voo play'. He even asked where they were from.

From their vantage point, they watched the street bustling with cyclists and scooters. When the food arrived, Rachael tucked her mother's scarf around her neck against the chill air, and kept her hands around her coffee cup for warmth. She would never have admitted it, but the coffee was awful. Nervously, she fingered the croissant, not wanting her hopes of that dashed too. It looked nothing like croissants back home. This one was nearly straight with the barest hint of a curve at each end, its crust caramel brown and its body puffed, as if it was the proudest croissant ever made. It weighed nothing, but when Rachael bit the end, she tasted a million flakes of wafer-thin crust supporting the silken lace of pastry and butter.

'Oh my,' she murmured, taking another bite, this one far more greedy. No, the croissant was fine. The croissant was king. 'I could eat these all day.'

'Then let's get two more for the road,' Sammy said. 'Now we just have to decide which way.'

They pored over the map. Rachael's choices kept returning to the river, whereas Sammy favoured heading for the nearest landmark. Rachael finally told Sammy to close her eyes and spun her on the spot. Sammy stopped, laughing and pointing, and they headed north-east. This led them to the Musée Rodin, where they spent half an hour wandering around the gardens amidst sculptures of stone and hedge.

'Mum would have loved this,' Rachael said, admiring the roses poised to bloom.

'They filmed some of *Midnight in Paris* here,' Sammy said. 'Right over there – look! Hey, what about we go find the Musée de l'Orangerie next? They have those huge rooms of Monet's water lilies.'

That was how they came to be strolling alongside the Seine. Rachael relaxed. Today, the river was inviting under a pale blue sky, pulling walkers and cyclists closer with its slow gravitas. They spotted the palatial Louvre upriver, and crossed over the water at the Pont de la Concorde, the gold top of the square's obelisk guiding them like a compass needle, the glass dome of the Grand Palais rising from the bare trees to the north.

'A bit bare and stark, isn't it?' Sammy said as they dodged traffic to enter the Jardin des Tuileries. The ground was mostly covered in a pale ochre grit, and puddles clung to the edges of the gardens. Even so, Rachael was buoyed.

'Maybe now, but it's like the fields right after the plant, when the old stubble is all grey and broken. Next week all the new shoots will come up and it'll look completely different.'

'We won't be here next week.'

Rachael turned. 'You okay, Sam?'

'Sorry, just tired – I think the jetlag's caught me up. Sore feet from last night too. But let's go see these water lilies. I've wanted to do that since we watched the movie.'

They ended up spending an hour gazing at the water lilies, which were just as amazing in real life as they had been on film. Afterwards, they explored the rest of the Musée de l'Orangerie with its Picassos and special exhibition, before wandering through the gardens. They passed children in puffy winter vests playing among the hedges, and souvenir sellers set up on blankets at the mouth of the Louvre's grounds. Rachael bought herself and Sammy silly matching Eiffel Towers, and they took a selfie with the Louvre pyramid behind, promising they'd come back to the Louvre itself another day. For now, they needed to head back to dress for the cruise.

They returned to the hotel the long way because Rachael wanted to stay near the river. When they finally had to cross over, Sammy stopped on the edge of a treed boulevard.

'What?' Rachael asked.

'I heard English.'

That was how they found a tour group about to enter a church: a monument of stone wedged between the surrounding buildings. Rachael gave Sammy a questioning look and she shrugged. They followed the group, and spent an unintended half-hour in the American Church in Paris, a peaceful retreat boasting magnificent stained glass, which glittered blue and red and amber in every vaulted wall. The two angel windows that faced the courtyard held Rachael's attention the longest with their earthy colours and exquisite details. The tour guide said they were Tiffany glass, and Rachael smiled, thinking of her mother's Tiffany glass lamp that still rested on her bedside table in the farmhouse. That connection to home was like an arrow of love shot straight through the earth, giving her strength. Her doubts dissolved. She had been right to come, and it was right to stay, despite the difficulties. She was sure of it.

Sammy smiled when Rachael told her and thanked her again for coming. For a brief moment, as they sat on the pews before the angels, Sammy rested her head against Rachael's shoulder, the way she had that day on the farm, and Rachael was sure that her friend needed to say something.

She was about to ask, when Sammy said gravely, 'Rachael, there's something I need to ask you.'

'What's that?'

'When did you start biting your nails again?'

Rachael looked down. Three of the fingers on her right hand had ragged ends, and all four on the left. 'Oh. I think that happened last night.'

'Come on. We have time to fix it.'

They made a short stop at the hotel, where Sammy connected her phone to the wi-fi and Google found them a nail bar just a few streets away, nestled inside a chic rendered townhouse with balconies of black wrought iron.

Rachael pulled out the guidebook, but nowhere did it tell her how to say, 'I need a French manicure.'

'I guess it's just a manicure here,' Sammy said, laughing. 'Anyway, you need acrylics. You haven't got any nails left to work with.'

So it was that by the time the cars were called to take them to the river for the cruise, Rachael had tiny talons extending from the ends of her fingers, each with an even crescent of soft pink polish. She'd avoided the more alarming lengths that would have been more at home on a wedgetailed eagle, and in an added bonus had discovered that she couldn't bite these nails.

The colour also went perfectly with her dress. She'd matched a fifties' bell-skirted dress pattern, with a simple V-neck and open back, to some dresses in the party photos in *Who*, and cut it with a slightly shorter skirt. She'd made it up in the soft pink slub silk, which was light and airy and held the skirt ruffles perfectly. The fabric had been a dream to work with, and even when she'd taken the time to bone the bodice and build the layers properly with felt and interfacing, and add two layers of underskirt, the whole creation hadn't taken as long as the oriental print dress.

When she stepped out of the car at the dock on the Île de la Cité, Notre Dame was visible to the east, catching the late afternoon sun as an apricot blush on its buttresses. Rachael smiled with genuine happiness, even when the view disappeared as she and Sammy passed through a tunnel of marquees. At three separate points, men in black suits, whose smiles seemed to have been surgically excised, checked their names off a list.

'What's with the tents?' she whispered to Sammy.

'Security,' came a familiar voice. Rachael twisted to find Beverley, wearing the blue chiffon dress Rachael had altered. 'I was talking to Walter last night and they're very concerned about the details of Bonnie's dress being leaked, so every event is tight. They're planning to auction the photos for charity. He was so interested in Milton too. Then Bernard had to come and muscle in, didn't he.' She held up a hand. 'But I promised myself I wouldn't let him bother me this week. So, girls, how was your morning? I was wondering where you'd got to.'

Rachael supplied Beverley with the details as they climbed aboard a long, sleek riverboat festooned with pink gauze and ribbons. On the lower level was a ring of covered lounges and a dance floor and bar, while the upper deck was completely open to the Parisian sky. The guests stood in pairs and small groups, clutching wine glasses, while servers moved around offering smiles and refreshments.

Rachael searched the crowd. This was her last chance to escape without having to brave the Seine. But Matthew was nowhere in sight.

Chapter 8

Sammy found them a group of Parkes invitees who were all admiring Paris, which spread out around them like a glorious painting.

'Can't believe we got an invite actually,' said Angus, whose knuckles were like the lamb shanks he sold, and made his wine glass look like a toy. 'Those Quinns must be absolutely loaded.'

'But they're lovely,' Beverley protested. 'Walter really seemed very normal to me.'

'Normal as a billionaire gets, I guess,' said Rodney, 'I mean, we are in Paris, Bev.'

'So we are. And isn't Rachael's dress amazing? Who would have thought we had such talent in Milton?'

Rachael pinked, wishing Beverley would talk about something else, but instead she went on to detail the history of what Rachael's mother, and Rachael too, had done for various theatre groups and debutante balls and other events around the district.

Desperate to change the subject, Rachael turned to Rodney's wife, Jeanette, who was wearing a pair of rhinestoned jeans, a crisp white shirt and red cowboy boots. Rachael thought she looked incredible and told her so.

Jeanette laughed. 'I've had three people ask me when I'm next on tour. They seem to think I'm some country music star they should know from Nashville. I started playing along. Bernie was in on it too.'

Bernie's face appeared in a gap, hair brylcreemed into Elvis wings. 'Heard my name!' He'd taken off his suit jacket, revealing a chambray shirt with *Blue Suede Choux* stitched over the left chest.

Beverley pursed her lips. 'Really, Bernard, couldn't you wear something a bit more appropriate?'

'What?' Bernie looked down at himself. 'It's a perfect conversation starter, and we are on a cruise. Can't be that formal. That bloke over there thought it was all terribly interesting. We were talking profits and investment. Come on, Bev, loosen up a little.'

A short beat of astonished silence greeted this; it must be the longest conversation Bernie'd had with Bev in years. Paris must have gotten to him, Rachael decided. Soon he was leading the group in their impressions of the city, and even Beverley's lemon face lost some of its sourness.

The boat slipped away from the dock and glided down the Seine, past the Louvre and La Grande Roue. Every time they passed under the arch of a bridge, the city disappeared and reappeared, as if it was being reinvented each time, even lovelier and more discoverable. Rachael was transported. The bubbles in her glass were smooth and delicious.

She noticed that more than a few male guests were looking in her direction and trying to catch her eye. The nearest had a charcoal-grey power suit and silvery temples.

'Have I got my skirt tucked in my knickers or something?' she whispered to Sammy.

'I told you, you look amazing.'

Rachael smoothed her skirt, faintly embarrassed. She'd thought she'd just blend in with a crowd like this.

'Oh, there she is. Rachael!'

Hearing her name, Rachael looked around, momentarily confused. Bonnie, tall and brown in a slip dress the colour of the sky, was waving in her direction.

Next moment, she had clicked across the deck and taken Rachael's arm. 'Sorry to cut in,' she said to the group. 'I'm just going to borrow her for a minute.'

Rachael had a second to see their looks of amazement before she was led towards a cluster of power suits and couture dresses. Among them, she was staggered to see Nicholas, raising a glass of orange juice in her direction.

'See, here she is,' Bonnie was saying, as though Rachael was an old friend. 'Rachael, I want you to meet Mike, Harrison, Gregory and Ferdie, and of course you know Nicholas.'

Rachael didn't really, and, awed by the power and entitlement wafting from the group, she turned to Nicholas and said the first thing that came into her head. 'I thought you'd still be in the hospital.'

'They let me out this morning, on the condition I didn't drink, hence the OJ.' He raised his glass again. 'Just a little heart issue. Nothing to worry about. Have it sorted out when I get home. You don't come to Paris to miss the party.'

He seemed so blasé. Rachael shook her head in amazement. 'That's dedicated.'

'Doesn't mean we're not keeping an eye on you,' Bonnie said, squeezing his arm.

'Wonderful dress, by the way,' Nicholas said. 'You look absolutely smashing. Thought I was having a vision yesterday. Now I know I was just seeing you.'

'Thank you,' Rachael said, taking the compliment as her mother had always told her she should, but colour crept into her cheeks. She suppressed the urge to bite her nails, instead fingering the cool stem of her glass. 'So . . . are you all from Sydney?'

'I have chambers there,' said Harrison.

Chambers. Rachael knew that had something to do with law.

'Melbourne,' said Mike.

'And I'm just from across the ditch, I'm afraid,' said Gregory in an English accent. 'What do you do, Rachael? You must be one of Bonnie's fashion friends.'

'Ah, no, actually. I'm from Parkes.' Silence greeted this, so she rushed on. 'Where Matthew's from. I . . . run a property out there. Wheat mostly.'

'Ah, primary production,' said Gregory with enthusiasm. 'I'm in the export business myself. Old pals with Walter from when we were both starting out. Terribly uncertain time at the moment, what with the dollar sliding around, don't you think?'

And soon, not quite understanding how it had happened, Rachael was involved in their conversation. Sometimes she struggled to keep up or understand what they were saying, but when she asked they explained without any of the judgement she'd feared, and she found herself talking about wheat prices and different markets and foreign investors, conversations she'd only ever had with her mother and other farmers. The fact that they were investment bankers and barristers and hedge-fund managers didn't seem to matter.

At one point, an incredibly attractive young man joined the circle, admired her dress and asked her what she thought of Paris, before Bonnie whisked him away somewhere else.

As he left, she leaned in to Gregory. 'Who was that? I feel like I've seen him somewhere before.'

'He's in that new superhero movie,' said Gregory. 'Been on telly in the UK for years and just making it in Hollywood. He's the patron of one of Bonnie's foundations. Nice lad.'

'Oh,' said Rachael, but she didn't get time to see where he'd gone because Bonnie was back, excusing herself.

'There's someone else I'd like you to meet, Rachael.'

Led towards the railing, Rachael spotted the diminutive form of Yvette, this time in sparkling black chiffon and velvet. She was standing alone facing the water, the lit end of her cigarette indistinct against the city lights.

'Granny, I want you to meet Rachael. You remember I told you about her helping out Nicholas last night? And I thought you might like to see her dress.'

Yvette looked at Rachael as though she'd never set eyes on her before. '*Enchanté.*'

'Lovely to meet you too,' Rachael stammered, unsure whether Yvette really didn't remember her.

Yvette took a puff on her cigarette, her gaze all haughty evaluation. 'Tell me about that dress. The fabric is exquisite.'

Bonnie smiled and slipped away.

The cigarette paused in its journey to Yvette's lips. 'Thank you, *chérie*,' she said softly. 'I did not want to have to explain to Bonnie how we met.'

'How are you?' Rachael asked.

'A tiny bruise on my hip, that is all. Not worth troubling anyone.'

'But don't you think you should tell someone? What if it happens again?'

'No, no. It is bad enough to have everyone think you are no good for anything anymore. I do not want them watching me too.' She gave Rachael an appraising look. 'You will understand one day. But for now I want to thank you for keeping my secret. And that is another beautiful dress— Ah, Bonnie. Rachael's work is very fine,' Yvette skilfully redirected as Bonnie came back.

'Sorry, Rachael, but Dad wants Granny to come downstairs.'

Watching Yvette being carefully steered away, Rachael was reminded of how her mother had often viewed her illness as a cage that had reduced her life to a small set of activities and caused other people to treat her differently. Age seemed to have done the same to Yvette.

Rachael looked into the sky, which was now a painting of a sunset. What on earth would her mother have said about all this? Her daughter on a riverboat in Paris, talking to investment bankers and movie stars and fashion icons. Rachael imagined her smiling, nodding sagely at the unexpected turns life could take.

The Eiffel Tower slid past, a silhouette hung with lights. A bittersweet tide turned in Rachael's chest. Ultimately she was here because of her mother, because of the unexpected cascade of events from her illness that had made it impossible for Rachael and Matthew to stay together. A heady mix of things that had gone wrong or were unfair or just awful. But after all that . . . she was here. A farm girl in the city of light and love.

She rubbed her arms as the cooling air slid over her skin, carrying a delicate bouquet of a dozen wines and perfumes. She could have been lonely in this moment, but instead a kernel of comfort settled inside her. She hugged her angora wrap closer about her shoulders, quietly tending this new feeling.

⟶

The moment was broken by a distant call of 'Rachael!'

Beverley.

Rachael instinctively shied away. She wanted to hold on to that kernel. And she needed to find Sammy.

There was no sign of her on the top deck, so she quickly picked her way down the stairs and circled around the lower deck's outside rail. No Sammy there either.

When she reached the stairs again, she heard footsteps coming down. In a momentary panic, she squeezed through a nook and found herself in a private corner with a little bench seat facing the stern, the Seine and Paris stretching out forever beyond. Shadowed by the top deck, she stood in the warm air flowing from the enclosed downstairs room. The footsteps clacked down the stairs and away.

Rachael eased her shoes off. Her aching soles hit the cool deck and she sighed in relief. The dark water soothed her, the boat running smoothly downstream with the current.

'And I thought I had this spot all to myself.'

Rachael jumped, nerves going off like a firecracker in her body. A man stood at the back of the ship, leaning against a pole that supported the upper deck. It wasn't Matthew, she saw that now. He was taller than Matthew, leaner, his face more intent. He had dark eyes, dark hair, and was dressed in black, his outer shirt suavely unbuttoned over a T-shirt beneath. He had a bag at his feet with *Nikon* stitched down one side.

'I didn't see you,' she stammered. 'I didn't mean to—'

A new clatter of heels came down the stairs and a woman called, 'Antonio?'

The man held up a finger for quiet.

The heels clipped towards Rachael's back. 'Antonio?' Then Evonne Grace, the wedding planner, leaned through the doorway. She stepped back when she saw Rachael. 'Oh, I'm sorry. Is anyone else out here?'

Rachael almost glanced at the man in the shadows, who was still out of Evonne's sight. Instead she shook her head. Evonne made a tutting noise and withdrew, her footsteps clacking away.

'Thanks,' the man said. His voice was husky, as though he'd been on a bender of cigars and bourbon. He was clean-shaven, but from the avant-garde way he wore his hair and his rebellious stance, Rachael suspected he would have been more at home with a chin of stubble.

Looking carefully, she realised she'd seen him across the room at the welcome drinks. 'You're the photographer,' she said.

'Guilty.' He extended his hand. 'Antonio Ferranti.'

'Rachael West,' she said, shaking hesitantly. She leaned down to guide her shoes back on. 'I'm sorry to intrude. I'll leave you be.'

'You don't have to go,' he said. 'Unless you're going to rat me out to Evonne. I'm just taking a break.'

Rachael found his accent hard to place. He mostly sounded American, but even with the gruffness some words were exotic and lilting, others broad, almost Australian.

He slid a camera from his bag and turned the lens towards the city, the machine a smooth extension of his body. The shutter clicked twice. Rachael watched, his attention wholly on his subject and his camera, as if nothing mattered but catching the world outside himself. He straightened, glanced around and caught her looking.

'You must be one of Bonnie's friends.' His tone was perfunctory, almost bored.

'Not at all,' Rachael said. 'I only met her this week.'

'But you work in fashion.'

'No. Don't know the first thing about it. Well, I mean, I can sew and someone told me the dress I wore yesterday looked like Tom Ford, but I have no earthly clue who that is.' Rachael's cheeks warmed. She was rambling.

He lowered his camera and scrutinised her with new interest. 'I remember that dress. I saw you yesterday.' He paused. 'Are you saying you made these dresses?'

'Yes,' she said, smiling slightly with satisfaction. Maybe she really did look the part. Maybe Antonio couldn't guess that she spent her days riding a quad bike, or walking through wheat fields. She turned her gaze across the water, shaking her head. The lights of Paris made her real life into the dream and this moment into reality.

Antonio raised his camera in a fluid motion. Rachael was too surprised to react before the shutter had captured her. 'Perfect,' he muttered, his eyebrows knitting in concentration.

'What are you doing?'

'My job.'

'You said you were on a break. I'd like it if you deleted that one.'

He lowered the camera, as if deliberating her request. 'Tell me who taught you to sew?'

'My mother, though I'm not as good as she was.'

'You wouldn't think that if I showed you this.' He pressed some buttons on the camera and held up the display screen. 'Here.'

Rachael recognised herself, but as if someone had photoshopped her face into a magazine ad. She had a soft ethereal smile on her lips, as though a beautiful but complex artwork had caught her attention, and the dress was an immaculate shining pink, its surface glowing like the lights of Paris. She shook her head.

'I often wanted her advice when I was making this,' she said sadly, touching her fingers to the screen. 'She died a few months ago.'

'I'm sorry,' Antonio said.

Rachael looked away, wondering why she'd told him. The Seine lapped around the boat, but she longed to hear the wind chimes at home and her mother's voice calling from the lounge.

'No one should have to lose their mother so young. I didn't mean to upset you,' he said, when the silence stretched too long. 'I'll delete the photo.'

'You didn't,' she said quickly. 'And don't. I'm just a little homesick. I almost went home early. Seems silly now when I'm only away a few days.'

'But you've been to Paris before.'

'No, never. Actually, this is my first time overseas.'

His eyebrows twitched as if he didn't believe her. 'You surprise me. Most of the people at this party,' he gestured to the top deck, 'have been everywhere, as long as it has skiing, racing or five-star hotels.'

'I'm one of the Milton guests.'

'Milton?'

'In Australia. It's a little town where Matthew – the groom – grew up. We're, you know, farmers and things like that. I run a wheat farm. Most days I'm in jeans and a beat-up hat.'

He smiled abruptly, and it gave his eyes an intense warmth she wouldn't have thought him capable of. 'I wouldn't have guessed. When I saw you upstairs, I thought you were in business.'

'I am. Just not the kind you thought, I guess.'

'I guess so.' He leaned back, more relaxed. 'Paris is beautiful, but nothing compares with home. I travel all over, even to Italy sometimes, and I still want pizza from the place I know down the street in New York. So I get you wanting to go home. But if you want some advice, give it some time. Paris isn't always great at first impressions. It's the details that get under your skin.'

Rachael considered. Even though it was seeing Matthew that had prompted her need to escape, Paris still felt as unfamiliar to her as a stranger would find the farm having only been in the house. They would never know about the inscription on her mother's gum tree on the rise, or that the dip in the middle of the east paddock made a black pool at sunset, or that there was a secret waterhole tucked in the rocks by the creek. The details were what made her home unique, special and beautiful.

She joined Antonio by the rail. 'I do love the river.'

The boat had turned and they were passing back under the low bridges to the Île de la Cité. Notre Dame slid into view with its buttresses dusky orange under spotlights.

'You're in good company there,' he said, and pointed to the cathedral. 'The Île de la Cité was the first settlement in Paris. That is the height of passion for a river – not settling on either bank, but on an island right in the middle.'

Rachael tried to imagine it: an empty landscape, more like home, with endless fields or forests, and a tiny seed of a city growing into the Paris of now.

'I can almost see it,' she said.

'Notre Dame took more than a hundred years to build. My nonna, she likes to say that love is like that. It should grow slowly.'

'She does, huh?'

'Yes, only she would talk about it with fire,' Antonio said, rubbing his hands together. 'You build a fire little by little, layer on layer, so the coals last through the coldest night. She says, be suspicious of hot romances because they burn out as fast as they start.'

Rachael glanced at him. He had a small smile of affection on his lips. 'She sounds like she knows a few things.'

'Oh yes,' he said, laughing. 'And she isn't afraid to tell everyone.'

'So . . . do you photograph weddings often?'

He shot her an assessing look, as if he didn't know if she was serious. 'Almost never. Believe it or not, last week I was in Syria, reporting on the refugee camps. Next week I'm flying to Africa with anti-poaching teams for *National Geographic*. These days I think I spend more time in war zones than at weddings.'

'So why are you—'

'Here? I know Bonnie. We met in Sydney a few years ago when I was there with my father. I like her charity work. She's no-nonsense, really believes in making a difference, not just saying you are. And I know her style. I started out in fashion photography years ago, so we agreed I would shoot her wedding as a favour.' He inclined his head. 'Besides, it's hard to pass up a week in Paris, especially when your next assignment involves body armour.'

Rachael raised an eyebrow. 'I was about to say, I wonder what sort of week Walter Quinn was expecting if he hired you?'

Antonio chuckled. 'You might be right. My papa always says that family is war. He's Italian, so he should know.'

'Oh, is that it? I was trying to work out your accent.'

'It won't help you. New York is home, but we travelled a lot when I was growing up. My father was a fashion photographer and we lived all over the world, so now my accent is like a camel.'

'A camel?'

'A horse built by committee. Too many conflicting inputs that results in something ugly and bad-tempered.'

Rachael laughed.

He straightened. 'Sadly, I must get back to work and find out what Evonne wants. I can't hide all night, pleasant as this is. *Ciao*, Rachael.'

He unexpectedly kissed her hand, his touch warm and sudden, then shouldered his bag and made for the stairs. Rachael swayed a little, as if his leaving had created a vacuum. She'd been enjoying the conversation.

She turned back to the city lights dancing in the white wake of the boat and thought about what he'd said. The Eiffel Tower was no longer visible, but beyond such a great icon, Paris must have so much more to offer. For the first time since she'd thought about going home, Rachael was grateful, really grateful, that she hadn't left.

She circled the lower deck and eventually found Sammy leaning on the railing near the bow, wine glass dangling in her fingers and talking to Peter.

'Here she is,' Peter said, tilting his drink towards Rachael. 'The woman everyone's talking about.'

'Everyone?' Rachael asked, looking questioningly at Sammy. Sammy shook her head and shrugged.

'Bonnie's taken with you, isn't she?' Peter went on. 'Likes your dresses and your quick thinking with that Nicholas bloke. She's been telling everyone what a gem you are.'

'Rachael looks like she needs a drink,' Sammy said. 'Shall we go to the bar?'

'No need,' Peter said. 'Must be one of those waiter fellas around. What'll you have, Rach? Tell me it's a real drink and not more of this wine nonsense.'

'I don't need one, thanks, Pete. Can I talk to Sammy for a minute?'

'Course.' Peter made an expansive hand gesture. 'I'm going on a mission. Man's got to be able to get a beer on this boat somewhere.' He tipped the remains of his wine over the railing and set off.

'Thank goodness,' Sammy said. 'If I have to hear any more about the price of seed this year . . .' She laughed, then leaned closer to Rachael. 'Don't leave me alone with him any more, okay?'

'Sure. Listen, Sam, I've been thinking.'

'Not about going home again?'

'Just the opposite. I want to go exploring again tomorrow. Really see things. I want to discover all the hidden details, you know?'

Sammy smiled. 'Glad to hear it. I was feeling a bit off when we got here, but it's pretty glam, isn't it? Like *An American in Paris* but with less ballet. Where will we start?'

Rachael leaned over the railing. The boat was passing under another bridge, the narrow portal creating a tunnelled view of the river ahead. Notre Dame was still just visible off the bow, its buttresses painted in light. She wanted to stand under those buttresses, wanted to walk through every street and park on the island. Wanted to build her own fire in Paris, and hope it would not only snuff out the lingering torch she held for Matthew, but light the way forward.

'What about there?' she said, pointing.

Chapter 9

Rachael woke the next morning sore in her body, like she'd been hauling straw bales all day. Even on the lush carpet her foot bones creaked under tender skin. That's what happened when you were more used to steel-capped boots than high heels.

She had a long, hot shower and dressed with excitement. Today, apart from a breakfast in the Maison Lutetia's dining room, was free, so she and Sammy planned to start with Notre Dame, then the Lady Chapel at the Church of Saint-Sulpice, while meandering in between to discover the intricacies that made Paris.

She knocked on Sammy's door but there was no answer. After waiting ten minutes in case Sammy was in the shower, she knocked again. 'Sammy. You awake?'

Sammy eventually cracked the door wrapped in a towel. 'So sorry, running late. I'll meet you downstairs, okay? Get us a good table!'

Rachael hesitated, then ventured downstairs to where the clinking of china and cutlery announced the dining room. She peered around an arrangement of deep red roses and saw covered chairs, white and silver centrepieces, silverware and napkins. It looked more like a wedding reception than a breakfast room. She considered her comfortable jeans and polo shirt and nearly went into reverse; then she thought of Antonio getting away with jeans at a cocktail party. So she took a breath and strode in with fake confidence, even when she appreciated the full effect of all that white and silver beneath the warm wood panelling, the chandeliers and ornate ceiling.

Many of the seats were still empty. She didn't want to sit down alone and wondered how long Sammy would be. She was hovering, undecided, when suddenly Matthew appeared through the opposite door, shrugging on a casual jacket as though he was late for a meeting. He saw her and stopped dead.

Rachael stumbled backwards into the hall. Shit. Shit! She'd completely forgotten this might happen, that she might just run into him somewhere in the hotel. Her confidence grew wings and fled. She spun for the stairs, and pulled up just in time to avoid crashing into the person coming down.

'I'm so sorry!' she said, trying to step around them, but all she managed was to trip.

'Whoa, easy there.'

A strong hand grasped her arm, and Rachael came face to face with Antonio. He was dressed in his black jeans and a black T-shirt, the camera bag slung diagonally across his lean torso. In the daylight he seemed more imposing, more raw and serious, than she remembered.

'Is there a fire?' he asked with a straight face.

Rachael straightened in embarrassment. 'No. I just . . . forgot something. I mean, I'm waiting for my friend, but I'm not sure how long she'll be. I just wasn't going to . . . wait . . . by myself.' Matthew had her so flustered she could barely string a sentence together. She took a deep, steadying breath. 'What I mean is, I'm sorry I nearly ran into you.'

'I'm not,' he said. It took Rachael a few seconds to realise he was amused, not offended. 'Perhaps you'd sit with me until your friend arrives?'

Rachael hesitated. A crowd of guests were descending the stairs and she didn't want to push through them. And she really didn't want Matthew to guess how he was affecting her. What better way to pull a veil over her distress than to walk back into the dining room?

So that was how she came to be sitting at a table in the far corner with Antonio. He took the chair facing the room, and Rachael sat opposite him, so she would have to look sideways to catch any glimpse of Matthew.

A smooth waiter materialised, filled their glasses with sparkling water, took their order and glided away again. Rachael took a sip and let the bubbles fizz in her mouth, cleaning away the sour taste of panic.

'I know I should have let you choose the seat,' Antonio said. 'But I need to watch the room.'

'Evonne looking for you again?' she asked, jamming her hands between her knees to stop herself chewing her nails.

'Not this time. I've had my meeting with her today. I'm just keeping an eye out in case Bonnie wants me. Ordinarily, I'd let you sit first.'

'Don't worry about it,' Rachael said, taking another slug of fizzy water that nearly made her sneeze. 'Chivalry's overrated. The last time a man opened a door for me, he spanked me on the way through.'

Antonio stared at her, eyebrows drawn together.

'I was seventeen,' Rachael explained. 'And he thought he was being funny.'

'You let him get away with that?'

'Not exactly. Sammy tripped him over. She's the friend I was waiting for.'

A quick smile and the eyebrows relaxed. 'I see.'

Remembering the event had the distracting effect Rachael needed. Her shoulders unknotted. She noticed the long muscles in Antonio's arms and wondered if he lifted weights, or if it was just from constantly holding a camera.

'You're not working this morning?' she asked.

'Not officially. This week is fluid like that – a few fixed times, but otherwise I'm free to come and go. It isn't a typical gig.'

'There's a typical gig when you're walking around in a flak jacket?'

Antonio grinned at her. 'Touché. Sometimes I think I prefer the flak jacket.'

'Why's that?'

He tilted his head towards the room. 'My father thought I would be a fashion and celebrity photographer like him. I tried it, but I didn't last long. Too many entitled people trying to outdo each other – who has the bigger yacht, who has the best clothes. It's empty, a waste. People could care about better things. I wouldn't want to do gigs like this all the time. I'm only here for Bonnie.'

'Oh,' she said, confused and surprised. Even though she wasn't exactly like the other guests, some of them must be Matthew's friends and they hadn't seemed like that to her. And Matthew wasn't a bad person.

Antonio's dark eyes gave her a swift assessment. 'You don't like me saying that?'

'You can say what you like,' she argued back. 'Doesn't mean you're right. Some of these people must care about important things. Matthew always wanted to fix children's eyesight, you know, like Fred Hollows. And I thought you said you liked what Bonnie does?'

'I do. Bonnie's a rare exception in a world that's built on appearances. Lots of people do that type of work because it makes them look good. The whole fashion industry is based on style over substance. Ball gowns and couture. Beautiful things with little value.'

The statement slugged Rachael in a soft spot. She thought about how much time she'd put into each of her dresses, how she'd loved doing the work and had taken such care over it, how proud she was of them. They held great value for her, and now his comment was turning her pride into guilt and ignorance, making her a silly girl out of place in the big world.

'You're uncomfortable,' Antonio observed, as if he was enjoying making her feel bad. 'You don't agree?'

Rachael shifted in her seat. Right now, he reminded her of Tess. She was conscious that, compared to him, she didn't know much about anything. What possible point could she make to a man who'd been to war zones? But at the same time, he'd invaded territory inside her of which she was fiercely protective.

She forced herself to look at him and said softly, 'I spent a lot of time making my dresses. It might not have been for some higher cause, but they mean a lot to me. I didn't ask someone else to make them. And it's not as though I live my life like this. I'm only here because someone else paid for it. It's a once-in-a-lifetime trip, and it's important to me. Really important. I don't want to feel bad about it. If you don't like that, you should probably find somewhere else to sit.'

The air between them pulled tight. Rachael's heart was thumping. She'd never said anything like that to anyone. The only time she'd come close was rehearsing comebacks to Tess, which she never used.

The waiter chose that moment to reappear with croissants, black coffee and orange juice. Neither of them paid any attention to the food. Rachael couldn't read Antonio's expression as he stared at her, his index finger slowly tapping the side of the table as if counting down to a deadline.

He picked up his coffee, took a gulp, and pushed the cup aside. 'I should go,' he said, pulling his camera off the chair. '*Ciao*, Rachael.'

Rachael almost had whiplash from the abrupt end of the conversation. She reached for her coffee, pretending to be unaffected, but her hand shook. As she watched him circling the room unobtrusively, observing its occupants as if he was stalking some large animal, she tried to reconcile the Antonio from last night, who had inspired her to see more of Paris, with this one, who was rude and who knew what else. She utterly failed.

Without meaning to, her gaze came to rest on Matthew's table. Peter was there, sitting straight-backed as his wife, Suzi, leaned in to talk to him. He nodded in a mechanical way, as if not really listening. Across the table, Bonnie and Walter had pushed their plates away and were looking through papers spread out before them. Bonnie had a pen in her hand.

Matthew was on Bonnie's other side. His expression made Rachael pause. He held his fork, but was completely still, staring into space. Some guests passed and slapped him on the shoulder in greeting or congratulations, and he broke from his contemplation, his smile lighting his face. But it faded like a shooting star as soon as they moved on.

Despite all the years they'd been apart, and all that had happened between them, Rachael yearned to comfort him. For a brief moment, she thought about doing it. Thought she was strong enough to waltz across the room, shedding the baggage of their past like a winter coat in spring, sit down beside him, smile and ask how he was, then reassure him that everything would be fine, the way he'd always done for her all those years ago. As if she was the strongest and most self-assured version of herself that had ever existed.

The fantasy lasted until he caught her eye. She managed a halting and desperate smile, catching at the dissolving ribbons of her confidence. Amazingly, he smiled back. Not the smile of a man who'd long forgotten her, but a kind smile, full of goodwill and acknowledgement, even a hint of apology. A smile of raw Matthewness. Rachael's heart tripped over him afresh.

Quickly, she looked back at the table and her untouched orange juice. She knew, feeling this vulnerable, that she should stand up and go wait for Sammy, or find Beverley or Bernie or anyone else from home to sit with. She never got the chance. The air shifted and a rush of achingly familiar scent filled her nose.

'This seat taken?' Matthew asked, pulling out the chair Antonio had vacated.

Rachael took one look at his face with its green eyes and kissable mouth and realised she was trapped in a corner with the man she most desired in the world, the very man she couldn't have.

Her whole body stiffened, preparing for the emotional blow that would inevitably come from this conversation. She tried not to stare, but it was impossible. She couldn't quite accept the cropped hair, the leanness of his cheekbones and jaw. Under his jacket he was wearing a casual blue shirt with a small horse stitched over the left breast, tucked into a fawn pair of trousers with a thick leather belt and matt silver buckle. The Matthew she'd known would only have tucked his shirt in for work. Rachael wrenched her eyes up and folded her hands in her lap.

'I feel bad about the other night,' Matthew said. 'I didn't get a chance to talk to you after the Nicholas drama, and I haven't been able to get away since.'

'Oh,' Rachael managed. 'You had your hands full. It was an emergency.'

'Yes,' he said, with a wry lift of his eyebrows. 'There seem to be a lot of those.'

He rubbed his face. Rachael noted his very clean, neatly trimmed fingernails. For the first time ever, she didn't have to hide her own. She reached for her water glass. Her hand wasn't altogether steady, but she wanted to show that he wasn't the only one who had changed.

Matthew wasn't looking at her hands. He was looking over her shoulder, tracking something in the room beyond, like he couldn't care less. Annoyance sparked in Rachael's chest. After the humiliating grief she'd endured when they'd broken up, then the long depression, then the renewed longing these last few months, the anger was as refreshing as a shot of lime on a treacle teacake.

She pushed her chair back and stood. 'I should be going.'

Matthew re-focused guiltily, put out a hand to stop her. 'Sorry. I'm always expecting someone to be looking for me. I didn't mean to ignore you. Please, stay.'

Rachael hesitated, then sat.

'Rach, I'm so sorry about your mum passing away. She was an amazing woman. The farm mustn't be the same without her.'

'Thank you. It's not,' Rachael managed after a long pause, her throat filling with tears at his unexpected familiarity and tenderness. She picked up her water glass and took a sip, trying to swallow the emotion and find a safer topic. 'Is work busy?'

'Manic. The program's really demanding, and I took up a research fellowship last year.'

'That sounds . . . important.'

He nodded. 'It's really good work, but setting up the protocol took an age. Then there's been all Bonnie's fundraising and this.' He waved a hand, indicating the wedding.

'You always said you didn't want to be on the treadmill for specialties, or be in demanding programs,' Rachael said, twisting her napkin in her fingers. 'What happened to the plan to come back to Milton and take over the surgery? Or join a practice in Parkes?'

He really looked at her this time, as if he'd only just remembered who she was, that they'd once had these conversations.

Rachael waited for a cutting reply. The Matthew she'd known could get defensive when his actions were questioned. In their senior year, they'd had an argument the whole drive back to the West farm because Matthew had bought a convertible ladder that extended to three-point-three metres and Rachael thought it was too short – they should have bought the three-point-eight. Even when Matthew, red-faced, discovered half an hour later that the ladder failed to reach the shed gutter, he'd defended his decision. He'd returned and replaced the ladder without uttering a word about being wrong.

Now, his eyebrows merely lifted, acknowledging her point. 'I don't know,' he admitted. 'After the second year of med school, I got caught up. A few years later, I'm working seventy-hour weeks and obsessing about journal impact factors, and working on flights instead of watching the movies. I don't know how that happened. Little by little, I guess.'

Rachael noticed how the smile lines around his mouth were less pronounced now, and the faint blue shadows of fatigue beneath his eyes. Her anger mellowed. Poor Matthew. He must be desperately tired. And she could appreciate how one thing could lead to another and suddenly years had passed and your life wasn't what you'd imagined.

She sighed. 'That's what happened with Mum too. Little by little.'

His voice softened. 'Right. I'm sorry. I keep forgetting what things must have been like for you.'

Rachael's goodwill wavered at this too casual remark. She couldn't help remembering the first time Matthew had visited after starting medical school, back when her mother could still cope for longer on her own. All Rachael had wanted was to talk to him about her fears, what would happen to her mum, how they were going to cope. But it had been impossible to engage him because he was so preoccupied with his Sydney life. The life she couldn't have. It had been the blackest spot in their relationship. He'd come home again at Easter and it had all been better again. They'd swum in the waterhole and he'd listened to everything, reassured her, helped around the farm. Three months later, he'd told her it was over. Rachael still didn't know what had happened in that short time.

'Matthew, I wanted to ask you—'

'Listen, I need to say—'

They each broke off with a sudden, stupid smile that was thick with memory.

Matthew said, 'That hasn't happened in a long time.'

'I know,' she said.

They'd once had an awful habit of both speaking at the same time, then taking ten minutes to decide who should go first. Sammy had once whacked Rachael when a *no, you go* exchange between her and Matthew had reached ridiculous proportions. They'd grinned about it at the time, safe in their love for each other. For it to happen again now was delicious, as if they were rediscovering some forgotten pleasure.

She enjoyed it right until the moment Evonne Grace tapped Matthew on the shoulder. The wedding planner was wearing another immaculate suit in cream with sensible square-heeled red patent shoes. Only a strand of blonde hair that had escaped her chignon, and a smear of coral lipstick on her front teeth betrayed a hint of stress.

'Mr Grant,' she said in a rush. 'I'm so sorry to disturb you but we really need to talk about those papers. Can we take a moment?'

Matthew's expression instantly closed down, any imagined flirtation gone. Rachael saw only the new Matthew in that face: the confident, commanding city doctor, the aspiring specialist. The person Matthew had always said he didn't want to be.

'Sorry about this,' he said, standing.

Rachael glanced up without hope and, unexpectedly, saw a glint in his eyes.

'Are you going to the photography class?' he asked.

'What photography class?'

'They're taking a tour bus over to the Eiffel Tower this morning. Can I catch up with you there?'

Rachael didn't remember seeing that on the program, and hesitated, thinking about the day she and Sammy had planned. Matthew held her eye.

'Yes, okay, I'd like that,' she found herself saying.

He gave her a quick smile. Then he was gone and it was too late to make a different plan.

She left her undrunk coffee and escaped to the foyer. Sammy was coming down the stairs wearing a pair of faux leather pants and a soft white cashmere top.

'Oh, thank goodness,' Rachael said.

'What's wrong?'

Rachael drew her into the salon off the foyer and hastily explained the whole story. 'I'm sorry, I know we were going to see Paris,' she finished.

'So, don't go.' Sammy shook her head. 'I don't like it, Rach. Doesn't it seem odd to you? Whatever he wants to say, he could have said it now. Why meet you later?'

'The wedding planner interrupted him.' Rachael bit her lip. 'I can't just say I'll do something one moment, then do something else and not give him any warning.'

'Rach, that's exactly what he did to you,' Sammy said gently. 'There'll be another time.'

Rachael was caught between the advice of a friend she trusted and remembering that sad look on Matthew's face. She told herself that maybe moving on meant trying to be friends with him, to reconnect. But if she was honest, she desperately wanted to know what he'd been going to say. The abrupt manner of their break-up all those years ago had left her with a yearning to understand what had happened. Maybe asking him would make the difference; finally allow them to part on good terms.

'I'll come back here afterwards and we'll go then,' she told Sammy. 'I can't just not show up.'

Chapter 10

An hour and a half later, however, Rachael realised that despite her determination to keep the appointment, Matthew hadn't reciprocated. There were only so many times she could say to herself *I'm sure he's just held up* before it began to sound ludicrous.

When he'd failed to get on the bus, she'd reasoned that he'd meet her at the location, especially as a few other guests showed up late in chauffeured cars, loaded down with shopping bags from Dior. But then the first hour became the second, and still no Matthew. Instead, Rachael had sat with Beverley, who was delighted to find Rachael alone on the bus and spent the entire trip reading parts of her guidebook out loud.

Now, Rachael was trying to pay attention to the instructor, who was a petite American woman in denim shorts, a knotted hiking shirt and a puffer vest against the chill. She'd brought a black duffel bag full of Nikon and Canon SLRs, and encouraged everyone to abandon their phones in favour of learning about f-stops and apertures and shutter speeds. Rachael tried to listen but Beverley kept interrupting with questions. What had the instructor just said? Oh, which button did she mean? This, combined with Rachael's constant checking for Matthew, meant she missed several critical points and became hopelessly lost.

As the instructor decided it would be fun to try some photos in pairs, Rachael slipped back in the group. All her photos were ugly or blurry. Or maybe that was just her misty eyes as the prospect of Matthew standing her up looked more and more certain. Sammy had been right. Rachael felt like a complete idiot. She almost didn't notice when the instructor paired a protesting Beverley with Bernie, who grinned like a great white shark.

Rachael sank onto a park bench, wishing she could just have a pencil and paper. They were camped only a few segments down the Champ de Mars, and while the surgically trimmed trees were still bare of leaves, the grass was lush and the opulent expanse of the park made the sky seem as huge as at home. Into that sky curved the Eiffel Tower, its feet straddling the cleared avenue like a giant sheltering the crowds. When they'd walked beneath it, the ironwork on its lower edges had reminded Rachael of petticoats, turning the tower, with its graceful curve, into an exaggerated skirt of steel. She had imagined sharing the image with Matthew, and showing him a photo that beautifully captured it. What a joke.

The instructor seemed to have abandoned any serious collaboration between Bernie and Bev, and was instead encouraging them to take a fun photo as if one of them was holding the Eiffel Tower in their hand. Good luck, Rachael thought, but she couldn't raise a smile. She was stuck here until the bus went back. She squinted at a nearby pine tree, the Tower looming in the distance, as colossal as her disappointment. Matthew clearly wasn't coming. She couldn't take a photo to save herself. And good lord, Bernie was actually posing for Beverley, Elvis style, one arm raised, the other holding a phantom microphone to his mouth. And even though Bev's mouth was pursed and Rachael caught her shrill complaint of 'completely anachronistic', clearly the natural order of things had been upended.

'So, here you are.'

With a shock of irrational hope, Rachael twisted around. Matthew had come after all!

Instead, she found Antonio, wearing a dark pair of sunglasses, his earlier black attire swapped for a white shirt and blue jeans. Despite the chill wind, he had no coat, just a thin scarf around his neck and a camera ready in his right hand. He was the last person Rachael wanted to see.

'What do you want?' she asked with uncustomary rudeness.

Without asking, he slid on the bench beside her. 'I shouldn't have said those things this morning. It was unprofessional. I wasn't trying to make you feel bad. I just forgot who I was talking to.'

'You forgot?'

'Hard as it might be to believe.' He hesitated. 'I don't pretend to be who I'm not, Rachael, but I do apologise. I enjoy talking to you.'

'Really.'

'Besides, you could have ratted me out to Evonne last night. I've got good friends who wouldn't have done that for me.'

Rachael warmed ever so slightly. 'You have friends?'

He laughed. 'Fair enough. But ask any of them – I like it when people have passion, when they have strong opinions. That's where all the interesting conversations start.'

'And probably a lot of the unpleasant ones,' Rachael muttered, thinking of Tess. 'Doesn't explain why you just walked off.'

'I know.' His voice became serious. 'Really, Rachael, I'm sorry. I came to Paris this week after a really intense assignment. It takes a while to find my manners again.' He pointed to her discarded camera. 'You're not enjoying the class?'

'Not really. My photos are all terrible.'

'May I?'

She handed him the camera, and with a few deft moves he scanned the images.

'Your aperture is too narrow,' he said. 'When you focus on something in the foreground, everything else blurs.'

'You have to focus? Oh dear, I missed that part.'

'Ah, but this is very nice.'

He held the screen out. Rachael made a face.

'That's my *feet*.'

'Nice composition: the feet in the foreground, Paris's greatest icon blurred in the background. It's a city for walking. Perfect metaphor.'

Rachael narrowed her eyes. 'Are you making fun of me?'

'Not at all.'

'I took it by *accident*.'

He laughed with genuine humour. 'Maybe you should try a few more of those.'

'Ha, ha,' she said, taking the camera back.

The earlier animosity had ebbed away and now Rachael kept looking at him, trying to work out what had changed in him since this morning. He smiled back and she paused, a tingle in her chest. That wasn't a perfunctory, professional smile. That was the smile of a man who didn't want to talk to anyone else.

'How's the instructor?' he asked.

He tipped his head towards the class, but kept his eyes on her. Rachael felt her neck flush.

'The American lady? She seems fine. I just missed a few things.'

'Like that she's Canadian?'

Rachael paused. 'You know her, don't you?'

'Avril. We've worked together before. She was a wildlife photographer, did a lot of assignments for *National Geographic*.

But now she has a residency in Paris and I recommended her to the Quinns. She's got the patience for groups.'

'And you don't?'

He shrugged. 'Not my style. I'm much better one on one. Twenty amateurs all over the place? No, thanks.' He waved in Avril's direction, and she gave him a friendly chin tip as her hands were full. 'I'm sure Avril would go over anything you missed. Or I can,' he offered.

Rachael didn't want a witness to her mortification. 'No, thanks. I shouldn't have even come to the class. I was planning to see Paris with Sammy.'

'So, go now. You don't have to stay.'

'I have to wait for the bus. My guidebook and all the passes are back at the hotel. I've only got my wallet. Besides, I'm meeting Sammy back there.'

'What room is she staying in?' he asked, pulling out his phone.

Rachael told him, and Antonio put the phone to his ear and broke into a torrent of French. From the few words she caught, Rachael gathered he had called the Maison Lutetia. She listened, fascinated and more than a little impressed.

He twisted the mobile away from his mouth. 'She's not answering her room phone. They think she's downstairs, so – oh, *oui. Merci, monsieur.*'

He held out the phone.

'Hello?' Rachael said. She could hear loud music, dulled as if behind a heavy door. 'Sammy?'

'Yes, it's me,' she said. 'How's the class?'

'What on earth is that?' Rachael asked. It sounded vaguely like a death metal version of 'Jailhouse Rock'.

'It's the Milton band. Matthew's asked them to play at the stag party tonight so they're having a panicked rehearsal. The hotel's been great – they converted the dining room into a practice studio and Peter and Angus are running around setting the gear up. Apparently the walls are so thick you can't even hear it next door. But the equipment's all hired and they're having some problem with an effects box. Ouch!'

Rachael winced as a wicked reverb hit her right eardrum. She stood and walked away from Antonio, cupping her hand over the phone.

'Matthew didn't turn up,' she said.

'What?'

'Matthew didn't turn up. I'm waiting for the bus to come back, but do you just want to meet me out here?'

'I promised I'd stay and help them sort out the music. When Bernie gets back from the class they want him to join in. Is he still there?'

'I can see him right now,' Rachael said.

Bernie had wrested control of the camera, though Bev had folded her arms and was refusing to pose.

'Well, they probably won't be ready for him for at least half an hour,' Sammy said. She paused. 'Pete did say that Matthew's sorting something out with the venue. I guess that's why he didn't turn up. I'm sorry, Rach.'

Rachael closed her eyes. Sammy would never say *I told you so*, but that didn't help her feel any less gullible.

'What time do you think you can get away?' she asked.

'Not sure. Apparently Matthew's coming back here with his parents after lunch, and they'd like Bernie to be ready to go then. I'll call you?'

'I don't have my phone. And it doesn't work anyway.'

'Oh, right. You could come back and watch? Or not. Up to you.'

Rachael said she would think about it, and handed the phone back to Antonio. But she knew there was no way she was going back to the hotel if Matthew would be there, not after he'd just failed to show up. One humiliation was enough for today. But alone . . . where would she start? Walk the rest of the way down the Champ de Mars, or try for the Louvre? She craned her neck to gaze down the long avenue, unenthused.

'What are you looking for?' Antonio asked.

'The nearest metro,' she said bravely. 'Is there one down there?'

'Where are you headed?'

Rachael sat back down. 'I'm not sure. I just realised I don't have my map.'

Antonio stood and offered his hand. 'What about a personal guide?'

'For what?'

'Paris. I know it very well.' He took the camera off her and deftly removed the memory card, which he handed over. 'Keep that photo. I'll be your guidebook.'

'You're serious?'

'Very. Now, where do you want to go?'

Rachael could have refused, but she'd been anticipating this day with too much enthusiasm to have it wasted. Besides, the prospect of taking the bus back and listening to Bev tell her all about the ordeal of taking photos with Bernie didn't appeal. Neither did sitting around the hotel. She grinned.

'Everywhere! Notre Dame, Saint-Sulpice, the Louvre—'

He laughed. 'Where first?'

'How about there?' She pointed to the Eiffel Tower.

'I recommend coming back in the evening, just before dark, so you can see the city at sunset. Glorious and romantic.'

Rachael raised her eyebrows. 'Romantic?'

He shrugged. 'If you like that sort of thing,' he said quickly.

Rachael took his offered hand and he pulled her up. Distracted by how his dark curls fell into place with nonchalance she only just avoided overbalancing into his muscular forearm. She let him go and spun in a slow circle, considering the options. Her thoughts kept returning to their conversation on the cruise and the glimpses she'd had of stone buttresses rising out of the Île de la Cité.

'Let's go to Notre Dame.'

Antonio grunted approval. 'It's about half an hour by metro, or an hour if we walk along the river.'

To Rachael, it was no contest. Thank goodness she'd worn sneakers.

———

In late morning, the Seine was a lazy, tranquil boat road, the bridges inviting exploration to every corner of the city. The path was a mix of cobbles and flagstones, and the sunny day had drawn out walkers with dogs and prams, tourists with maps, and cyclists, all passing each other in a slow dance as the tour boats floated past. Antonio pointed out that the current could be strong, the white wakes trailing the bridge pillars, but Rachael still found it glorious.

On both sides of the river, the park and avenue trees showed budding branches.

'One more day and all the leaves will be out. You came to Paris right on the cusp of spring,' Antonio said.

Rachael was buoyed. Spring was a time of renewal, just like she hoped this week would be for her. Maybe Matthew not turning up this morning was for the best.

Antonio was the ideal guide, his love of Paris as obvious as the turning season. He told her how the city had once been all cramped medieval streets, and how they'd been opened up later into the great boulevards. How the city had been remodelled and changed over time, affected by wars and revolutions. As they were passing the Louvre on the opposite bank, he told her how the Place du Carrousel was used for executions during the French Revolution.

'What, right there?' Rachael asked, pointing across the river.

'Yes, in that exact spot.'

'Sammy and I were standing there yesterday. Amazing. But bloodthirsty. I'll never look at it the same way again.'

'That's the double side of history – it's often brutal. How about a change of topic?'

'Like what?'

'Tell me about your farm.'

'What do you want to know?'

'Describe it to me.'

'It's about five hundred k's west of Sydney—'

'No, no, I mean describe it like a story.'

Rachael stopped and thought. 'Well, if you drive there on a summer's day, your legs stick to the seats because the sun is baking and the air conditioner's never enough. The sky's so blue it looks like an ocean, and the heat makes the distant road into a grey mirage. There's wild wheat growing in the road drains, and the ford across our drive has a permanent pothole, so you bounce coming over it. The house looks like a white block from the road, a square in the middle of the fields, and you can tell the time of year by whether the land is green or gold or grey.'

She went on, telling him about the acres of tree-dotted fields, the sheds, the house with its border of gardenias, the bruised colour of the sky on a winter's morning, the golden sun on a summer's eve. The waterhole with its orange and red striped boulders, the green water so clear you could see almost to the bottom. He listened with his eyes half-closed, as if picturing it all.

'And who else is there?' he asked finally. 'Husband? Boyfriend?'

Rachael shook her head. 'Just me now, since Mum passed away. And no boyfriend since—' She almost said his name and pulled up short. 'Well, I'm still getting over a break-up.'

She hadn't meant to add that last part. Antonio glanced at her and she wondered if he was imagining her all alone on the farm with no one else for miles around.

'What?' she demanded.

'Your descriptions are very beautiful. You make me want to see it myself – I felt like I was miles away from Paris. You have the soul of an artist.'

'You saw my photographs, right?'

He laughed. 'So photography is not your medium. But I want to know – your mother ran the farm, and now you do. Is that what you wanted?'

'Actually,' she said, 'when I was at school I wanted to be a journalist. I was going to study in Sydney.'

'And what made you want to be a journalist?'

'Um.' She thought about it, but couldn't remember where the idea had come from, only the thrill of planning her life with Matthew. 'I'm not sure. That must sound so stupid.'

'Not at all. Some things are just in us, part of us. I think photojournalism is like that for me. I have to take pictures, tell stories with them. So why aren't you a journalist now?'

'My mum got sick. When I finished school, I stayed to look after her instead.'

'Ah. That must have been hard.'

'Not really,' Rachael said. 'Can we talk about something else?'

'Okay.' He stopped and stared at the river flowing far below them. 'Do you know the story of L'Inconnue?'

'What's that?'

'More than a hundred years ago, a drowned woman was pulled from the river, not far from here, and she was so beautiful that one of the morticians made a mask of her face.' Seeing Rachael's expression, he shrugged. 'It was the Victorian age – everyone was a little obsessed with death. Regardless, her mask had an easy, peaceful smile, much like the *Mona Lisa*, and many copies were made. She even became the face of the first resuscitation manikin. That's actually how I first heard the story – from an army medic in the Sudan.'

Rachael tracked a leaf floating downriver, trying to imagine the unknown woman drowning right here, more than a hundred years ago, when Paris was a darker, colder place. A peculiar loneliness lapped inside her.

'Who was she?'

Antonio shrugged. 'No one knows. No one ever identified her. After I heard the story, I became preoccupied with it for a while. When I next came to Paris, I found one of the original mask-makers still in the city and saw the copy they had of her. I photographed that place in the river where they pulled her out a dozen times, and researched anything written about it. If the story is true, she was probably a stranger in Paris. Had no family here. Maybe she got into some difficulty and killed herself. However you look at it, someone unclaimed in death probably didn't have a happy life.'

Rachael couldn't help thinking of the number of people who had packed into her mother's funeral. 'I guess that must be true.' She hugged herself, wondering if the unknown woman had ever stood right in this spot and looked down on the river with dark thoughts. Antonio caught her eye. 'Yes, it used to make me feel depressed like that too. Which is why you always have to get to the end of the story. You see, parts of the account don't make sense. Doctors have said the mask isn't the face of a person who drowned – the expression is wrong, and the detail preserved is too good for someone pulled out of the water. Perhaps the mask was simply modelled on a living girl. It's a true mystery. That's what makes old cities fascinating.'

'Layer on layer of people's lives,' Rachael said.

'Yes, and all the complexities of those lives. Far more unseen than seen. This is what I love about Paris – looking for those stories, as much as the ones in the museums and galleries. Think of how many people have lived here and visited, all the experiences they've had.'

When they finally crossed to the Île de la Cité and stood before Notre Dame, Antonio had inspired Rachael to imagine what it would have been like here in the Middle Ages when the cathedral was first completed and dwarfing everything around it. How would the soaring towers have looked then, rising out of the river? Probably as awesome as they did now, given the crowd waiting to go inside.

They joined the queue, and after a short delay slipped inside the stone walls and into silence.

The cold air under the vaulted ceilings had the ability to hush all voices. Rachael had only ever been inside St George's in Parkes, so she was utterly unprepared for the reverence the cathedral commanded. Her feet swished over the flagstones with a sound that reminded her of walking through fields, but the landscape here was paintings and candles and chapels. The glorious blues of the rose windows looked down on Joan of Arc's statue. Rachael slid out of the stream of tourists to sit in a simple wooden chair and let the ambience soak through her. She wasn't religious, but somehow this church was transcendental, demanding an awe that went beyond belief and faith and into a place without words.

Eventually, she continued on, only stopping when she saw votive candles under the paintings of Mary. Antonio lent her two euros and she lit a candle for her mother.

'I'll pay you back,' she whispered.

He shook his head.

She noticed that he dipped his finger in the font of water and crossed himself in a practised way, and wondered if it was something he'd learned growing up, and what he believed now.

She didn't think once of Matthew.

When Rachael reluctantly re-emerged into the sunny square, the brilliant light warmed her body and her heart, infusing her with an energy she hadn't felt in years.

As it was nearing one in the afternoon, Rachael assumed this was the end of their tour. She thanked Antonio and prepared to walk back to the hotel.

'You need to go?' he asked.

'Well, not exactly.'

'Because if you like, we can see the other side of the river.'

Rachael gazed down towards Pont d'Arcole, where a whole other part of Paris waited, happy in her heart. 'Let's go.'

They crossed the Seine, pale green in the sunshine, and walked the first block along the river. Trees lined the high wall to the road, and what Rachael at first thought were two-toned trunks turned out to be carvings in the silvery bark. She stopped at one tree that was dense with hearts and names and wishes; nearby an iron ring set in the wall was festooned with love locks.

'It's so romantic,' she said.

Antonio shook his head. 'I suppose. If it's romantic that love doesn't care about defacing public property.' He pointed. 'You think that tree wanted all those names carved into it? Or that anyone stopped to think about what that ring is used for before they snapped a lock on it? They've had to remove railings on the bridges here because they collapsed under the weight of all the locks. But all anyone says is how sad it is that they're being removed.'

Rachael frowned, then looked back at the trees. 'I suppose I see your point.' She even felt a little better at having no reason to be carving names herself. But she still wondered if Bonnie and Matthew would add their own lock somewhere among the thousands in Paris.

When they finally climbed away from the Seine and into the old city, Rachael stopped to investigate every laneway and café they passed, as if she needed to stay close to the river.

'At this rate it'll take you fifty years to see Paris,' Antonio said, but lightly.

'Fine, I'll speed up. Oh, what's that?' she asked, as the street ahead opened up to a large building of glass and steel.

'In Australian, "Les Halles",' he said, giving a good imitation of a broad Australian accent murdering the French. When Rachael gave him a mock glare, he continued, 'It's a shopping centre. You have those in Australia, I think?'

She gave him an exasperated look, wanting to punch him on the arm. Antonio smiled, clearly enjoying riling her.

'Okay, I'll stop. Traditionally it was a huge market area. Now, there's a park, and a large church on the other side, which happens to be at the foot of Rue Montorgueil.'

'What's that?'

'A street full of fancy patisseries, boulangeries and cafés. Very touristy,' he said with disapproval. 'Now, to the right, the Pompidou Centre is—'

'Patisseries? That way!' If he was going to make fun of her and be judgemental about what constituted romance, she wanted to drag him into this touristy place he so clearly disdained.

Despite Antonio muttering under his breath about her being 'impossible', he led her into a narrow paved street whose every window was full of delights – tiny pastries, plump cheeses, blueberries the size of grapes. By the time they reached the top of the street, dodging scooters and footpath tables and delivery vans parked half on, half off the road, Rachael had eaten two croissants and a choux bun stuffed with cream and strawberries, and was itching to bring Sammy back here as soon as possible.

'What's up here?' she asked as they crossed the road, leaving the patisseries behind and moving uphill into tightly packed five-storey buildings.

'It's the dressmaking district,' Antonio said. 'And then if we go east, we come to the site of the original city gate – more of an immigrant quarter now, but interesting.'

Dressmaking? Rachael moved forward, her senses piqued. There were no wide avenues here, just a network of narrow roads crowded with delivery vans and more scooters. The vans were offloading bolts of fabric, and through the windows of the seemingly tiny shops she could see every permutation of clothing: bridal gowns and day dresses, smart fashion and sports clothes. These weren't the big fashion houses' boutiques with expansive glass facades; many seemed to be manufacturers and not open to the public. Rachael could sense the industry behind every door.

Antonio indulged her and they wandered along street after street, in and out of stores that took her interest. Down one particularly kinked lane, Rachael discovered a tiny haberdashery set into the stone blocks of a basement and crowded with racks of button tubes, lace cards and braid loops. A painted sign over the door read *La Mercerie des Rêves*. In a basket of covered buttons carefully sealed in plastic bags, she found a set of ten in white silk, their surfaces shining with fine gold-threaded lace. The handwritten price said twenty euros. Rachael bit her lip. They were gorgeous, but the fabric required to do them justice probably cost more than the last harvest had brought in. She sadly put them back.

'Very restrained,' Antonio said, once they were back on the street. 'When I saw that look on your face I was sure you'd buy them.'

'I wanted to. At home, I have this small collection of buttons and lace and other things my mum collected overseas, and they all have these little labels about where they're from. I thought I might start a collection too, one day.'

'So why didn't you buy them? You don't want to start with something from Paris?'

'They're for a wedding dress,' Rachael said, as if that explained it. 'I'll find something else.'

They meandered on, the sun sinking lower until it made sunbursts on the windows and a golden sheen across the cobbles. For Rachael, walking in that light with Antonio was a living painting, just as beautiful as the Monets she'd seen in the Musée de l'Orangerie.

'Imagine living here,' she said, peering up at a lacy roofline five storeys above, with its chimneys and gable windows.

'I do, sometimes.'

'You know what I mean. Actually having a place here.'

'I do,' he said again.

'What?'

'Well, it's a friend's place, but he's almost never here. I borrow it when I'm in Paris – I much prefer it to a hotel. The view from the terrace is unique, and there's no security, no pretension. Do you want to see it?'

'How far is it?'

He shrugged. 'Three minutes this way. But I warn you: you'll need some stamina.'

Rachael didn't appreciate what he meant until they reached the building. The apartment was on the top floor, which meant climbing the most uneven, creaking spiral staircase she had ever seen. It looked as if it belonged in a dungeon rather than an apartment block.

'Eighty-seven stairs,' Antonio said as they neared the top.

'Why would you count them? That makes it so much worse,' she panted. 'How does anyone ever move house?'

'It's Paris. There's no lifts anywhere. Besides, who would want to move from here?'

When he opened the door, she acknowledged his point. Though the apartment was cosy – just a kitchenette with a small lounge, a bedroom off to the side, and a bathroom – it had gorgeous thick wooden beams exposed in the ceiling and a terrace that offered a stunning view across the rooftops.

'Pity we don't have champagne,' Antonio said as they stepped out into the afternoon.

Rachael stared across the rooftops and sighed with satisfaction. She almost wanted to fling her arms out, like Rose in *Titanic*. 'I don't mind at all. This is amazing.'

Here, far from the luxurious hotel and the crowds at the monuments, she had a sense of Paris as a living, moving thing. All around and below her were people making their way in the city. People unloading bolts of cloth and cutting patterns and making clothes, and baking, and sailing boats, and taking photos and writing and meeting and being. It was so different from the farm and yet it gave her the same feeling of purpose, of things to do. She tried to explain it to Antonio.

'Do you get used to it?' she asked, when his expression remained unmoved. 'When you travel so much, do you forget how exciting everything around you is?'

'Things are less exciting when people are shooting near you,' he said, but he paused, examining her as if he wasn't sure she was serious. 'I guess I don't think about it like that.'

'Maybe it's just because it's new for me.'

'Maybe,' he said, his husky voice deepening. 'Or maybe I've seen too much.' Then he shook his head.

'What?' she asked. Did she sound like an unsophisticated hick?

'You're very interesting,' he said finally. 'When you look at the world and at other people, you seem to see their best parts. I haven't met anyone like you before.'

Rachael frowned. 'You say that like it's a bad thing.'

He laughed. 'No. Refreshing. Watching you today reminded me about when I was young and still excited by everything, including the fashion business. You made me realise I often see the bad in everything now. It's a failing, I think. Or maybe I've been doing my job for too long.'

Rachael was quiet a minute. 'Mum used to say that everyone is more than their worst faults.'

She didn't mention that her mother had often said it about her father. That it had been Marion's reason for Rachael to forgive both her father for his shortcomings, and Tess for going with him, which Rachael had never quite managed.

'You must be thinking about her a lot since she died so recently. Were you very close?'

'Yes,' Rachael said simply. 'She was amazing, and she'd had this whole other life before she came to the farm. She travelled all around the world after she left school, and did all these different jobs. Worked in cafés and hotels, in dive shops and casinos, and made clothes for people on the side. She met my dad when she was travelling, then followed him back to fruit-pick together, and then they settled on the farm, and then came me and my sister. She didn't know anything about farming at first, but she learned fast, so when Dad left she just kept running it.'

'She sounds very adaptable.'

Rachael smiled, thinking of her mother equally at home in gumboots in a paddock or wearing a silk gown at a CWA fundraiser. 'She was. She told me once she didn't regret any of it, because once she got sick she had all the memories to go back to.'

'What kind of sick?'

Rachael explained briefly about the primary progressive MS, how it had taken Marion's mobility and stability and muscle tone, and how that led eventually to pneumonia. 'She was really unlucky – the type of MS she had is rare. Most people live years longer than she did. But somehow she knew last year would be it. She was so calm about it, but I miss her and it doesn't feel like it gets any easier.'

Antonio was silent a while, then said, 'If I've learned anything from my work, it's that most of us aren't good at grieving, particularly in western countries. We're so conditioned to think sadness and sorrow are bad, that they should be fixed as soon as possible. But you can't fix them. Someone you loved has gone, and nothing will replace them. You can only carry the sorrow. You shouldn't feel like you have to make it go away, especially before you're ready.'

'Yeah, that's it,' Rachael said slowly, holding his gaze, unexpectedly moved. He was the first person to really understand that. His expression, normally so watchful and intent, was now full of compassion, as if a great understanding had passed between them. Rachael felt drawn towards him, from right in the centre of her chest. Abashed, she looked away across the rooftops. 'Um, tell me about how you became a photojournalist.'

'I learned photography before I could walk, in my father's studios. He photographed celebrities there, even royalty. Then I decided it wasn't for me.'

As they leaned against the terrace rail in the fading sunlight, he explained how he'd decided to study journalism instead. She watched his face as he told her how he'd pretended to be someone else so people didn't judge his work by his father's name. The space between them gradually closed, until his shoulder was brushing hers, and neither of them moved away.

'They always found me out in the end. My father knows too many people. But I just kept working. I think I've done enough now to not be just his son, but so much of my success was an accident – the right person seeing one of my photos at the right time and choosing to use it. Happy accidents. Like meeting you.'

The wave of longing caught Rachael off-guard. So when Antonio dipped his head and kissed her gently, she could think of nothing but kissing him back. Slowly, and carefully, as good a kiss as she'd ever had.

He paused to smile, his voice soft. 'Whoever this man is you're getting over, I think he's a fool.'

Rachael's heart was wholly his in that moment. He kissed her again, more insistently, passionate and unmistakable. She was so absorbed in rediscovering kissing after so many years, revelling in the taste and touch of him, that when a set of bells rang out she jumped with a loud gasp.

'It's just the church in the next street,' he said, not letting her go.

Rachael snapped out of the dream. 'What time is it?'

Antonio checked his watch. 'Five.'

Rachael paled. 'Oh no, Sammy. I didn't mean to be out so long. We were supposed to meet up eventually. I have to go.'

'Don't worry,' he said, his lips grazing her cheek, 'I'll see you again. Tell me your room number so I can call you.'

Rachael did, hoping she'd got it right as she scrabbled for her shoes and bag. But all the time she was thinking what a rotten friend she'd been.

Chapter 11

It took Rachael half an hour to make it back to the hotel, which she never would have accomplished without Antonio. He'd pointed out that it was peak hour and the traffic would be gridlocked, so there was no point taking a taxi or calling the hotel for a car. Instead, he guided her back through the metro, a dizzying blur of stairs and turns and trains.

All that was left of the band practice in the salon were a few coils of unneeded cables. Rachael knocked on Sammy's door, her heart thumping, expecting to be met with remonstration. Instead, Sammy opened the door blinking, shading her eyes from the hall light. She was dressed in a singlet and yellow pyjama pants covered in tiny pink hearts.

'Rach,' she said. 'What time is it?'

'Quarter to six. I'm so sorry. I meant to be back much sooner.'

Sammy rubbed a hand across her forehead. 'It's all right. I had a shocking headache so I lay down for a while. Blame the loud music.' Her smile was wan.

'Do you want to go out for dinner? Maybe to the Eiffel Tower? Antonio said it's the best view of the city at night and the desk might be able to swing us a booking. Or we could go to the Pain de Sucre patisserie and eat everything in sight.'

'Antonio?' Sammy tilted her head. 'You mean Antonio Ferranti, the photographer?'

'Well, yes. I, um, ended up walking around Paris with him today.'

'Ah, suddenly I see how time slipped away.' Sammy leaned on the doorframe, a smile on her lips. 'So how is the getting-over-Matthew plan coming along?'

Rachael blushed. She hadn't thought of Matthew all afternoon. And when Antonio had kissed her, she hadn't thought of anyone but him. 'He just asked if I wanted to go sightseeing after the class this morning.'

'And?'

'And . . . I couldn't work him out at first. But he seems . . . nice.'

Sammy pressed a hand to her forehead in disbelief. 'Nice? You're turning the colour of beetroot and that's all you're going to say?'

Rachael shrugged. She didn't know yet how to encapsulate Antonio. She'd barely broken the surface; and the kiss felt too new and intimate to tell Sammy about.

'He's a photojournalist,' she said finally. 'He's doing this week for Bonnie as a favour. Most of the time he works in war zones, and in Africa. But he grew up in lots of different places, and he knows heaps about Paris.' She broke off, knowing there was a stupid smile on her face.

'Sounds promising,' Sammy said. 'So . . . ?'

'So, are you coming out?'

Sammy sighed. 'Honestly, Rach, this headache might be turning into a migraine. I feel a bit funny even in these hall lights.'

'Oh. Well, we could stay in. Just hang around the hotel, go up and check out the bar on the roof?'

'I'd love to, but I'm not going to be good company. I'm just going to crash early, stay in the dark room.'

Rachael was back in her room a minute later with no Sammy and no plans. Disappointed, she paced around the bed, smoothed the bedspread. The curtains were still drawn back, the street a river of lights. She didn't want to spend the evening alone.

Her room phone rang with a surprisingly soft, musical sound. Rachael laughed; even the phones were refined.

'Hello?' she answered.

'Tell me all your plans for tonight are cancelled.'

Rachael's heart thumped at the sound of Antonio's voice. 'Actually, they are.'

'Dinner?'

'Dinner sounds great.'

'I'll pick you up in an hour.'

He took her to a little restaurant called Aronnax only a few blocks from the hotel. In good jeans and a new black shirt, Rachael worried she might be underdressed. But as they walked to the restaurant and Antonio's hand drifted to catch hers, she no longer cared what she was wearing.

The room was lined with dark wood, and the low ceiling reflected starbursts of warm yellow light. As soon as they were seated, Antonio ordered champagne.

'To your first time in Paris,' he toasted when they clinked glasses.

Rachael accepted his recommendations from the menu, and the meal began with escargots swimming in butter and herbs. She had never tasted anything so delicious: nutty and tender and creamy all at once. A rosemary sorbet followed.

'I was thinking about what you said this morning,' she told him. 'About couture having no value.'

'Yes?'

'Well, you seem to like other kinds of art. We walked past dozens of sculptures today, and elegant architecture, all those little details that make Paris what it is. You must think they all have value.'

'Sure,' he said, carefully, as if he saw where she was going.

'Well, when I make a dress, I think about it in the same way – what the shape will be like, how it will look on someone, what the fabric is like in my hands, how to cut it to best effect. That's like what a sculptor does. Why does a dress have no value just because it's something that gets worn?'

'I didn't mean you,' he said quickly. 'You're the creator. But people wear fashion without thinking about those things.'

'But if someone hangs a painting in their house when they don't know how it was painted . . . that doesn't change the value of the painting.'

He grunted. 'Maybe you would make a journalist after all.'

'You think?'

'A journalist can't be afraid to stand up for themselves. I think you have that down.'

'You wouldn't say that if you'd seen me with my sister,' Rachael muttered.

She paused as a plate of rustic boeuf bourguignon landed before her, giving off a rich aroma of herbs and wine. She'd never tasted anything like it.

'Tell me about some of the things you've seen in your work,' she said.

He thought about it for a few minutes while deftly boning the fish he'd ordered. 'I don't think it's really dinner conversation,' he said finally. 'Have you got a strong constitution?'

Rachael nodded, a little warily.

'I've seen demonstrations of a hundred thousand people standing up to their government, and one man defending an old elephant against poachers. And then I've seen rich men step over starving children, and wealthy governments turn their backs on desperate people, and my own country's government bombing hospitals. You've never seen horror until you've seen war.' He shook his head. 'But I've also seen poor families who can barely afford to eat taking in those worse off, and doctors leaving safe jobs in their home countries to work in dangerous places. Great passion and bravery and kindness, and cruelty and malice. Everywhere.'

Rachael's skin chilled and she put down her fork. Not because her stomach was turned, but because he'd highlighted how privileged she was to be sitting here.

He gestured for her to eat. 'Look, don't get me started on all that. I'll sound like a philosophy major. I think you're asking because you're interested in journalism?'

Rachael nodded.

'So let's talk about that. Journalism is about cause and effect. And it's most powerful when the cause is universal – war, disaster, governments – and the effect is hidden. The journalist's job is to uncover and connect the causes and effects. A photojournalist can do it in one picture. Here, you recognise this?'

He showed her a photo on his phone: a young girl, her hair shrouded in a red cloth, her eyes the most striking shade of green Rachael had ever seen. Angry eyes, defiant and haunting.

'I've seen that photo before,' she said in surprise. 'Somewhere.'

Antonio nodded. 'It was on the cover of *National Geographic* years ago. She was an Afghan refugee in a camp in Pakistan. It became one of the most famous photos they ever published, a symbol of that conflict. I could show you others and you'd recognise them too. Our job isn't fixing things. We shine a light on them.'

Rachael could easily appreciate his passion and was carried along by it. He made journalism sound so dynamic and significant.

The whole evening was pure enjoyment, right down to the light dessert of meringue and creamy citrus custard. After coffee, they walked the streets, and instead of going back towards the hotel, Antonio led her to the Eiffel Tower, lit up for the evening.

He took her hand. 'I have a little surprise. I got the hotel to pull a few strings.'

To Rachael's amazement, they were soon clanking up in the elevator, jangling with nervous excitement. And then she was there: standing above the city as it moved like stars in the night sky. She gazed at all of Paris in silent awe, etching the grandeur into her memory. Her heart was pink with happiness, and then Antonio kissed her again. A kiss that promised a whole world of discovery.

'You're freezing,' he said when she shivered in the breeze.

'I don't care.'

He gave her a wry smile. 'Tough too.' And he kissed her again.

Rachael didn't remember the walk back to the hotel, or entering the foyer, or the staircase. She came back into herself when they were standing outside her door, his arms around her as she fumbled for the key. When she dropped the card on the floor, she abruptly realised what she was doing. She hadn't been on a date in ten years. Hadn't been with anyone since Matthew. And here she was, with a man she'd known for all of a day.

'I can't,' she said softly, searching his face for his reaction. 'It's been a long time and this is all too fast. I can't.'

Antonio pulled back, watching her with his dark eyes. He said nothing, but took her hand, squeezed her fingers. He leaned in and kissed her gently.

'I'll go. Goodnight, Rachael. I'll see you tomorrow.'

She watched him retreat down the stairs before she retrieved the key and let herself in. Then, for a long time, she leaned against the wall, amazed at the whole day. Glad she'd been able to apply the brakes before things went too far.

When she lay down, she was asleep in five minutes.

⤙

She woke to a knock. Slow and soft at first, then louder. Insistent. Groggily, she reached for the bedside lamp. The clock said 12:06. Was it Sammy, having a bad night with her migraine? Was it Beverley, unable to wait until morning to relay the latest horrors Bernie had inflicted? Was it Antonio?

More knocking as Rachael stumbled from her bed to the door. She yanked it open, and almost fell over. Matthew leaned on the doorframe in a black suit, looking incredibly attractive and also incredibly drunk. His bowtie hung loose, and his top three shirt buttons were undone, showing an expanse of smooth muscled chest.

Rachael just stared. When she'd known him, his chest had been covered in soft curls. Now, it was as naked as a shorn sheep. The shoulders of his jacket were spotted with raindrops, and by the exposed ankles beneath his narrow trouser cuffs, he'd lost his socks somewhere. His eyes were horribly bloodshot and squinty.

'Hi, baby,' he said, too loudly.

'What are you doing here?' she hissed, aghast, but her legs had traitorously turned to squirming eels. A hot rush spread through her body.

She peered around him down the hall, which was thankfully deserted. A creak sounded from the floorboards overhead and her stomach leapt.

'Let me in,' he said, swaying and holding the wall for support. 'We need to talk.'

'No,' she hissed, glancing at Sammy's door. Perfect. Just when she could use a best friend, she was sleeping. 'Go away,' she added, all too aware that, despite his state, he still had the old effect on her. She could smell the dusky cologne he'd always worn and it transported her back to being held in his arms, being kissed and loved.

Matthew stared at her. Well, it would have been staring if he could focus. Instead, he fixed on something ten feet behind her.

'I really want to talk,' he slurred.

Rachael dropped her voice to a furious whisper. 'You could have done that earlier today, but *you* chose not to show up.'

His brow furrowed, as if he couldn't remember anything that had come before his last double. His hand slowly lifted and pressed against his suit jacket, right over his stomach. 'I don't feel so good.' He suppressed a hiccup that turned into a gag.

'Oh, for god's sake.'

With one more furtive glance along the hall, Rachael grabbed his elbow and hauled him inside, then marched him across the luxurious and vulnerable carpet to the en suite. She pulled up the toilet seat, pointed him towards the bowl, and walked out again. Whatever happened, she was not going to spend the rest of the night with carpet that smelled like vomit. Nor did she want to explain to the front desk how such a thing had happened.

She moved as far away as possible, to the door of her room, and rested her back against it. The seconds dragged like hours. She had to get him out of here, fast. Let him vomit, then check the hall, and toss him out like the last lingering patron at a B&S ball. Hopefully he was so pissed that he wouldn't remember any of it tomorrow.

After five minutes, when she didn't hear any evidence of throwing up, she padded back to the en suite and peeped inside. Matthew had put the toilet seat down and was sitting on it with his forehead in his hands. Against the marble tiles and the expensive avant-garde wall print, he looked like a model in some sordid fashion shoot. All that was missing was a woman in streaky mascara and a crushed expensive dress.

Rachael pressed the heel of her palm into her forehead. This was not happening.

'Whatever possessed you to come here?' she asked.

After a short pause, he said, 'I was thinking, at the party.' He sounded almost sober. 'It was the band that did it. All those songs. I remembered dancing with you at the Elvis Festival. How much we laughed that day.'

He leaned back, his hands falling into his lap, his head unsteady against the wall. His throat bobbed and he licked his lips.

Rachael took pity on him. As if he was a dangerous exotic animal, she marched a wide arc around him to the sink, filled a water glass and set it down on the counter just within his reach.

'You always knew how to take care of me,' he said. No trace of a slur now.

'Don't say things like that.'

'It's true. I couldn't say it this morning, but I feel so bad about how we ended. I was stupidly busy with med school and the exams were tough. I panicked, thinking I'd never be able to come home on breaks, and it wasn't fair to make you wait.'

Rachael crossed her arms across her chest, guarding herself, wanting to scream that he knew she would have waited for him.

'I've heard all this before,' she said instead, but her voice wavered.

'I was wrong. I was wrong to do that to you. I want you to know that.'

'If you really wanted to say that, you could have turned up at the photography class. I felt like an idiot waiting for you,' she said furiously.

'I'm so sorry. I couldn't get out there and back in time, and I had no way to contact you. That's why I'm here now.' He put his head in his hands. When he raised it again, tears were rolling down his face. 'Rachael, I miss you. I miss . . . us.'

Rachael jammed her hand over her mouth, moved by his distress and impossibly conflicted. She *wanted* him to say this. And didn't. Wanted to put her arms around him. And punch him right in the face.

Matthew gave a broken laugh. 'I never thought I'd end up here, in this life. Bonnie and I have a house in McMahons Point, for fuck's sake. It's all too big, bigger than I imagined. Too busy and public.' He looked at her, his eyes lighting. 'We should run away together. You and me, tonight. Wind the clock all the way back. Do it all over.'

'You don't mean that,' Rachael said, scared now, chills running through her body. She was dangerously swayed by his words, his offer of the very thing she'd wanted. But the idea was just a fantasy. Wasn't it?

She edged towards the door, but where could she go? He might be still here when she came back.

'I know I hurt you,' he said softly, reaching a hand towards her. 'I know I broke your heart, and I didn't mean to. Do you remember that night we were out in the fields at your place, in that dip, talking about all the things we'd do together? We were such a good team. I think about that all the time. I can't stop thinking—'

'Shut up!'

Rachael spun away as fresh tears burned into her eyes. She'd almost reached out and touched him. A tiny wedge of clarity fell like sunlight across her thoughts.

'You're drunk,' she said, her eyes fixed on the tiles. 'You're going to regret this tomorrow. I hope you had a nice party, but you need to go and sleep it off. Right now.'

The next minute was the longest of Rachael's life. She heard the tink of the water glass on the marble countertop as he picked it up. Heard him swallow, and replace it. The rustle of expensive clothes as he stood. She worried he might make some kind of move towards her, but he didn't. Didn't say anything, didn't touch her. He just stumbled right past her. Twice, she heard a thud as he careened off the wall, then came the whoosh of air as the heavy door opened, and the soft snick of the latch. He was gone.

Rachael crept to the bed and sat on its edge, tears slipping down her face. With them went all the confidence and energy of the day. One stupid act and she was back down in the pit, shaking with despair, because though she'd thrown him out, she'd wanted him to keep talking. Wanted to hear what he'd say. Clearly, she was still hopelessly in love with him; an infection that had stayed alive in the deep niches of her soul. It was hopeless. She was hopeless. What other word was there for someone who went on loving a man who had left her ten years ago, even when he was about to marry someone else?

The clock said 12:26. Twenty minutes. That's all it had taken for him to drop by and muck her up again. What did she have to do to cure herself?

Chapter 12

After she'd stopped crying, Rachael wiped her eyes on her pyjama sleeves. She retrieved the water glass from the bathroom bench and washed it, then replaced it carefully behind the sink.

She checked her room's peephole. The hall was still empty. She quietly eased the door open and stepped across to Sammy's room. She knocked softly and waited. No reply.

She tried again. Still nothing. Was Sammy even there? For a moment, Rachael wondered if her friend was walking the illuminated Parisian streets, just like Owen Wilson in *Midnight in Paris*.

It only took two minutes to swap her flannel pyjama pants for jeans and pull a jacket over her shirt. She crept down the hotel stairs, worried that Matthew might be lurking in the salon. But there was only the night desk attendant, looking absurdly fresh for the midnight hour, who discreetly nodded but made no enquiries as Rachael headed for the door.

The street was bathed in moonlight. Rachael was drawn towards the river and eventually she reached a flat stone courtyard across from a bridge, its entry flanked with two gold sculptures, now dulled bronze by the night. The Seine flowed by, dark and silent. In the distance, she could just see the top of the Eiffel Tower glittering with lights. How was it possible that just a few hours ago she'd been up there, feeling her life was finally about to bloom with the spring, and now she was back in the dark of winter?

She pulled her coat around her. However much she might wish it, no strange cars would appear to carry her away like in the movies, even if she'd gone all the way to Saint-Étienne-du-Mont church, which Sammy had marked on the map before they'd even left Parkes. No, time travel was a fantasy. She would go back to her room and probably spend the rest of the night lying awake instead.

When she reached the hotel, the security man nodded in her direction.

She paused. 'I'm looking for my friend Sammy, one of the other wedding guests. Short blonde hair, about my height. Did she come out here?'

'Not that I've seen, sorry, ma'am,' he said in a surprisingly growly British accent.

'Oh. Thanks.'

So if Sammy wasn't in her room, she'd never left the hotel. Wearily, Rachael climbed the stairs to the third floor. The gym was empty; a bank of televisions playing music videos on mute. She climbed three more floors, and pushed out into the night. The rooftop bar looked out towards the Eiffel Tower, the great lit sea of Paris all around.

She was surprised to see the bar was still open. A barman buffed glasses behind the counter, and the tables were set under the sky.

'Rachael!'

Thinking it was Sammy, Rachael turned. Then she spotted a waving hand at a far table. It wasn't Sammy at all. It was Bonnie.

Her first instinct was to run. Not to avoid Bonnie, but because in her flannel PJ top she was as embarrassed as she would have been to be caught walking around naked. But she couldn't pretend she hadn't seen them.

Bonnie and a large group of women were spread across three tables, Bonnie wearing a pink gauzy veil with an LED-lit tiara, and a white sash that said *Bride* over a short pink-sequinned couture mini-dress. At least four other women had tried to emulate her look, sans tiara and sash, and had fallen short, though they'd obviously spent a great deal to do so. The table was decorated with wine and cocktail glasses full of colourful liquids, and everyone was red-cheeked and giggly.

Bonnie leapt up, remarkably steady, and met Rachael near the bar. 'Is everything all right?' she asked, glancing at Rachael's top.

'Fine,' Rachael said, trying to ignore the other women who were falling out of their seats trying to see. Her heart was also hammering thinking about the fact that Matthew had been in her hotel room only an hour ago, drunk and saying things that Bonnie would never want to hear. 'I couldn't sleep. There hasn't been a fire alarm or anything.' She tried to smile.

Bonnie, amazingly, laughed. 'That's funny! But do you need something to sleep? We've got a doctor on call after Nicholas the other night.'

'Oh, I couldn't do that,' Rachael said hastily.

'It's no trouble. Why don't I give him a call? The jetlag is hell. Mum was just on the phone to him about the same thing.'

Bonnie glanced over her shoulder at an older woman in sparkling black and a good deal of diamond jewellery sitting at a table apart from the main group. Rachael recognised her from the stage at the welcome drinks. That must be Marguerite de Richelieu, Bonnie's mother. Rachael knew little about her, except that she was estranged from Walter and kept a low profile. At the same table, Rachael was surprised to see Yvette, the end of her cigarette glowing.

'Well, if you're sure,' Bonnie said. 'But don't be brave. I half-expect I'll need a Valium on Friday night. I can't believe this is all finally happening.'

She was so like a small girl in her happiness, imagining her perfect wedding day, that Rachael pushed away the uneasy vibe Matthew's appearance had left and attempted a smile.

'I'm sure you'll be fine,' she said, hoping it would be true.

'The wedding's been put off so many times already,' Bonnie confided, 'because Matthew's always so busy in Sydney. Daddy and I joke we had to come to Paris to get him far enough away from his patients. But I so think a big traditional ceremony is the only thing that matters. Plus the photos for the fundraising, of course.'

Rachael nodded, but her smile was slipping. She was caught in some kind of no-man's-land, unable to escape without being rude.

'Bonnie,' Yvette called. 'Don't just stand there gossiping. Ask her to sit down.'

And that was how Rachael ended up sitting on a Parisian rooftop after midnight with her ex-boyfriend's new fiancée while wearing a pyjama top. The only available seat was in the gap between Yvette's and Bonnie's tables. Yvette issued a flurry of French to a passing waiter, and soon a glass of champagne landed in front of Rachael. She gave up cataloguing the oddities of the day and picked it up, but didn't feel the least celebratory. Everyone was looking at her.

'So,' she said. 'How was the hens' party?'

'Very silly, but Bonnie enjoyed it,' Yvette said, tapping ash onto the ground.

Her acceptance of Rachael seemed to satisfy the other women, who lost interest and dragged Bonnie's attention away too, one of them showing her some photos on her phone.

'I heard it was at the Moulin Rouge,' Rachael said, trying to pull her jacket lapels more tightly closed.

Yvette's lips formed a wistful smile. 'Yes. The only place in the city older than I am. I was there in 1944 when I was fifteen. I saw Edith Piaf when she returned after the Liberation.'

'Mother, please.' This from Marguerite, across the table.

'She was an amazing singer,' Yvette continued with a dismissive hand gesture.

'And a traitor. We don't talk of such things.'

A snappy exchange occurred in French. Rachael replaced the champagne glass and sank into her seat, trying to pretend she hadn't noticed the family spat. Marguerite finally pursed her lips, and Yvette shrugged. Whatever it had been was over.

'Are you one of Bonnie's fashion friends?' Marguerite asked, her eyes taking in the pyjama top.

Rachael took a breath, trying to find the right words to explain she was from Matthew's side without stammering, when Bonnie called, 'She's Rachael, Mum, you remember? The oriental dress? Uncle Nicholas?'

Rachael was saved from further explanations when Yvette stood to bid Bonnie goodnight.

'I am an old woman,' she said, her pearls swinging. 'I must be in my bed by two. Make sure you sleep, *chérie*, or you will be yawning through the rehearsal tomorrow.'

Rachael seized the opportunity to excuse herself as well. Despite not drinking the champagne, she was feeling distinctly giddy with lack of sleep. Yvette requested that Rachael escort her back to her room and they slowly descended the stairs together, Yvette leaning on Rachael's arm.

'What are you wearing to the rehearsal tomorrow, *chérie*?'

'Oh, another fifties-inspired dress with a full skirt.'

'An old pattern?'

'Yes, but I made a few changes again. I cut a more tapered waist, and made the belt buckle a bit more modern.'

'*Belle*,' approved Yvette. She paused as they reached the door of her suite. 'Have you ever thought of applying to a fashion design school? There are good ones here, and in London. You have skill, *chérie*. Or you could take an internship with a designer instead.'

Rachael laughed, surprised by how casually Yvette had made such a huge suggestion. 'But that's not a career,' she said, gazing down at her manicured nails, which looked odd alongside her tatty pyjama top.

'Who told you this?'

Rachael hesitated, because her mother had, a long time ago. Sewing was a hobby people did on the side. She'd always been clear about that.

'Everyone,' she said finally. 'Besides, I don't really know anything about fashion.'

'But you can learn those things. And I could introduce you to some people. Come in for a moment, *chérie*.'

Yvette's suite was a step up in luxury from the rooms downstairs, everything done in white and cream with splashes of red. An antique chaise longue stood under one of the windows, all of which were dressed with cream silk curtains embroidered with burgundy fleurs-de-lis. A thick pale carpet ran throughout the suite, and the bed was made up with white linen. A glass vase of deep red roses stood on a side table, and a blond-wood desk against the far wall was covered in sketches.

'Look,' Yvette said, gesturing towards them. 'Tell me your thoughts.'

'Lovely,' Rachael said, admiring the confident lines of the silhouettes: clinging dresses with classic scooped necklines and asymmetrical details, alongside sweeping ballerina skirts with ruched bodices. 'They remind me of something I've seen before, but the details are exaggerated – bigger buckles, pleats, things like that?'

'I did these ten years ago,' Yvette said, sounding wry and sad. 'For the last two years I can think of nothing. I am ... blocked. I am supposed to show a collection, but it is long overdue now, and all my staff have left. I am finding it hard to draw. Everyone thinks I am finished.'

Rachael glanced up. Yvette's long fingers gripped the back of the chair. 'But you're still so elegant,' she said. 'And you have so much experience.'

'In this business, all that matters is what you did last. I am still missing the centrepiece of the collection – the wedding gown.'

'Well, what ideas do you have?' Rachael asked.

'I am thinking about the fifties, like you. The classic silhouette, the promise of the new, after the war. I wanted to play with that.'

'In the same way? Like a bigger skirt, but smaller waist – something like that?'

'Yes, perhaps.' Yvette tapped her chin with her cigarette holder. 'You know, I like to watch your face when you talk about dresses and patterns. Your enthusiasm gives me ideas, as if maybe I can find my youth again and finish this collection.'

Rachael didn't know what to say.

Yvette smiled at her. 'It is very late. Thank you for humouring me, *chérie*. Think about the design school and let me know. Give Bonnie your number before you leave.'

The idea was so ridiculous that Rachael shook her head as she returned to her room, her feet aching after all the walking, her eyelashes heavy as bricks. She stumbled on the last step to her floor and nearly crashed into a man in a dinner jacket coming down the hall. After a stupid fright that Matthew had returned, Rachael realised it was Peter. He also looked dishevelled and unsteady, but nowhere near as drunk as Matthew had been.

'Rach,' he said, pulling up, his face shocked. 'Man, I must be wasted.'

'Must have been a good party,' Rachael said. 'I didn't mean to scare you.'

'Got off at the wrong floor,' he said, rubbing the back of his head, his eyes seeming to have trouble focusing. 'Must be half-asleep. Don't know what we were drinking.' He brightened momentarily. 'How's about the penguin get-up, eh? *Suits* me, right?' He did a slow turn, grinning at the pun.

'It does,' Rachael said, suppressing a laugh.

He tipped an imaginary hat. 'Catchya later, Rach.' With only one stumble, he dodged around her and up the stairs.

Rachael shook her head. Closing her room door, she headed for bed for the second time tonight.

⌐

The next morning, Rachael woke groggily to her room phone softly chiming in her left ear. The clock said just after eight. The previous night rushed back and she rolled over in the soft sheets, instantly awake, her stomach diving as she snatched up the receiver. Would it be Matthew?

'You didn't call.'

Tess.

Rachael rubbed her eyes and sat up. A sliver of marble wall was visible through the en suite door. Had Matthew really been in there just eight hours ago?

'N-no,' she stammered. 'Sorry.'

'So what happened yesterday?'

'Well,' she began. So much had happened since she'd last spoken to Tess. 'I saw the Eiffel Tower, and had dinner in this wonderful restaurant, and I saw—' *Antonio's apartment*, she almost said. 'Some medieval streets,' she substituted. 'And—'

'So everything's under control then? You won't be calling me from Sydney tomorrow?'

'I guess so.'

'I'm very glad to hear it. This call is costing a fortune so I'm going to go,' Tess said, then added almost as an afterthought, 'Have a great time.'

Rachael replaced the receiver and snuck another glance into the bathroom, just to assure herself Matthew really was gone. His presence had had such a powerful effect on her, his words utterly unexpected. But he had only come here because he was drunk.

She ran the shower and turned her face into the spray. Matthew *might* still feel something for her, but it couldn't be serious. Not after this long, not when he'd changed so much. Not when he was about to marry someone else.

She shut off the hot tap and made herself stand the cold for ten long seconds. She emerged gasping and more clear-headed. With her hair in a towel, she fumbled with the itinerary, needing a thump of reality.

There it was. *Rehearsal* was printed across the afternoon, then *Rehearsal Dinner* in the evening, venue undisclosed. Cars would collect them from the hotel foyer at three, and following the rehearsal there would be entertainment from a London show, then the dinner, marked *Informal*. That left hours of free time.

Before even bothering to dress, Rachael crossed the hall to Sammy's room, hoping her friend was keen to venture out.

'What's wrong?' she asked as soon as Sammy opened the door. Her eyes had sunk into deep, shadowed sockets and the corners of her mouth were uncharacteristically turned down. She looked gaunt, almost ill. 'Bad night?'

Sammy tried to smile, but Rachael knew. Something had happened.

'I went looking for you when you didn't answer your door last night,' she added. 'I wanted to check you were all right.'

'Ugh, I took a Valium.' Sammy stretched, and the action seemed to pick up the edges of her face and pull them into a closer approximation of her usual self. 'Always makes me feel scattered in the morning.'

'Is that why you didn't answer the door?'

'Must have been. I've been here the whole time. What did you need?'

Rachael paused, suddenly needing to blurt out her secrets. 'Can I come in? I need to tell you something.'

'Better go to yours. Mine looks like a bomb's gone off.' Sammy dragged Rachael back across the hall and closed the door behind them. 'What is it?'

Rachael took a huge breath, then let go of the words. 'Matthew came here last night. At midnight.'

Sammy's eyelids popped open. 'Oh, he didn't.'

'He was hammered after the bucks' night. I only let him in because I thought he was going to chuck everywhere.'

'You let him in? Oh, Rach. What did he say?'

Rachael shrugged. Relaying it now, she seemed able to bend what had happened into a more favourable tale. No need to mention how upset she'd been, or Matthew's drunken suggestion about running away. As she told Sammy, she almost believed she'd been completely in control of herself.

'He was apologising for how we broke up – you know, in a drunken rambling way. I threw him out,' she added, thinking it made what had happened seem more on her terms.

'I can't believe it,' Sammy said. 'I thought you said he acted like he hardly remembered you the other day, then he didn't turn up to that class?'

'He was drunk. I'm sure he won't remember anything about it today.'

But she couldn't entirely fool herself. Couldn't help thinking about what Matthew had said over and over. The lure of his words, the promise of reclaiming their lost years and for all Rachael's sacrifices to have meant something, was difficult to ignore.

'Let's hope not. What an idiot move.' Sammy rubbed her face. The atmosphere was decidedly tense.

'Sam, what's going on? You haven't been yourself all week – something's really bothering you.'

Sammy shook her head, but her voice was all hard fractured edges. 'I want to hear about your plans for today. Sticking around Mr Photographer?'

'Is it because I didn't listen to you yesterday – about not going to that photography class to talk to Matthew?'

'Geez, not everything is about you, Rachael.'

Rachael was shocked into silence. She took a breath. 'I didn't mean it like—'

'Let's just forget about it.' Sammy stood, rubbing the blue smudges under her eyes. 'I'm sorry I said that. I didn't mean it. Are you going on the bus tour?'

'What bus tour?'

'To Versailles.'

'I wasn't intending to. But if you're going . . .'

'I'm not going anywhere except back to sleep right now.' Sammy's tone left no room for negotiation.

Rachael bit her lip. Something awful was happening between them, something that had been creeping up over days or weeks. 'I think we should talk about this.'

'I don't want to!' Sammy burst out. 'I don't want to talk about it. I just want to go back to bed.'

The door slammed behind her. Rachael was left sitting on her bed in her robe, the map of Paris and the itinerary in her hands. She was so confused, she couldn't move for a long minute, then she dried her hair, threw on old jeans, a shirt and cardigan, and thought about whether she should try again with

Sammy. After deliberating another five minutes, she decided she would, then heard the muffled click and thud of a door closing across the hall. Throwing open her own door, Rachael was just in time to see Sammy disappearing around the turn in the stairs, a pair of dark glasses covering her face. Rachael let her go. It was clear enough she wanted to be alone.

That didn't stop her diving for the phone when it rang five minutes later. 'Sammy?'

'*Non, mademoiselle*. This is Henri, the concierge. Madame de Richelieu is waiting in a car downstairs. She asks if you can spare her some time this morning.'

Chapter 13

The car in the hotel driveway was midnight black. A tinted window was lowered to reveal Yvette's cigarette sending a plume of blue smoke skyward. A hotel attendant held open the other passenger door for Rachael. Inside, the car was all cream leather, and smelled of cigars and floral perfume.

Yvette was resplendent in a square-cut suit of burgundy slub, the jacket pockets detailed in dark trim, and a matching pleated skirt.

'*Chérie*,' she greeted Rachael. 'Can you give me an hour? I want to show you something.'

Rachael couldn't have refused. As the car took them across the Seine, she peered out the window. 'Where are we going?'

'After you left me last night, I could not sleep. I had so many ideas. Today, I want to discuss them with my friend, and I thought you could see her showroom.'

The car turned onto the elegant Champs-Élysées, took another turn at the Arc de Triomphe, then pulled up outside a stone building with black iron Juliet balconies. Rachael was confused when the burly driver left the car and followed them inside.

Yvette said, 'You must forgive me for this, *chérie*. It is five floors to the top. And you must not breathe a word to anyone.'

The driver scooped her up and carried her up the stairs.

On the top floor, an unassuming wood door opened into a sunlit studio and showroom. Mannequins lined one wall wearing creations in different stages of construction – two Chanel-style suits, an unhemmed cocktail dress, a longer silk dress, and what looked like the beginnings of a wedding gown. The other walls were lined with cutting benches, racks for bolts of fabric, three sewing machines, and a floor-to-ceiling mirror. Rachael smelled tailor's chalk and machine oil and the clean scent of newly opened packaging.

A round woman with cropped greying hair, a tape measure and glasses around her neck, greeted them. '*Yvette! L'escalier! Tu ne devrais pas! Ça va?*'

The two women exchanged kisses and Yvette beckoned Rachael.

'*Chérie*, this is Martine Bertrand. She is one of the *petits couturiers* still working in Paris. A beautiful dressmaker and a good friend. Martine, Rachael is a dressmaker from Australia, but she thinks it is not a real career.'

'No?' Martine drew herself up with raised eyebrows, then laughed heartily.

Rachael knew she had turned red.

Yvette patted her arm. 'Do not be embarrassed, *chérie*. But look around. Ask questions.'

So Rachael did. The room was heaven, the kind of place she could disappear into for a week, time standing still as she worked on something beautiful.

'How long have you been here?' she asked Martine.

'I am back in Paris for fifteen years. Before that I was in America, making costumes for theatre and film. Here.' She pulled a heavy album from a shelf.

Rachael turned the pages. Photo after photo of Martine with costumed actors, mostly grand medieval and Regency dresses and coats.

'Now I make couture suits and gowns better than the *grands couturiers* for less money. New Yorkers come to me straight from the airport!' She laughed.

Rachael was astounded. She pored over the photos, the fabrics, the patterns on the cutting table, spending a delicious hour while Yvette and Martine conversed in French. Could this really be a future for her? But how would she even start? She didn't know about trends and designers. All she knew was what her mother had taught her.

Yvette finally came to stand beside her. 'I hope you have enjoyed seeing this studio,' she said. 'The driver will take you back to the hotel. I do not want to occupy your day, and Martine and I will be a long while.'

'That's fine,' Rachael said. 'I know where I am. I was going to go walking today anyway.'

She descended the five floors in a daze, then paused on the footpath, gazing up at the unassuming building that held such a wonderland. She then walked all the way to La Grande Roue before she could even focus on the present moment. The riverbank was in view – she always seemed to come back to the Seine – but she didn't want to cross over and go back to the hotel yet.

She bought a crepe at a tourist stand under the wheel, and crunched a second time through the Jardin des Tuileries. The air was still biting, but true to Antonio's prediction, the trees were unfurling delicate pale green leaves, the splendour of new life opening right before her. Spring was finally here.

Warmed by the sun, she contemplated the river and the unfamiliar territory of the right bank. Finally, she veered around the souvenir sellers and the Louvre and headed uphill into the first arrondissement and then the second, through street after street of stone facades, some grey, some white, some with iron balconies. Eventually, footsore and hungry, she stopped before what looked like an arcade – a covered, narrow passage between buildings. Inside was the oddest mix of shops: toy stores and cafés – one whose window sported a taxidermied wolf wearing a crystal necklace – antiques and military memorabilia shops, and wine sellers.

Rachael meandered deeper, discovering, and at the end of the first passage found another, and then another across a street. Finally she stumbled on Le Valentin, a *salon de thé*, *chocolaterie* and *pâtisserie* in one luscious store. She was soon seated with a pot of tea that smelled of roses and orange blossom, a plate of *macarons* and something called a *jouffroy*, which was hazelnut heaven on a fork.

Savouring the tea, Rachael leaned back, reflecting on the morning with an odd sensation stirring in her chest. Excitement, she decided. Paris – and more particularly Yvette – had shown her new possibilities. Even though her heart still fluttered when she thought of Matthew sitting in her bathroom, she had glimpsed life beyond him.

⤙

Keeping better track of time than yesterday, she boldly descended the stairs to the metro like a local and managed the trip smoothly, even without Antonio. The different lines were numbered and coloured, the ticket machines gave English instructions, and every train had a map above the doors.

She bounced into the hotel with plenty of time to change, thinking that nothing could damage what she had gained today. And she could build on it all again tomorrow.

The only blot on her joy was worry over Sammy, who didn't answer her door when Rachael knocked.

With that niggling stone in her heart, Rachael pulled on her red polka-dot dress. This had taken almost as long as the oriental dress to make, with its flouncy underskirt, reverse-faced sweetheart neckline, and white sash at the nipped-in waist. Standing in front of the mirror to do up the buckle, she scrutinised her work, wondering what Yvette would think. She'd taken inspiration from the fifties' *Vogue* magazine, but changed the sash buckle and the neckline to make it fresher. She'd even managed to find a pair of red heels to match.

Dispensing with any attempt at putting up her hair, she simply tucked one side of the now-wavy bob behind her ear with a red slide. She wanted to ask Sammy if her lipstick shade was all right, but ended up having to go down to the foyer alone.

There, she found Beverley deep in conversation with the other Milton guests, a pamphlet on the gardens of Versailles still in her hand.

'Oh, Rachael,' she said, waving the pamphlet as she detached herself from the group. 'What a magnificent dress. I feel like I haven't seen you all week. I was expecting to see you on the bus this morning, but only Sammy came along. You weren't sick?' Rachael could only manage a quick no before Beverley went on. 'I also saw you talking to the photographer on Tuesday at the class.' Her eyebrows raised in a question. 'Is he as interesting as he looks?'

'That's funny,' Rachael said, for once quick with a deflection, 'I saw you talking to Bernie.'

Beverley's lips compressed. 'I've had to make an exception. I'm trying to convince him not to move his bakery and destroy Milton.' Then she gave Rachael a quick smile. 'I do believe you just avoided my question. Might there be a Parisian romance for you?'

Rachael's protests would have been far more effective if Antonio hadn't chosen that minute to show up, murmuring, '*Belle, très belle*,' in a soft, admiring voice.

Rachael flushed. Beverley wielded a knowing smile.

'Another creation of yours?' Antonio asked, and Rachael blushed further as she met his gaze, memories of the previous evening rushing back.

Today he had forgone black and was in a pair of dark blue jeans, his white shirt sleeves rolled to his elbows, and the bright colour set off his dark eyes and hair. He looked professional and commanding with the black strap of the camera bag across his chest, but his interest was as clear as the summer sky.

'Yes, isn't she brilliant?' Beverley said, giving him a very embarrassing once-over look.

'Would you excuse us, please, Bev?' Rachael said, feeling utterly rude but holding Bev's eye.

After a tense moment, Beverley broke. 'I'll just find you over there, shall I? I want to hear all about your week.'

'You didn't introduce me,' Antonio said after Beverley had turned away. He gave Rachael a slow, teasing smile.

'Antonio, Beverley; Beverley, Antonio,' Rachael mumbled, moving forward in the line for the cars.

'Beverley Watkins?' Antonio asked.

Rachael gave him a sharp look. 'Yes. How do you know?'

'She has some kind of feud going with another guest. I remember that from a security meeting.'

'Why did that come up?'

Antonio shrugged. 'This is a big event. The security firm assessed all possible threats. If their dispute had ever made a media report, the security guys would have found it.'

'Wow,' Rachael said, thinking of an international security firm chasing down copies of the *Parkes Champion-Post* to read about accusations of Bernie's dog vandalising Beverley's garden. 'Everyone at home thinks it's a joke. No one can even remember why it all started.'

They reached the front of the queue and Antonio gestured Rachael into the next car and slid in after her. The door closed with a soft thunk.

'I thought you'd have been there already,' Rachael said, her heart doing a good job of trying to punch through her chest.

'Secret locations are secret, even from me.'

'That must make it hard. How do you prepare?'

She didn't know where to look, much less what to say. A whole lifetime had passed since they'd seen each other yesterday, and she was hopelessly muddled.

'They've allowed time for light and test shots. But it's all a ruse. Wherever we're going to rehearse won't be the wedding location.'

'It won't?'

'No. Too hard to hide with this many people. It's a decoy.'

Rachael peered out the rear window. The long line of black sedans leaving the Maison Lutetia would be harder to hide than a presidential motorcade. 'Then why bother keeping it secret?'

Antonio laughed. 'I don't know – misdirection, I guess, but I don't particularly care for games. And I don't see the point of pretending.' He deliberately took her hand and gave her a smile that made her weak with longing. The muddy feelings in her heart settled. 'Would you come out with me again tonight? We could see the Tower after midnight when it sparkles with lights.'

'Tonight?' Half Rachael's mind was on the warmth of his hand on hers, half trying to form sentences.

'Sure. The dinner will be over by nine. Plenty of time for going out. Do you like dancing?'

And despite Matthew's drunken declarations, despite all her tangled feelings, Rachael found herself relaxing in the simple directness of Antonio, the promise he offered.

'That's risky,' she said. 'You haven't seen me dance.'

He grinned. 'True. But in that dress, all would be forgiven.'

Rachael shook her head. 'Not a good idea though. My feet are so sore after yesterday and all the walking this morning, and I still have to make it through today in these heels.'

'Ah. Where have you been this morning?'

She told him how she'd considered visiting the Louvre, but instead had found the arcades and the *salon de thé*.

'Ah, *les passages*,' Antonio said. 'They're the original shopping malls – authentic Paris. So, forget dancing. Tomorrow we should see the Louvre. And I'd like to hear about your plans after Paris. Such as, you're moving back here to pursue a torrid affair with a handsome photojournalist.'

Rachael laughed. 'Did you actually just say that?'

He shrugged. 'Worth a try. Seriously, Europe is an interesting place in an interesting world. If I hadn't lived here when I was young, I'd be completely a different person.'

'I'm hardly young.'

He frowned. 'Of course you are.'

'I'm twenty-eight. Most people I went to school with at home are already married, have families, mortgages, all that stuff. My sister has three children and she's younger than me.'

'Who cares about that?'

Rachael had no answer. How could she explain to him the pressure the last ten years had created? How right those two women had been at her mother's funeral? She no longer had time to play around and experiment.

'I don't know what I want yet,' she said.

'And that's fine. My point is, in Europe it's not unusual to not have a family, a career, or a mortgage before thirty.'

Rachael stared at her skirt, smoothing the perfectly pressed seams. 'You know, someone asked me last night if I'd consider applying to fashion design school. Or for an internship with a designer.'

'Really.' He sounded unimpressed. 'Who?'

'Yvette, Bonnie's grandmother. She even took me to see a dressmaker's studio this morning. It was wonderful.'

Antonio raised his eyebrows. 'I know a little about Yvette. She and my father knew each other years ago. But she's been retired a long time. Are you considering what she said?'

'Well . . .' Rachael felt both cautious and vulnerable. It was fine for Yvette to make suggestions, but reality was different. 'Do you think it's a bad idea?'

He shrugged. 'Is that what you want? To make dresses for other people?'

Rachael frowned. She pulled her hand back from his. Somehow he'd turned what she loved into something unworthy.

'I like sewing,' she said. 'It all just feels so weird.'

'What?'

'Trying to start out now. I feel as if I'll never . . .' *Catch up. Be anything. Make up for lost time.*

He found her hand again and squeezed it, and his voice turned kind. 'When else are you going to do it? Come out with me tomorrow. Let me show you the Louvre and we can talk about journalism at least.'

'I guess I could.'

'Good. I'll come by the hotel at nine. And tonight . . . shall we just see what happens? I'll be working most of the time.'

They shared a brief smile, and Rachael allowed the promise of yesterday to flow out of her memory and into this moment.

Antonio glanced out the window. 'I think I know where we're going. They've thought of everything.'

A few more turns and the car entered a park, pulling over beside a lake lined with willows. A posse of ducks patrolled the grass, and across the water was a lodge.

'Where are we?' Rachael asked.

'The Chalet des Îles,' Antonio said. 'It's an island. Nice and controlled.'

The guests were chattering, stilettos and leather soles clacking on the path as Evonne Grace herded them down to a dock festooned with ribbons. Alongside were half a dozen sleek white rowing boats. The water was a royal blue wash over a rich grey canvas, the island waiting and mysterious.

'You can choose to take the ferry,' Evonne said, 'Or, if you're feeling adventurous, row across with a guide.'

Rachael searched for Sammy, but she hadn't yet arrived.

Antonio offered his arm. 'Does the lady want to brave the water or take the ferry?'

A few guests were already climbing into the rowing boats, shrieking with laughter as the small crafts tilted.

'The lady will take the ferry,' she said.

'Are you sure? I thought you were adventurous.'

'Yes, but I don't want to start the day soaked through. I can have adventures later.'

Antonio's hand slid briefly over hers and a flurry of butterfly wings beat in her chest. 'That sounds even better,' he said, his voice low with amusement. 'Will you do me a favour?'

'What's that?'

'Would you be my assistant? I need someone to help me for just a few minutes when we reach the other side.'

Rachael examined his face, looking for traces of mockery or deception, and found none. 'Fine. As long as it's on dry land.'

⟶

The chalet was situated on one of two islands in the middle of the lake within a great public park that was clearly popular with joggers, walkers and ducks alike. Security had redirected the joggers and walkers, but could do nothing about the ducks that waddled fearlessly through the crowd. Evonne Grace kept trying to discreetly shoo them off. Rachael caught Antonio taking photos and had to hide her smile.

The classic Swiss A-frame building looked as if it had been transplanted directly from the Alps, which turned out to be pretty much true. The park, Rachael overheard, was a remnant of oak forest once used for hunting and had been the idea of Napoleon III. The chalet was a re-creation of one built for his wife, the Empress Eugénie, and became a popular literary café during the Belle Epoque. Even so, Rachael guessed it might be the first time it had met with the likes of Walter Quinn, who'd booked out the site, brought in a decorator, and filled the whole place with enough black-suited security guards to protect an important state official.

On the ferry across, the guests were served miniature flutes of clear sparkling liquid with tiny program cards attached with a red ribbon. The rehearsal only required the bridal party, so the guests were encouraged to explore the island and enjoy the open bar and the many street performers. Later would come a highlights show of *Les Misérables*, with performers flown in directly from London's West End.

Mistaking the drink for water, Rachael took a slug and tasted fire. She nearly gagged. 'What is this?'

'Sparkling vodka,' supplied a woman on her other side. 'Seen everything now, huh?'

When they disembarked, the work of Walter's Quinn's decorator was evident everywhere. A broad clear deck flanked with green shrubs and flower gardens jutted out from under the chalet's balcony, with chairs in bright primary shades arranged around low tables. Steps led into a pavilion, where technicians in black were setting up rows of chairs before an improvised stage. The only obvious nod to a wedding was a plinth on the deck crowned with an arch of flowing white gauze, the water and the park providing the perfect backdrop.

In the chalet itself, one room downstairs was set with comfortable couches, the other with tables prepared for the dinner. Delicious scents drifted down to the deck: basil and tomatoes, roast duck, caramelising sugar. The whole place seemed miles from any city, let alone one like Paris. It was as though they'd slipped through space and found timelessness here beside the lake.

The ferry turned back to retrieve more guests, and the few brave occupants of the rowboats landed, pink-cheeked, and were helped up the slope by more security guards.

'So, what is it you need help with?' Rachael asked Antonio. 'Do you want me to carry your bag?'

'No,' he said, lowering it to the ground and taking out a camera with a slim lens. He nodded towards the plinth, all business now. 'Would you stand up there?'

'Up there? Why?' It was the most visible spot on the entire island.

'To test the light and the perspective. With this much sun, the sky can be overexposed.'

Rachael's hand went automatically to her mouth to chew her nail. Instead she stabbed herself in the lip with one of the acrylics. She wiped a smudge of lipstick off her finger, then gripped her hands behind her back. 'No, thank you.'

Antonio closed the space between them. 'You're shy?'

'Well, yes, a little,' she admitted in a low voice. 'I don't want to be up there in front of everyone. It's for the bride and groom.'

She didn't mention that she was worried what people would think of Matthew's ex-girlfriend being up there.

Antonio wasn't giving up. 'Can I give you some advice?'

Rachael gripped her hands harder. 'You're the one behind the camera. It's different for you.'

'I know. But this is something my mother told me when I was young.'

'All right.'

'She said, when you're frightened and it's only a small thing, laugh and pretend you're having a great time. No one will notice and the moment will pass.'

'What about when it's a big thing?'

'Then you ask for help.'

Rachael bit her lip, remembering the time she'd been too shy to try out for the school play, then been devastated when the parts went to other girls. 'Everyone's nervous all the time,' her mother had told her, taking Rachael in her arms. 'We all care what other people think of us, and yet they really don't spend any time thinking about us at all! Think of nerves as a give-way sign on the road. Pause, have a look around, make sure there's no danger. They're not a sign to stop.' She'd had a kind, knowing smile.

'Besides,' Antonio said now, 'no one's looking. They're all heading for the champagne. It's just you and me. Plus, of course, the paparazzi camped down the river.'

'What?'

'Joking.'

Rachael looked around and saw he was right. People were clustered inside the bar or exploring the grounds, and the ferry was still loading passengers on the other side. No sign of Matthew.

'All right. But just for a minute.'

She climbed the two steps up to the plinth with wobbly knees. The lake shone with captured sunshine, reflecting warmth into her cheeks like a kiss.

Antonio raised his camera. 'Very nice. That red is magic against the green. Can you imagine this place in the fifties? You in that dress, swing music, a long afternoon in Paris . . .'

Rachael smiled, his words transporting her into the pages of the *Vogue* magazine that had inspired her. She unclasped her hands, plucked the edges of her skirt in her fingers and dropped a curtsy.

Antonio laughed and she heard the camera click. 'Very nice! But too demure for you. What about a can-can?'

'No way!' But she spun in a circle, swishing her skirt as she moved her feet, a dance step she'd done with Matthew once.

The thought flew through her mind like a sparrow, small and quick, barely disturbing the air. She almost chased it, but Antonio was still encouraging her. She turned to face the lake, looking back at him over her shoulder. The look that passed between them was surprisingly intimate, as if they'd spotted each other across the room at a party.

'Beautiful,' he said, his camera forgotten. 'So beautiful.'

Rachael held his gaze, felt his eyes lingering on her, the fire of attraction catching and spreading inside her. The world shrank to just his dark eyes, the anticipation of his kiss. She imagined meeting him at the lake's edge after dinner, the island dark but for the chalet lit up beyond the shadows. His hand sliding around her waist, his lips warm against hers . . .

She glanced away, without knowing why, and saw Matthew. He stood at the end of the chalet's balcony watching her, his face still and stony.

Rachael's stomach went over a cliff. She stumbled and reached a hand out for the arch. She grasped metal and gauze, swaying towards the water below. She felt giddy and sick. And guilty. As if she'd been caught doing something wrong with Antonio. As if she was somehow being unfaithful. Which was utterly stupid. She huffed a breath, shaking her head.

'Are you all right?'

She heard the concern in Antonio's voice. The two men couldn't have been more different: Antonio, the raw photojournalist; Matthew, the polished doctor.

'Just dizzy for a second,' she said, but then her head really did swim because Matthew was striding towards the plinth.

'Thought I could help,' he shot over his shoulder to Antonio, a grin on his lips. But his eyes bored into Rachael as if he was staking a claim. 'After all, we want these photos perfect.'

Rachael froze, skewered between Antonio and Matthew, terrified of what Matthew was about to do.

'Dedication, I like it,' Antonio called back, clearly unaware of the tension. 'Lucky you're the one getting married or I'd be jealous!'

Rachael's fear beat like an execution drum, but Matthew simply unbuttoned his suit jacket and struck a pose. A few claps and cheers came from the restaurant balcony. Rachael turned away in embarrassment. Great, so people were watching now.

'Hey, work with me here,' Matthew whispered.

When she looked at him, he raised his eyebrows, an appeal to play along. So, despite her dry and parched tongue, Rachael folded her hands under her chin and made a silly pose. Matthew countered with an Elvis move, toes turned in, one arm raised. Whoops from the balcony. Rachael stepped back to give him room, but clapped with delight.

Antonio laughed and stepped away, saying he needed to go over the photos.

Matthew gave the balcony a show's-over bow and the applause died away as people lost interest. He slid his hands into his pockets and looked around discreetly to check they were alone.

'I'm sorry I made you feel uncomfortable last night,' he said. 'I can't apologise enough. That wasn't my intention.'

Rachael pretended to inspect her nails. 'I wasn't even sure you'd remember.'

He gave her a sharp glance. 'I meant what I said. I regret how things ended between us, especially that you had to go through all that with your mum alone.'

'I wasn't alone; I had Sammy,' Rachael said quickly, to cover the hurt that came hurtling up from where she'd buried it deep inside. Many times when her mother had been ill, when she'd been lonely or frightened, she'd wanted Matthew. Wanted him with a soul-destroying pain that had left permanent marks on her.

She watched the ferry pulling up, the next batch of guests alighting from the rowboats, so she wouldn't have to look at him. She knew she would lose it if she did. She *wanted* him to feel bad about abandoning her, wanted him to experience something of the torture she'd gone through. But if she told him all that, she would cry.

'Do you know why I asked my parents to invite you?' Matthew said abruptly. His hands were still in his pockets.

Rachael imagined they looked like a pair of unconnected people chatting idly, more interested in the scenery than each other. How perverse that internally she ached for him to show her whether he meant the things he had said.

'You invited a few people from home,' she said.

He nodded. 'I'm proud of where I come from, even though I live in Sydney now. I wanted Mum and Dad's friends from Milton here, and mine from school. And the Quinns know so many people I had to make up the numbers.' He said it with a smile, as if embarrassed, then the smile vanished. 'At least, that's what I told Bonnie. Truth is, I wanted you to come. I wanted to see you.'

Rachael's heart drummed in her throat again. The other night he'd been stinking drunk, but now he was clearly sober.

He shot her a sideways glance, assessing her reaction. The lake was still, the clouds frozen overhead, as if the whole world had paused just to hear what he would say next.

'Rach, I still—'

'Matty!'

The stillness shattered into tiny pieces. Bonnie had appeared, a vision in a gauzy white mini-dress and blue heels. Antonio had evidently been showing her the photos.

'Ant says the light is perfect. Daddy's just bringing the pastor down. You ready?'

'Yeah,' Matthew said, turning away.

Rachael swayed as he left her standing on the plinth, his incomplete declaration still resounding in her head. It was several long seconds before she could trust her legs to step down.

Matthew might not have finished his sentence, but her mind had done it for him. *I still love you*, it whispered, tormenting her.

Sure he did. He'd probably been going to say, *I still feel bad about last night* or *I still think the Swans are an ace team*. But she couldn't know. And as much as she hated herself for feeling it, hope clung fast to those two unsaid words.

Chapter 14

The rehearsal began. The priest was short, round and balding, but had a warm smile, and spent several seconds facing the lake with his arms spread, no doubt remarking on the view. Bonnie stood with two women who Rachael recognised from the hens' party, and Yvette sat to one side, perched on a chair while a black-suited security man held a parasol over her. Antonio appeared to be having a disagreement with Evonne, who kept pointing in one direction while Antonio shook his head. Everyone else was watching from a respectful distance, or ignoring the rehearsal all together as they drank and sought out seats for the performance of *Les Misérables*.

Despite the fact Yvette raised the end of her lit cigarette in Rachael's direction, Rachael knew when she wasn't needed. She went searching for Sammy. After two trips around the terrace and the lower bar, now filled with a noisy crowd, she found Sammy leaving the bathrooms on the far side. Sammy's black dress made her face unusually gaunt, though she'd styled her hair into short waves, just like at her own wedding four years ago.

Rachael approached with trepidation. 'Sam.'

Sammy's face flooded with relief. 'Rach. I've been looking for you. I'm really sorry about this morning. I didn't mean to bite your head off.'

'I don't care about that. I want to know that you're all right.'

Sammy glanced around, then led Rachael to a quiet corner of the terrace, where the woodland encroached on the chalet. 'It's been a bad week,' she admitted.

'It's more than that,' Rachael said. 'Is it Marty?'

Sammy's face wobbled and she took a breath that was clearly a stopper on a flood of emotion. 'Things . . . things might be a bit worse there than I told you.'

'How much worse?'

'Bad. Like so bad I can't see how we get out of it.'

Rachael was aghast. 'But back home you said you were going to counselling.'

'We should have done that a year ago.' She shook her head, a single tear escaping. 'I love him, Rach, and I've been trying to find ways to hold it together, but he's just not engaged with me. No matter what I do, he's just drifting further away. We don't even really talk to each other any more. Every time I've called this week he's made an excuse after five minutes.'

'I can't believe I didn't realise. And now you're here without him. You should have said something.'

'It's given me time to think,' Sammy said, straightening her back as if regaining control. 'This is my problem. Shall we get a drink?'

'I guess.'

They took glasses of wine to one of the high tables, Sammy attempting to steer the conversation onto more neutral topics, and both of them working on reconnecting. But Rachael didn't want to mention anything about seeing the dressmaker's showroom, or her solo adventures in Paris. It seemed too much to set her own hopes alongside Sammy's turmoil.

Eventually, they sat in silence, until Sammy said, 'I saw you down there with Matthew before.'

Rachael gave her a furtive glance. 'You remember what I told you about the other night?'

'Drunkgate?'

'Yeah. So, we were standing up there before and I got the feeling he was going to say something important.'

'Like what?'

Rachael blushed. She didn't want to say it out loud. 'Like something about *us*,' she mumbled. 'Then he was interrupted, and I can't stop thinking about what it might have been.'

She tried not to show her despair, to pull herself together.

Sammy squeezed her arm, a little too hard. 'People get cold feet before weddings all the time, and when it's this big and involved it's probably worse. It's probably just that. Rach, really, be careful. You shouldn't give him opportunities to throw you like this. You came to see him get married, to get over him. Let him get on with it.'

'I'm sure you're right,' Rachael said, hoisting her spirits with great effort. At the end of the week, Matthew and Bonnie would go home to their plush Sydney life with its parties and opportunities, and Rachael would go back to the farm. Unless she was careful, she'd end up with a freshly broken heart. But the tiny kernel of hope that had been watered by Matthew's attention was still persistently sprouting.

'Now, do you want to stake out a seat for this *Les Mis* show,' she asked, 'or go exploring? I heard there's a bridge across to the other island.'

'Unless you want our heels sinking into the ground, I vote the show,' Sammy said. Then she put a hand on Rachael's arm, her expression grave. 'Rach, I want to talk to you about something. Later on, okay?'

'Of course. What about now? There's lots of time.'

Sammy shook her head emphatically. 'No, later. After dinner. I want to enjoy the afternoon.'

⌒

The professional cast did an amazing job of *Les Misérables* without their usual sets and a limited live band supporting them. Rachael teared up during 'I Dreamed A Dream', and by the final rousing chorus she and Sammy had agreed they simply *had* to go and see every show the West End had to offer.

On a post-show high, they followed Evonne's direction to move into dinner. The round tables had gold candlestick centrepieces with streaming ribbons, and a giant projection screen was set up at the front. Rachael and Sammy ended up on a table with Bernie, Rodney and Jeanette, and Matthew's parents Greg and Evelyn, who'd been circulating and seemed tired. There was also a couple from Bonnie's side of the guest list, and Beverley, who sat herself next to Rachael.

Everyone was jolly, ordering cocktails and gushing over the immaculate duck pâté that arrived for entrée. Bernie kept trying to fill Bev's wine glass across the table, which she refused with unaccustomed politeness.

'Don't look so amazed,' she said when she caught Rachael staring. 'Bernie's finally agreed to listen to my arguments about not moving the bakery, that's all.'

Rachael's own drink sat untouched, and she only ate half her food. Once, she saw Yvette across the room, but didn't quite have the courage to approach her. Every time she thought she might, one of the sideshow acts that were circling around the tables would get in the way, producing a dove from a hat, or tearing money into pieces before making it whole again, or juggling the silverware. They created a festival atmosphere, full of goodwill, but the conversation was so loud that Rachael didn't hear half of what Beverley was saying to her.

By the time the final plates were being cleared, Rachael had calmed down. She could only see the top of Matthew's head from her table, so didn't have to worry about catching his eye, even when Peter stood and tapped a fork on his wine glass.

'I've been asked to introduce the formal part of the evening,' Peter said, making air quotes as he said 'formal', which generated a smattering of laughter. 'My little brother is a pretty slick and successful guy, but I think you're about to see that he came from some humble roots. We were sheep farmers, after all.'

More guffaws. Rachael sat up straighter.

'And, Bonn, don't think you're getting away with it either, because I've been assured that fashion sense of yours wasn't always so developed! I think we'll be presenting some evidence, so prepare yourself.' Peter tipped his head towards the projector.

The crowd were laughing with anticipation now as Bonnie covered her mouth in mock embarrassment.

'So, without further ado, I give you the gorgeous Bonnie – oh, and this guy right here, what's his name?' A mock scuffle with Matthew ensued, which drew an 'awww' from the crowd. 'Just kidding. My little brother, Matty.'

A round of applause swelled as the lights dimmed, and over the top of the clapping, 'Baby Love' began playing, and the screen showed a dimpled baby with a pink jewelled headband smiling from a highchair. The screen flipped to another baby, this one clearly Matthew, his face serious as he destroyed Christmas wrapping paper under a tinselled tree. The photos kept rolling, all with the washed-out look of age, showing Bonnie and Matthew growing up separately, obviously worlds apart. He appeared in landscapes around the farm – as a six year old on a quad bike, as an eight year old wearing oversized gumboots and a cowboy hat and attempting to drag a sheep. Bonnie's surroundings were much more sophisticated – lounging in a tiny bikini beside a blue pool, wearing a Madonna-esque costume for an eighties' party, holding her grandmother's hand on the catwalk at age ten. Rachael glanced in amazement at

Yvette, who looked nearly the same in the photo as she did now, except for deeper hollows in her cheeks.

This wasn't so bad. The dread Rachael had been anticipating wasn't real. But the moment she thought it and let go of her protective tension, a punch slugged her in the soft centre of her heart. Gradually, as they moved into the teenage years, she noticed she was missing from Matthew's photos. She caught sight of herself in a few group shots, but in this critical period of their lives, when she and Matthew had been inseparable, there was no evidence of her.

The song switched to 'Hound Dog' as Matthew flashed up in an Elvis suit, caught mid–crazy legs at the Parkes Festival. Then in his school formal suit, but without Rachael. There was one shot where she was sure she had been cut out, carefully and professionally. Interleaved were dozens of photos of Bonnie on the arms of various boys, but no one watching this show would have any idea that Matthew had even known Rachael.

She could accept that she was no longer in his life, that she had to find a way to move on. But this complete denial of her existence cut deep. Not only had she lost the last ten years of her life, but the two before it as well. That defining time, when she'd understood who she was and what she wanted because she was with Matthew, had vanished with the click of a mouse. Feelings of inadequacy, insignificance, of simply *not mattering* slammed through her like bullets. She was so ashamed of how she'd clung onto her memories of that time, and her heart shrank like cellophane under a hairdryer, cracking and crumbling to dust.

She couldn't watch any more. Especially not now the pictures had moved on to their early twenties, when the lives of the bride and groom had collided. The music changed to 'Chapel of Love', and now Matthew and Bonnie were skiing together, hiking, diving on a reef. Matthew stood proudly in a gown and mortar board, Bonnie beside him.

Rachael pushed out of her chair. That was the life she and Matthew were meant to have. She couldn't bear it.

Sammy caught her eye, mouthed *Are you okay?*

Rachael headed for the bathrooms, which meant squeezing down the side of the room so she didn't block people's view. The photos moved on to this week in Paris, but she held up a hand to avoid seeing Bonnie and Matthew posing with their friends before their hen and stag parties. She didn't look back, didn't stop, until she was through the doors and into the quiet outside.

The deck was deserted now, but for the floating lanterns and party lights that made bubbles of soft colour between the shadows, and the silhouettes of lurking security guards patrolling the perimeter of the complex.

Rachael swore as only a true Aussie farm girl could. Of course she would have to be on an island. In a red dress.

She slipped off her shoes, which were clacking with every step, and flopped down on a patio seat, pretending to rub her feet as she looked for a way out. The ferry that had brought them across had disappeared, and as desperate as she was to leave, she wasn't stupid enough to swim. The flounces in her skirt would be a death trap, and besides, these James Bond security men looked extremely capable of rescue, which would create an even bigger scene, completely defeating the object of leaving.

On the way over, she'd seen a bridge to the other island. She didn't know what was over there, but maybe there would be a boat—

Wait a minute.

She stood, shoes in hand. Yes! The rowboats were still pulled up along the bank on the far side of the dock, where trees grew almost to the water's edge.

Rachael padded towards the outside bathrooms, but as soon as the security man in view discreetly turned his back, she slipped through the gap between the pavilion and the terrace, and trotted down the slope through the trees. The air rushed coolly past her cheeks, and the smell of greenery and muddy water meant liberation. She'd made it. And this time she wouldn't go back. She'd take a train to London and get on a waitlist for a flight home if she had to.

The party was a receding collection of lights, an island within an island, Rachael an escaping shadow. She made for the furthest boat, reasoning she'd be better concealed, hissing as she stumbled over rocks and sticks on the path.

Fumbling with her shoes in her hand, she shoved the boat. It didn't budge.

'Shit,' she muttered, leaning all her weight against it. It slipped an inch and she nearly ended up face down in the water. Great. That would be the perfect way to end the night – dripping wet and ruining her dress.

She threw her shoes into the boat and climbed after them, her skirt rustling. The oars were long and sturdy, so she planted one against the bank and pushed. The boat creaked and rocked on its axis. Rachael swore again, especially as she could now see a suit coming down the hill between the trees. She'd been spotted.

She gave the oar one last heave, straining as all the blood rushed to her face, and the boat lurched another inch. Not far enough. James Bond was nearly on her now.

She flopped miserably back on the seat, ready to accept her fate. Maybe she could appeal to him to take her across. But then she lifted her eyes and saw short-cropped brown curly hair in a shaft of moonlight.

Worse than James Bond. It was Matthew.

'What the hell are you doing?' he asked.

'What does it look like?'

'Did something happen? I saw you run out.'

'Oh, no, I just fancied a nice little row down the river,' she hissed at him, furious. She'd only wanted to get away, and now here he was again, making her legs weak and her pulse race just by looking at her.

Leave me alone, she wanted to yell, but she couldn't quite make her tongue form the words. How was it possible she could be so drawn to him and so repulsed at the same time?

She stared across the water, reconsidering the idea of swimming.

'Why don't you come back?' he said. 'There's going to be dancing.'

She rounded on him. 'When have I ever liked dancing?'

To his credit, he paused. 'You never did, not really. You pretended to though sometimes, just to please me.'

Rachael's anger cooled a few degrees. 'I'm not going back in there. It's humiliating having to watch all that.'

'What? Those stupid photos?'

Tears welled in Rachael's eyes. 'They're not stupid to me, Matthew. You were my life for those years. Those photos made it look like I never even knew you. And then I have to see photos of . . . of . . .'

She couldn't finish. Couldn't say *of you and her*.

Matthew gripped the edge of the boat and said, 'Hang on.' The craft rocked as he easily swung himself over the side.

'Now what are you doing?' Rachael's voice was shrill, her knuckles white around the oar.

'Rowing you across,' he said, extracting the oar from her grasp. He planted it in the bank like a javelin, and with two shoves the boat slipped from the bank.

'I loosened it up for you,' she muttered.

Matthew grinned, his teeth shining in the low light as he slid the oar ring back into its keeper.

Oh, don't do that, Rachael thought. That smile melted her insides. It transported her instantly back to the time when Matthew's hand seemed perpetually in hers, his lips were always available for kissing, and their future was uncharted but bright and exciting. Now, in the dark, those memories were cruel.

Matthew sculled slowly away from the bank. Out on the water, the air was alive with croaks and gentle lapping, the earthy smell was more pungent, the sky a great ceiling of stars. The chalet lights burned brightly on the island, plunging this part of the lake into an even greater darkness.

As they reached the middle, Matthew stopped rowing. The boat glided to a halt.

'What is it?' Rachael asked.

Matthew gently stowed the oars. He dropped his head into his hands, rubbing at his temples before he straightened again.

'I think I've made a huge mistake,' he said.

For a brief moment, Rachael thought he was talking about the boat. That he couldn't reach the other side, or he'd remembered something he was supposed to be doing back at the party.

'What do you mean?' she said, her voice wavering.

He looked wretched, as though he might be sick. 'This wedding . . . it's a huge mistake.'

Sammy's voice was loud in Rachael's head. 'You've just got cold feet,' she said, her voice barely a whisper.

He laughed, then gave her a crooked smile, full of anguish. 'I still love you, Rach.'

Rachael's heart stopped. 'What?'

'I didn't realise until I saw you again this week. I was so jealous of that goddamn photographer, all over you today. I wanted to hit his smug face.' Matthew leaned back, as though having to restrain himself.

Across the lake, the bright lights of the party seemed mocking. No one over there knew. Everyone, including Bonnie, was preparing for a wedding. Bonnie's father had poured thousands and thousands of dollars into this week – he'd flown the cast of a West End musical out here just for an afternoon's entertainment, not to mention guests from Australia – and all of it hinged on the willingness of two people. And now here was one of them saying he wanted no part of it. The magnitude of that turned Rachael inside out. Right up until this moment, she'd been able to convince herself that she was only imagining his feelings for her. That safety net was now gone.

'But you haven't seen me in years,' she said, her heart thumping in her chest. 'You didn't even come to Mum's funeral.'

'I felt awful about that. I was at a conference, but I could have come. I got caught up. In this life, I mean. Like I said the other day. Living in Sydney for so long, I forgot what it's like back home. What you're like. You were right what you said the other morning about Sydney not being what I wanted. It's not. I want what we talked about in that wheat field – being together, staying near Milton.' He shook his head. 'You're as beautiful as I remember. You look amazing.'

'It's just the new clothes,' she whispered.

'No, it isn't. You *are* amazing. When I think about what you did for your mum, how calm you were with Uncle Nick the other night. I can't believe I forgot. Bonnie thinks you're wonderful.'

Rachael was simultaneously buoyed and nauseated. 'What about Bonnie?'

'Bonnie is . . . great,' he said carefully. 'Really driven. I admire her a lot. But we're both so busy working we hardly spend any time together any more. We don't want the same things. She loves the big-city lifestyle – events and parties, working around the clock, flying overseas. It's all so intense.'

He shook his head sadly. 'I don't think it's been real love between us for a long time now.'

Rachael hugged herself. Her fingers were freezing against her arms. He was saying all the things she'd wanted to hear. But she'd never imagined they could make her so . . . unhappy.

He picked up the oars again and began rowing towards the opposite shore. A tiny part of Rachael was relieved, vindicated that she hadn't been crazy to still be in love with him. For the first time since the invitation had arrived at the farm, the crushing sense of being left behind and unwanted, of being lonely, lifted away.

Soon, the bow ran up on the shore. Matthew sat staring at her.

'What happens now?' Rachael asked.

'I don't know,' he said, and looked over his shoulder at the chalet jewelled with lights. 'I have to go back.'

'I guess so.' Rachael clambered out of the boat, her skirts rustling.

For three heartbeats, they shared a lingering look, past dreams and present reality stoking both longing and regret.

'Rach . . .' Matthew began. Rachael's heart broke as he closed his eyes, controlling himself. Finally, he spoke again, his voice choked. 'At the dock just down there you'll find one of the security guys. They'll organise a car for you.'

He rowed away on the gloomy water, and was soon too distant to see.

In desperation, Rachael nearly called after him, *I love you too!* She hadn't told him. And now she might never get the chance.

Chapter 15

Rachael closed the door to her room at the Maison Lutetia, hobbled to the bed and peeled off her shoes. Her feet looked as though they'd been crushed in a vice. Both heels were blistered, the balls red and tender. But it was a relief to be back in the room and alone. The cushy carpet and heavy curtains muted every sound, even the rustle of her skirt as she dropped the damp red dress on the ground. She walked stiffly to the bathroom and ran three inches of water into the tub, swirling in a tiny bottle of bath salts. Then, in her underwear, she sat on the edge and soaked her feet.

The scene in the boat with Matthew replayed itself over and over. He still loved her. He didn't love Bonnie. He was making a mistake.

But what did that mean?

She didn't know.

He didn't even know.

Rachael could imagine what her mother would say. That it wasn't her place to intervene between two people, however unhappy they might appear to be. And to take care, because Matthew hadn't seen her in years, which meant he could only be in love with an idea of her. The last time he'd truly known her, he'd broken it off.

Rachael argued back. She couldn't bear the idea of him remaining trapped in his life in Sydney. The anguish on his face when he'd talked about it, as if all the fears he'd confided in her years ago – of being stuck on the big-city career treadmill – had come true. And the solution was so obviously simple. He had to leave Sydney and come home.

Then time truly would have turned back, and she – they – would have everything they were meant to.

When the guests returned from the Chalet des Îles before midnight, Rachael had a momentary surge of hope when a furtive tapping sounded on the door.

She found Beverley on the other side.

'You never came back to dinner,' Bev said. 'Are you ill? Was it the fish? Bernie said the fish tasted funny.'

'I'm fine,' Rachael said.

'Because I'm happy to organise the doctor. Or if you need to talk to anyone, I'm always at the ready.'

'Thanks, Bev. I'm just going to get some sleep.'

Rachael closed the door only to hear another knock a minute later. This time Sammy stood on the threshold, shoes in hand, brow wrinkled in concern.

'What happened to you? I looked everywhere. I was so worried!'

'I couldn't watch any more,' Rachael said, guilt swimming up at the anguish on Sammy's face. 'I had to get away.'

'So you just left the party? What, did you swim across the lake?'

'I took a rowboat.'

Sammy clapped a hand over her mouth, then burst out laughing. 'Oh, Rachael.' She shook her head. 'I almost had security start a full search.'

Rachael paled. 'You didn't.'

'No. Against my better judgement. There were so many security guys around I thought nothing bad could have happened. I figured you didn't want to be found. Then I couldn't see Matthew for a while and . . .' She heaved a sigh.

'And what?' Rachael asked, holding her breath.

'Let's not worry about it. It's late.'

'Wait, you wanted to talk to me about something?'

'Later,' Sammy said, turning for her room.

⟶

The next morning, Rachael woke early in a state of nervous energy. She waited in her room, obsessively spot-cleaning and packing the dresses she'd already worn, and staring at the black Audrey Hepburn-inspired dress she'd kept for the wedding ceremony, wondering what to do with it. She wasn't usually superstitious, but would it be tempting fate to pack it too?

Her mother would have laughed at such nonsense. Rachael ironed the dress again, carefully replaced the plastic hanging bag, and hung it in the wardrobe.

Finally, desperate to talk to someone and not wanting it to be Sammy, she picked up the room phone.

'Sorry if I woke you,' she said as Tess answered, sounding groggy.

'It's three in the afternoon,' her sister replied. 'I was sneaking a nap while the baby's asleep. Why are you so breathless?'

'I've got a problem,' Rachael began, and then paused because what could she say? She couldn't mention Matthew. 'I met this guy.'

'Hallelujah. I bet he's some dark, handsome Italian.'

'Well sort of . . . as it turns out.'

Tess snorted. 'And you wanted to come home early. What's the problem? His eyes too dreamy?'

'I'm just not . . . sure about it. I mean, this is only one week. What happens next?'

'What do you want to happen?'

Rachael threw up her hand. 'I don't know!'

Her whole life for the last ten years had been reactive, driven by what her mother needed, what the farm needed, in that order. Now everyone kept asking her what she wanted like it was the easiest thing.

Tess sighed. 'Look, if a man's interested, he'll let you know. At least, he will if he's got any backbone. So if you don't like him, don't string him along. Be honest. You should know if you like him or not.'

When Rachael put down the phone, all she could think was, what if the man can't let you know? Tess hadn't been any help at all.

At eight forty-five, she could wait no longer. She emerged from her room in jeans and a checked shirt and padded downstairs. The lobby was empty; she assumed the guests must be sleeping off last night's excesses. Everything was as it had been yesterday: the rich red and wood-panelled walls, the potted palms, the gold-framed portraits, the same scent of lemon and rosemary and polishing wax. It was surreal when the world had moved so much inside Rachael's head.

When she heard a man's voice, Rachael snuck across the empty lobby and peeked into the salon. There, she found Bernie and Beverley sitting across from each other on the plush leather sofas, two glasses of orange juice between them. Bernie was gesturing expansively, his juice nearly finished, and while Bev had her arms folded and hadn't touched her glass, she was nodding as he spoke. Rachael crept away before she was seen, wondering what they could be talking about.

Only a few tables were occupied in the dining room, none with Matthew. She should check the gym.

She was just heading for the stairs when a red-jacketed attendant opened the front door and a man came striding through. Rachael's chest burst. Matthew!

No, wait, it wasn't. It was Antonio.

The antique hall clock showed five minutes to nine. Panic rushed through Rachael like icy water. She'd forgotten all about agreeing to meet him.

'Good morning,' he said with a broad smile. 'Ready for the Louvre?'

'Um, I'm not sure I can go,' she said quickly.

'Oh?' Clear disappointment in his voice. When she couldn't form an excuse, he said, 'Pity. I was going to tempt you with an opportunity you won't want to miss.'

'What do you mean?'

'A chance to fulfil your journalistic aspirations. Are you interested?'

Rachael just stood there stupidly. What could she say? *I'm waiting here in the hope that my former lover will turn up and tell me his wedding's off and he wants to run away with me.* She kicked herself. She could have just said she wasn't feeling well.

Antonio was offering his arm. Rachael saw no choice but to take it. The only thing she could think to do before she left was to ask the hotel desk to tell Sammy – or anyone else who was looking for her – that she would be at the Louvre.

⌒

They left the metro at Monnaie de Paris, Antonio explaining that this way they could walk across the river. Rachael said nothing. They emerged under a broiling sky the colour and texture of her thoughts, and walked across Pont Neuf in silence. Antonio didn't try to take her hand. The wet pavements and leaden sky made the city's buildings seem more luminous, and the shaggy coat of lovers' locks at the mid-bridge more ominous. Jewel-like raindrops hung on every symbolic declaration of undying love. Rachael averted her eyes.

Finally, after they'd walked the last block along the Seine, crossed the street to the Louvre and reached the inner courtyard, Antonio faced her.

'Something's up,' he said. 'I missed you last night after the dinner.'

His face was so concerned, Rachael took pity on him.

'It wasn't you. I just went home early.'

'But you have something on your mind.'

The Louvre's glass pyramid was a perfect mirror for the soft grey and white sky. The palatial building that wrapped around it was heavy stone. The two structures were completely different in time and architecture and yet a perfect marriage of opposites: weight and lightness, old and new. Rachael wanted to be free from the tumble of thoughts inside her head so she could appreciate it. She despaired that Matthew had simultaneously provided the opportunity to see such things and taken her ability to enjoy them.

'Yes,' she said to Antonio. 'I have a problem I'm thinking about.'

'Ah. Is it deciding whether to move to Paris, or London, or New York? Because I can understand how that would be difficult. Personally I vote for New York, but only if Paris is out.'

Rachael laughed. 'Don't be ridiculous.'

'I'm not. They're all good bases for a journalist.' He paused. 'Can I tell you about this opportunity now?'

Rachael stiffened, abruptly fearful. She didn't know if she could handle anything else at the moment. 'What is it?'

'A job. But don't look so worried,' he said, as if he could sense her tension. 'We'll talk about it later. For now, you wanted to see the Louvre.'

After they'd cleared security and stepped inside, Rachael did, temporarily, forget Matthew and the wedding and every disappointment she had ever endured. The famous pyramid soared over her head, breaking the daylight into compartments and creating a space that seemed vast for something underground. A stairway spiralled down into the sunken foyer, as though the museum was paying homage to an ancient tomb. The air was thick with discovery, and despite the milling crowd, there wasn't even a queue for tickets.

When Antonio pulled Rachael forward, she squeezed his hand with genuine excitement.

'Are you desperate to see something in particular?' he asked. 'Or can I show you the most interesting piece here?'

'Is it the *Mona Lisa*?' Rachael scanned the gallery entrances, wondering where to go first.

'I'm very glad to hear you have an appetite for Italian artists,' Antonio said, with a slow smile that made Rachael laugh. 'And Leonardo was a genius, but no, nothing so clichéd.'

'Okay, what then?'

'This way.' He led her into a wing, through a series of wide hallways and up a long flight of palatial stone stairs, then another, and another. Each time they reached a landing, Rachael glimpsed galleries to each side holding marble statues, glass cases of vases, tapestries and ornate furniture, but Antonio kept climbing. Finally, on the second floor, they turned into a narrow gallery crammed with paintings. Antonio stopped before a gold frame.

'There,' he said simply.

The painting was of a doorway, with chequered tiles outside and terracotta ones inside. At first, the picture seemed to show nothing – there was no person or animal in view. A broom was propped outside the door, and a length of cloth hung from a peg alongside it. The door was ajar, showing the room beyond, but the room was empty.

Rachael glanced at Antonio. He was rapt in the picture. She must be missing something. She looked again.

First she noticed the keys: an old skeleton-type key stuck out from the painted door's lock, and others hung below from the iron ring. One of the old sheds on the farm had a key like that, and after rain the doorframe would shift and the lock would jam. She imagined the feel of the smooth metal shank in her hand, the weight as she lifted the door to relieve the pressure, the *thunk* as the key finally turned. At home, that key was left permanently in the lock. But why were the keys in the door in the painting?

Next, she saw a pair of yellow slippers, discarded right on the threshold of the doorway. Her mother would have ranted about them being a trip hazard. Rachael had been messy as a child and she remembered the remonstrations. That had all changed the first time her mother had tripped after her diagnosis. Now, Rachael tucked all her shoes away and kept the floors clear.

Other details sprang out. A book and a lit candlestick on a table inside the room. A painting on the interior wall showing two figures. A chair, but no other visible furniture. She searched, flummoxed, unable to fix the purpose of the room. Was it a bedroom? A dining room? Where was the woman who had left behind her shoes and candle and keys? Had a pot on the stove boiled over? Had her a visitor arrived unexpectedly? Or a message that someone was ill? Was it joy or sadness or anger or fear that had drawn her away? What did the world hold past the edges of the painting?

'I think you see,' Antonio said softly. 'For me, this single frame tells so many different stories. I can look at it again and again and find something different.'

Rachael nodded. She was struck suddenly by the idea that if Matthew decided he wanted to run away, their hotel room might look like this to Bonnie. What might he forget in the rush that she would puzzle over?

The idea stuck, going round and round. 'What do you think happened?' she asked, desperate to break the loop.

'Today, I think an old woman lives there, with no one to help her, and she's opened the door, then gone back outside to bring in her bag, because she couldn't carry it and turn the key at the same time.'

'What about the book? And the candle?'

He shrugged. 'She's old, she doesn't sleep well. She's used to reading at night, so the book and candle are always there.'

Rachael made a contemplative sound. The idea was somehow so sad. She thought of Yvette, and her mother, especially in the last two years.

Antonio touched her shoulder. 'What do you see?'

'I think she found someone waiting for her, and now they're both just out of view, catching up.'

He arched an eyebrow. 'Someone waiting behind the locked door?'

Rachael shrugged. 'Sure. Maybe they came in the window.'

'A secret lover perhaps?'

Rachael had the urge to lean towards him. She glanced up to find him watching her, a smile in his eyes.

'Maybe,' she said.

'Hmm. I like that idea.'

They held each other's gaze for a long while, until, finally, Antonio's fingers brushed the back of Rachael's neck, giving her chills. 'Did you want to see the *Mona Lisa*?' he asked.

Rachael did, so they strolled together down a grand staircase, then through room after room with glorious painted and carved ceilings. Their hands drifted together again and again, almost, but not quite, healing Rachael's anxiety.

They crossed a sunken gallery where the headless *Winged Victory of Samothrace* stood above a ring of camera flashes, and across a creaking parquet floor emblazoned with stars. Then into another long, long gallery where the ceiling was a plain grid of transparent blocks. Here the crowd swept them along with the force of a flooded river into a side room halfway down. And there, behind a barrier and a glass case, was the *Mona Lisa*.

Antonio left Rachael to press forward alone until, finally, she reached the front. A minute later, she found him at the side of the room.

'Well?' he asked.

She shrugged. 'To be honest, she's rather small and dark. I'm not sure what the fuss is about, but I still had to see it.'

'True. Paris wouldn't be complete otherwise.'

She glanced back at the small painting, the object of so much intrigue. 'I keep thinking I want to look again, and I'm not sure if that's because she's famous or because of the painting itself.'

He nodded. 'That's because you're still looking for the best parts. Now, can I tell you about this job?'

Rachael raised her eyebrows.

'I know a magazine editor who wants a cadet for six months. It's a good publication and she's a good editor. I think it would be a great experience for you.'

'A cadet at a magazine?' Rachael blinked. 'Why on earth would she want me? I haven't written anything in years.'

'You're interested in the world. What else does a journalist need? And this editor's looking for someone with good sense, not someone just out of school. She would take a recommendation from me.'

'But don't I need to, you know, have experience?'

'Cadetships are about learning as you go. You don't like the idea?'

Rachael shook her head. 'But I don't speak French, much less write it.'

'The magazine is in London.'

London. Rachael thought of the farm and laughed. 'That's insane!'

'There'd be difficulties, sure. The pay is terrible. But Rachael, listen, this editor is very good. The magazine is highly esteemed. If you do well, other doors will open for you. The magazine may want to hire you. And if not, you could use the experience to apply to anywhere in London, New York, even Sydney.'

Rachael slowly shook her head. This was just more fantasy. She couldn't leave the farm. And what about Matthew?

There it was: the sneaky thought that kept returning, that told her to wait to see what Matthew would do. Whether he was really going to come home with her.

'I'm happy to send her your details,' Antonio said, squeezing Rachael's hand. He drew a card out of his pocket. 'Let me know? Talk to her, at least.'

Rachael tried to smile, to be grateful for this amazing opportunity he'd put in front of her. She turned his card in her hand: simple white with black text – his name and number and addresses. She swallowed, not blind to the possibilities he presented. Here, in the magnificent Louvre, a handsome man was offering her what she'd once dreamed about, and was looking at her as though he wanted to put thoughts of any other man out of her head forever.

And yet. Matthew.

She slid the card into her pocket.

Antonio's features flickered. 'You don't seem interested.'

'I don't know.'

'Why not?' Impatience crept into his voice. 'Are you still thinking about design school?'

She hadn't been, but his attitude rubbed sparks off her. 'What if I was?'

'Design school is a remote possibility,' he said with a shrug. 'You don't know if you'd be accepted, or what may or may not come afterwards. This is in front of you right now. Don't miss it through indecision.'

'Indecision?' she hissed, keeping her voice low in the crowded gallery. 'This isn't a small thing. Maybe I couldn't do it. Did you think about that?'

'Of course. All big leaps are scary.'

Rachael's hands had clenched into fists. She forced herself, finger by finger, to relax. Antonio's expression was neutral, his eyes understanding.

'The worst part is deciding,' he said. 'Once you do that . . .'

Rachael sank onto a bench, knowing he wasn't going to give her the argument she'd wanted. 'It's not just that,' she admitted. 'There are personal factors.'

'Your farm?'

'No, something else. I'm not sure what to do.'

'Ah.' His eyebrows lifted. 'Tell me about it?'

'I don't know if I can,' she said, miserable that he was so considerate while she held on to her unspeakable secret.

'Let's go and see Michelangelo's *Slaves*. Less crowded.'

Ten minutes later, they were sitting on the stairs before two nude marble statues, unfinished and yet exquisitely polished, that exuded a sexual energy Rachael found uncomfortable.

'They were commissioned for a pope's tomb,' Antonio said when she remarked on it. He scratched his head. 'This one's meant to be dying, but he looks more like he just forgot to get dressed, or is searching for his keys.'

Rachael couldn't laugh.

'This must be a bad dilemma if that's not funny,' he said. 'Come on, spit it out.'

Rachael bit her lip. Tess had said to be honest with him, and she'd already spent the whole day mulling it over. She needed to come clean and tell the truth . . . at least, a close version of it, scraped bare of any specifics. She plunged in.

'Recently, I saw an old boyfriend and he said he's still in love with me.'

Antonio grunted. 'Understandable. But unexpected?'

'Yes. I thought he'd forgotten all about me. And now he doesn't know what to do either. You see,' she went on, gathering speed now she'd started, 'I hadn't seen him in a long time, years actually, since my mum got really sick. It was a bit of a shock.'

Antonio was quiet a moment. 'Why doesn't he know what to do?'

Rachael daren't mention a fiancée; that was too obvious. 'It's complicated. He lives in a different city and has a very busy job. He's been married before,' she added, to try to throw off any suspicion.

'And what do you want to happen?'

Rachael shook her head. She traced the edge of the marble step with her finger. How many feet had crossed this point? How many of those people had felt indecisive about their love like she did?

'I think you must have been deeply in love with this man,' Antonio said carefully, 'to feel like this after so long.'

'It didn't work out the first time because my mum was sick, and I couldn't move to where he lived. But now . . .'

'Now you think you might have a second chance,' he finished. His dark eyes were hooded as he stared past the statues and into the next long hall.

'Well, yes. Only I keep thinking it must be a dream.'

His eyes were on her now. 'Why's that?'

'Because things like that don't happen in the real world.'

'The world is a very big place,' he said, his voice flat. He didn't meet her gaze. 'Lots of things happen all the time. But I will say one thing.'

'What's that?'

'A man should know what he wants. If he's telling you he doesn't know what to do, I'd be worried there's something else going on. Maybe he already has a girlfriend, or a wife. Otherwise, what would stop him? I wouldn't like to see you get hurt, Rachael. He's had his chance with you once.'

The edge in Antonio's voice dragged Rachael's eyes to his face. She could see the hurt hiding behind his words.

He saw her searching his expression and abruptly stood, offering a hand to pull her up. When she was standing, he let go.

'That's why you aren't sure about the cadetship,' he added. 'You have to talk to him, Rachael. If it's real love, you'll find a way to support each other's dreams. Otherwise, what's the point?'

Rachael had nothing to say to that and Antonio was clearly upset. He didn't move to take her hand again as they left the Louvre, or attempt to kiss her. Should she apologise? But for what? For being honest? Or for allowing him to kiss her while she was thinking about Matthew?

⌐

They were soon back at the hotel, any further sightseeing plans scuttled. She watched Antonio leave, his dark curls catching a sunbeam breaking through the rainclouds. He didn't look back. She thought about the offer he'd made. But that had been before her disclosure and he hadn't mentioned the editor again. Had she made a horrible mistake?

She almost raced after him and all the possibilities he represented, but the weight of Matthew and her lost years held her rooted.

Desperation burned her chest like a hot brand. She could think of only one thing to do.

Chapter 16

Sammy wasn't in her room when Rachael knocked, so she went into her own room to change her shoes. When she pulled open the door again to leave, she found Sammy with her hand raised, about to knock.

'Oh good, I was coming to— What's wrong?'

Sammy's face was blotches of pink and cream, the tip of her nose and eyelids were red, her hair was unbrushed. Her breaths shook.

Five minutes later, Rachael had her seated on the edge of the bed, a hot tea pressed into her fingers.

'What is it?' she asked. 'Did something happen back home?'

Sammy shook her head, eyes dull.

'Talk to me?'

Sammy laughed bitterly. 'I still don't really want to.'

'Why not? It's me.'

'Because if I tell you, you won't like me any more,' Sammy said in a small voice.

Rachael sat back. 'You're my best friend. I'll always like you.'

Sammy put the tea down with a shaking hand and rubbed her face. 'I'm not so sure about that.' She paused. 'What if I told you that for the last six months I've been seeing another man.'

Rachael was amazed. 'Who?'

Sammy looked away. 'Peter.'

'Peter? You mean—'

'Yes, that Peter. The best man, Peter. Matthew's brother, Peter.'

'And by seeing each other you mean . . . ?'

'Yes, that too.'

'Oh.' The sound was a puff of air covering all the things Rachael thought but didn't say. *But he's married. But what about Marty?*

'You must think I'm horrible, and I didn't intend it to happen. Geez, don't people always say that.' Sammy looked up to the ceiling. 'I've been trying for such a long time to work out where Marty and I went wrong. We used to have all these dreams of opening a business and building a house, but he's not interested any more. I don't believe in giving up, but he won't talk to me . . . And then one day Peter was there, and we started talking about what businesses the district needs and he was so interested—' She broke off, sniffing. 'I've tried to stop seeing him. Every time I've told him, and told myself, that's the last time and I'm going to fix things with Marty. Then it doesn't happen, and a week goes by and Peter calls . . .' She lifted her hands, helpless.

'I had no idea,' Rachael said, still so surprised. She'd never heard even a whisper about Sammy and Peter. About Peter's volatile marriage, yes, and comments about Marty's work prospects, but never about Sammy and Peter together.

'That is the general idea with affairs,' Sammy said with a bitter laugh. 'Peter would stay out later than he had to when I was doing shifts at the motel. And sometimes, when I couldn't sleep, I'd go for a drive and he'd go out checking for wild dogs. It wasn't hard to meet up. I thought about moving town so I didn't have to see him. I should never have gotten into this mess.'

'Oh,' Rachael said, horrified, 'that's why you didn't want to come this week. Because he'd be here and Marty wouldn't. And I made you come.'

Sammy's lips lifted in a grim smile. 'You didn't make me. I made that decision. I don't understand how it's possible to enjoy something and hate it so much at the same time.' She looked away. 'It can be so confusing. One time, we just spent the whole night talking about your mum, what we remembered about her. Pete was really devastated about her passing away, and Marty didn't want to listen to me go on about it. I think I really loved Pete for that. Then, other times, I couldn't get away fast enough – I didn't want to be that person, cheating on my husband. Sounds ridiculous, but I was happy and repulsed at the same time.'

Rachael took a slug of tea, wincing as the hot liquid scorched her tongue. 'I met Peter in the hallway the other night. He said he'd got off on the wrong floor.'

Sammy made a face. 'Yeah, he told me about that. I told him it was stupid taking such a risk with Suzi here. He'd get caught. You hate me, don't you?'

'Of course not,' Rachael said, pushing away her cup and hugging Sammy fiercely. Sammy who had passed notes to Rachael in primary school. Who'd comforted her after Matthew had left. Who'd cooked dinners for her and her mother when she was too tired after harvest. Who'd held her mother's hand in the hospital, and then held Rachael long after her mother had died, when she'd thought the world was falling in.

'But something's clearly happened,' she said. 'Have you had a fight?'

'Sort of. This is the best part . . .' Sammy's voice broke, and she glanced at Rachael, her eyes terrified. 'I think I'm pregnant.'

Rachael's gasp was audible. 'Are you sure?'

Sammy's shoulders hunched in misery. 'No,' she whispered. 'But maybe. Probably.'

Rachael put her arms back around Sammy, who was shaking. 'Have you told him?'

'Who?' Sammy asked, with a bitter laugh. 'My husband or my boyfriend?'

'You mean you don't ... ?'

Sammy shook her head. 'No idea. Probably Peter, but I just don't know.'

'Peter wasn't happy?' Rachael guessed.

'I think he's in shock. I guess it's not what he had in mind, despite things he said to the contrary.'

Rachael tried to process it all. Before, her mind had been full of Matthew and Antonio. She'd felt her problems had an urgency that had made her all jittery, as if she'd not slept in days and had drunk two strong coffees to stay awake. She'd wanted Sammy's advice. Now, she had to force her problems into the *small things* compartment and think about Sammy.

'What exactly did he say?' she asked.

'Not much. Just that he didn't want to talk about it now, not with the wedding tomorrow. He did hint about leaving Suzi though.'

Rachael's heart abruptly sped, as if she'd had a fright. Tomorrow. The wedding was tomorrow.

She forced her mind back to now. 'What are you going to do?'

Her mother had often asked that question. Marion had believed in letting people solve their problems themselves. If they wanted your help, they'd ask for it. Anything else was presumptuous.

Sammy's voice was frail and wavery. 'I have no idea, Rach.'

'What about Marty?'

Sammy screwed her eyes shut, shaking loose tears. 'I love him,' she said softly. 'But I don't know how to save us. Maybe I can't.'

'So you don't want to be with him any more?'

'I guess.'

Sammy put her hand over her mouth, as though she'd just glimpsed the consequences of her whole life unravelling. How people would talk about it, about her. Peter's family was widely known and respected. If he left his wife, it was Sammy who would be crucified. On the other hand, Rachael realised that if Sammy was unclear about the baby's parentage, the situation might be more complex than she was letting on. She and Marty really might just be going through a bad time.

She sat rubbing Sammy's shoulder, and holding back other questions.

'What can I do?' she asked finally. 'Do you want to talk some more? Get something to eat? See a doctor? Apparently there's one on call.'

'No, please, Rach, you have to promise me – don't say anything to anyone.'

'You know I won't.'

The secret sat heavily in Rachael's mind, competing with her own problems and making her impotent. What *could* she do?

She was putting her mind to the question when a knock came at the door. When she glanced through the peephole, all her thoughts collapsed.

Bloody hell. Matthew.

She opened the door a crack. Matthew gave her the kind of smile she'd last seen in the wheat field over ten years ago, full of joy and expectation. It broke Rachael into two selves: one who thought fervently about how she could slip away with him in that instant – was there a convenient broom closet on this floor where they could huddle like teenagers? – and the adult one, who shook her head.

The terror of discovery tightened every muscle. 'Sammy's here,' she warned in a frantic whisper.

His joy and expectation slipped back behind the mask she'd seen him wear all week. He took a step back, glanced once down the hall. 'I'll go out to a café for a while, and come back,' he murmured.

His words squeezed all the blood from her heart. When would he come back? What had he come to say?

He blew her a kiss and Rachael reeled as if it had been a dart.

By the time she hesitated and leaned out the doorway again, Matthew was already out of view, only the fading sound of his steps on the stairs evidence that he'd been there at all.

She closed the door, almost giddy. He'd turned up at her door. He'd blown her a kiss.

'Who was that?' Sammy asked.

'Just housekeeping,' Rachael said swiftly. 'I told them it wasn't a good time. They said they'd come back.'

'Okay.' Sammy's face fell. With a twisted smile, she said, 'For a second, I thought it must be Pete. How sad am I?'

'Not sad,' Rachael said, resuming her seat on the bed. 'But you've had a terrible shock. It's going to take some time to work out what to do.'

'You sound like your mother,' Sammy said, though in a gentle way, as if she missed Marion West just as much as Rachael did.

'Why don't you have a shower?' Rachael said, fetching a towel from the bathroom. 'You'll feel better and then we can talk some more.'

Sammy hesitated before taking the towel, then grabbed Rachael in a wordless bear hug.

When Rachael heard the water running, she slipped out of the room and down the staircase to the lobby, hoping that Matthew might be waiting in the salon. She only managed to slow her speed by sternly telling herself that it would help no one if she appeared frantic.

The salon was empty. She checked the smoking room, and found two older men she didn't know, reading papers and with glasses of amber liquid at their elbows. They gave her a cursory glance.

Rachael pushed through the front door and into the grand entrance. The day was still grey with a light drizzle, the pavement stones dark islands in a grid of water. At the end of the hotel driveway, Parisians in smart boots and tailored coats passed by, some huddled under umbrellas but most with their faces open to the raindrops. No sign of Matthew anywhere. Would he have come out into the rain?

She stepped out from under cover, then wavered between going further and returning inside.

A porter approached. 'Pardon, *mademoiselle*. Are you waiting for a car?'

Rachael realised she must look a fool: standing out in the rain with her eyelashes gathering droplets, spinning back and forth, a magnet between two like-poles.

'No, thank you,' she said, and retreated.

Back in her room, the shower was still running. She sat on the bed drinking cold tea and mulling on Matthew's brief appearance. Had he really meant he'd come back? When? In an hour? Today? Tomorrow?

By the time Sammy emerged from the bathroom, looking brighter despite her wet hair and the same old denim skirt and black top, Rachael was nearly hysterical.

'You all right?' Sammy asked.

Rachael felt like a rabbit caught in a spotlight. She tried to relax her face. 'Fine.'

Sammy frowned. 'Did you go outside?'

'No . . .'

'Your shoulders are wet.'

'Oh, yes. But only for a second. I was seeing if it was still raining,' she said lamely. Then an idea occurred. 'Do you want to take a walk and get some food?'

'I don't think I can eat,' Sammy said, then sighed. 'But I can't be like this all day. I'll just have to make the best of it. You go eat. I'm going to try to have a nap. I didn't sleep much last night.'

'Are you sure?'

Sammy's distress was so contained now, it was only evident in the severe way she'd brushed her hair down onto her head. Even though Rachael knew this was what her friend tended to do – after all, she'd been playing down the problems with Marty for months – her heart leapt traitorously at the chance to go after Matthew.

⟶

As soon as Sammy had gone to her own room, Rachael changed her shirt, which was sweat-soaked under the arms, and brushed her hair, glancing only briefly in the mirror to check that her face was clean. Her bag and scarf whipped around her legs as she simultaneously tried to turn the corner out of the en suite and collect her things. She dropped the room key twice before she managed to stuff it in her pocket, and then she was flying down the stairs.

She raced around the block to the first cafe, expecting to find Matthew right there. He wasn't. But that was fine; there were more.

The skip fell out of Rachael's stride after the second, and the hope from her heart after the third. On sheer dogged disbelief, she walked another two blocks to a different place, but when Matthew failed to be there either, she finally stopped, out of options. Matthew didn't even have her number. She couldn't turn up at his room, even if she knew where it was. She only had one remaining idea.

'Excuse me, any messages for Rachael West, room 107?' she asked the young man on the front desk.

'*Non, mademoiselle.*' His smile was apologetic and warm. 'May I assist you with anything else? A phone call?'

'No, thank you.' She could hardly call Matthew's suite.

Back in her room, Rachael sank onto the bed, deflated as a balloon three days after the party. Losing hope was the worst; her ribs ached as though they'd overstretched her whole chest. She couldn't confide in Sammy. She wouldn't understand, and besides, she had bigger problems.

God, Sammy. Rachael pressed her hand to her forehead. Never would she have imagined her best friend having an affair, especially after she'd been so adamant Matthew shouldn't give Rachael ideas.

Looking for distraction, she flicked on the television and, after several minutes of channel hopping, found CNN. An interview with an American political commentator was just ending, and a new story began about the ongoing Syrian crisis, the journalist wearing a flak jacket and helmet.

Rachael tried to be interested, remembering the things Antonio had told her about his work in war zones, but she jumped at every little noise. A room service cart went down the hall and she pushed mute, listening as it passed her door and stopped a few rooms up. Un-mute.

The journalist was now interviewing a desperate refugee, the translation dubbed over the top. Rachael felt horrible. While she was sitting here in this luxurious room, all those poor people were fleeing for their lives, and no one wanted them.

Wait, what was that? She thought she'd heard a knock. Mute.

As she swung her feet to the floor, it came again. She sped to the door, relief like steam pressure driving her forward.

She opened the door, expecting Matthew. But the smile froze on her face.

Antonio stood in the hall light.

'Hi,' he said. His face had lost its guarded expression from earlier in the afternoon. 'I didn't like the way we parted. I want to apologise, and to explain.'

He appeared to have come straight from the shower, his curls damp and artfully mussed, his face clean-shaven, smelling of something spicy and alluring. His customary black shirt was back, tucked into clean blue jeans.

'You don't have to do that.'

'No, please. I'd like to talk. We can go somewhere else if you prefer.'

Rachael wavered, then swung the door open. 'Come in.'

She followed behind him, suddenly embarrassed by the wrinkled bed and the tea still on the bedside table. Hastily, she straightened the covers and took the cups to the bathroom.

Antonio seemed not to notice. When she returned, he was watching the silent TV. 'I know this guy,' he said, gesturing to the man in the flak jacket. 'We were in the same place together once, in the Sudan.'

Rachael offered him the remote. 'Do you want the sound?'

Antonio took it, but shook his head and turned the screen off. 'I'll try to call him later. Do you mind if I sit down?'

He pulled out a chair from the ornate table directly across from the end of the bed and sat, leaning forward, his elbows on his knees, waiting. Rachael finally sat across from him on the bed.

'You might not like me for saying this,' he began. 'But don't go back to your old boyfriend.'

A steel rod slid into Rachael's spine.

He rushed on. 'My reasons, I confess, are purely selfish.' When Rachael began to speak, he held up his hand. 'Please, let me finish. I think you're a wonderful woman. Smart. Talented. I like that you argue with me, and that you're excited by new things. And that's just what I know after a few days.'

Rachael had the strangest feeling. No one had ever called her a woman before. Matthew had always referred to her as 'his girl', and Rachael and Sammy talked about themselves as girls too. Rachael wasn't a woman; her *mother* was a woman. But from Antonio, it seemed a natural description, as if he'd never dream of using any other word.

'Do you know what I thought that morning I walked out on you at breakfast?' He searched her face, his own intent and honest. 'I thought, screw this, I'm leaving again in a week. Why do I want to waste my time arguing with someone I just met?' He shook his head. 'I tried to forget about you. Then spent the next hour thinking about nothing else. I knew I'd made a mistake. I knew I had to find you. The front desk told me where you were.'

'I had no idea,' Rachael stammered.

He held her gaze, unabashed. 'I might have opinions you don't like, and I know I spend a lot of time travelling. But I like you, and I know you see the best in people. I want to know if you see anything you like in me.'

Rachael had ceased straining to hear what was going on in the hallway. Her senses were full of whatever cologne Antonio was wearing, the way his chocolate eyes seemed to see her like no one else did. They held her accountable, refusing to let her look away. She wasn't sure at all what this was between them. Antonio reminded her of an unfinished masterpiece, with raw edges and rough patches to negotiate. When she'd spent time with him, that had seemed possible. But what did she really know about him? Nothing. She and Matthew had a long and familiar history.

'I like you, yes,' she said. 'But we just met. And you said yourself, you're leaving next week.'

His gaze flickered. 'I think what you mean is, I don't make you feel like your old boyfriend.'

'You're right,' she admitted, though she remembered the gentleness of his kisses and where they might lead.

'Hmm,' he said, sitting back. 'But your old boyfriend has had time with you and I haven't. It's not a fair contest. I wonder if we can't try an experiment.'

'Like what?'

He stood and offered her a hand. When he pulled her to her feet, he kept her hand in his and she found herself face to face with him. Matthew was a head taller than her and she'd been forever looking at his chin. But Antonio's nose was only just above hers, so he only had to dip his lashes to look into her eyes. His palm was warm against her waist.

Rachael's breaths were tiny soft gasps, and her heart thrummed. She couldn't move enough air to say anything, and wasn't sure what she could say. The space around them was a maelstrom of sensations – warmth and softness and adoration, somehow all communicated through the touch of his hand and the smile in his eyes.

When she made no protest, he dipped his head and kissed her. A feather touch at first, light and smooth. A tiny retreat, and then again, more insistent.

Rachael swayed against him and the warm touch of his hand spread along her body. She was caught, and kissed him back, because this felt somehow so easy, so natural. Except she would be going back to the farm in two days, while he would no doubt be off to South America, or Iraq, or somewhere equally unbelievable.

He pulled away, cradling her face as he spoke. 'Rachael, you would have such amazing experiences in Europe. I don't think you would ever regret it. I'd try to convince you to come to New York, but you know yourself better than I do. So choose fashion, or journalism, or something else. I'll encourage you in whatever you do.'

Rachael could almost see it: that glimmer of a dream becoming reality.

Then another knock broke into the moment. Her lungs froze into slabs of ice. Was it Matthew?

She had to tell Antonio to wait. Her breathing shook as she peered through the peephole.

When she saw a dress, she first thought *Sammy*. But the figure was too tall. Spying slender arms, one with a gold cuff around the wrist, she realised it was Bonnie. Nerves fired like cannons through her chest. Bonnie was bouncing up and down and glancing around anxiously.

What if she knew? What if Matthew had told her?

Bracing as if she were about to be shot, Rachael inched the door open.

'Oh, thank god,' Bonnie said. 'I was hoping you'd be here. I've got a— Oh, I'm so sorry.' She stared over Rachael's shoulder, and Rachael realised she must have seen Antonio. Bonnie's gaze darted back to Rachael's face and she dropped her voice. 'I didn't realise you had company.'

'I'm just leaving,' Antonio said smoothly, slipping past Rachael without touching her.

He elegantly kissed Bonnie on both cheeks, and confirmed that he'd meet the driver at seven in the morning. Like this kind of thing happened every damn day. He mouthed *Talk to you tomorrow* behind Bonnie's back before disappearing down the stairs.

As soon as he was gone, Bonnie dropped her jaw like a schoolgirl. 'Wow, Antonio Ferranti,' she hissed conspiratorially, as though she and Rachael were the oldest of friends. 'Good for you!'

'It's not like that,' Rachael said quickly.

Bonnie nodded as if Rachael was just being modest. 'I won't say anything then. Our little secret. But, Rachael, I have an awful problem. Evonne's sick and can't leave her bathroom apparently, and Granny's fingers just can't do the work any more. All the stores are closed by now, and it'd be a dreadful security issue taking it out anyway. Can you please please help?'

'What are you talking about?'

'The dress. It's damaged. I need you to fix it. Please.'

Rachael experienced one of those moments when the full ironic absurdity of the universe blasted at her from stereo speakers set to eleven.

'I almost brought it down with me, I was so out of my head,' Bonnie was saying.

Rachael's stomach dived. Bloody hell, that would be great: Matthew appearing to find his fiancée and her dress in her room.

'But then Granny calmed me down and suggested you. So, please, take as long as you need to freshen up and then come to the suite – 501. There'll be a security man at the end of the hall, but he'll let you through. Thank you so much!' And she dashed off up the stairs in a pair of slingback heels.

Rachael couldn't move for ten long seconds. Then she closed the door, washed her face, and changed into clean trackpants and a T-shirt. If she was going to sew, she wanted to be comfortable.

Chapter 17

Fifteen minutes later, Rachael was ushered into a room in Bonnie's opulent suite, where the furniture had been moved to the side to make room for an enormous starched white sheet spread out on the carpet. Yvette sat in a spindly-legged chair flanked by two bridesmaids, their hair in curlers under scarves. Rachael tried not to look at the four-poster bed visible in the adjoining bedroom; tried not to wonder if this was where Matthew and Bonnie planned to spend their wedding night.

'They can bring a table,' Bonnie said, 'but I thought maybe you should have a look first, see what you can do.'

'All right.'

Bonnie went into the bedroom and returned with a huge black bag, which she laid on the floor. When she opened the zip, the fabric showing through glittered like fire-filled diamonds.

Rachael gasped, and brushed the fabric on a fine scalloped edge. 'How amazing,' she breathed.

It was the understatement of the week. Bonnie's dress was made of a fabric Rachael would never dare go near in a store for fear of damaging it by proximity. It must cost hundreds if not thousands per metre. It was layer on layer of fine hand-woven lace stitched through with gold thread and tiny crystals gathered into flowers. Underneath the lacework, the dress was stitched silk, the lustrous fabric folded and sewn into long seams at each centimetre, creating an incredibly light but stiff base.

Bonnie pushed the bag apart, picked up the top and shook the gown loose: a striking Queen Anne neckline, fitted through the waist and hips and flared into a skirt like an inverted lily with a chapel-length train.

'I shouldn't have tried it on,' Bonnie explained, 'but of course I did, and Bethany stepped on the back. See?'

Rachael assumed Bethany was the bridesmaid currently biting her lip and hunching her shoulders in an effort to make herself as tiny as possible.

'I'm so sorry, Bonnie,' she squeaked.

Rachael saw the damage: the silk had split in a horizontal line straight across the back, creating a huge grin of satin lining. When she looked closer, she realised it was the fabric itself that had torn, rather than one of the many seams. The lace over the break was only stretched, not broken, but she had no idea yet how she might repair it. Maybe it could be coaxed back into shape to cover stitches in the silk, but it was so thin and delicate that any clumsiness would show straight through.

'The silk is antique,' Yvette put in, her hand held in a way that suggested her cigarettes had been forcibly removed. 'You run these risks with old things.'

Rachael was only managing not to chew a nail because she didn't want to get a wet fingerprint on the dress. She almost expected Bonnie to hand her a pair of white gloves.

'I don't have any tools,' she said.

'Here, *chérie*.' Yvette brandished a small package in her knotted knuckles.

The package was a silk envelope the size of a coin purse, embroidered with fine flowers and tied with a string of gold thread. Inside Rachael found a gold-plated thimble and scissors, a weave of yarns in forty different shades of white and cream, and several cards of buttons, press-studs and needles. It must be an antique itself, but was absolutely pristine. It looked as though the threads had never been disturbed.

She glanced fearfully at Yvette. 'This looks expensive.'

'This is what it was made for,' Yvette said, gesturing towards the expanse of priceless lace and silk.

Rachael swallowed, but the butterflies in her stomach had become pinned down with lead stakes. As she stared at the dress, she was suddenly certain that Matthew wasn't coming back to repeat the things he'd said in the boat. He'd had a moment's weakness, that was all. Maybe, somewhere deep in his soul, he thought he loved her, but it was probably only in the same way that he felt nostalgic for anything from home. The power of his life with Bonnie was so great, it would carry him to the altar and all the way back to Sydney.

Rachael's fingers were as heavy as her heart as she tried to match a thread to the gown. A perfect shade of light cream slipped easily from its fellows and she threaded the needle awkwardly, her acrylic nails getting in the way. She peered at the damage under a spotlight, trying to forget that Bonnie, the bridesmaids and Yvette were all watching her. In that moment, Rachael missed her mother so much that tears sprang into her eyes. Marion West would have known just what to do, and would have produced from her sewing chest all kinds of delicate interfacings that she could have stitched behind the tear to support it. Rachael needed something like that.

She appealed to Yvette. 'Do you think we could find something to stitch behind, then run a wide hand-stitch through the holes from the seams above and below? That might be invisible behind the lace.'

'I cannot even see it that well, *chérie*,' Yvette apologised. 'And the designer kept the remnants. We could send someone to his house, but the stupid man doesn't answer his phone.'

'Granny, it's Louis Charles. He's got even more security than Daddy. Besides, someone might take photos. I don't want to jeopardise the auction.'

'Auction?' Rachael asked.

'Of the photos and the exclusive story. We're hoping for at least half a million for the dress photos. Louis Charles hasn't done a bridal gown in ten years. I want to fund a whole child literacy program with the money.'

Rachael put down her tools. 'Wouldn't he come in the morning perhaps?'

Bonnie shrugged. 'We're trying him. But the timetable tomorrow is so tight. I have to be ready to leave the hotel at eleven, and it takes two hours to do the make-up.'

'Louis is an old Valium addict who will be out of his head until noon,' Yvette said dismissively. 'He might have designed you a beautiful dress, *chouchou*, but one of his star dressmakers will have cut and sewn it. He will barely remember who it was before he's sober.'

Bonnie gave Rachael a look of appeal. Helplessly, Rachael thought about what to do.

'Would you put the dress on again?' she asked. 'I want to make sure I don't change the fall.'

Once Bonnie had wriggled into the gown, and the bridesmaids had done up the laces – Bethany standing so far away from the dress Rachael was sure she was about to pitch over on her face – Rachael could fully appreciate the mastery of the design. The dress was pure art, its undulating skirt evoking the sense of a furled flower, its perfect petals shimmering with dew and about to bloom. She was grateful to find that the split had occurred near the edge of one of the lace pieces, which might improve the chance of covering the defect.

'You want the veil too?' Bethany asked timidly.

The veil was a simple raw-cut length of tulle that flowed like water two feet beyond the end of the train. Gorgeous in its simplicity, it was unfortunately so light that it didn't do anything to conceal the tear.

Rachael fingered the texture. 'You don't have any offcuts of this, do you? It would make a good backing. I'd only need an inch.'

Bonnie considered a moment, then said, 'Cut it off the end.'

'What?'

'It's a raw edge anyway. Cut it off the end. It's long enough.'

When Bonnie insisted, Rachael, feeling like a heretic, took up the golden scissors and tried to maintain a crisp line as she cut off an inch of tulle.

'I'll have to sew up the edge seams,' she said. 'They're overlocked on a roll hem, and you don't want a ragged end. There's a gold thread in the overlocking that will catch on everything.'

She overlaid two pieces of the tulle to create more stiffness, then hefted the silk and lace out of the way so she could access the back of the fabric. How would she press it when she was done? The dress wasn't light, and it might pull out of shape on an ironing board.

With the bridesmaids holding up the heavy skirt, she used four needles to pin the tulle in place, and a bright blue thread to roughly tack the ripped edges together and take the weight off the tear.

'Clever,' said Yvette, who'd produced a magnifying glass and was peering over Rachael's shoulder.

Rachael took the matching cream thread and began to stitch as much behind the tear as possible, passing the needle through the existing seams in the silk.

'Hardly any fraying,' she muttered as she worked, two needles clamped between her lips. 'That's good. Don't slip. Ah, yes. Now you.' She'd picked up this habit from her mother, who'd maintained a continual stream of commentary as she hand-stitched hems – which was almost the worst work in the world – or unpicked mistakes, which was the worst.

Miraculously, the rent came together like a healing wound, the repair stitches holding strong through the tulle stiffener. Rachael used the finest needle to finish off with two rows of tiny catch stitches along the tear itself, just grazing the silk from behind to hold the edges down but not show through.

She checked all the ends of her threads three times before carefully pulling them through to the back of the fabric and snipping them off. Only then did she cut and pull out the blue tacking stitch.

Yvette made a triumphant noise. 'You must look at this miracle,' she told Bonnie. She angled the spotlight onto the torn section and handed Bonnie a mirror that the concierge had brought up.

Bonnie peered. 'I can't see from here. Quick, help me take it off.'

While the bridesmaids helped Bonnie out of the dress, Rachael peeled herself off the floor, her knees and shoulders aching. She wound the blue thread around and around her finger as she waited for the verdict. Bonnie collapsed into a chair in just her slip and stockings to pore over the repair.

Next moment, she leapt up and flung her arms around Rachael. 'I wouldn't even know it was there! You are a miracle!'

'I was just lucky. The way it tore was fixable,' Rachael said, pulling away.

Bonnie's radiant smile was right before her, tears in her eyes, but Rachael felt unable to accept the thanks and praise. All her energy was spent, and next to Bonnie she felt icky and

guilty and out of place. The world Bonnie lived in was so alien
to her: half a million dollars for photos, a wedding dress of
antique silk and hand-woven lace. No wonder Matthew felt
caught up and out of place himself.

The reality of that, of the vast difference between her and
Bonnie, sank through Rachael like a river stone. Goosebumps
crawled up her arms. She was sickly sure Matthew wouldn't
come back to her, just as he hadn't come to the photography
class the other morning. She was angry with herself for brooding
on him, and for opening her mouth to Antonio, jeopardising
any chance she might have with him.

'I might go,' she said weakly.

Bonnie nodded. 'Yes, I interrupted earlier, I'm sorry.
And it's late. Thank you, thank you again. I'll make this up
to you, I promise. But whatever you do, don't mention this to
anyone, okay?'

'It was no trouble,' Rachael said faintly.

'I know – maybe you'd like to be an assistant for a charity
fashion show we're doing in September? The theme is *Fashion
Through the Ages*. Actually, that's a great idea – don't you
think, Granny?'

Yvette raised a hand as if toasting Rachael.

'I'm not sure,' Rachael said, really wanting to escape so
she could cry in private. 'I've never done anything like that.'

'You'd be great if what Matthew's told me is anything to
go by. We'll talk about it back home.'

⌒

By the time Rachael extricated herself, the cold chills had
given way to hot despair. Her hands were cramped and her
body was stiff from holding the weight of the dress. She went
straight into the shower to wash away the aches and to try to
make sense of her sadness.

Why was she so terribly surprised? She'd come to Paris this week expecting to see the love of her life marry someone else. Expecting to have to move on and get over him. Tomorrow, she would finally have to accept it. Matthew might not love Bonnie, but there was no way he was going to give up his life in Sydney for Rachael.

When she flicked off the bathroom light, she was surprised to see it was eleven o'clock. Her bare feet were silent on the plush carpet. Standing at the window in her pyjamas, she peered down at the street. People were still walking the pavements, the rain had stopped and the streetlights hung like captured stars.

You should go out there, her mind told her. *Have a late dinner at a café, and who the hell cares if you're alone?*

But she didn't want to be alone.

Fine, then call Antonio, tell him you're sorry and the cadetship sounds amazing and can it still happen?

But Rachael didn't want to speak to Antonio.

Fine, then at least tell Sammy about all of this.

Sammy. Shit. What the hell was Sammy going to do? What would Peter do?

Rachael couldn't help thinking, look what happens when you marry the wrong person. Matthew was already having doubts. He shouldn't have to go through with it.

A knock.

Rachael froze, and all the thoughts that had been churning around her head slid away like melted butter. Her hand trembled on the door handle.

Outside, she found Beverley holding two dresses.

'Oh, Rachael, I thought I saw your light on. I really need some advice. Which one do you think I should wear tomorrow?'

Rachael's mind spun until she thought she was actually going to pass out.

'Either,' she said faintly, then chose at random. 'This one.'

'Really, are you sure? Maybe I should show you them on. Have you got time? It'll only take five minutes.'

So Rachael found herself letting Beverley into her bathroom to change. She was jumpy the whole time, and had to work hard to appear normal as Beverley twirled first in a black chiffon gown, then a striking blue print with a flattering tapered skirt.

'I don't think black is right for a wedding, but I thought the blue might be too much,' Beverley said.

'No, it's perfect.' Rachael could hear that she sounded breathless. 'Where else are you going to wear it?'

'Funny, that's just what Bern—' Beverley broke off with a quick smile. 'Well, I'd better take it off before I wrinkle it.'

She bustled back into the bathroom.

Two days, Rachael thought. It was only two days since Matthew had been in that same bathroom.

'Are you really all right, Rachael, dear?' Bev asked when she re-emerged. 'You are pale.'

'Must be jetlag still,' Rachael said with over-brightness. 'And it's late.'

Beverley left her to sleep, and Rachael pressed her back against the room door, trying to calm herself. To accept that what she wanted would never happen.

When the knock came it was right between her shoulder blades. She jumped.

Then she opened the door, and this time it was Matthew. For a moment, she blinked, unbelieving, as every other detail of her life flew away. The door closed behind him with a soft thunk.

'Sorry,' he said. 'I couldn't get away until now.'

'It's fine,' she said quickly. Her heart was hammering so hard it was an effort to speak over it.

She prepared herself for him to tell her he'd made a mistake, for them to talk about old times, cry a bit maybe.

She turned, thinking to put the kettle on, but he caught her wrist and spun her back. Surprised, she found his arms around her, his eyes searching hers. In the soft lamplight, the edges of his green irises were gold, and everything about him was right. His shoulders were a familiar shape under her hands, his scent was that same cologne he'd always used. The memories were sown so deeply in her they were almost unconscious, raw and powerful. More powerful than anything potential or possible or promised. With Matthew, it was all sure and known.

'I'm not going to muck around,' he said, smoothing his thumbs down between her shoulder blades and stoking a heat that rushed south into her thighs. 'I've told you what I feel. I want to know if you feel the same. Tell me.'

'I love you,' she said, willingly, easily, as she'd wanted to since last night in the boat. 'I've loved you every day since you left.'

His eyes closed and he swallowed so hard his throat bobbed. His breath huffed with relief and he crushed her to him.

'Oh, Rach,' he moaned. 'What an idiot I've been.'

Then he was kissing her and it was like they were alone in the fields again, warm and secure and wonderful. He hadn't changed, and neither had the way they fitted together, the way he held her and pulled her into him.

He broke away with clear reluctance. 'I've wanted to do that all week,' he said, his voice husky with desire.

Rachael took his hand then and pulled him further into the room, wanting to lead him to sit down. They needed to talk about what to do now, how it might be possible to find a way through all this without . . . what? Without hurting Bonnie? Without casting an embarrassing and very public spanner into the grand machinery of this wedding?

'We should talk,' she said.

Instead, Matthew opened her fingers and placed a folded note in her palm. 'I can't stay long. But I'm deadly serious. I want the life we were supposed to have. Tell me you do too.'

She nodded frantically, unable to speak.

He squeezed her hand. 'Then I'll see you tomorrow.'

Rachael's fingers curled around the piece of paper as he closed the door behind him, leaving her with all those *what now?* questions they needed to talk about. But he wanted her. She had no doubts about that now.

She thought about the offer Antonio had made. How unknowable and uncertain it was. He could tell her tomorrow that it was all smoke. And even if it was true, how could she afford to take some cadetship in London? She wasn't like her mother, who'd been young and fearless about heading out into the world. All she knew was the farm. And Matthew.

Her body shook with terror at the idea of losing him a second time. All the shine and promise of unknown tomorrows seemed nothing without him in them. So she plucked out any remaining doubts like weeds. Occasionally she missed one, and it would grow and make her stomach flutter. Like, what will everyone say when they find out?

She clenched her body until the flutters were still. To hell with other people. She'd lost him once. He didn't want to get married to Bonnie, so he shouldn't.

This was just what was meant to happen.

Chapter 18

Rachael woke the next morning wondering if she'd simply had the most vivid dream. But no, she could still smell Matthew's scent on her clothes. And though the early light bleeding through the curtains was dim, she could see his note propped on her bedside table.

Meet you in hotel lobby at 12. Be packed.

She crushed the note to her chest, her skin flushing hot, then cold, then hot again. Twelve o'clock seemed so far away. And the ceremony was supposed to be at twelve thirty – how was she going to organise herself around that?

Matthew might already have called it off. But when she stuck her head out into the hall and saw how quiet and normal everything seemed, she was sure that hadn't happened. For one, if it had, Beverley would surely already know about it and would have come to tell Rachael.

She hung onto the door handle, her fingers white, her head spinning. She pinched the skin inside her wrist and read the note again. Yes, this was happening. He meant it.

Timidly, she knocked on Sammy's door.

To her surprise, Sammy answered looking ten times better than yesterday. 'Morning,' she said brightly, gesturing Rachael into the room. 'D-day, huh?'

'What?'

'D-day. The wedding.' Sammy frowned. 'You okay? You look terrible.'

'I do?' Rachael's hands probed her face.

'Bags under your eyes like stuffed pillows.'

'What about you? After yesterday?'

Sammy's face was tight with the effort of holding herself together. 'I'm not thinking about it until after the ceremony. Peter said we'll talk then. He doesn't want to make a big deal of it for Matthew's sake.'

For Matthew's sake. Rachael's stomach lurched. 'And what about—'

'Don't,' Sammy said, jumping up to gather discarded shirts and shopping bags off the carpet. 'Please. I just need to get through today.'

Rachael's teeth came down on one of her acrylic nail tips. She glanced at the clock: 8:19. In less than three hours, they were meant to assemble downstairs for transport to the ceremony. In less than four, she would be meeting Matthew in the lobby, which should long be empty by then. Her heart stuttered with longing, even though the day's pressures felt like a wave pushing her fast towards a rocky shore.

'I'm still thinking about leaving early,' she said, teetering on the edge of coming clean. Would Sammy think it a brave and exciting thing to do? After all, she was having an affair with a married man and talking about him leaving his wife.

Sammy's head appeared around the bathroom door. 'Early like when?'

'Later today maybe.'

'And miss the reception?'

Rachael shrugged.

Sammy frowned. 'You made it this far, Rach. The flight home is tomorrow. How much difference will a day make?'

Rachael was about to say it. About to say: *Matthew's not going through with it. I'm meeting him at noon today. Wish me luck, Sam*. But she didn't.

And then the moment was lost, because Sammy came out brandishing hair straighteners and said, 'Wish there was time to go grab another one of those croissants.'

'What? Oh, yeah, they were great.'

'Let's go tomorrow morning before check-out. Now, you go have a shower in your room, then I can straighten your hair. And you have to help me decide what to wear.'

She held up two dresses on their hangers: one, a body-hugging fire-engine red; the other, a shimmering midnight blue.

'Where did these come from?' Rachael asked, inspecting the delicate overlapping panels on the blue dress's skirt. It was real Italian silk.

'Mail order, using up my pay for the next three months.' Sammy sighed. 'You're going to say blue, aren't you?'

Rachael nodded.

Sammy carefully hung both dresses on the back of the bathroom door, then unexpectedly threw her arms around Rachael, momentarily crushing all the twisted nerves in her chest into nothing.

'I'm sorry about everything,' she said. 'I'm sorry that you had to stay home with your mum, and that Matthew left. I'm sorry you had to come here to get closure on it. And I'm sorry for dumping my problems on you in the middle of it all.'

'That's what best friends are for,' Rachael replied, but the words set off twinges of guilt.

Sammy squeezed once more before she let go, then wiped under her eyes quickly with her thumbs.

Rachael retreated to her room to shower, feeling wretched after Sammy's speech, but still committed to Matthew's plan.

Her bed was neatly made with her packed case resting on top, only her toothbrush and make-up were still in the bathroom, and the black Audrey Hepburn-inspired dress hung perfectly pressed on the back of the door. The clock read 8:32.

A frisson bloomed beneath her ribs. Whatever was on that rocky shore rushing towards her, she knew Matthew was there too. She no longer had to wonder whether he still loved her. The tide of their love was stronger than anything else, and it would carry her forward until they were together again.

❧

Rachael and Sammy were ready by 10.50 am. Sammy looked amazingly sophisticated in the blue silk. She'd clipped a tiny flower hat into the side of her hair, which was coaxed into soft blonde waves. Her mouth was a scarlet kiss of bright red that drew even more attention to the deep blue of her dress.

Rachael was very glad that her friend's outfit stole the attention as they descended the stairs, though Sammy had made jealous noises about the simple chicness of Rachael's dress. Even Rachael herself had spent a good minute admiring it in the bathroom mirror – a classic black slip of satin with a scooped neck and slim skirt, and delicate sleeve caps of black lace. Sammy had done Rachael's make-up, with dramatic smoky eyes and the palest coral lipstick, before tucking the ends of her straightened bob behind her ears. After all the primping, Rachael had to sternly remind herself that none of it mattered as she wasn't going to the ceremony.

She hadn't been able to find a way to escape going with the others to the venue. It would be ludicrous to claim she was feeling unwell now. Besides, Sammy would probably insist on staying back to make sure she was all right. She'd contemplated faking a faint, but it carried the same risk. It would be easier to go along as expected, then take a taxi back.

As they joined the swirling finery in the hotel lobby, her legs had all the strength of cooked noodles.

One of the hotel concierges called for attention in such an adorable accent that everyone hushed immediately. '*Mesdames et messieurs*, Monsieur Quinn welcomes you all to this day of celebration. I will read the groups for the cars, and if you would please make your way outside, we may begin departure.'

'I heard they were doing this,' Sammy said. 'Allocating groups to the cars. Probably to stay on top of the timetable.'

Maybe that would be good, Rachael thought. If she ended up in a car with people she didn't know, she could more easily slip away at the other end. Oh, but what if the venue was miles and miles away? What if they drove for an hour to some country *château* where there weren't any taxis and she couldn't possibly get back by twelve? She hadn't considered that. Shit. She'd better get out of here.

'Samantha Voss, Rachael West,' the concierge called. Sammy grabbed Rachael's hand. 'With Beverley Watkins and Bernard Collins.'

'Oh, no,' Sammy said, 'that's all we need. Bev shooting daggers at Bernie the whole way.'

The concierge checked them off a list printed on thick cream parchment. 'Beverley Watkins?' he repeated. 'Bernard Collins?'

No response. A moment's confusion passed between the staff, then they waved Rachael and Sammy through to the waiting limousine.

Inside, they found name-tagged gift bags waiting for them. As the car drove away, Sammy pulled a Bvlgari bracelet from hers, and a miniature bottle of champagne.

Rachael pressed her own gift bag between her knees, sick with nerves. She couldn't even bear to look inside it. Any moment she was going to have to tell the driver to stop and let her out. She just had to hope that Sammy would accept she couldn't go through with the ceremony, and leave her to catch a cab. The very idea of it made her want to vomit.

'What's in yours, Rach?' Sammy leaned over to peer in the gift bag. 'Hey, it's going to be okay,' she added, squeezing Rachael's arm. 'Remember, this is why you came.'

Rachael rummaged in the bag to hide the sudden welling of tears. Maybe she couldn't go through with this. She'd miss the rendezvous and everything would come undone . . . And then her fingers closed on something heavy.

'Wow, a *watch*?' Sammy said.

In Rachael's fingers was a very expensive-looking steel Bvlgari watch, but it was the dial that had caught her attention – both hands nesting together right on twelve. Attached to the steel band was a small jeweller's tag that read *Rachael* in a shaky cursive script. It was unmistakably Matthew's handwriting. Rachael quickly removed the tag and dropped it in the bag, her doubts melting away in a flood of warmth through her chest. He really wanted her. He'd left her a sign, and it was all she needed.

She slipped the watchband over her wrist. A perfect fit. And when Sammy held Rachael's arm up to her ear, commenting that the watch wasn't running, Rachael wasn't deterred. She knew why.

Five minutes later and the car entered a long tunnel of snowy-white tenting. The doors were opened for them, and they walked along a thick red carpet to where the tent ended at a set of stone stairs. Once they'd climbed up, they stood on an elevated walkway overlooking a sunken courtyard. A church with a soaring spire formed one side, its door immediately to the left. To the right, after steps that led down, an elevated stone cloister wrapped around the other side of the courtyard.

The whole scene was instantly familiar. Rachael had been here before. The security tent had thrown her off, but now she recognised it: the American Church where she'd admired the Tiffany glass windows that day she and Sammy had gone out.

Black-suited security men stood like statues at every corner, intermittently talking into their wrist mics. Rachael and Sammy's car was one of the first to arrive, and without a crowd the cloisters and courtyard seemed an elaborate prison. Rachael would never be able to slip away unnoticed.

The polish chipped on her right index finger as she bit down on the nail. It must be after eleven fifteen. More cars were rolling in, spilling guests up the stairs to the balcony and down to the courtyard. Rachael hovered in the cloister, but couldn't resist Sammy's determination to lead them down to the cloakroom in the courtyard, staffed by outrageously handsome men in suits. Rachael kept the watch on, but handed across the gift bag. She wouldn't be seeing that again. The clerk winked at her.

'I'll just go find the loo,' she told Sammy.

'Great idea. I'll come with you.'

'You don't have to do that,' Rachael said quickly, her hope fraying.

'Don't be silly. I'm not going to stand here by myself.' Sammy narrowed her eyes. 'You're not going to jump out the window, are you?'

The courtyard was filling. Rachael saw camera flashes going off as several wandering photographers snapped the guests. Antonio was nowhere to be seen. No doubt, he was currently photographing Bonnie in her dress, creating the pictures that would be auctioned for the foundation and using his skill to keep the repair out of shot.

'I'm fine,' she said. But she couldn't shake Sammy, and the bathrooms turned out to be in an annex down a blind corridor, with only a tiny high window. Rachael knew there was no way she could get through it, especially not in a cocktail dress. She looked a second time anyway.

A clock in the hallway said eleven twenty-five. Panic was simmering in her now, like the first bubbles in a cooking pot.

They re-emerged to find the courtyard half-full. As Sammy leaned in to talk to a circle of Matthew's old school friends, Rachael took her chance. She would have to leave the way she came in. Maybe she could push through between the white tent and the stone wall.

She'd just made it to the balcony when a man in a morning coat and top hat appeared in her way. She dodged him, and trotted down the stone stairs and back into the tent. The last cars were arriving and the security men had their backs to her as they opened doors. She kept her gaze straight ahead, her walk purposeful. If only she'd thought to bring her phone, she could have feigned taking a call.

But suddenly, she was there. She rounded the corner, slipped outside the tent, and made it to the street. Her heart was thumping so hard she was sure she'd break a rib at any moment.

She strode away without looking back, until a street opened on her right and she turned the corner, out of sight. And glory of glories, there was a taxi. Another sign.

In halting French, she asked for the Maison Lutetia and was on her way. Rachael counted every second of the twelve-minute trip. When she realised she would be back at the hotel just after eleven fifty, her panic simmered down and flutter-winged nerves took off instead.

She experienced an ice-bath blast of horror when the driver stopped and read the meter. She didn't have any money! Somehow, she made him understand that she needed to run in for the fare. He glanced at the hotel's expensive facade and shrugged.

Rachael lurched out of the cab and up the entrance steps. The lobby was deserted except for the usual potted palms and the sound of a vacuum cleaner somewhere overhead. Even the front desk was vacant.

She flew up the stairs and let herself into her room – thank goodness she'd remembered to bring the key – and rifled through her bag for her credit card. By the time she'd sorted the fare, tendrils of damp hair were congealing at the base of her neck, but she still had time to go back to her room, towel off, and spray on some deodorant.

She tugged her skirt down as she trotted back inside, saw someone standing at the front desk, and quickly pulled up. It was a woman in an elegant mint-green suit, one hand resting on the marble countertop. She looked around and Rachael saw it was Evonne Grace, the wedding planner. Her face was grey-tinged under her light make-up, a thin sheen of sweat visible high on her forehead.

'Oh,' she said. 'It's Rachael, isn't it?'

'Yes,' Rachael said cautiously. She hoped Evonne was about to leave. 'You don't look too well.'

Evonne's lips twitched and she pulled an embroidered hand-kerchief from her jacket pocket to dab at her forehead. 'Just a little stomach bug. I wouldn't miss today for anything. It's too important and I've worked too hard.' Her English accent was prim, as if she was standing by pure force of will. She nodded her head as if acknowledging Rachael. 'I must thank you. Bonnie told me about the dress. I would have been there last night to help if I hadn't been . . . indisposed.' She dabbed her mouth, and slotted the kerchief away. 'Louis Charles came by himself this morning and was very impressed with the repair. I'm sure Bonnie will want to thank you personally again after the ceremony.'

'Great.'

Evonne checked her watch. 'Did you forget something?'

'What?'

'Did you forget something? Everyone's supposed to be at the venue by now. I'll have the desk call for a driver.'

'No, please don't. I just didn't feel well,' Rachael said.

'Really? Oh dear god, I hope you don't have what I had. I thought it was my lunch yesterday. Please don't let everyone come down with it. That's all I need.' She glanced around, but seeing no staff, plucked a smartphone from her pocket and began typing with two practised thumbs. 'You wouldn't believe what a nightmare planning is here. It's so competitive. This week was my enormous break. Then the photographer doesn't want to listen to me, and the administration is a nightmare. I can't have people saying they all came down with food poisoning too.'

'I'm sure that's not it. And it's not your fault,' Rachael said, almost hopping from foot to foot. Matthew could appear at any moment. Hopefully he would spot Evonne and hang back.

Evonne seemed in her stride now. 'Oh, it's always my fault. The planner's in charge of everything. I mean, even the legal stuff that we tell everyone, they don't do it and then they want us to work miracles. I tell them time and time again, if you're an overseas resident you have to be married at home first and send through the paperwork. We have to lodge it in time here, otherwise you can't proceed with the wedding. I had to chase Bonnie and Matthew for their certificate. Another thing for me to do!' Evonne stopped abruptly, as if realising she'd gone too far. Her features adjusted back into the serene, controlled planner.

Rachael watched through a thick haze of dawning realisation. 'What did you say?'

'I shouldn't have said anything. That was unprofessional. Lord, please don't tell anyone.'

'No, no,' Rachael said, shaking her head, her voice trembling so much she could barely get the words out. 'What you said about needing to be married.'

'Oh. In France, you either have to be a resident or you need to be married at home first before you can be married here. Most people opt for the latter, because residency's hard to prove if you're not actually living here. Why? You thinking of a Paris wedding too?' A small, hopeful smile.

Rachael's haze was clearing, leaving a fever of disbelief. She could hardly breathe. She remembered tiny details now, as if a playback reel had paused for her to notice them. Evonne asking Matthew for the papers that first morning at breakfast. Bonnie talking about how you weren't properly married without a big ceremony.

Matthew had said all those things to her . . . *promised* all those things . . . and he was already married.

Rachael stumbled back, looking for an exit. She couldn't be here.

Evonne peered at her, concerned, but Rachael couldn't hear a word. This wasn't what she'd wanted. Maybe if she left now, if she went back to the church or even to the airport, if she left a message with the desk for Matthew to say good luck, she could put things right.

A black-suited clerk slid out of the room behind the front desk. Rachael only had time to think, good, salvation, before she heard voices on the stairs – a woman laughing and a man's familiar deep chuckle. Rachael had nowhere to hide.

She watched, astonished, as Bernie Collins and Beverley Watkins, arch enemies, appeared side by side on the staircase. Beverley was trying to untangle her sequinned handbag from a tassel on her coat hem, and Bernie's tie was askew as he shrugged on his suit jacket.

'We're horribly late,' Beverley hissed.

'And whose fault is that?' Bernie laughed, giving her a playful nudge.

'Oh, god,' whispered Rachael. This couldn't be happening.

'What's going on?' Evonne demanded, standing so tall her heels popped out of her designer shoes. 'I've got a bride due down here at any moment. They're already an hour late. I can't have guests not at the church. Quickly,' she said, turning on the clerk, 'you get them into a car. I'll try to stall Bonnie.' She punched at her phone.

'Oh, god,' Rachael said again as the clerk disappeared into the office and Bernie and Beverley skulked through the lobby like teenagers.

Bernie paused when he saw Rachael, his expression confused and bashful, then he shrugged and waved. Rachael limply waved back. Beverley simply looked horrified and guilty and turned a red to match the wallpaper.

Evonne was tapping her foot, her phone pressed to her ear, waiting. More voices drifted down the stairs.

'Shit,' she hissed.

With what appeared to be a supreme effort, she composed her features, plastered a brilliant smile on her face, and strode towards the staircase. 'Oh, Bonnie, you look immaculate.'

Chapter 19

Time crawled at a pace that allowed Rachael to watch the whole wreck in slow motion.

There was Bonnie, lily-like in her gown of antique silk and lace, her hair swept up with diamond-studded clips, the veil flowing behind her like captive mist, her smile the dazzling unmuddied happiness of a woman truly in love.

Flanking her, Yvette was chic in a tailored pale grey silk skirt suit accented with her huge pearls and a cameo brooch. Marguerite was a perfect foil in a pistachio embroidered gown. The two bridesmaids wore baby-pink chiffon.

Evonne mounted the stairs. Rachael knew she only had a few seconds to act. The smoking room was all the way across the salon behind her, but she might be able to make it. She retreated and in her haste, hit a side table and stumbled.

Before she could right herself, someone steadied her shoulder. 'Hey.'

'Oh, god.'

She spun, straight into Matthew. His arms folded around her, and before she could stop him, he kissed her. Evidently he had no idea what was going on. Had no idea that Bonnie hadn't already left for the church.

Rachael struggled, which seemed to confuse him. He pulled back, stroking her face and asking her what was wrong.

Rachael was only frantic to be free, his touch burning her like acid. He wasn't the man she'd fallen deep in teenage love with, or who she'd wanted to run away with last night. He was someone else entirely. All the changes – the haircut, the suit, the serious expression – she saw them now as his real face, a morphing of the Matthew she'd loved.

'What's gotten into you?' he said, a playful smile still on his lips.

Finally, he glanced past her. Rachael didn't need to turn to know that Bonnie had appeared and was staring straight at them. That she, and the others in the bridal party, and Evonne too, must be trying to make sense of why the groom wasn't at the church, but rather standing in the hotel foyer kissing another woman.

No one said anything.

Finally, Rachael turned around. The antique hall clock ticked through five painful seconds.

She saw the individual lights come on in Bonnie's mind as she took in Rachael and Matthew standing together.

Rachael was stripped raw by that look. Her lips still burned from the kiss he'd given her, a kiss of unparalleled destruction, and the only one she hadn't wanted. She pressed her fingers to her forehead. 'Oh, god.' Her head swam. Maybe she'd faint.

The silence was torture.

'Bonnie,' Matthew croaked. 'I—'

'You're already married,' Rachael rushed out, her voice low, before Matthew could say any more. Maybe if she spoke quickly and got out of here, she could somehow still claim her innocence.

'What?' Matthew said.

Rachael's voice steadied. She wouldn't have this chance again. 'You're already married. You have to be, for French law. Aren't you?'

Matthew's gaze flickered towards Bonnie. 'Well, technically . . .'

Rachael closed her eyes. For a fraction of a second, she hoped she could open them and find this wasn't happening.

She had done the same thing when her mother died. Then, the world had been all hospital white: white walls, white ceiling, white curtains. Now, it was rich with colour – royal burgundy, blue and gold. And yet the experience was the same: the dreadful knowledge that something had happened that could never be reversed. She knew she wouldn't walk away from this the same person. The damage she had done was irreparable.

When she opened her eyes, she dared to look at Bonnie. She had the urge to sink to her knees, to beg for forgiveness.

Instead, she then saw Antonio, standing at the banister, his camera loose in his hand. A moment passed between them and Rachael heard the doors of possibility slamming closed in her mind.

The atmosphere was so pressurised, the only thing Rachael could think to do was leave. So, without another glance at Matthew, she made for the front door. Bernie and Beverley were still waiting there, eyes agog at the unfolding drama. Hot shame burned tears into Rachael's eyes. She only made a few steps before Bonnie's voice came down the stairs like a dart.

'Don't you go anywhere.'

Rachael froze and slowly turned back.

Her elegant pink wisteria bouquet in one hand, Bonnie swished down the stairs to face Matthew. 'In there,' she said, pointing to the office behind the front desk. Her voice could have cut glass.

Before the door closed, Rachael caught sight of them in profile: Bonnie in her spectacular gown; Matthew wearing a pair of jeans, a polo shirt and a defiant expression. They looked like a matador and a bull facing off across a ring, the audience waiting to see what would happen.

Yvette slowly crab-stepped down the stairs in her long gown, steadying herself between the banister and Antonio's arm. Her lips were thin and bloodless. She didn't look at Rachael once, as if she didn't exist. Marguerite wore an expression of disgust. The bridesmaids whispered to each other behind their hands.

The office door opened and the desk clerk appeared. 'Miss West? Your car is here.'

Rachael moved silently down the hall to the front entrance. She didn't look back as the dark car pulled into the kerb, as Bernie and Beverley climbed in first. She would accept whatever fate was now hers.

Chapter 20

Rachael half expected to find the hotel had loaded her luggage into the car, and would take her straight to the airport. Instead, it was much worse. She, Bernie and Beverley were driven directly back to the church, where a silent security man flanked her for the rest of the day. Instead of being able to run away, Rachael had to watch as Matthew arrived, now wearing a dark blue suit with a baby-pink tie, and managed to put a smile on his face. At one point, she saw him deep in conversation with Peter and wondered what he was telling his brother. She would never know. So many things she would never know.

Bonnie had arrived thirty minutes late, but that was expected for the bride. The whole ceremony played out as though the incident in the lobby had never happened, making Rachael wonder if she really was in a dream.

Sammy found her when all the guests were erupting from the church into the courtyard. 'You disappeared. Again.'

Rachael's eyes were full of tears, but she couldn't say anything with the security man hovering.

'If you could step away, miss,' he said to Sammy.

Rachael could only watch Sammy realise that something bad had happened, and that the two of them couldn't talk about it.

The lavish reception was held in the Maison Lutetia's grand ballroom, where a sophisticated light show on the ceiling and walls, all covered with gossamer cloth, made it seem as though the building was transparent and the full glory of Paris, the city of lights, was all around them. A few days ago, Rachael would have been wowed by it. Now, she could imagine Antonio saying it was a clever and beautiful forgery, as false as her connection to Matthew had been.

Antonio. He was there at the reception, of course, circling through the guests, taking photos. He didn't come near Rachael, who was seated alone at a table in the far corner, the security man beside her, now changed into a dinner suit but ever present and ominous. She understood. It was easier for them to keep tabs on her if she stayed at the party. A few guests gave her odd looks, so Rachael kept her eyes down. Besides, she couldn't bear to see Antonio's assessment of her written on his face.

When the happy couple finally departed and Rachael was allowed back to the hotel, the security man stood vigil outside her door. She saw Sammy through the peephole, attempting to argue her way in. The man was very polite as he turned her away, only saying that there had been a security breach.

The next morning, some critical window must have passed because the security man was gone. Sammy took a long time to answer her door. Just when Rachael was about to give up and take her case downstairs, the door opened. Before Rachael could speak, Sammy gave her a look of hurt and betrayal, then muscled past with her carry-on, leaving her case for the porter.

Rachael took her own bag downstairs, cowed and silent, trying to be invisible in a black shirt and jeans and dark glasses. She endured the drive to the airport alone. Once through security, Bernie and Beverley tried to encourage her to have a coffee with them, but Rachael was too embarrassed and huddled herself in a corner of the gate lounge. She didn't see

Sammy anywhere. She hugged herself as she waited to board, just wanting to get home.

Now, still hours and hours before they landed, Rachael went to wash her face in the tiny bathroom. Her chest felt bruised, as though she'd been in a car crash. She kept expecting to see evidence on her face; two black eyes seemed about right. But inexplicably she looked the same as normal.

She dried her face and resisted checking the time. When she opened the tiny bathroom door, she was surprised to see Sammy before her, arms folded.

'I know you're angry with me,' Rachael said. 'I'm sorry—'

Sammy grabbed her hand and pulled her into the tiny alcove between the toilet modules that only the flight attendants were supposed to use.

'I want you to explain to me what the hell happened,' she said. 'Why you disappeared and then turned up again under watch, and why I got interrogated by two guys in black suits about things I have no idea about. And then why Peter comes and tells me it's all over and never to call him again because he can't possibly leave his wife after what happened with Matthew and you.'

Rachael swallowed.

'Why didn't you tell me?' Sammy's whisper was barely audible. 'Were you just going to run off and say nothing? I told you about Marty and Peter, and I never wanted to do that.'

'I'm sorry about Peter,' Rachael began.

Sammy held up a hand. 'You were the one who said you wanted to get over Matthew, and I was so glad about that. What possessed you to listen to him? What did you think would happen? That he would leave Bonnie Perfect Quinn in the middle of their Paris wedding?'

Rachael was speechless. In retrospect, it sounded ridiculous. But the hope had been so powerful.

'I just wanted him back again,' she said in a small voice.

Sammy rubbed her face, avoiding Rachael's eye. 'I remember. I never thought you'd actually try to break them up.'

'Sammy—'

'I'm going back to my seat,' Sammy said. 'I'm angry and I'm tired. So I want you to leave me alone.'

Rachael returned to her seat with tears spilling over her lids, her sobs barely contained. Her insides were a worse mess than they'd ever been over Matthew. Sammy was her best friend. The loss of her trust stripped Rachael to the bone.

The kindly lady in the next seat patted her hand. 'You okay, love?'

'Mmm,' Rachael said, swiping at her eyes.

'Had a shock? Or man trouble?'

'Something like that,' Rachael mumbled.

The lady made a comforting sound. 'Best have a gin then, lovey, and avoid the soppy romance movies. After crying comes getting mad, and then you know you're close to getting over it.'

Sure enough, half an hour into an action movie featuring The Rock, and halfway down her second gin, the unfairness of the whole situation began to simmer within Rachael until she was boiling with indignation. *Matthew* was the one who'd sought *her* out. *Matthew* was the one who'd told her he still loved her, still wanted to be with her, when all the time he was unavailable. And yet here she was, copping the blame for the whole debacle.

Why had she listened to him? Because she'd believed him. Because she'd wanted those two women at her mother's funeral to be wrong. She'd wanted her life back as it was supposed to be. Besides, she'd always listened to Matthew. Their future together had been his idea. Even her plan to be a journalist – that had been Matthew's idea too. Only now did the reality of all that seem so stark.

Rachael didn't believe that it was all her fault, but that didn't stop the consequences falling more heavily on her, and she couldn't take back what she'd done. Couldn't Sammy understand that? After all, she'd been having an affair with a married man. She thought she was pregnant. What right did she have to judge?

As Dwayne Johnson on screen shouldered a particularly large weapon and went in search of the man who'd wronged him, Rachael marched up the cabin to confront her friend. She would tell Sammy that this was stupidly unfair, that they needed to work it out, that Sammy needed to listen to what had happened.

But Sammy's head was tilted over as she slept, her headphones askew. On her screen was the same movie Rachael had been watching, the action now playing out in a series of explosions. Sammy's eyes were deep hollows and her mouth tugged down at the edges. She looked deeply unhappy.

The fight went out of Rachael. She wasn't going to make a scene on the plane. They had both kept things from each other. They'd both lost their loves and their dignity. Rachael heard her mother's voice in her mind, telling her not to worry, that true friends would always find a way to make up. That Rachael could be the bigger person in the argument.

She spotted Beverley seven rows ahead, her eye mask down, and Rachael's shame over the whole episode in the lobby rushed back. She crept back to the toilet so she could cry without the woman next to her making any comment.

⟵

They landed at six on a rainy Sydney morning. Disembarking, Rachael was stuck for an age behind an old man with a cane and a tweed hat. By the time she made it to the baggage carousel it was already full of cases. She didn't see Sammy, or Bernie and Beverley, anywhere. Finally, she made it through customs, hoping to catch them on the other side. Nothing.

After half an hour waiting near the exit doors, Rachael realised she was truly alone. With a heavy sigh, she turned for the train station. It was going to be a long journey home.

Chapter 21

Tess picked Rachael up from the station at five that afternoon, after a train journey across the mountains and out to Parkes that had seemed as long as the flight from Paris.

'Why are you on the train?' was Tess's greeting when Rachael had called ahead. 'I thought you were getting a lift?'

'There wasn't room,' Rachael had lied.

The first five minutes of the drive to the farm passed in painful silence. The fields slid by, some newly planted, others showing the remains of the harvest stalks still standing as they waited. Rachael had scheduled her own plant to start in a couple of days, pending a weather check. She'd planned it like that partly as an insurance in case she needed something to take her mind off the wedding. Her fancy Parisian nails were all gone now, and she'd chewed the newly grown stubs underneath back to pink.

'So,' Tess finally said, 'aren't you going to tell me how it was?'

'It was okay.' Rachael's voice was flat.

'You go all the way to Paris and it's just "okay"? What happened to the handsome man?'

'Later, Tess.'

When they rolled into the drive, Rachael could see her niece Emily and nephew Felix playing outside the shed. She told Tess she was exhausted, which was true. As she carried her case into the house, her body ached as though she'd aged twenty years. A food-splattered highchair was half-pulled into the kitchen table. Toys were strewn across the lounge, a dump truck sitting in her mother's chair. Rachael turned away from the window so she wouldn't have to look at her mother's tree.

In her room, she pulled the curtains closed. After the opulence of the Maison Lutetia, the simple bed frame, hand-made quilt and threadbare carpet seemed to belong to an entirely different universe. She imagined her room in Paris still strewn with the evidence of her swift departure, the Bvlgari watch left on the bed, and wondered whether someone might puzzle over what had happened, like the picture Antonio had shown her in the Louvre.

She tried not to think about the offers that Yvette, Antonio and Bonnie had made. The idea that she'd lost those opportunities through her own stupidity was too awful to contemplate. Would she otherwise have been heading to London to work at a magazine? Or helping Bonnie organise the fundraiser fashion show? Or applying for an internship with a designer? She'd been offered so many different new lives and given them all up for a lie.

Rachael bit her lip and snorted back the tears. Maybe she could drive out of town in a flurry of dust. Turn up the highway and just keep going – past Dubbo, all the way to the Queensland border and beyond – and never come back.

Only her ties to the farm stopped her. Unless a tornado blew in overnight, the planting would start in two days and she couldn't leave Tess and Joel to do everything. Joel had already managed the pre-planting weed control so she could go to Paris. No matter how ashamed she was, Rachael would always have the fields to care for, and the sooner she resigned herself to that fate, the better off she'd be. She had to harden up and get on with it.

⟶

After a restless, jet-lagged night, she dragged herself out of bed just after six thirty, the sun still a squashed apricot on the eastern horizon. Today, all the equipment needed going over and the plans and seed-density calculations had to be rechecked.

Tess was already in the kitchen with the news radio turned up, dropping batches of bread in the toaster as the kids climbed on and off the kitchen table chairs, spreading crumbs. The baby was in the highchair, happily smearing Weet-Bix across the tray.

'Is Joel up?' Rachael asked.

'Good morning to you too,' Tess replied, dropping a teabag into the bin. 'He's been up for an hour already making a start.'

'He didn't have to do that. You could have gone home. I had ring-ins booked for this.'

'Well,' Tess said, her ponytail swinging as she turned around to spread Vegemite on another slice, 'lucky we did stay. What would have happened if you'd run off? Just let the fields sit fallow?'

Rachael blinked, wondering how on earth Tess knew. 'I don't know what you're talking about.'

'Really? You know I don't like listening to gossip, but for pity's sake, what were you—' Tess broke off and held up a hand. 'It doesn't matter. I'm not going to repeat anything I've heard. Let's just forget it.'

Appetite lost, Rachael poured her tea away, hot shame burning her up. Crumbs stuck to the soles of her feet. Emily was feeding a piece of toast into the slot of Marion's Heinz 1957 money box. Rachael extracted it, and was rewarded with screaming.

'Just let her have it,' Tess said.

'It's Mum's vintage money box,' Rachael protested, wetting a cloth to wipe away the globs of butter.

'She shouldn't have had it down there with kids around,' Tess argued. 'And don't hover with a cloth like I don't know how to clean up.'

Rachael wanted to yell that she didn't need Tess hanging around, judging her too. She'd planned for the planting weeks ago and Tess had been so strident about them leaving as soon as Rachael was back. She didn't understand why they were staying longer. Instead, aware of her nieces and nephew watching, Rachael capped her boiling temper and backed out.

She found Joel in the office poring over the weather report, his big shoulders hunched awkwardly in the chair.

Still shaking with annoyance at Tess, Rachael pulled down a sheaf of plans. 'Don't let me hold you up if you want to get back home,' she said. 'I'm okay to run the plant myself.'

'Boss is in control on that one,' Joel said. 'Think she likes the place. Besides, with the rain situation we're still a few weeks off any planting at home. And cleaning the equipment after is a shit job. Happy to lend a hand.'

Rachael went out into the fields. Her feet crunched through the stubble as she turned her face into the gusting wind, trying to read the indecisive sky. The rhythms of the farm, the sunrise and set, the wind and rain – they had always defined the edges and substance of her life. Yet now the smell of the earth and the air, the shape of the clouds, even the colour of the fields, seemed veiled and foreign, as if the part of her that understood their meaning had withered to the root.

She didn't go back to the house until lunchtime, and found everyone around the kitchen table.

'Do you normally just mosey around the day before planting?' Tess demanded. 'Joel needed to run some errands.'

'It's fine,' Joel said around a wad of bread.

'It's not fine. We came to cover for you so you could go to Paris and now you're taking us for granted.'

Joel shot Rachael an apologetic look.

She glanced at Felix and Emily, but they seemed occupied with putting holes through their bread and making moustaches with slices of cheese. The baby watched her siblings, giggling with glee.

'If you need to go home, I'm not stopping you,' she said, and retreated to the study, trying to get her mind back to the planting.

She could hear Tess crashing dishes around the kitchen sink, muttering. The children had been banished to the verandah. Rachael stared at a list of seed densities and soil moisture content results, all the time wondering how long Tess would take to leave.

'Knock, knock.' Joel stood in the doorway. 'She doesn't mean it, so don't take it personal,' he said, as if he'd heard her thoughts. He glanced over his shoulder, then stepped inside and gently pulled the door shut behind him. 'She's just stressed about things up north.'

Rachael slid the sheet of paper back into the pile. 'On the farm, you mean?'

'Yeah. We're pretty close to the wall there, Rach.'

She looked up in surprise. 'I know you said you were going to be late to plant, but—'

'We've had lean years these last few. We didn't get enough rain, and then prices were low – you know the story. I bought new equipment to help us plant faster, but that drained the capital, and the place was only marginally profitable in the good years. I should have waited. Or used the money on some new bores. But that's all hindsight now. We can't take on debt with little hope of repaying it, so I've been looking for a buyer the past year. No takers yet.'

Rachael paused, letting it sink in that Tess and Joel were about to lose their home. 'I had no idea.'

'Yep. Well, we didn't want to say anything. Been hoping it would turn around. Your mum did the right thing here going to no-till. She was a smart woman, how she slowly built things over the years. Production's still good here even in a dry year.'

'What are you going to do?'

He shrugged. 'Depends if we can get a fair price. Whoever buys it will need to put some money in.'

Rachael's mind raced to her bank balances. They weren't huge, but if it would help. 'If there's anything I can do, Joel.'

'I know. But I'm not telling you 'cause I want something. Just didn't want you thinking Tess is on your case. She was really levelled by your mum's passing, but she's been trying to hold everything together, pretending it doesn't matter so much. Don't say anything – you know how proud she is.'

The plans rested in Rachael's lap, forgotten. Instead, she saw Tess crying in their mother's room two days after the funeral. She sighed.

The kitchen had gone quiet. A moment later, the door swung in and collected Joel in the back.

'Oof!'

'Why're you standing behind the door?' Tess demanded.

Joel ducked out without a word, leaving the sisters facing one another.

'Thought you were planning for tomorrow?' Tess said, wiping her hands on a tea towel.

'Just finishing.'

'Well, good, because before we go I want to sort out some of Mum's things.'

'Tess . . .' Rachael tried to find the words to approach her sister about her own farm without ratting out Joel for telling her, but nothing would come.

'Rachael, it's been months. Her walk-in cupboard is still full, and her dressing table hasn't been touched. This isn't healthy.'

'I'm not ready,' Rachael said. 'There's no rule about how long that takes.'

'It's all gathering dust. And mould. Tell me the last time you looked at any of it? I'm not waiting any more.'

'Tess, no!'

Rachael leapt up and ran after Tess. She overtook her in the hall and made it first to their mother's room. She stood stupidly in the doorway.

Tess uttered a frustrated noise. 'I don't understand why you don't want to sort it out. You had your trip overseas. Now you need to move on. Find a man, have your kids.'

Rachael saw tears in Tess's eyes. Any retorts she might have thrown at her sister to mind her own business dissolved like rainclouds in a dry year. She knew how proud Tess was to be a farmer's wife, and now that life was falling away from under her. Rachael could understand what that was like. For the first time, she saw Tess's fear and hurt and uncertainty. That her intrusions were a way of controlling the things she could while being at the mercy of everything else.

Rachael counted her own blessings. Joel was right – this farm was doing okay. She might have wished to reclaim her lost years or go to university, but she'd made a grave mistake in Paris, and those dreams were the price. Her mother had made a good life for herself here on the farm. Maybe it was time to give in and make peace with that.

Rachael let the tension out of her body, and conceded. 'Maybe you're right. I know it was a while ago, but what was that you mentioned about Joel's cousin?'

Tess paused, clearly flummoxed. 'I thought you'd forgotten about that.'

Rachael firmly closed the door to their mother's room. 'Maybe you could set us up after all.'

—

'His name's Harrison. He'll call you,' a delighted Tess told Rachael after she'd hung up the phone not ten minutes later.

Harrison did, before the hour was out. Rachael wasn't sure if he was overly keen or just scared witless of Tess, but on the phone he had a deep voice and sounded amiable enough. She was slightly encouraged.

'I'm sorry, the plant's about to start,' she had to say when he asked when they could meet. 'It's going to be flat out for a while from tomorrow.'

'How about dinner today then?'

Rachael glanced at Tess, who was hovering in the doorway, and agreed. They arranged to meet up in Parkes for an early café dinner.

Harrison rolled up in a dusty Hilux wearing a good check shirt with his hair still wet from the shower. 'You must be Rachael,' he said, climbing down. He wasn't bad-looking. Nice eyes, and he smelled of aftershave and soap. 'Thanks for making it short notice. Might not have managed to meet up for weeks otherwise. I know how it can get around plant.'

'Must be a good sign,' Rachael said with a small kernel of hope.

They took a table, talking shop because that was safe. Rachael could hear herself speaking about the farm, about the advantages of dedicated tramlines or their weed-control regimen, but she wasn't quite within her own body. She wished she wasn't constantly reminded of how this wasn't Paris and it wasn't Antonio sitting across from her. Her heart dipped a little each time she thought of him.

'Jailhouse Rock' began pumping through the café speakers and Harrison – or rather Harry as he'd asked to be called – said, 'Elvis is a big thing around here. I looked in on the festival back in January. Never seen anything like it.'

'It's a Parkes thing,' Rachael said. 'Up in Milton we've got Bernie Collins and his bakery.'

'That's Blue Suede Choux, right? I remember it. Did you know they had an Elvis dinner out at the big Dish? It was good fun. Nice to be in a place with some personality.'

Rachael smiled around the ache in her chest. She loved home, but Paris had shown her how much bigger the world was. The conversation faltered for ten minutes.

'Tess says your farm's been running no-till for a good while,' Harry finally said, trying to steer back to neutral ground.

They recovered slightly, talking about the relative virtues of ploughing versus not, and then more about Harry's cherry orchard, then a bit more about their families.

Then he said, 'Tess mentioned you just had a trip to Paris.'

Rachael pushed her half-eaten pasta around her plate. 'Yes.'

'Must have been quite something.'

'It was.'

He waited expectantly, but Rachael was incapable of describing any of the things she'd seen. It all reminded her of Antonio, or Yvette, or that little dressmaking studio near the Arc du Triomphe. Her reluctance put him at a distance and so the little kernel of hope never germinated. Conversation dwindled until she and Harry were both politely looking out the windows, or talking about the weather. Rachael knew it was her fault; she kept imagining herself in Tess's life – on the farm with a husband and children – and couldn't shake a need to run away.

They parted amiably, but without organising to meet again.

＊

'What happened?' Tess asked when Rachael walked in the door. 'I thought you'd be out for hours yet.'

'It was okay,' Rachael said, but her disappointment was dark and deep. She went to her room and didn't come out, despite Tess sending Joel to ask if she wanted tea.

Tomorrow's work loomed. Rachael paced around like a prisoner, straightening her bedspread, reorganising her drawers. Finally, needing some kind of catharsis, she dropped to the carpet and opened her dresser's bottom drawer. She pulled out a photo of her and Matthew from their last school dance. Rachael looked absurdly young, her face soft and round and unlined. Her cheeks didn't have that roundness now, and a curved line was etched from the outside edge of her nose down to her mouth.

She put the photo aside and dug underneath for more. She found Matthew, Bernie and a group of friends all dressed as Elvis; and another of Matthew in just his shorts about to jump into the waterhole, head back and arms spread, brave and carefree.

She pulled out the pile of letters. Some were just notes they'd passed in school; others were from the first half of the year he went away, when Rachael had written every week and so had he . . . at first. After a while he'd argued that email was so much easier, even though the farm's connection was often on the blink. She re-read some of them, but couldn't feel any fondness now. They just sounded immature and dreamy, thoughts from another life.

She added them to the photos, and the rest of the drawer followed: little velvet bags and boxes of jewellery he had given her; a smooth river stone she'd picked up the first time they'd gone to the waterhole; a dozen other obsessive reminders of their relationship.

What a joke. Matthew had never apologised for his actions, for misleading her. Had never even tried to make it right.

In the very bottom of the drawer was Matthew's senior jersey, carefully folded and wrapped in acid-free tissue paper. He'd given it to her when he was accepted into medical school, the same night they'd made love out in the field. Rachael had fallen asleep holding it for months afterwards. Now, she didn't want to touch it. It smelled of the same cologne he'd been wearing in Paris.

She bundled all of the keepsakes into a bag, wanting to burn them. And yet she couldn't bring herself to do it. Despite everything – leaving her, lying to her, leading her on, undoing all her chances of something new – she remembered him sitting in that rowboat and saying he still loved her. All the wrongs he'd done her should have burned him out of her like fire through stubble. Instead, the sadness of what could have been, and her own lack of insight, lingered.

Rachael put the bag back in the drawer. She would keep it to remind her in five years, in ten, in twenty, what a folly it was to think you could go back.

She stood, and stretched. On the dresser was a framed photo of her and Sammy as teenagers, grey with mud after swimming in a low dam, both squinting their eyes and grinning at the camera. For the third time, she picked up her phone, and again the call switched straight to message bank. Rachael hung up – she'd already left two messages – and sank onto her dresser chair. She was rigid with jet lag and despair, incapable of sleep. She might be able to bear losing everything but the farm, but not without the friend she'd had since school.

She tore out three pages from an old exercise book and uncapped a pen with fingers that trembled with fatigue. *Dear Sammy*, she began.

An hour later, the letter was done. Rachael pushed it into the pocket of her jeans. Tomorrow, she told herself, after the long day of planting, she would drive over to Sammy's. If her friend wouldn't talk to her, maybe she would read the letter instead.

Rachael woke at dawn. When she went outside, the sky was all gold and pale blue, the fields rolling away all around, the air crisp on her cheeks as the birds sang their chorus. Planting day had always inspired her – going out and running over every inch of the fields, coming back in the breaks to update her mother on their progress. In earlier years, Marion had watched with binoculars from the verandah, or even hobbled down to the shed with the aid of her walking stick, bringing a thermos of tea and a packet of biscuits, which Rachael, hot and dry, would polish off without guilt. Last year, Marion had slept until after noon, and Rachael had paid a ring-in to take over in the middle of the day so she could get her mother up, showered, dressed and seated in her chair. Still, she had determinedly worked until dark.

Now, despite the glorious day, Rachael could summon neither inspiration nor enthusiasm. She was running purely on habit. She checked the weather reports, and was backing the tractor to hitch the drill when Joel came down to the shed with two mugs of coffee.

'Keen,' he said. 'You want me to kick off?'

Rachael climbed down from the cab. 'No need. I'll take it until ten, then could you take over for thirty? I'll take it back after that.'

'You'll need a longer break than half an hour.'

She paused. 'Well, maybe an hour, and I can make a trip into Milton.'

She didn't make it through to ten. Just before nine, when she turned the drill for a run back towards the house, she saw Sammy's green hatch with the mismatched door panel coming down the driveway. She instantly killed the tractor engine and was down from the cab in a second, running across the field. The car pulled up on the drive, and Rachael skidded to a stop when Marty unexpectedly climbed out.

He squinted at her like someone who'd been flushed out of a dark place by torchlight, his cap pulled low, brow furrowed. But unlike the last time Rachael had seen him, he was also clean-shaven, his shirt tucked in, and clearly on a mission.

'Have you seen Sammy?' were his opening words. 'She didn't come back last night.'

How much had Sammy told him?

'Ah, no.'

'Shit. I thought she'd be here. I've checked everywhere else.'

'I haven't seen her since the plane from Paris. I don't know if she said anything, but we had a fight. She hasn't been answering my calls.'

Marty took off his cap and rubbed at his hair. 'Us too, yesterday. She wasn't happy after she got back. Did something happen over there? She rang me almost every day and said she was having a great time. Made a change from the last year. She's been upset about this business thing for a while, you know, 'cause money's been tight and we had to wait, but I thought she was over it. I don't understand.'

'Um . . .' Rachael couldn't say anything about Peter; that wasn't her place. 'I'm not sure. She didn't say anything?'

'Not a word. Took off after the spat. I guess she caught a lift with someone. I mean, it's Milton. Where's she gunna go?'

'Did you check at the motel?' Rachael asked. 'And with Bernie?'

'Yeah. The motel says she's supposed to be on this arvo, but Bernie says he hasn't seen her since they drove back from Sydney. The cops reckon it's too soon to worry, especially as it's happened before.'

'What did— Wait, it's happened before?'

Marty shrugged, then looked away, embarrassed. 'Uh, yeah. Twice in the last few months. But she said she'd stayed at the motel.'

Rachael put a hand to her forehead. She stank of sweat and dirt, and dust and straw coated the inside of her nose. Her hands were numb from the vibration in the cab. She glanced at the drill, immobile in the field, at the acres and acres left to go. And yet all she could think was, where the hell was Sammy? She obviously hadn't said anything to Marty about Peter or the baby.

'I'll look,' she said. 'I'll call you.'

Marty thanked her and turned for the car.

The letter was a lump in Rachael's pocket. She dropped her pretence of calm and made for the big shed, where she ran straight into Joel.

'Whoa,' he said. 'Don't tell me the drill's packed it in?'

'Sammy's missing. I know there's so much to do, but no one's seen her and—'

'You want to split?' Joel said, holding up the keys for the Hilux. 'Needs fuel anyway.'

'You're the best,' she said, kissing him on the cheek.

Two minutes later, she was flying down the drive, alive for the first time since Paris. She couldn't do anything about her own wrongs, but she could find Sammy.

⟵

Rachael's first idea was to head to the motel in Parkes and wait for Sammy to come in for work.

'Called in sick,' complained the owner, who was manning the reception himself and seemed rather oversized for the job, his generous gut upsetting the printer tray every time he turned for his coffee cup. 'Though can't say I'm that convinced.'

'When did she call?'

'An hour ago. Which gives me such ample time to call in someone else.'

Rachael left him to his sarcasm. While she was relieved Sammy wasn't lying in a ditch somewhere, she still wasn't answering her phone. Her parents lived in Bathurst, but Rachael knew Sammy wouldn't go there even if she was paid. But after fuelling the ute and visiting all her favourite places in Parkes, Rachael was running out of ideas. Maybe Sammy had bought a bus ticket after all.

She even drove out to the Dish, and found the visitor centre deserted except for a small clutch of tourists.

'You want to buy a ticket?' called the counter staff as Rachael stuck her head inside the theatre.

In desperation, she turned back for Milton and, after a slow drive past the shops, and taking a moment to bury her shame, pulled up in the residential streets behind. Bernie answered the door wearing a half-finished rhinestone Elvis suit, a set of bifocals balanced on the tip of his sweating nose. 'Rachael!' he said with a grin that held no trace of reserve or disapproval.

Rachael let go of a huge tension she'd been carrying. Even after seeing her in the lobby with Matthew, Bernie was exactly the same.

'New costume?' she asked.

'Started it yonks ago,' Bernie said, rolling a fat crystal between his fingers. 'But these things and the hot glue are sending me bats. Stuck three fingers together already. Come in. I'll put the kettle on.'

'Thanks, but I won't stay. I'm just looking for Sammy. Marty says he can't find her.'

'I know, he asked me already. We thought she was out at your place.'

Rachael shook her head.

'I did wonder if you'd had a tiff when she said you were making your own way home,' he added.

'Do you have any idea where—'

'Your eyes are better than mine,' Bernie interrupted, proffering the rhinestone with glue-spattered fingers. 'Is that blue or cobalt?'

'I couldn't say.'

'And this? Yellow or amber? I got the packets all mixed up.'

This was all very odd. Bernie didn't seem at all worried about Sammy. Almost like he knew he didn't have to be.

Rachael reached into her pocket. 'Bernie, can you please give this to Sammy if you see her?'

He took the letter with his gluey right hand, then, finding it stuck, transferred it to the clean left one. He frowned. 'Rach, it's not serious, is it? This argument between the two of you?'

Rachael's lip wavered. 'I hope not. But it's really important I find her.'

Bernie offered the letter back. 'When a man gives his word not to say anything, it's important not to break it. But if you were to ask me if I'd given Sammy a lift to the creek drive and I didn't say anything, well, I wouldn't have said anything, would I?'

Rachael stared at him. 'Are you saying . . .'

'I'm not saying nothing,' he said, tapping his nose.

Hope bloomed in Rachael's chest. 'If you see Beverley, tell her I'm sorry too.'

'What for?' he called after her, but Rachael was already gone.

She raced the Hilux back home. The creek drive was one turn-off up the highway from the farm gate and had once led to a pump station at the river. The road had been disused for years and was overgrown and undrivable, but it provided an easy walking track to the waterhole if you knew where you were going. But the walk took at least half an hour.

Rachael ran to the shed and leapt on a trail bike. Across the far field, she could see Joel running a straight line with the drill, swirling dust obscuring the tractor's wheels like a magic trick.

She pulled up at the edge of the river trees, knowing that if Sammy was here she'd have heard the bike. Rachael climbed to the highest rock over the water and scanned the area. The breeze softly whistled between the rocks, and the creek burbled into the pool. It was such a long way from the Seine: this was a wild waterway, one never likely to be settled, at least not by many. But Rachael only needed one person.

Please, she thought, please be here. She couldn't fail at this too. A real friend would have known that something was badly wrong in Sammy's life, and Rachael hadn't. She would have given up again every chance she'd squandered on the Paris trip to spare Sammy feeling that she needed to run.

'Sammy!' she called.

An echo came back, but no reply.

Rachael couldn't see any signs of someone being here – no tent or scraps or wet marks by the pool.

She climbed down and circled through the trees. The tumbled boulders and trunks made lots of blind spots, but she found nothing in any of them. Once, she thought she heard a nearby crunch of leaf litter, but when she stopped to listen, nothing else came.

Just as she was climbing back, she spotted a patch of freshly turned earth the size of a scraps burial or a bush toilet. Definitely made with a camping trowel.

'I know you're here,' she called.

No response. Sammy clearly didn't want to talk.

Rachael took the letter from her pocket and weighed it down with a rock in an obvious place. Then she plucked another stone from between two boulders and cast it into the water with a wish. The resulting ripples sparkled in the sun, inviting, but she had to get back. Joel had already done longer in the cab than he should have.

⟶

By the time blue twilight was dwindling into night, Rachael's bones hurt. She drove the tractor into the shed and trudged back to the house, tasting grit between her teeth and wondering how long she could stand under a hot shower before falling asleep. Through the kitchen window she saw Tess stirring a pot while the kids ran around the table. Joel, fresh from the shower, took turns to catch them and lift them up above his head.

After her shower, Rachael yawned as she tried to pull a brush through her hair, listening to the shrieks and squeals floating down the hall. Then she heard Tess telling them to be quiet, and the verandah door being opened. Rachael put her brush down as footsteps came down the hall. She turned and there was Sammy standing in the doorway.

Rachael's fatigue evaporated. Three steps crossed the distance between them, and she crushed Sammy in a hug.

'I was so worried,' she said. 'And I'm so sorry.'

Sammy said nothing, but she held on in the same way Rachael remembered doing the night her mother had died.

'Was it Bernie?' Sammy asked finally.

'He told me that a man doesn't go back on his word.'

Sammy grunted. 'How ironic.'

'I was starting to worry you weren't there at all.'

'Good thing I had the quick-fold tent or I'd never have hidden in time. I didn't want to talk to anyone.' Sammy held up the creased sheets of paper, a small smile on her lips. 'You're lucky. I might have mistaken this for loo paper.'

'So you read it?'

She dropped the letter onto the bedspread. 'You really mean all that stuff about me being as important to you as your mum?'

Rachael nodded.

'Wow.'

'I also meant it when I said I'd tell you everything that happened if you want to hear it.'

Sammy nodded, so Rachael laid out every detail between when Matthew had left her room on the Wednesday night in Paris until the drive to the airport.

'He was already married?' Sammy repeated when Rachael had finished.

Rachael nodded.

'That dirty bastard.' She shook her head. 'Not that I'm really surprised. I never liked what he did to you. But you know that already.'

'You were right. I shouldn't have let him in again.'

Sammy sighed and pulled up the desk chair. 'Don't do that.'

'What?'

'Go thinking it's all your fault. He played his part. Believe me, I understand that. But I wish you'd told me.'

'I wish you'd told me.'

Sammy looked away, then stepped back to the door and closed it. 'Shit, what a mess.'

'What are you going to do? Are you really . . . ?'

'Yep.' Sammy tipped her head back, clearly trying not to cry. 'I'm terrified, and I have to tell Marty.'

Rachael bit her lip, thinking about everything that had happened in the last weeks. 'Do you really want to do that now? You don't even know what you're doing yet. How is Marty going to feel about it?'

'I can't keep it from him.'

'Do you want to stay with him?' Rachael asked softly.

Sammy's voice was tiny. 'Yes. I didn't know how it was going to work out, but I never wanted to leave him.'

'You can't take it back once you tell him. I don't mean that you shouldn't, just think about what might happen. I wish Matthew had kept his trap shut.'

'It's not the same thing. How could I possibly let Marty think the baby's his?'

Rachael sighed. 'You don't know it isn't. You could get a test done or something.'

A long silence sat heavy between them. Rachael plucked at the bedspread, catching a ragged nail on the coil of an embroidered rose.

Finally she said, 'Is it over with Peter?'

'Yes. He's worried sick that his business will be affected if people find out. Should have seen that coming. He offered me hush money, can you believe it? I told him to piss off.'

'I can't believe he'd do that. What a jerk.'

Sammy made a helpless gesture. 'And I thought I knew him. I was so insulted. And then I was mad at you. Peter was covering his own arse, and my best friend had left me in the dark. I felt so utterly alone.'

'I know,' Rachael said, tears threatening to spill down her cheeks. 'Sammy, I'm so desperately sorry.'

'I know.'

They hugged for a long minute before Sammy stood. 'I have to go. You look like you're about to collapse.'

'Going home?'

'Yeah. I have to. I can only hide out for so long. And if I want to make calls at the waterhole, I have to scramble to the top of the rock pile and hold the phone in the air.' She paused. 'I'll think about what you said, but I have to tell him. Peter might have played his part, but I have to take responsibility for mine.' She scooped up the letter.

Rachael nodded. 'I'll give you a lift back. And remember, I'm here, no matter what.'

She trailed after Sammy through the house, which was now in the midst of the kids' bath time. Sammy glanced towards the sounds of splashing and laughter, and Rachael wondered if she was thinking about her own child and what the future held.

They drove back to town in relative silence. When Rachael had pulled into the kerb just down from Bernie's place, Sammy paused with her hand on the door catch. 'Were you really offered two jobs?'

'Yeah.' Rachael tried to smile. 'A magazine editor friend of Antonio's was looking for a cadet. And Bonnie wanted to talk about me helping with some kind of fashion show for charity.'

'Seriously?'

Rachael shrugged. 'Doesn't matter. I screwed up, so they're gone. The cadetship wouldn't have paid much anyway, and like Bonnie's ever going to talk to me again.'

'True. But what's the problem with the cadetship? You could afford to do it, couldn't you?'

'Umm . . . Antonio was there when Bonnie caught me and Matthew.'

Sammy leaned back in her seat. 'So there *was* something going on with him?'

Rachael pressed a hand to her forehead, awash with regret. She could now barely remember his face across the table from her, or the warmth of his arms around her as Paris glittered all around. All she could recall was feeling like they were at the centre of the whole world.

'I think there could have been, but not after what happened. Besides, I don't know if that's really what I want. I think journalism was something Matthew thought I should do. Maybe that's why I couldn't focus on it.'

Sammy watched her carefully. 'Are you happy here, Rach?'

'Oh, I'm fine. Just tired. The plant is always so draining.'

'I should go.' Sammy opened her door.

Rachael reached out to touch her arm. 'Good luck.'

After Sammy had vanished down the driveway, Rachael slumped. She was desperately tired, but not exhausted enough to quiet her troubled soul. Sammy was taking responsibility for her actions, coming clean whatever the consequences. Rachael knew she had to make amends too, assuage the shame, or she would never escape it.

She drove home under the gathering night, the stars appearing overhead like tiny eavesdroppers.

Later, as she lay in bed, still restless, an idea drilled a seed into her mind, one that grew as she worked the next day in the tractor cab.

The day the planting finally finished, she knew what she had to do. She told Tess and Joel she would be gone for a day, and early the next morning she fuelled the car in Milton and took to the highway.

Chapter 22

The first part of the drive was four hours down the winding highway that passed through Bathurst and then rose up and up through the Blue Mountains. After the climb and descent, the road opened up like a river reaching its delta, and Rachael entered the motorway hell of Sydney. Her plan had been to start early, get there, do what she had to and be home by five, but the traffic had other ideas. She spent two hours crawling along the first motorway because of a truck accident, or so said a glowing sign that she read twenty times before she crept past it. Once that was done with, she mistook the directions in her GPS, whose maps clearly hadn't been updated since 2003. Soon she was seeing signs to the airport, which was completely the wrong side of the city.

Another two hours passed in further misadventures, one including an unexpected tunnel, until Rachael was nearly in tears. When she finally saw and crossed the Harbour Bridge heading north, she would have cheered if her mission hadn't been so cheerless.

Finally, she turned into a street where heavy brick pillars, manicured hedges and lush gardens concealed the harbourside mansions within. Learning the right address hadn't been easy;

Sammy would have been horrified if she'd known what Rachael had done to get it.

She was hoping – counting in fact – on neither Bonnie nor Matthew being home. They were supposed to be on their honeymoon. Rachael tried not to think about how that was going. Was Bonnie pretending nothing had happened? Was Matthew?

The fence at her destination was an orderly row of slender iron spikes, as if a phalanx of soldiers had gone on a tea break and left their spears behind. The grass verge was as plush and spotless as a green rug, silencing Rachael's steps as she padded from the kerb to the gate. Her heart thumped, not least because the rooftops almost looked fortified, as if snipers were targeting her. But she had to do this.

Set into the side of the gate was a security intercom with a camera lens and a single stainless-steel button. She pressed it.

'Name and appointment?' A man's voice, bored.

'I don't have one. I just have a package—'

Click.

Rachael waited, but nothing happened. She pushed the button again.

'No access without an appointment,' the man said. 'Packages are not received at the house. We call police for repeated—'

'It's Rachael West.'

Silence, but no click. The man was still listening.

'I want to pay back the money,' Rachael rushed on. 'For the trip to Paris. I have it here for Bonnie right now and I was wondering if I could leave it—'

'No access without an appointment.' Click.

The old Rachael wouldn't have pressed that button again. Hell, the old Rachael would never have come in the first place. She would have accepted the obstacle and endured it, while wishing that things had gone differently.

Her fingertip blanched as she mashed the button a third time. The new Rachael knew this was the right thing to do, and she was determined to do it, no matter how uncomfortable it made her.

'We call the police for persistent entry attempts without an appointment. Please leave now.' Click.

Rachael fingered the thick packet in her hand. She couldn't see a letterbox. Should she leave it on top of the intercom and hope someone picked it up and gave it to Bonnie? Knowing her luck, they'd think she was planting some kind of bomb and then she'd be on the national evening news. Wouldn't that be a fabulous development.

She'd assumed the repayment would be welcome, justified, even necessary. Now, she realised that from the security people's perspective, she probably looked like just another unwanted caller – a canvasser, admirer, or any other time-waster. They probably had a dozen every week.

Embarrassed, she slunk back to her car and drove away. Desperation and conviction had made her foolish. She could have saved herself the trip.

⟵

Rachael didn't make it home until midnight. She spent the next two days cleaning the planting equipment and doing all the post-plant chores. After that, she peeled four notes off the pile she'd intended for Bonnie and sent Joel, Tess and baby Georgia away for a break, promising to mind Felix and Emily. For once, Tess accepted without a fight.

The next afternoon, Rachael and the kids were trudging back from the waterhole through the freshly planted fields. Well, Rachael was trudging. The kids were running while she called after them to walk in the tramlines and avoid compacting the seed. It was Emily who spotted the glinting windscreen coming up the drive.

When the car came into view it looked distinctly out of place: low-slung, black and sleek, gliding on flawless suspension even on the rutted driveway. Dragging a dust cloud, it vanished behind the house.

Rachael's stomach dived. Who was it? Had Bonnie's security people tracked her all the way back from Sydney? She glanced at the children; they were tired and dirty and needed a bath. Should she tell them to go hide in the shed?

'Who's that?' asked Emily.

A figure had appeared on the verandah: a tall woman in flowing white trousers and a Prussian blue singlet. Despite the warmth of the afternoon, a cold horror gripped Rachael between her ribs. It could only be Bonnie.

'Let's go and have some lemonade,' she said bravely, which was enough for the children to find a burst of energy up the hill.

'Hello!' Felix called towards Bonnie as the two of them hurtled into the house, slamming the screen door in their haste to reach the fridge.

Rachael slowed to a stop, knowing how she must look. She was dressed in cut-off shorts, muddy boots and an old holey singlet, and had three wet towels over her shoulder. She'd raked her hair back into a band and knew the top was all lumpy and the short underneath escaping. Her face was red, and dust clung to her damp legs. Bonnie looked ready for a runway; Rachael was only fit to bed down in a sheep pen.

'Hi,' she said, before an awkward silence. 'Do you want to come inside?'

Bonnie glanced towards the house. 'Are those your cousins?'

'Niece and nephew. I'm looking after them while my sister and her husband have a break.'

Bonnie shaded her eyes. 'Will they be all right by themselves? I'd like to talk to you alone.'

The children didn't care, especially when Rachael allowed them to put on *Toy Story* and take the lemonade bottle into the TV room. Tess would never know.

Rachael led Bonnie into the lounge, which seemed so worn and diminished in her presence. For moral support, Rachael sat in her mother's chair, heedless of how dirty she was. Bonnie seemed to consider before she folded her long legs to sit on the facing couch and tucked her ankles underneath. She'd refused tea, and Rachael noticed the big engagement ring was loose on her finger. She made her own hands into fists to stop herself chewing her grubby nails.

'I guess you must have heard about me coming to Sydney,' she began. 'I wanted—'

'Yes, that's why I'm here.'

Rachael fell silent.

'I'm a direct person,' Bonnie went on. 'That's how I run my business. So I'll be direct. How much do you want?'

Rachael blinked. 'What?'

'How much do you want? You'll have to sign a non-disclosure, of course. I told Matthew we should have done this in Paris, but he said the whole thing was his fault.'

Bonnie made it sound as if she was talking about Matthew dropping his socks on the floor instead of him nearly running out on their wedding. It took Rachael an age to realise what she meant.

'I don't want your money!' she said. 'I came to give it back, not ask for it.'

Confusion knitted the space between Bonnie's perfect brows. 'Give it back?'

'I didn't want you paying for my trip after what happened. Look, I'll go and get it now.'

Rachael jumped up and made an undignified exit by tripping on the carpet edge. The packet was still in the top drawer in her room, crumpled and looking like a bribe in a cop drama. She managed not to trip on the way back, and held the money out to Bonnie.

'That's all of it, except a few hundred I gave to my sister. I'll put that back when I can get to a bank again.'

Slowly, Bonnie took the envelope and folded it in her palm. The confusion lifted, replaced with a small smile. 'Richard must have misunderstood. I have to admit I was surprised. I didn't think you were that kind of person.'

'I'm not,' Rachael said, but softly, because she didn't feel she had the right to protest anything Bonnie might think of her. She sat down again. 'Bonnie, I'm really sorry. I know it doesn't make it better, but I am.'

Bonnie didn't meet Rachael's eyes. The words seemed to glance off her as she gazed out the window. 'I suppose I should have come out here years ago,' she said. 'Matthew offered enough times. It's pretty.'

'You should see it next week when the wheat comes up.' Rachael's voice was rough. Sadness had wedged in her throat like a sharp stone. Her apology had meant nothing. How could it?

Bonnie stood as if she was leaving, then turned back. 'He's my husband, Rachael. He was before we left Sydney. I'm not going to be another celebrity couple divorced after forty-eight hours and give people more reasons to talk about us. I believe in letting people redeem themselves. He can do that. And that's as much as I'll say to you about my marriage.'

Rachael was about to apologise again, to say any number of platitudes she'd carefully practised before going to Sydney, but they all died in her throat. She could see the hurt in Bonnie's eyes. No matter how much money Bonnie had, how many fancy clothes, she was as vulnerable to love as anyone else. And Matthew was hers now – her love, and her problem, in whatever balance those things would be. Rachael's time with him had ended long ago, and the moments in Paris had been stolen from some other life that wasn't hers. She found no peace in the realisation, but it did allow her to understand what wouldn't help.

'I'd say I didn't mean to hurt you,' she told Bonnie, 'but my mother would have said that's a cop-out, because hurting other people is always the last thing we think of when we're only thinking of ourselves. And that's what I was doing. I wanted to believe I could do my life over. But I can't. I don't know if you'll believe me, but I liked you. I still do.'

Bonnie turned the packet over in her fingers. 'I'm sorry she died. I can't imagine how hard that must have been, and what you did for her. Matthew told me about it, and I try to remember that. I try.'

Rachael stood as a blast of Woody and Buzz echoed from the TV room. This felt final. She could only hope that, in time, Bonnie could forgive her . . . or perhaps forget her.

Bonnie handed the money back. 'I don't want it. Take it for fixing the dress. Then that's the end of it.'

After a pause, Rachael took it, and followed her as far as the front door. The sky had come over heavy with clouds, and in the diminished light Bonnie's Audi gleamed like a rough gem under its coat of dust. Rachael glimpsed the cream leather of the interior as Bonnie opened the driver's door.

She pushed a pair of sunglasses onto her face. 'I liked you too,' she said.

After she'd gone, Rachael went back inside and cried in the hallway. *Toy Story* was still running, both children sprawled on beanbags, immobile and unblinking. Rachael's mind was similarly occupied, busy replaying the conversation with Bonnie and unable to complete other tasks, like thinking what to do next.

Eventually, she peeled the children away from the closing credits and into the bath. She kept hearing Bonnie saying she believed in letting people redeem themselves. That had been in her mind when she'd tried to return the money, but maybe she had to go further. She paced about the house, thinking it over.

After the children were asleep, she went into the study and took out a block of writing paper. Her hand had cramped by the time she'd finished the two letters, and rain was spitting down over the fields.

During the night, a storm drummed on the roof and lightning photoflashed outside the window. Rachael opened the curtains and listened to the water tumbling through the blackness. A literal watershed. The letters would mark the end of the Paris chapter. She would never forget what had happened there, and she must endure it. Just as her mother had endured her father pushing off, and her illness, and everything else. Endured it because there was no other choice.

The last thing she did before sleep was to tiptoe out to the sewing table, which, after her frenzy before the Paris trip, was buried under threads and offcuts. She bagged all the excess fabric, repacked the boxes, and defluffed and oiled the machines. In a few months, the school or the theatre would be looking for costumes again.

She sighed, pushing away the memory of Martine's studio in Paris. If she thought too much about it, she would start wondering if this tiny corner – in this house, in the world – could ever be enough.

⁓

Tess and Joel returned at lunchtime the next day. Rachael instantly noticed the difference in Tess, who appeared calmer, unpacking the car with no sign of impatience. She was soon drawing out of the children what they'd been doing in her absence.

'Aunty Rachael took us to town and bought us cream buns,' put in Felix.

'Felix!' hissed Rachael, utterly betrayed.

Her nephew put a contrite finger to his lips as if he'd forgotten it was meant to be a secret.

'Well, weren't you lucky,' Tess said, much to Rachael's surprise.

'A white lady came to see Aunty Rachael too,' Emily said.

Tess raised her eyebrows.

'Bonnie,' Rachael said quickly.

'Why would she come here?'

Rachael then had to explain to Tess about her attempt to return the Paris trip money. They sat in the family room, and Tess listened without making any comments.

'How did you even know where they live?' she asked finally.

Rachael blushed. 'I, um, asked Peter.'

'And he just told you?'

'Not exactly.'

In fact, Peter had been extremely reluctant to talk to Rachael. She'd only managed it because she'd turned up at AgriBest and caught him alone in the warehouse. She'd told him that she just wanted to return the money, and when he still said no, that it wasn't worth his life to tell her where Matthew lived, she'd had to imply what she knew about him and Sammy. It wasn't her proudest moment, but she'd left with the address.

Tess sighed. 'I can understand you wanting to, but was that really the best way to go about it? You could have been arrested or something.'

'For what? Besides, she wouldn't take it.'

'Humph,' Tess said, but with none of the judgement Rachael had come to expect. 'Well, you tried, and I'm sure the money is better put to use out here.'

She broke off as the children came in to go through the carrier bags, demanding to know if there were any presents.

'Did you do your chores?' Tess asked them.

'Yes,' they chorused.

She nodded, and didn't even react when Felix tugged on Rachael's hand and asked if they could watch another movie. Tess simply stuck the baby on her hip and shooed Emily and Felix into the spare room to check their bed-making, telling them they could have more movies if everything was in order.

Rachael stared after them. Just as she was thinking that now would be the time to talk to Tess about her own farm, when she was in such a good mood, the phone rang in the study. When Rachael heard, 'It's me,' from Sammy, she pushed the door closed.

'How's babysitting?' Sammy asked, so brightly that Rachael instantly knew something was wrong.

'What happened?'

'I told Marty,' she said, her voice breaking. 'I'm sitting in an empty shed.'

Rachael knew this wasn't a conversation for the phone. 'Come over,' she said.

'Isn't your sister still there?'

'Yeah, but I need to check the fields after the storm. We can do the rounds.'

An hour later, Sammy and Rachael trekked slowly down the rows, the ute parked up the hill, Sammy huddled behind her sunglasses. Rachael had her eyes open for standing water that might kill the seeds. So far this section seemed fine, which was more than could be said for Sammy.

'The instant I told him, I regretted it,' she said. 'I know what I did was awful, but now he has to live with it too. And what about . . . ?' She gestured helplessly to her middle.

'Peter wouldn't be any help?'

'Complete radio silence.'

'Do you know where Marty went?'

Sammy shrugged. 'When he didn't come back yesterday, I checked the credit card. He bought fuel in Bathurst, and went to a café near Katoomba, so I guess he's heading east. He won't answer his phone. Must have been a hell of a shock – I didn't think he'd go that far for anything – and he left a mess when he packed.'

'I'll come and help you clean up,' Rachael said. 'And stay so you're not by yourself.'

Rachael didn't know why, but Sammy abruptly stopped and spun towards the house, her hand held up against the glare. Rachael followed her gaze and found her mother's tree, standing alone at the top of the hill.

'Come on,' she said, dragging Sammy by the hand to another tree nearby. 'Let's get out of the sun. I need to ask you a few things.'

They hauled themselves up on a low branch, just as Rachael had when she was a child. Those times felt so long ago.

'First, have you been to the doc?'

Sammy pulled a face. 'No. Been too much of a coward.'

'Do you want me to come with you?'

'Maybe,' she said in a small voice. Her lip trembled. 'I was hoping that maybe Marty would, but that's just wishful thinking now, isn't it?'

'Oh, Sam.'

A cloud rushed across the sun and the sky momentarily dimmed, before the dappled brilliance lit through the leaves again.

'But you want to stay with Marty? And you want the baby?'
Rachael asked.

Sammy nodded. 'I don't know if I can do anything to
convince him to come back, or to ever make it right again.'

They sat in silence.

Finally, Sammy said, 'Rach, do you wish you had run away
with Matthew? What would you have done if you hadn't found
out about him being married?'

Rachael's shoulders twitched as if hundreds of tiny creatures
were crawling over her skin just thinking about if she'd learned
that information later. 'No idea. I wasn't thinking that far ahead.'

Sammy grunted. 'Because the present moment is more
powerful than tomorrow. Been there.' She slid down to the
ground. 'There's one thing I didn't mention.'

'What's that?'

'When Marty left, he said, "I need some time to think about
all this". That doesn't sound like he's absolutely decided not
to come back, does it?'

'Sounds encouraging,' Rachael said, though she didn't dare
suggest that everything would be fine. Instead, she hugged
Sammy and told her to call anytime.

⌒

Rachael went back to the fields. With each step, dozens of *what
ifs* streaked through her thoughts like shooting stars.

When the sun had sunk and she was returning to the house,
a real shooting star burst overhead, a match struck on the
heavens right above the tree on the rise.

In that moment, she knew the farm would never be enough.

Chapter 23

A week later, at eleven in the evening, Rachael was yawning in the study. Tess and Joel had already turned in, and she ought to have been in bed herself three hours ago. She stumbled taking her tea mug back to the kitchen, and was returning carefully with a refill when the study phone rang.

Rachael leapt on it, thinking it must be Sammy, but heard the three short beeps of a long-distance call. She frowned, wondering who it might be.

Hesitantly, came an ''Allo?' The voice was thin with distance but the accent was unmistakable.

Rachael sat in surprise. 'Yvette?'

'Ah, is that you, *chérie*? This is a terrible line.' Crackles and pops overlaid every word.

'I didn't expect to hear from you. How did you even get my number?'

'I have your letter,' Yvette said, and Rachael heard a rustle of pages. She imagined Yvette holding up the letter Rachael had mailed care of Martine Bertrand's showroom. 'It is not hard to find a number when you are listed in the directory. You left so quickly after the wedding.'

Rachael's breath caught. 'As I said, I'm so sorry for what happened. I'm . . . ashamed of myself.'

'Well, the idea is usually to be discreet. But you are not French, so perhaps you have not had enough practice.'

Rachael put a hand over her face at the idea she might have been so calculating. 'I honestly didn't mean it to happen. I hadn't seen Matthew in years. I went to Paris thinking I'd get over him if I saw him get married.'

'Well, Matthew is not French either. But, *chérie*, I do not think you would make a good mistress. You are too young with too much talent to be ruled by a man like that.'

'Why are you being so nice to me?'

'When you are old, you will understand that so much of life is a farce. I do not sleep much any more. Instead, I lie awake and think about my life. You are not the first person to do something reckless out of love and regret it. And I remember the kind things you did for me. My own family sometimes are not so accommodating. They think an old woman is to be protected, or ignored.'

Rachael bit her lip. 'But Bonnie ... she would have been standing there at her own wedding thinking the whole time about what Matthew had done.'

'Yes. Then again, if you had not been there, her dress would have been ruined, and she cared very much about those photographs for her charity.'

'Someone else could have fixed it.'

'Maybe.' Yvette paused. 'Rachael, I have done many things in my life that I was ashamed of. Everyone has such things. Yet I still made a good life. I had a long career, and I still find surprises even now. The same can be true for you. At the end of your life, you will look at what happened very differently. Time changes everything.'

'I know,' Rachael said. She suddenly remembered the conversation with Antonio. 'My mother used to say that people are more than their worst mistakes.'

'This is very true,' Yvette said. 'And now she is gone, have you any other family, *chérie*? Father? Sisters and brothers?'

'My sister.'

'Good. Are you alike?'

'Completely different,' Rachael admitted.

Yvette laughed. 'This is good too. It keeps life interesting.' A pause. 'I want to tell you something. Before the week you were here in Paris, I had not made anything new for a long time. Now, the collection is complete. I want to send you the pictures. Your work inspired me, and your kindness. I can only imagine how much you meant to your mother.'

A tear rolled down Rachael's cheek.

'But, *chérie*, perhaps now you can give some kindness to yourself. Love will make us do wonderful and stupid things in the same day. Write to me again, if you would like. Tell me what you are doing. Tell me what you are making next. I am an old woman and no one writes letters any more.'

'I guess I could,' Rachael said, though she couldn't imagine having another sewing project for herself for a long time. She only needed jeans on the farm.

When Yvette had rung off, Rachael crept down the hall towards her bedroom. She paused by the guest rooms filled with Tess and Joel's things. The house had been so quiet last Christmas. Quiet, empty and lonely. Rachael missed her mother with a piece of herself that was larger than her dreams had ever been. But with Tess here, the house had life again. Rachael was grateful her sister had stayed as long as she had.

The next day, Rachael was returning to the house intending to speak to Tess when Felix appeared in the doorway waving the cordless phone. 'For you, Aunty Rachael!'

Bernie was on the line. 'Rachael, love, I have a question for you,' he said, puffing.

'Sewing machine or overlocker?' Rachael asked, wondering which costume he was working on now. 'Have you been running?'

'A little. Listen, your mum had some heart trouble in the last few years, didn't she?'

'Mmm, sort of.' Marion had had a few episodes of angina.

'So I have this pain,' Bernie huffed. 'Sort of in my stomach, and my shoulder a bit. Does that sound worrying to you?'

'Bernie, why didn't you call the doctor, or the ambulance?'

'Oh, no, no, don't want to bother them with it. I was on the rowing machine, see? Probably pulled a muscle.'

Rachael pressed her hand to her forehead. Bernie sounded really out of breath. 'How long ago were you on the machine?'

'Ten, twenty minutes, something like that.'

'Hang up and call the ambulance. You don't know with these things.'

Despite her insistence, Bernie protested it wasn't necessary. Rachael pulled her keys off the kitchen hook and jogged out to her ute.

'Bernie, I'm getting in the car and coming over. But I expect to see a damn ambulance when I arrive, okay?

'Bloody man,' she muttered as she sped down the road, nudging the speedo over the limit.

Throwing out all the rules, she dialled Beverley on her mobile, expecting the highway patrol to pull her over at any moment as she left a hurried voicemail.

She made the drive in under twenty minutes. No sign of an ambulance, or any activity at all. With a glance through the windows, she thumped on the door. 'Bernie?'

He answered wearing a pair of stubby shorts and an Elvis Festival T-shirt. He had a glass of water in his hand, and his jaw was working.

'What are you eating?' she said, aghast. His face was flushed, sweat drops at his temples.

'Antacid,' he answered, after a big swallow. 'Found them in the third drawer and figured I'd give it a go.'

'Is it working?'

He grimaced. 'Not really.'

Rachael extracted the water glass. She'd been in enough hospitals with her mother to know a few things. 'No more food or drink. If you had to go into surgery, that's important.'

Bernie collapsed on the couch, saying he just needed a minute and for Rachael not to worry. Rachael turned for his phone – she'd left hers in the car – and found it out of the cradle.

'Bernie, where's the phone?'

'In the kitchen, I think.' He swallowed. 'I actually don't feel that great.'

She muttered under her breath as she went to find it. 'Bernie? It's not there.'

'Rach, can you bring me that glass of water? Feel a bit sick.' He'd turned grey, his fingers laced over his beer belly. 'Ooof,' he moaned. Was he about to pass out? Then colour touched his face again. 'Easing now. That was a bad one.'

'I'm just racing out to the car for my phone,' Rachael said.

'Before that, maybe get the de-fib from the hall cupboard, love.'

'You have a defibrillator?'

'Course. Don't want to go out like the King, do I?'

Against her better judgement, Rachael jogged into the hall. She threw open the cupboard and was greeted with piles of sheets and towels, a boxed foot spa, and a whole shelf of puzzles.

'Where is it?'

'Next to the first aid box. Though I suppose I should have put it on the wall in the loo. You don't see it?'

Rachael scanned the shelves. There it was. She'd just thrown it down on the floor next to the couch when she thought she heard sirens. Ten seconds later, an ambulance pulled into the drive. Five minutes of intense activity followed as the paramedics checked Bernie over, and another five minutes later, a car screamed into the driveway and Beverley tumbled out. Seeing the scene in Bernie's living room, she hung back with the dignity and poise of Milton's last postmistress, but her anguish was clear from the hand gripping her handbag.

'I'm sure he'll be fine,' Rachael said, trying to be reassuring. 'I didn't mean to worry you.'

Instead of a cutting remark, Beverley only said, 'You did the right thing. I called the ambulance straight away.'

When the paramedics decided it was best to transport Bernie to the Parkes hospital, Rachael told Beverley she'd follow in her car. As Bernie was loaded up, dotted with sticky pads and wires leading into a machine, he was still trying to encourage the paramedics to drop into Blue Suede Choux tomorrow for a freebie.

Rachael met up with Beverley again in the hospital's emergency waiting room.

'He's stable and they think it might be his gall bladder, but they're going to keep him a while to monitor his heart. It's all those sweet things he eats,' Beverley said, but her voice shook. She extracted a tissue from her handbag. 'Listen to me, going on like a schoolgirl.'

Rachael sympathised; she'd spent enough time in hospital waiting for news of someone she cared about. But she still suppressed a smile. 'I didn't realise you meant so much to each other.'

Beverley chortled. 'Oh, I know what people are going to say after the last few years. But it turns out we have more in common than I gave him credit for.'

'Who'd have thought?' Rachael laughed.

'Goodness knows, I didn't expect this to happen to me at my age,' Bev said, then looked Rachael squarely in the eye. 'Your mum did though. She said I'd find someone again.'

'When did she say that?'

'In her letter. The one you gave me with the quilt. I'm only sorry she didn't get the same chance.' She put her arm around Rachael. 'I know it isn't the same as her being here, but read her letter again, lovey. I'm sure she left you some good advice.'

Rachael frowned. 'What letter?'

'The one she wrote you.'

'There wasn't one.'

Beverley pulled away to look at her. 'Yes there was. You mean you haven't found it?'

The hospital decided to release Bernie after an hour. Rachael spent the whole time going over in her mind all the papers her mother had left – the piles of envelopes and lists – and where a letter might have been lost. At the back of a drawer? Stuck to another letter? She would have to check.

The doctor recommended that Bernie have a full review with his GP within the week, including a discussion about diet.

'Haven't seen the doc in years,' Bernie said. 'Fit as a fiddle. Can't be that serious.'

'Thank you, doctor, I'll make sure he does,' Beverley said. 'After that, we're going to have a *talk*.'

Bernie affected a terrified expression as Beverley bustled off to fetch her car and bring it round to collect him. 'Better ask the doc to give the old prostate a poke,' he complained to her back. 'At least he'll wear a glove!'

Rachael saw a nurse hide a smile behind her hand, but she was too frantic to find it funny. She couldn't wait to get back to the farm.

⟶

When Rachael arrived home, Tess and Joel were down in the shed with the children. She went straight to her room and rummaged through the desk drawer where she'd kept her mother's lists and letters. She found nothing but a frightened daddy-long-legs.

She was halfway down the hall to the lounge when she abruptly stopped. Ten seconds later, she stood in the door of her mother's room. The bed was neatly made in white linen, the knitted blue throw undisturbed across the foot, trailing tasselled ends to the blanket box. The Tiffany glass lamp on the bedside table was unlit. The walk-in robe was quiet with its thick carpet, hanging fabrics and coat bags and no windows to admit outside noise. It smelled of mothballs and wool.

Rachael flicked on the light and took a deep breath. Tess had been right – the racks were full to bursting. Underneath the hanging bags were rows of shoeboxes, and the shelf overhead was two-deep with white plastic storage tubs holding papers, school photos and knick-knacks her mother had grown tired of dusting. Beverley had helped Marion organise it all.

Rachael sat on the ottoman, just as Tess had done, and stared at the clothes and shelves. Where was the letter?

She pulled down a box at random. Papers. Another held old books, the pages tea-brown. Rachael opened every box and found nothing.

She went back to the bedroom and hauled open the blanket box. Maybe there were items to donate in here that she'd missed, and the letter would be with them. The box was stuffed with winter woollens. She frowned. They'd always lived in the red-silk ottoman before.

She rushed back to the walk-in robe and lifted the ottoman cover and found the inside transformed. The usual wool jumpers and mothballs had given way to an incredible haberdashery collection: ribbons in packets or rolled into spirals, buttons in tubes or sewn onto cards, netting, feathers, braiding, pieces of fine lace wrapped in tissue. Each piece bore a tag or a label. It was like the collection Rachael had out in the pattern box, but these came from around the world, some of them decades old; so old it was impossible her mother had been the one to collect them. One tartan ribbon read *1980, London, found in the tube station at Covent Garden*. Another, a particularly beautiful piece of beaded lace, said, *Calais, found in remnant bin, Rue de Vic*.

And there, nestled in the centre, was an envelope. *For Rachael* read the front. Her mother's writing, the letters uneven and jerky, showing the time and effort it had taken. Rachael swallowed as tears rushed into her eyes. When had her mother written this?

With shaking fingers, she slipped the unevenly folded page from the envelope. *Dear Rachael* was written by hand at the top, the same hesitant script as the outside. The next part was typed.

Dear Rachael, if you are reading this then I was right about this year being the one. If I made it through Christmas I was intending to destroy this and write something more up-to-date. I thought many times about whether to have this conversation in person, but I guess we have had it all before, just in little pieces over the years. I asked Beverley to help me with writing it down. This way it will be legible, and I can write as fast as I remember it.

I have never shown you this collection. I've kept it hidden away because much of the time I didn't want to look at it. It reminds me of the life I used to want, which is so different from the one I led. I imagined using all these things one day, but I never have. Some of them came from my mother, and when I travelled I added things I found and loved. There are notes about each piece, and I've

added some photos with what I can remember from my favourite
places. When you go yourself (because I know you will), you
might have a laugh at what I did, or see how much has changed.
Those were odd times (the travelling) – it was wonderful, and
lonely, and exhilarating, and scary. Sometimes madly interesting,
sometimes a complete bore. A bit like living on the farm (with
better coffee). But I knew myself more because of it. You will too.
I always thought I was picking my way towards tomorrow, and
every day was something new.

At this point, the typing stopped and the handwriting took
up again, that careful shaky script. It must have taken hours,
Rachael thought, imagining her mother writing alone, without
Beverley or anyone else to witness what she was saying.

You're sleeping now, just down the hall, like you did when
you were a little girl. I can scarcely believe you're all grown up.
I often feel guilty that I've taken these years from you. You should
have been out in the world – living, finding your way, making
mistakes – instead of looking after your mother. But you stayed,
and I have loved you so fiercely for that.

People say all the time that their children are their greatest
achievements. I've always viewed that as foolishness. We each
make our own achievements. But I've had so much more time
with you than a mother can expect of her daughter. I am sorry
to leave before I meant to, to not be there to see what you'll do
in your long life. You still sit at my feet to tell me about your
day, just as you did when you were small. You can't imagine
how it breaks my heart to miss that now. But you will have your
freedom as you should. I want you to have the chance at things
I was too scared to do.

My own mother was wonderful, but she told me not to be a
seamstress, and I think I said that to you once too, in haste and
without thought. I don't regret the life I had, but it isn't the one

I imagined when I was standing in castles or drinking wine in a trattoria in Rome. I wanted to be a dressmaker. That is why I have never touched this collection – it's for another life. I don't know what you will do, but don't make that mistake. Ignore anything I ever said to you, because I am not your heart. You wanted to go to Sydney once. Maybe you still do. Maybe you want something else. Find it. Bind yourself with love to all you do. Life can be long or so short, and we don't know which it will be. There is no time for looking back.

And so I have only one thing left to say. You are generous and courageous, my lovely daughter. Go. Live.

With love unending, Mum

The last four words were written with no hesitation at all. Rachael swiped at her eyes, sniffing back tears before her nose ran. She read the letter again. Then she picked through the collection and found a thick packet of photos.

'Oh, Mum,' she said, clapping a hand over her mouth.

Right on top was a picture of her mother in a scarf and beanie with the Eiffel Tower rising behind her into a grey Parisian sky. Rachael had stood right there during the photography class. It was where Antonio had sat down beside her.

On the back of her mother's photo was a printed sticker that read: *Paris (duh!). Horribly ill after catching the flu on the train. Was terrified of the metro but made it here eventually after two wrong stops. Asked a young man called Pierre to take the photo – we had lunch! Fantastic day, even after finding bed bugs at the hostel (be warned, photo later).*

On it went: more photos from Paris; then Barcelona and the Sagrada Família, and a shot near the coast labelled *Barcelona – eating cheese and drinking wine at the beach with Frankie, Susan and Scott. Spent the night sketching dresses inspired by the cathedral.* Then a photo in a London pub, where Rachael recognised a very young version of her father. Her mother had written: *With Andrew and pint at the Spaniards Inn. He didn't know who Dickens or Keats were (perhaps I should have known better?) but had a great time anyway.*

Rachael had never before appreciated that time in her mother's life. Marion had never mentioned that she'd been afraid of the metro, or fleeced by train conductors for buying the wrong ticket on an overnight train. To Rachael, her mother had always seemed sure of herself, no matter what happened. She'd never seemed regretful. Now, with the letter and these photos, she saw Marion as . . . young, before everything that Rachael had seen happen to her.

One photo, taken in a pristine Swiss village, was labelled: *Lucerne – bored. So bored. And out of money. Thought I would have to eat my hat that night.* Rachael giggled.

She read the letter again. When she'd finished, the sun was sinking over the fields, kissing goodnight the tiny shoots that would soon push through last year's stubble. She stood on the back verandah, the breeze lifting her hair. Her mother's tree crowned the rise, its leaves all golden in the light. Rachael was filled with the same light, and absolution settled on her softly as a feather.

She could see Tess outside the big shed, supervising Felix and Emily as they helped their baby sister walk, while Joel worked at the bench, mending a panel. He'd insisted on doing it. Rachael watched them with entirely different eyes. The whole farm was different. The shadows were the colour of the cobbles on the Île de la Cité, and the horizon was so clear that she imagined she could almost see the whole world in the grey smudge between land and sky.

She had a decision to make. It demanded a ritual.

Without bothering to take a towel, she rode a quad bike towards the river, calling to Tess she'd be back in an hour.

The swimming hole was already in long shadows, but the rocks were warm from the sun. Rachael peeled off her clothes and slid into the frigid water. Her skin contracted with cold, and when she ducked her head under, chill fingers probed her scalp. She re-emerged with a gasp, the droplets on her eyelashes making jewelled sparkles of the last of the sun.

After ten minutes – longer than was sane this time of year – she sat on a warm boulder to drip-dry, etching the place in her memory. She realised then that the decision had been made long ago. She'd just never had the courage to act on it.

Chapter 24

She found Tess in the kitchen, stirring a pot, while the children chased each other around the TV room.

'Bloody hell, where have you been?' Tess said when Rachael appeared, then took in her wet hair. 'Oh, I see. The rest of us have to work, but you can take off to go swimming and just mosey on back when you like.'

For the first time, Rachael didn't feel anything at the cutting tone. She saw the fear in Tess re-emerging and understood it. Really understood it.

'Could you leave that a minute and come into the lounge? I need to talk to you and Joel.'

Rachael didn't wait for an answer. She found Joel scrubbing his hands in the laundry. Two minutes later he and Tess were seated on the couch. Tess folded her arms.

'I went through some of Mum's things today,' Rachael began. She'd decided not to mention the letter. She might one day, but Tess would probably find it hurtful if she hadn't had one too. 'She had a huge collection of lace and buttons and other things, and some photos of her time overseas.'

'Great,' Tess said. 'I'm glad we're finally getting to clearing out. How can I help?'

Rachael almost smiled. She tried to choose her next words carefully.

'It's not about that. Look, you guys like this place, don't you? I know you have your farm, but I'm sensing you might not be keen to go back there.'

Tess shot Joel a look. 'You told her, didn't you?'

Obviously Rachael hadn't been careful enough.

'Not everything,' Joel protested. 'Just didn't want Rach thinking—'

'What?' Tess demanded.

Rachael couldn't believe she'd ever missed it. Tess wasn't just scared and angry, she was embarrassed. She didn't want Rachael to know their farm was in trouble, that they were trying to sell. Tess, who'd always wanted to be a farmer's wife, who had made it happen, and now had three children to think about. Tess, who thought she was going to lose all that and instead have to watch Rachael keep their family farm, all because she was the one who'd left with their father all those years ago.

Rachael held up her hand. 'I'm glad Joel said something. You're looking to sell, right?'

Tess glared at Joel. 'Didn't say much, huh?'

'Do you want to move here?' Rachael asked. 'I'll sell this place to you for whatever you get for yours. We're turning a profit most years. Not always a big one, but still.'

Tess's expression was genuinely shocked. Then came disbelief, joy and denial in a series of microflashes, in that order. She wouldn't give in to hope so easily.

'And how is that going to work? You'll get sick of the kids after a while.'

Rachael glanced down, then out the window. This was hard for her to say, despite how right it felt.

'I'm going away. I'd love to come back to visit, but . . . I want to do other things.' She dropped her voice. 'I stayed for ten years with Mum. This part of my life is done. It's not for me.'

Tess was silent. Really silent, in a way she never ever was, for a whole minute, until Rachael wondered if she'd misunderstood.

'Are you really sure?' she said finally, her voice meek and trembling with possibility.

Rachael nodded, then stood. 'You'll want to talk about it. I'll go and wash up.'

She got a towel and ruffled the rest of the water from her hair. The bob had grown out just enough to catch it in a band behind her head. With her hair pulled back she looked grim, so she shook it out again and let the drying ends crinkle against her neck. There, better. Now she looked as she felt – light, free, and a little ragged around the edges.

What would she do if Tess said no? This whole madcap plan of hers could fall over before it even got going.

She found the abandoned pot in the kitchen – stroganoff, Joel's favourite – relit the gas and checked on the rice. Unexpectedly, a pair of arms flew around her from behind and she smelled the faint trace of shampoo on Tess's hair. Her sister hugged her hard, longer than any time Rachael could remember in their lives. Rachael stopped stirring and held the arm she could reach, almost scared that moving would frighten Tess and the moment would collapse.

Tess finally pulled away, sniffling. She wiped under her eyes and dabbed a tissue to her nose. Rachael had never seen her hardy, sharp-edged sister this way, except that glimpse in their mother's wardrobe last year.

'Where will you go?' Tess asked. 'Sydney?'

Rachael laughed. 'No way. Europe, I think. I want to make dresses. I don't even know how to begin, but that's what I want.'

She waited for a sharp comment, for remonstrations, but Tess simply looked thoughtful.

'What about the travel agent in Parkes? They would help. And you know Dad's mum was Irish – you should see if you can get an Irish passport.'

'How do you know that?' Rachael asked, astonished.

Tess shrugged. 'Dad loves talking about the family tree, which is funny because he hasn't shown much interest in his grandchildren yet. But Felix and Emily's friends all seem to have grandparents, so I thought they should at least hear me talk about him now and again, even though "Grandma" isn't much older than us.'

Tess glanced out the window towards their mother's tree, now a silhouette against the last of the twilight.

'I missed her when I left,' Tess said softly. 'I missed here. I missed you both.'

'Why did you go then? I never understood it. Mum was heartbroken.'

Tess closed her eyes and shook her head gently as if Rachael understood precisely nothing. 'I thought that if I didn't, Dad wouldn't love me any more. Mum, I was sure of. I knew she loved me. But I thought I'd lose Dad if I didn't go with him. So I did.' She shrugged. 'Look how that turned out. If I had my time again—'

'Don't,' Rachael said, putting her arms back around Tess. 'Don't do that. Just make the best of tomorrow. I'll need to hear all about it when I'm gone.'

Tess straightened. 'Suppose we'd better eat this dinner then.'

Rachael knew her sister wouldn't say anything more, it wasn't in her nature, but she could see contentment settling in her. Cautiously, because Tess didn't count chickens, but settling all the same.

⌒

At dinner, Tess and Joel asked Felix and Emily if they'd like
to live here.

Rachael watched their disbelief become excitement, then
the bargaining that ensued about who would have what room,
while the baby threw rice on the floor. Rachael was full of
happy dread: she wanted to go, and yet never leave. When Felix
started to say that Emily could have Aunty Rachael's room,
and Tess swiftly told him, 'No, Aunty Rachael needs her room
for when she visits us,' she had to get up from the table to
fetch some water, so they wouldn't all see her crying about it.

After dinner, she told Tess and Joel to leave the washing
up. Slowly, she cleared the kitchen, putting away each dish in
its proper place, saying goodbye to them too. When she next
came back, who knew how Tess would have organised things?
It was her sister's place now.

The clock showed nine thirty when she finished. The children
were all asleep, and Joel and Tess had turned in too. Rachael
opened the back door and stood among the gardenias at the
edge of the verandah. She caught a waft of familiar scent. One
creamy flower had opened in the centre of the row. She bent
and trailed a finger along its silken petals. Her acrylics might
be gone, but her nails were smooth. She hadn't bitten them in
days. Sammy would be proud of her.

Her mobile buzzed and Sammy's face appeared on the screen.

'Hey,' Rachael said. 'I was going to call you tomorrow
morning.'

'Why are you whispering?'

Rachael smiled – at the great fields running into the darkling
sky, at the hidden waterhole and its memories, at the scent of
gardenias; the joys of a home she would leave and yet carry
with her everywhere. The idea was a just-lit flame, vulnerable
to disturbance.

'Everyone's asleep,' she said.

'Sorry.'

'It's fine. I actually have something to tell you, and I'm not sure you'll be happy about it.'

In fact, Rachael was deeply worried. Sammy was at a low point and her instincts said this wasn't the time to be going away. But perhaps there would never be a good time.

'I'm selling the farm to Tess and Joel, and I'm going overseas, at least for a while.'

Rachael thought Sammy's exclamation was probably audible at the Dish. It took five minutes to explain that she didn't have any details yet, but hoped to go for six months, maybe longer if she could find some work and top up her savings.

Sammy was silent for a time when Rachael had finished. Finally, she said, 'I'm completely jealous. But it sounds like something you need to do. You'll probably meet some gorgeous prince and he'll whisk you away.'

'Yeah, right.' Rachael laughed, but she was done with the idea of being whisked away. 'But you called me. How are you?'

'Well . . .' That one word was stuffed with relief and hope and a dozen other things. 'I have something to tell you.'

'Mmm?'

'Marty called from Sydney. I don't want to pretend things are great. But he's coming back. That's something, right?'

After they'd ended the call, Rachael leaned back on her hands, closed her eyes and tried to record this moment on some kind of internal tape. The faint background pulse of insects calling, the rustle of tiny creatures in the dry leaves, the wind blowing dust against the shed, then gusting across the verandah. The breeze pushed on her cheek, like she was a sailing ship bound for the sea. Home had been her anchor, and now it was time to cast off. Some day she would come back and tell her mother what she had done.

When she finally went inside, the study door was ajar, the computer still running. Going in to shut it down, she found a single email in her inbox. Her heart trembled when she read the sender as *Ferranti, Antonio*. The subject said: *Your letter*.

Should she open it now and spend the night dwelling on whatever it contained? She remembered her mother's letter. *Courageous*, it had said. With one eye open, she clicked the email and found only a single line.

Got your letter. Call me. A

With a shaking hand, Rachael found his battered card and dialled the number. When the click of pick-up came and Antonio's voice answered gruffly, she couldn't speak.

'Who is it?' he demanded after the too-long pause.

'It's me,' she rushed out.

'Rachael.' Surprise in his voice. And warmth. And something else. 'I didn't expect to hear from you so soon.'

She bit her lip. 'I tried to call you before, but after it kept going to voicemail I figured you didn't want to speak to me, and I'd write instead.'

'My phone always does that when I'm away.'

'Oh.'

'I've been in Africa the last few weeks. I just got back today. I probably have fifty voicemails waiting, but I read your letter instead of listening to them.'

'I meant it,' she said simply, thinking of all the apologies and confession she'd poured into the letter, not expecting she would ever hear from him.

'I guess you can see the bad things in people after all, even if it's yourself,' he said. A pause. 'That job is still going if you want it.'

Rachael began to protest. She didn't want him to think that was why she'd written.

'And I sent you something in the post,' he interrupted. 'If you like it, I want you to call me back.'

⟶

A week later, when Rachael collected the post from Milton, it included a small white package addressed in neat ballpoint handwriting. Tearing it open, she found a card of silk and gold lace-covered buttons, the same ones she'd admired that day in Paris. On the back, Antonio had written, *La Mercerie des Rêves, Paris.*

Rachael cradled them to her chest, relief and amazement competing for supremacy. He'd remembered. And though she and Antonio were far from the promising beginning they'd had, she sensed there was room to move forward.

She didn't know if she would ever use these buttons, but no matter where she went, she wanted to remember. She searched in her drawer until she found the memory card he'd given her at the Eiffel Tower, planning to print the photo when she was next in Parkes. Then she took out a pen and added to his note, *Gorgeous day with Antonio in Paris. Kissed him at the top of the Eiffel Tower. First day of the rest of my life.*

Epilogue

December had been mild and dry and the rolling hills of the farm were silver with cut stubble. Rachael was heavy with the exhaustion of the flight from London and the long drive, and sweating as though she'd never lived here through twenty-eight summers. After the dead-winter of Europe, the heat had a wallop like a sledgehammer. But when she spotted the familiar band of trees before the drive, one of them hung with tinsel and a huge banner that read *Welcome home!*, none of the discomforts mattered.

Antonio aimed his camera through the open window. 'We're finally here?'

'I did warn you it was a long drive.'

He shot her a crooked smile. 'Not complaining. These colours are amazing. Make it longer.'

Rachael's chest filled with pride. Even after seven months in Europe, the drive home was eerily familiar – she could have been coming back from a trip into Milton or Parkes instead of all the way from Sydney. The only difference was the sense of freedom: coming home was so much more wonderful when you knew you had the choice to leave again. And after freezing London, the baking heat would be a luxury once she acclimatised.

The house appeared around the bend, its verandahs and pale roof promising cool relief. Rachael saw the children rushing in and out of the doors; no doubt they'd spotted the car. She remembered a time when she and Tess had done that, excited by every vehicle that came through the gate, running to find their mother.

Emily and Felix were waving; little Georgia, now nearly two, copying between them. Tess appeared just as Rachael pulled up, preventing the children swarming over the car in a bid to greet her first.

'What a reception!' Rachael laughed as she slid out of the seat and Emily and Felix grabbed a leg each. She leaned down and hugged their warm bodies, feeling their soft hair against her cheeks and breathing in their smell of bubble bath and dust.

'We missed you, Aunty Rachael,' said Felix as Rachael kissed him on the cheek. Shyly, he rubbed the kiss away.

'Did you bring us presents?' asked Emily.

They both peered around her at Antonio, who had climbed out of the passenger seat.

'Hey,' he called to them, then crouched so they were eye to eye. 'I'm Antonio, but you can call me Ant. What're your names?'

'Is that your camera?' Emily asked after the names had been supplied.

'Would you like to see? Perhaps you can both take some photos of each other?'

'Let Rachael and Antonio come inside,' scolded Tess.

Rachael hugged her sister amidst the chaos. Tess had changed. Her face had smoothed out – the pinching around her eyes and mouth was gone – and she'd grown her hair longer. She was thinner, but in a muscled way that made Rachael wonder if she'd taken up running.

'You look great,' Rachael said.

Tess gave her a quick smile. 'Too busy to eat,' she said, but in a jovial way that told Rachael it was only half the truth. 'What have you done to your hair?'

Rachael gave it a self-conscious scrunch. It was shorter now, falling in a bob just below her ears; it was easier to keep that way, and she was experimenting with fashions.

The first month overseas had been a whirlwind of culture shock: the change from wide open spaces to a huge city, from driving to catching the tube everywhere, and finding a place to live without bankrupting herself – all while starting a cadetship she felt woefully unprepared for.

She'd viewed it as a gateway job; something definite to go to in a strange place rather than hoping to land something once she got there. The work involved a lot of fact-checking and taking minutes of meetings and helping with research for the journalists working on feature stories. She was slow at the research, and hated calling people to ask for interviews or to clarify quotes. She'd spent several nights in her first room in a dingy hostel silently crying and wondering what the hell she'd been thinking. In those moments, her mother's letter and the photos had been the only things helping her through to the next day.

Slowly, the bumps had evened out. She worked out how to research faster, avoiding all the dead ends she'd got trapped in at the beginning, and who in the office was the best person to teach her different skills. That was when she began to sew again, at night in her apartment with a second-hand machine, and went hunting all over town for high-end remnants for her projects.

Around the same time, Rachael had met three other Australians on working holidays in London – Liz from Perth, Ethan from Melbourne and Ruby from Sydney. They were doing the pub quiz together at Rachael's local one night when she walked in on her own, and heard her accent when she ordered dinner. Soon, Liz, the group's natural social secretary, was organising weekend trips to Avebury, Sherwood Forest, Ely Cathedral, and Paris. On that last trip, Rachael had wandered past the Arc de Triomphe and stared up at the little showroom on the top floor. Two months later, she'd posted a letter to Martine Bertrand with samples of her work.

Now, she hauled her case from the car boot.

'I'll take it,' Emily said, extracting the handle from Rachael and dragging it towards the house.

'Gently!' Tess said.

Then Rachael started, because standing in the doorway was Sammy, clutching a tiny sleeping baby to her chest. Rachael ran, stopping short only because she didn't want to crush both of them.

'I thought you were coming later?' she whispered.

Sammy smiled. 'You don't have to whisper. Nothing seems to wake him. And I wanted to be here when you got in. Tess has been great helping out.'

'Can I see?' Rachael peered at the sweet snub face, only a few weeks old. She'd seen a photo Sammy had emailed around, but it hadn't captured the long eyelashes or the sweet curve of his lips. 'He's beautiful. Are you getting any sleep?'

Sammy shrugged. 'Not much. But I've still got energy. Ask me again in a month.'

'Right, all you kids, inside,' Tess said. 'I thought you wanted to make White Christmas?'

Soon the children were installed at the kitchen table, a plastic drop sheet underneath them, happily stirring a vast bowl of copha, rice bubbles, glacé cherries and white chocolate, and rolling spoonfuls into patty pans.

Antonio proved himself indispensable by slipping easily into the circle, claiming that he was used to it from all his Italian cousins. He and Joel kept the peace while Rachael, Sammy and Tess sat in the lounge, catching up.

Rachael couldn't help noticing how at home Tess looked in their mother's old chair. The room itself was cosy and homey, with the big Christmas tree set in the corner, two stars now on top.

'I've told the children they can open one present each tonight, because tomorrow they have to wait until at least six,' Tess said.

A crash sounded out in the kitchen. A pause, then crying.

Tess rose. 'Better go see how the world's ending this time.'

As soon as she'd gone, Rachael squeezed Sammy's arm. 'How is everything? Really?'

Sammy's hesitation was only slight. 'All right. Marty's been staying to help with Olly. Things aren't great, but we are actually talking. I asked him if he wanted to do a test.' She paused, her lip in her teeth, then swallowed tears away. 'He says he's thinking about it, but he wants to know Olly better first. He admitted he was really ego-bruised about losing his job, and he shut down after that happened. He's tired of being depressed about it though, and he's looking properly now, and considering the business idea again. The motel owner's going to sell, so we're even thinking whether we could buy that, as a start. So at least we're working on everything, slowly. I don't for a second think we're all fine, but there's hope.'

Rachael nearly cried herself, she was so relieved.

Sammy kissed Olly's sleeping head and rested her cheek briefly against his downy hair. She craned her neck to see if Tess was coming back, then said quickly, 'I'm sorry to ask this, but have you heard anything about Bonnie?'

'Not really.'

It wasn't quite the truth. Bonnie had recently flown into London to launch a clothing label, and Rachael's friends had been talking about it. Rachael had bitten her tongue and watched with interest. She knew that Bonnie and Matthew were still married, but noted that they were never seen in public together. She'd once come across a tabloid magazine speculating about what was happening between them, complete with long-range photos of them on holiday somewhere in the south of France. Her heart still skipped if she heard either of their names, but the butterflies of attraction were long gone. She knew she'd been incredibly stupid, and then incredibly lucky.

Antonio was helping. He'd been on assignment for two months when she'd landed in London, embedded with anti-poaching teams in Africa. She'd been apprehensive about his return, but he was pleased to see her and Rachael had felt more confident. After several weeks, they'd gone on a date. Then another. And another. And the slow burn of love he'd once talked about had gradually taken hold of her.

Finally, Rachael had been able to ask him about that week in Paris.

'I hadn't realised the man you were talking about was the groom,' he'd said. 'But you're a beautiful woman – I don't blame him.'

'You're coming back tomorrow for lunch?' Rachael asked Sammy.

'Me and everyone else. Bernie and Beverley too, can you believe it?'

'That's still going on?' Rachael was surprised.

'Yep. They're even collaborating these days. Bernie's decided not to move the bakery, but he's opening a second store in Parkes.'

Olly stirred, and Sammy stood to walk around, shifting the baby's weight to her other shoulder.

'So are you chucking it all in and coming home?' she asked.

Rachael glanced out the window before she answered. 'Things have been touch and go sometimes. I was worried what I'd do when this job was over.'

'But?'

'But ... I have an interview with a dressmaker in Paris in January, and I've applied to intern in dressmaking with two designers in London. Antonio gave me the photos he took of my dresses at the wedding to use as a portfolio. The pay's even worse than this last job, but if I'm careful I might be able to come home once a year.'

'Woohoo,' Sammy said softly. 'I knew this would work out for you. I really did.'

Rachael smiled, and sent silent thanks to the tree on the hill. There had been times on the farm when she'd thought she would never leave. Now, she wasn't sure when she would return. She knew that whatever Sammy thought, things were far from worked out.

She missed her best friend dreadfully, and was still learning about herself and what she could do, but at least she was on her way. Tess and Joel's farm had sold, so she had some money to keep going, and she could see they were the right ones to live here. Her mother would have loved to see the family together again, however briefly. Rachael's home would always be here, but next week it would be time to fly again and see where her dreams might land.

'You just have to promise me one thing,' Sammy said. 'Make sure you invite me to your wedding!'

Acknowledgements

The Paris Wedding was a challenging book to write. I would like to thank the many contributors, especially Paula Ellery and Rebekah Turner for their notes, my Sisters of the Pen writing group for all your help (Kim, Meg, Liz, Fi and Nic) and all the staff at Hachette. Special thanks to Bek for being the best writing buddy ever.

As extended from the dedication, I would like to thank my mum, Isabella Nash, for her endless patience in teaching me to sew when I was young. I am not as good as Rachael in the story, but it's a skill that has been invaluable, as has Mum's continued support and encouragement in my adult life. Further thanks to my step-dad Vic Blake for the same.

Thanks also to Elizabeth and Albert Lecoanet for the mates' rates on your gorgeous apartment in Paris, on which I based Antonio's apartment; and to Shannon for your wonderful care of Alec while I worked, and for the discussions about parental estrangement and the reasons children have for their choices which informed Tess's character. Much appreciation to Kate Kleinworth and Bella Ridout for French checking (and to Sarah Ridout for facilitating).

As always, love and thanks to my husband Kevin for making this difficult business so much easier and for believing that following interests is life's greatest purpose.